*Acclaim for N*

# THE SONG OF NAMES

"*The Song of Names* vividly brought back to me the horrors of war-torn England, where I spent my childhood years. In spirit it is reminiscent of Dickens, and in temperament of Dostoyevsky and Isaac Bashevis Singer. Yet it is entirely unique as well as gripping—a masterpiece of a novel."
—Ida Haendel, violinist and author of *Woman with Violin*

"Having judged Norman Lebrecht somewhat imperfectly through his trenchant, occasionally acerbic observations of my profession, I was surprised and delighted by his fastidious, sensitive and unvarnished tale of the life and times of a young musician. Such good writing."
—Neville Marriner, Founder,
Academy of St. Martin in the Fields

"Anybody who takes music seriously has been reading Norman Lebrecht for years—but who knew he was a novelist? What a pleasure to read a serious work of fiction with such deep underpinnings in history and aesthetics."
—Tim Page, Pulitzer Prize–winning music critic,
author of *Dawn Powell: A Biography*

"Compelling humanity . . . deliciously caught. . . . Conjured with exceptional vividness."
—*The Evening Standard* (London)

*Norman Lebrecht*

# THE SONG OF NAMES

Norman Lebrecht is one of the most widely read modern commentators on music, culture, and politics. His Wednesday column in the *Evening Standard* (London) and on the Internet has been described as "required reading." His BBC Radio 3 show, *Lebrecht Live*, attracts Web Listeners from Buenos Aires to Budapest. His many books include *The Maestro Myth*, *When the Music Stops*, *Mahler Remembered*, and *Covent Garden: The Untold Story*. *The Song of Names* is his first novel.

**Also by Norman Lebrecht**

*Mahler Remembered*
*The Maestro Myth*
*When the Music Stops*
*The Complete Companion to 20th Century Music*
*Covent Garden: The Untold Story*
*The Life and Death of Classical Music*
*The Game of Opposites*
*Why Mahler?*

# THE SONG
# OF NAMES

*A Novel*

*Norman Lebrecht*

Anchor Books
A Division of Penguin Random House LLC
New York

FIRST ANCHOR BOOKS MTI EDITION, DECEMBER 2019

Library of Congress Cataloging-in-Publication Data
Lebrecht, Norman, 1948–
The song of names : a novel / Norman Lebrecht.
p. cm.
1. Missing persons—Fiction.  2. London (England)—Fiction.
3. Holocaust, Jewish (1939–1945)—Fiction.  4. Friendship—Fiction.
5. Violinists—Fiction.  I. Title.
PR6112.E27S66 2004
823'.92—dc22
2003067451

**Anchor Books MTI ISBN: 978-0-593-08248-5**
**Anchor Books Trade Paperback ISBN: 978-1-4000-3489-5**
**eBook ISBN: 978-0-307-42938-4**

*Author photograph © Sam Long*

www.anchorbooks.com

Printed in the United States of America
10  9  8  7  6  5  4  3  2  1

For Beatrice, Myriam
and Pauline

# 1

# Time Out

Swimming in a double-breasted suit against the Monday morning incoming tide, I feel a double misfit. The whole working world is flooding into town while I am heading out, and for no good reason. What is more, I am just about the only man on the forecourt in a respectable suit. Times have changed, and chinos are worn to work.

Or whatever they call work. Sitting at a flickering screen, hunting and gathering data, strikes me as a poor substitute for the thrill of the chase, the joy of the kill, the kiss of conquest. There is no romance, no mortal struggle, in digitised so-called work. It is a virtual pursuit, without real vice or virtue. Mine, on the other hand, is a people profession, hence almost obsolescent.

It would not do to enquire too closely into the purpose of my trip. 'Is your journey really necessary?' nagged the railway hoardings during the war. No, not enough to convince the auditors, who will slash my expenses claim on seeing the negligible returns. Nor to satisfy Myrtle, who will raise a quizzical eyebrow and register a connubial debt. There is no pot of gold at the end of my trail nor, truth be told, enough profit to interest a Sunday boot-saler – which is not, of course, what I tell the accountants ('must keep in touch with consumer trends'), or Myrtle ('meeting a familiar face can make all the difference when money's tight'). What matters is that *I* know why I am going, and I don't have to make excuses to myself. Escape, or the illusion of it, is what keeps me alive and my business more or less solvent.

Survival instinct propels me through the Euston crowds towards a reserved first-class seat on the nine-oh-three Intercity Express, my chest pounding with unaccustomed effort and an absurd anticipation of adventure. Absurd, because previous expeditions have attested beyond reasonable doubt that any prospect of adventure will get scotched at source by my innate reserve and speckless propriety – attributes that are bound to be mentioned in my none-too-distant obsequies, alongside the Dear Departed's musical expertise, mordant wit and discreet philanthropy.

Adventure is, in any case, antithetical to my nature and inadvisable in my state of health. Furred arteries and a fear of bypass surgery have imposed severe restraints. I am limited to six lengths of the health-club pool and half a mile on the electronic treadmill; excitement is strenuously avoided; conjugality is conducted rarely and with the circumspection of porcupines. 'Take care of yourself,' are Myrtle's parting words and, for her sake, I do try. In the absence of marital ardour, it's the least I can do.

Yet, even a rackety, unbypassed old heart can be stirred by departure fantasy. As I board the train, my pulse picks up ten points in fake anticipation. I look ahead breathlessly, with a reassuring sense of *déjà vu*. It's like watching televised football highlights on a Saturday night when you've already heard the classified results on the radio. The programme may reveal some fine points of form and skill, but any tension has been ruled out by an incontrovertible foreknowledge of the outcome.

Watching stale soccer from the snug of a prized deco armchair is the limit of my permitted thrills – a sad comedown for one who was groomed to make things happen. Sad to have slipped from motivator to spectator, from the wings of great stages to a piece of high-winged furniture. Still, there are compensations. By staying out of the thick of things, I have acquired an aura of what, in small-business circles, passes for timeless wisdom.

Lifelong prudence has reaped its rewards. My town house has a heated indoor pool, I holiday winter and summer in wickedly overpriced Swiss resorts and my pension arrangements are structured to keep me in comfort for three lifetimes. 'Comfort ye, comfort ye, my people,' said the prophet Isaiah – so we made it the tribal aspiration. What greater calm can a man find on earth than the quiet rustling of gilt-edged assets?

At Rotary and Bnai Brith you cannot tell me apart from the rest of the Lodge, and that is how I like it; none of the other brothers has, to my certain knowledge, been invaded by genius and ruined by its defection. Forget I mentioned that: not many people are meant to know about it. 'Mustn't grumble,' my father used to say, when asked how he was; and so do I. Normality is my nirvana. Only within, deep within, at the clotted edge of irreparable loss, do I feel the need for an unnecessary journey that will allow me to avoid devastating self-contemplation and the acceleration of inherited arteriosclerosis.

I wouldn't be surprised if the railways were mostly run for people like me, half-wrecked psyches in perpetual flight from the missing part. I can just see a Development Director springing his brainwave initiative at a board meeting. 'Why don't we run extra Monday-morning services to the boondocks?' he proposes brightly. 'There must be thousands of useless deadweights, dog-ends and waiting-for-godders who are just dying to get away.'

Settling in my window seat I pop two pills, a brand-name sedative and a homoeopathic palliative, shutting my eyes for ten minutes of yogic meditation. My Harley Street consultant (the cardiologist, not the naturopath) advises daily exercise and the avoidance of agitation. Being of a responsible disposition, I eat warily and carry a kidney-donor card. If I see a pretty girl or a police chase, I look away. In Michelin-starred restaurants, I order steamed fish. I have many friends but no recent lovers, vague interests but no driving passions.

Myrtle, my partner in life, has a life largely of her own. A large-boned lady of healthy appetites, she lunches sparingly in good causes and plays bridge for her metropolitan borough. She took it up in her thirties, after having children, discerning in the pastime an outlet for her formidable memory and jugular instincts. Myrtle can remember the seating plan at every chicken-schnitzel wedding we have attended, the Order of Service at Her Majesty's Coronation, the universal symbols of the periodic table and the entire line-up of the Hungarian football team that inflicted England's first home defeat, 3–6, in the aforementioned Coronation Year, which was also the year of our marriage. Many's the time I have urged her to apply her remarkable mental powers to a worthier object than a pack of cards. But Myrtle's tolerance for ladies who lunch on behalf of the starving and homeless is limited.

Our two sons have grown up and apart from us, triumphs of private schooling and canny marriages. One is a Kensington obstetrician with a trophy wife, the other a libel lawyer with a traditional spouse. Over dinner, I prefer the barrister's scurrilous gossip to the manicured sanctimony of a society abortionist. But I feel no satisfying patrimony when, on Friday nights, we play a charade of happy families around a table groaning with murderously poly-saturated fats. Monastically picking at my wife's heedlessly prepared dietary dynamite, I retire dyspeptically to bed with a glass of camomile tea and the *Spectator*, a lifelong habit, while coffee is taken in the lounge. My apologies are accepted with a wince of scepticism. Some in the family, I suspect, ascribe my medical condition to chronic hypochondria.

A decent Omm-trance is pretty much unattainable on a train that starts and lurches through a thicket of signals, then spurts past outer suburbs like a runaway horse. Once the speed settles to a steady rocking, incomprehensible announcements splutter forth about the whereabouts of the refreshment car and would the chief steward please make his way to first class, thank you.

Giving up the quest for inner peace and undistracted by the silvered February landscape, my attention turns to business, which barely needs it. The company I keep going is a spectre of the firm that my father founded in 1919 'to advance the appreciation of music among men and women of modest means'. In its heyday, Simmonds was a household name, to be found in the nation's living rooms among the Wedgwood teacups, Hornby toys and grafted aspidistras in Robertson's jampots. Simmonds (Symphonic Scores and Concerts) Ltd manufactured piano reductions of orchestral masterpieces, issued in noble purple covers for the uniform price of sixpence. We also produced popular lives of the great composers, albumised folk-songs and approachable novelties by uncelebrated living composers. But the heart of Simmonds was the concert division, which organised orchestral nights for all the family, grannies to toddlers, at group discounts that worked out at less than the price of a cinema seat.

Simmonds' suite of offices, nuzzling the old Queen's Hall at the top of Regent Street, buzzed seven days a week with unprofitable ideas, artistic aspirations and fatally entrapped wasps. No window was ever opened, for fear of diluting the fug of inspiration. Elbow-patched pianists in pursuit of unpaid fees jostled students and factory workers waiting for last-minute penny tickets. Trilby-hatted newspapermen interviewed stateless conductors in secluded corners – on one occasion, apparently, in the left hand stall of the ladies' washroom where the cistern drip-dripped so relentlessly that an idle wit attributed the metronomic tempi of that night's Tchaikovsky Fifth to the inadequacies of Simmonds' plumbing.

My father, hunched behind a pyramid of unread contracts and uncorrected page-proofs, presided at all hours over his musical emporium, seldom locking up before midnight. 'I can't leave the place empty,' he would say. 'Who knows when the next Kreisler might walk in?' Half a century before open-plan offices, he took his door off its hinges, the better to observe all comings and goings. No artist ever entered unnoticed. As mail piled up and secretaries resigned in tears, my father juggled three telephone receivers simultaneously, virtuosically and without ever raising his voice.

Mortimer (Mordecai) Simmonds had the manners of a gentle-man and the abstraction of a scholar – though he was neither, having been sent to work 'in the print' at thirteen years old to support a widowed mother and four sisters in Bethnal Green. In the inky-stink din of a newspaper press, he befriended the lower echelons of journalism and ascended the proof-readers' ladder to join the sub-editors' desk of a literary supplement, itself a passport to Hampstead salons. There he met in mid-war and was persuaded to marry my mother, the dowried and somewhat dowdy eldest daughter of an Anglo-Sephardic dynasty, the Medolas, who offered to set him up in the business of his choice. Bookishness beckoned, the more so after two years on the Somme, but he failed to find the kind of books that would give him aesthetic satisfaction and would also make money. His business career was going nowhere when a friend gave him a spare ticket to the Queen's Hall on 4 May 1921, a date he would commemorate every year of his life. The soloist was Fritz Kreisler, back for the first time in eight years. Hearing him play an innocuous concerto by Viotti moved my father more than all the words he had ever read. Kreisler, with his bushy moustache and flashing eyes, ran off dazzling cadenzas as if they were child's play while holding listeners, one by one, in the grip of a limpid glare. 'I was seduced,' my father would recall. 'It was as if he played only for me. From the moment his eye caught mine, I knew that my life was destined for music.'

Unable to read a score or play a scale, my father hired a tutor to instruct him in the difference between crotchets and quavers and the significance of pitch relations in concert programming. He frequented student recitals at the Trinity College of Music, behind Selfridge's department store, sniffing talent by instinct. One violinist he picked off the pavement, busking in Oxford Street. With a handful of hopefuls, he put on chamber recitals at the Aeolian Hall, a churchy room on Regent Street; and with the newly formed Birmingham Orchestra, bussed in for the night, he staged the first of his family entertainments at the marbled Royal Albert Hall, on the southern edge of Hyde Park.

No critic was ever invited to his concerts, but the halls were full and admission was universally affordable. An outraged music industry condemned Simmonds for 'lowering the tone'. My father laughed, and halved his top-price tickets. He refused to join collegial committees to discuss unit costs, credit lines and entry controls on foreign performers. He could not countenance anything that imposed restraint on an interpreter of music, a bringer of light and joy. He revered artists, almost without reservation.

No Balkan pianist with three Zs in his name would ever come under pressure from Mortimer Simmonds to adopt a new identity for English convenience. No fat singer was ever required to slim. He gave second chances to panic-frozen beginners and blamed his own shortcomings when a concert flopped. He had no time for snob-appeal or seasonal brochures, for copyright niceties and entertainment tax – least of all, let it be noted, for his wife and son, whom he only ever saw in daylight over Sunday lunch, and not with undivided attention or unfailing punctuality.

So when the phone rang one winter Sunday with the roast beef charred in the oven and my mother muttering over her petit-point, I failed to react in any way, hysterical or practical, to news of his death at the desk. My father belonged to Simmonds (Symphonic Scores and Concerts) Ltd, not to me; he died at his post, as it were, amid a mound of unopened mail. He was sixty-one, my present age. At the funeral, the rabbi spoke of his love of art, his humility and self-deprecating wit. He left me wishing I had seen more of him.

Hauled out of Cambridge, where I was sitting my history finals, I took charge of the firm and swiftly secured its future. On to my father's hyperactive disorder, I imposed financial rigour. The rabble of loss-making unheard-of composers, most of them Hitler or Stalin refugees, was parcelled off to a modern-music publisher in Vienna, who kept three and unsentimentally sacked the rest. The family concerts were wound up and the soloists redirected to rival agencies. Two became famous; the rest vanished into marriage, music-teaching or orchestral drudgery. I was sorry to lose the artists, for their eagerness was infectious and their egotism endlessly amusing. Some I had grown up with, others were so daunted by the challenge of tying their shoelaces that I did not like to think what would become of them without our unstinted protection – but what else, in the circumstances, could I have done? There was a pressing personal reason for me to terminate our involvement with talent, a reason I try very hard, on medical and legal advice, not to dwell upon or commit to print.

I got a good price for the offices from a Dutch merchant bank, retaining a corner space for myself, a spinster secretary called Erna Winter and an occasional junior. The revenue from these rapid disposals provided for Mother, who fell silent after Father's death and required periodic care in a private psychiatric hospital. During a remission she helped arrange my introduction to Myrtle, the bony daughter of Hispanic cousins, and morosely graced our solemn nuptials before overdosing on anti-depressants – whether deliberately or accidentally I neither knew nor deeply cared.

When my rationalisation was completed, what remained of the firm was a publishing division, producing purple-backed low-priced study scores for amateur and professional use. In less than a year, I had made Simmonds (Symphonic Scores and Concerts) Ltd profitable and risk-proof, reducing its operations to the point where they would never demand of me the sacrifice that my father had so willingly offered.

My shortcomings would be exposed in time, though not emphatically enough to dent my sage-like reputation. What I did not know at twenty-one years old is that risk elimination is bad for business. You have to take chances to have a shot at winning but I, unfamiliar with life, applied the dusty theorems of Cambridge economists and the jerky responses of a trauma-tised mind.

Before very long, one of the composers I had sold off wrote a million-dollar theme song for a Hollywood movie; another had an opera staged in fifteen German cities. My father's favourite, Vladimir Kuznetsov, was found hanged from a light-fitting in a Dalston bed-sitting room. His 'nephew' and room-mate, a costermonger called Steve, assured me that the poor chap's death had nothing to do with losing his publisher, but was the result of an auto-erotic experiment taken to an unfortunate extreme. Smitten with regret, I endowed a Kuznetsov Prize in the wretched creature's memory.

Simmonds' family concerts continued as cheerily as before under new ownership, enticing ordinary people to hear the music they loved and new artists to test their mettle away from critical ears and cultural commissars. My withdrawal made my competitors rich.

As for publishing, the bedrock of our business, I failed to anticipate a collapse in the demand for printed music. Radio and recordings – tapped, like water, with the touch of a finger – destroyed domestic music-making and fostered musical illiteracy on a scale so vast that, when people now talk of 'playing' music, what they mean is shoving a tape into the car dashboard. Few wrestle with a reed for the joy of hearing its wail and fewer still consult a pocket score during the course of a concert. Schools have stopped teaching children to play anything more elevated than penny whistles and dustbin lids. The 'popular score' has become a contradiction in terms.

Demand for printed music persists only in those parts where a semblance of Victorian values somehow prevails. In churches that keep up a trained chorus for Sunday worship and community halls where brass bands come together of a Wednesday night to practise early-industrial traditions. Towns and scrubland villages where tots can blow a tune before they read or write and teens discover sex in the coffee breaks of choir rehearsal. Often as not, these are the most derelict and violent corners of the kingdom: Ulster streets where the pipes play in sectarian bombings, Welsh hill-farms where counterpoint and lonely alcoholism are common-law co-habitants, Humber fishing ports where the cod has been fished out but the trawlermen's songs live on.

These are Simmonds' last resort, the relics I shall nurse until retirement or death, whichever comes the sooner. It is to one of these regions that I am heading now, to a downtrodden part of northern England where, in a wilderness of closed mines and disused shipyards, choral societies spend their year working up *Messiah* for Christmas, colliery villages have band calls twice a week and the roughest of rugby tacklers can play rude ballads on a pub piano, two-handed and with passable accuracy. Behind the coal-blackened fascias of terraced houses and defaced concrete council blocks, kids are made to play their scales before they have their tea. Beyond the electronic gates of executive lawn estates, music forms the first line of class-war defence: 'If snot-nosed Kayleigh with a single mum can get Grade Three with merit in piano *and* violin, I want our Charlotte to show what she can do at the Easter AIDS Awareness Concert.' Music took a bashing when Margaret Thatcher crushed the miners, but men who may never work again still approach me with urgent requests for a *Trumpet Voluntary* or singalong *Elijah*, and indigent single mothers with barely enough in their purses to put food on the table somehow manage to shell out for one of the tacky fiddles, made in China, that I carry as a tenuous sideline.

Unfailingly on my quarterly visits, I get asked to audition pre-matriculants who have applied for a place in one of London's famed music colleges and academies. Invariably, I advise them to consider a different vocation than one that will take them no higher than the rear desk of an insecure provincial orchestra. 'No matter,' say the mums dismissively. 'At least he won't go down the pit like his dad.' That cliché has rung all the hollower since the mines were shut, the shipyards became marinas and Dad was reduced to terminal unemployment or a demeaning 'service industry' existence as a waiter or tele-sales clerk. There will never be real work again around these parts for real men, let alone the dignity of labour.

The quick and the bright make an early escape, the quick to professionalised sport, the bright to chase musical dreams in rock groups and classical conservatories. My immediate destination, which must remain nameless, has never launched a star, but it has contributed any number of foot-soldiers to the musical army: boys who blow horns in opera orchestras and women who saw at violas as far afield as Sydney and Singapore, not to mention keyboardists for any number of backing groups. It yields the occasional ballet conductor and, once in a while, a contralto steeped in sacred oratorio. Stout and dependable performers, the soul and sinew of musical industry they are – a triumph of application over inspiration. I admire their grit as a dodo might nod to a dinosaur, two anachronisms trudging against the tides of fashion towards certain extinction.

Dismissing these maudlin reflections, I hear my station called – mumbled, rather – over a crackly address system by a Punjabi ticket-inspector unversed in English cadences. The clipped consonants of crisply uniformed conductors have been abolished, mashed into a multicultural blur by a soon-to-be privatised rail network that has begun to call its passengers 'customers' and treats them like cattle. Mine is not the only occupation in modern Britain that has lost its point and purpose. The whole lackadaisical country is slouching into sloppiness. Bloody Germans could teach us a thing or two.

Chewing a *Cham. Rad.* homoeopathic sedative, I grab my suitcase and stumble off the train, into the sour blare of a brass band playing, as if by macabre request, V. Kuznetsov's *Dawn on the Dnieper*. At the centre of the platform stands the Lord Mayor in full esoteric regalia, all gowned and chained. I know the fellow. His name is Charlie Froggatt and we once hacked our way through the Mozart clarinet quintet with two schoolmasters and a visiting undertaker in the empty Temperance Room of Bethesda Methodist Chapel – a hip-flasked impromptu performance on a blank August bank holiday. Froggatt, a grocer by trade, is a whiz on the woodwinds.

'It's sodding Simmonds, innit?' he bellows in my direction. 'Welcome to Tawburn!' though that is not the name of the place. Time for some pseudonyms. Can't use X and Y – too Conan Doylish. Let's call the area 'Tawside' and its towns 'Tawburn' and 'Oldbridge'. Anything more readily identifiable could provoke a reopening of police files, and that's the last thing I need. Tawburn Station is where I stand, amid the usual debris of empty crisp packets and polystyrene cups.

'Your Worship,' I address Froggatt with mock pomp, 'how good of you to come out and greet me – and in full fig, what's more.'

'Cut it out,' growls Froggatt. 'This isn't for you. It's bleddy Tawside Music Day and we're trying to raise a bit of consciousness in public places. Band's been practising that modern sunrise stuff for weeks and still comes unstuck on high E. Come to think of it, you're just what I need. Jump in car and I'll give you lift to the town hall.'

There is no polite way out of this. Froggatt grabs my elbow and steers me ceremonially down the platform to his black Daimler, the band switching to the safer chords of 'Hail the Conqu'ring Hero' from Handel's *Judas Maccabaeus*. My luggage is picked up by a porter, whom I point to the Royal Tawburn Hotel across the square. Rather than use one of the health-club inns that have sprung up around the marina, I stick with the lugubrious old station hotel, where no amount of air-freshener can ever dispel the day-long stench of breakfast kipper.

'Don't get all worried,' says Froggatt, pouring us a pair of malts from the back-seat bar, 'this isn't gonna cost yer. It's just a little favour I need off you tonight. Dinner, black tie, all that.'

No excuses come to mind. My nights on Tawside are mostly free, ever since I learned to avoid amateur musical evenings, where the playing is almost as excruciating as the semi-defrosted canapés. I tend to spend my evenings alone in the Royal's saloon bar, unwinding with the intake of roughly twice the Health Department's recommended alcohol consumption. The bar is oak-panelled, uninvaded by satellite TV and one-armed bandits and therefore half deserted – leaving me to do the *Daily Telegraph* crossword in peace. If I crave conversation, there is a barman who is knowledgeable about football and numismatics, and a spot of passing trade, nothing too taxing. One distant night, before my first heart murmur, a breezy blonde who popped in for a pack of fags tipped my double Laphroaig all over the *Telegraph* and my trousers. This led to a round of drinks each and a soggy stagger upstairs, ostensibly to clean up, culminating in spontaneous carnal combustion. It was an event of no consequence – the sort of thing that happens to a travelling salesman when his luck is in. An occupational digression, occasioned by *ennui* and opportunity. Like the deal that got away, you put it out of mind and hope there is no comeback. Hardly worth mentioning, really.

Froggatt's sand-dry accent drags me back to tonight's obstacle, the Mayor's black-tie dinner. Sitting in a stiff collar surrounded by small-town tradesmen is not my idea of a good night out, and I cannot cope with a late night if I'm to do any business tomorrow. Worse, what if he expects me to make a speech? Public speaking gives me the stutters, a regression to boyhood reticence.

'Fret not,' says Froggatt, anticipating my objections, 'we'll have you tucked up in bed by eleven and you won't have to get up and perform. Just be chairman of our jury and present the prize for the telly cameras in time for the nightly news.'

'What jury?' I demand.

'Tawside Young Musicians' Competition,' sighs the Mayor. 'Not heard of it? I'm not surprised. We've hardly any prize money and I can't afford PR. Couldn't get local telly to cover the semis and the best we can hope for tonight is ten seconds at the end of the regional news. But at least it'll show we care about music up here, and that we've bred some of the finest musicians in the world. There are some good youngsters coming up. They're about the only export commodity we've got left.'

'And I'm the best chairman you can get?'

'Don't flatter yourself,' rasps Froggatt. 'I invited Sir John Pritchard, the conductor chappie; he has cousins in the town. But we got a call last night that he's "unwell" and you can't get a big name at short notice. I was bleddy wetting myself – until you stepped off the train, and I thought, He'll do.

'Simmonds is a big name around here. Everybody sees it on the front of their music sheets. Mr Simmonds of Simmonds as chairman of the jury? That'll do nicely, and I'm not taking no for an answer.'

'But I'm not in the least bit qualified,' I protest. 'Judging a competition calls for specific instrumental expertise. I play the fiddle and piano a bit but you know me – I'm just a commercial traveller in musical goods, a cog in the music machine.'

'Don't give me that,' says the Mayor, with a hint of metal. 'No false modesty. Your family has worked with Kreisler and Heifetz, your name's almost as famous as theirs. You can tell a decent fiddler from a fake, a flash of talent from a teacher's pet.

'Anyway, you won't have to judge the technical stuff on your own. We're calling in two professors from Manchester. You'll also have two council men, our head of Music and director of Arts and Leisure Services, to broaden the perspective. What you do is chair the panel and throw a casting vote only if the profs and the officials can't agree on a winner. You'll have six of the best under-eighteens in all England. Just pick one, declare the result before half ten and I'll do all the speeches. Any problems?'

We have pulled up at Tawburn town hall. Waiting for me indoors are the directors of Education and Libraries who, I hope, are about to sign replacement orders for lost and damaged scores that will cover my overheads to the end of the financial year. I badly need those orders. Knowing that refusal can offend, and that offending the Mayor can have an adverse effect on library sales, I quickly acquiesce. 'Yer an ace bloke,' says Froggatt, charging up the steep front steps in a swirl of robes. 'My car will call for you at six. Be there.'

It is a relief to switch to the sigla and ISBNs of professional librarianship, the furtive codes of scholarly commerce. The day passes in a pleasant blur of ur-texts and catalogue prices, book-trade gossip and musical trivia. By the time the tea-trolley comes round, I have secured the biggest orders and could well go home, mission accomplished. But I am committed to the evening's dinner and have arranged in my mind to spin out the rest of the week with a tour of small accounts that will justify my absence to Myrtle and the taxman. Small shops, small change. But it gives me the sense of stealing time for myself, time that is mine to own and to squander.

That's what I lost when the genius left – the mastery of time. Like death, it is a loss that cannot be repaired, a hole in the heart of things. I trudge back to my hotel in slashing rain, the shop-lights twinkling on glossy pavements. It is a two-minute trudge, not long enough for reflective anticipation of the evening ahead. When the blow falls, it will fall without warning. Nothing in this final day of normality has deviated from the norm, nothing warns me that the monotony of my half-life is about to be shattered, that I am to be brought face to face with the thing I most fear and long for – the golden part that was gutted from my subsequently empty existence.

# 2

# It's About Time

I always pack black tie and tails, just in case. Also a spare three-piece business suit and a woolly muffler to ward off chill winds from the polluted Taw estuary. 'Take care of yourself,' was Myrtle's instruction, and I do my best.

It has been, all told, a subdued day, punctuated by hourly reports from a war in the Persian Gulf, a fight that demands no great act of national sacrifice but none the less exposes bitter national divisions. 'They send five armies to reconquer a Kuwaiti sheikh's oil field, but won't lift five fingers to save our coal industry,' grumbles the Director of Education, a phlegmatic polymath with a night-school degree. I mutter something politically ambiguous as he signs my order in laborious triplicate.

'What a farce,' observes the director of Libraries, his patched jeans betraying fashionably leftish sympathies. 'First we sell arms to Iraq, then we bomb them to bits, then we'll sell 'em some more.' It won't be long before he is signing *Socialist Worker* petitions demanding western aid for ruined Iraq. I bite a lip and nod hypocritically until the signed order is tucked into my slightly tremulous hand.

'Good day, sir?' asks the Royal Tawburn barman, as he pours me a quick one.

Not bad, I reckon. Four thousand pounds' worth of business in the murk of recession and the thick of war is better than a pack of excuses. 'I suppose I have earned myself a drink,' I tell George, the barman. 'Why don't you have one too?' In the snug of a saloon that has not sniffed fresh air since Lloyd George lolloped through on his last campaign, I cast a quick eye over the small print of tonight's contest:

. . . open to boys and girls born on or before 1 December 1978 in the Tawside administrative region or continuously resident there from 1 January 1985 . . .

The six winners of preliminary rounds will qualify for the Grand Final where they will be required to play a solo work of Johann Sebastian Bach on piano or violin, followed by a work of choice, which may or may not be accompanied on the piano by a person nominated by the contestant.

No finalist will play longer than fifteen minutes, except by special request of the chairman of the jury . . . chairman will vote only in the event of a tie . . . jury's decision is final and irrevocable. Judging procedures will follow the rules of the Queen Elisabeth International Music Competition of Belgium (copies available on request from Director of Arts and Leisure Services). Members of the jury will not divulge details of their deliberations or maintain any contact whatsoever with the news media during the contest and for seven days thereafter without written permission from the chief executive, Tawside District Council.

Standard stuff. The Reine Elisabeth is just about the longest-running and best-run music competition in the world, founded by a music-mad Queen of the Belgians who was herself a useful violinist. Sensible of Tawside to take up her fair and impartial rules, like the Marquess of Queensberry's in boxing.

The mayoral Daimler purrs up on time and shuttles me back to the town hall, where a wall-eyed receptionist gives a sullen nod towards the Wordsworth Room. I am the last of the adjudicators to arrive. The two Mancunian professors, male and vaguely female, stand out like frayed cuffs on a funeral suit. They have taken up positions at either end of the mantelpiece, beneath an oil portrait of the Lakelands poet, wearing the musty air that provincial academics adopt to protect their ivoried tenure from real-world intruders. They greet me wanly, wine-glass in hand, as if welcoming a fresh corpse to the pathology lab.

Tawside's head of Music is a good deal friendlier. Fred Burrows, organist of Tawburn Cathedral and conductor of the Tawside Youth Orchestra, beams hugely and comes barging over. He is a big, bumbling bachelor, good with kids, no threat to women. 'I'll get you a drink,' bellows Fred, only to find himself outflanked by a portly, full-bearded personage of obvious self-importance. Our fourth judge, in a poly-yellow tie with green stave lines bearing the purpled motto 'Play To Win', introduces himself as Oliver Adams, 'call me Olly', Director of Arts and Leisure Services.

Above the forested slopes, Olly's fortyish face has the tender sheen of a newborn's cranium, complete with cradle rash. He foists on me a glass of hypermarket chardonnay, a warmed-over canapé and a gift-wrapped exemplar of his corporate cravat, all of which

I deposit discreetly on the mantelpiece. 'Great to have you with us, Mr Simmonds,' he booms. 'Good to have a chairman who knows the score, unlike some I could mention who only count wrong notes. What we're looking for here is a real winner, someone who can get out and sell himself, sell the region, Play To Win. I came up with the competition slogan. D'you like it?'

Olly is new to cultural affairs – 'moved over from Marketing last year,' he confides. He'll learn. Behind him, half a pace behind, stands a handsome, fair-haired woman in a printed silk dress, quite stylish. She appears to be some kind of personal assistant or *aide-de-camp*. 'My wife, Sandra,' declares Olly, causing my senses to swim and swoon as I half-recognise her – surely not? – as my long-ago one-night stand from the Royal Tawburn saloon bar.

Now, it is not uncommon for men of my age and proclivities to run into someone with whom we may, or may not, have once-upon-a-time kicked off restraint and garments in panting coition, sharing orgasms but no phone numbers. If there is an etiquette for such occasions, I have yet to discover it. Someone should write a how-to book for aging roués. What does one say to an ex-quickie, or not, as the case may be? No point in venturing, 'I say, haven't we, er, met before?' Because if you have, she won't believe you could have forgotten her. And if you haven't, she'll catch the wink in your eye and write you off as a drooling old pervert – that is, if she doesn't squawk sexual harassment and summon Security.

What to do? I could be mistaken. Time can turn ancient gropes into grand passion and rejection into gentle acquiescence – every near-miss a full-blooded winner. For want of certainty, I resolve to stay neutral and hope that something she says or does will trigger a confirmatory memory cell. Some hope.

Sandra, if that's her name, rings a faint bell but not enough to jangle the recollection belfry. I might have bumped into her once at some cocktail party, or across the counter of a Tawburn music shop. I try to imagine her as she must have been a dozen years ago, before marriage to Marketing polished her social skills and multiple childbirth broadened her bottom to Rubensesque dimensions. I strive to picture her as the giggly, up-for-it sec who, half pissed and half for a laugh, stumbled with a smart-suited salesman in similar condition up the Royal Tawburn stairs and on to a creaking bed, bumpety-bump and sound asleep. And then once more, piston-smooth and with cobwebbed eyes, in the curtained light of morning-after. Then shower together, blow-dry, dash of lipstick, must dash, no time for coffee, see you later, not a chance.

'Sandra has kindly agreed to serve as rapporteur to the jury,' declares Olly. 'She used to do the books for Mr Burrows' band, so she's familiar with musical terms, and all that. If there's anything you need, Mr Chairman, just ask Sandi and she'll be happy to oblige.'

Gratefully, I search Sandra's garrulous green eyes for something obliging but find only the blank smile of a civic spouse. 'I'm sure we won't make excessive physical demands on Mrs Adams,' I venture, seeking a flicker of ironic response to my dusty joke. Nothing, not a shadow on her verdant iris.

That could mean one of four things. Either she doesn't recognise me. Or she doesn't want to. Or she is biding her time for a private word. Or it wasn't her at all – and, if it wasn't, I wonder what the real girl looks like, and what *was* her name? I shall have to rely on luck and wit to get me through the evening without making a prat of myself.

All vanities aside, I could forgive an old flame of a decade ago for not recognising me. Although still trim, I have lost most of my wavy hair, three back teeth and that brisk patina of benign middle-agelessness that passes for anything from thirty-five to sixty. Never much of an Apollo, I used to possess a lightness of spirit that, allied to an attentive ear, proved attractive enough to women to make me feel sexually desirable, albeit relatively inactive beyond (or even within) the marriage bed. What I now resemble is a man on the brink of his pension, dried out and beyond revival. The glow has gone from my skin, the spark from my eyes, to such a degree that my devoted secretary, Erna Winter, now retired, recently walked right past me on Regent Street without her customary greeting – 'Good morning, Mr Simmonds, and did you have a good concert last night?' As memory wanes, how I miss the omniscient Miss Winter.

And what of Mrs Olly, if she is who I think she was, or might have been? The girl at the bar might not have seen much of my face in the forty-watt gloom and I might have given her a false name, if any, out of habitual caution. 'Don't be a grouchy bear,' she laughed, I seem to remember, mopping up the spilled drink on my trouser-leg. 'Tighter, Daddy Bear, tighter!' she cried, at a climactic moment, I suddenly recall. 'Hold me tighter.' Funny how memory flashes up fragments and withholds the essence. I have no image of the girl, no name; all I know is that she has a thing about teddies and grizzlies.

Perhaps I was one of a caravanserai of closing-time pick-ups that she scored in pursuit of some ursine ideal, a grail that (if she is the same person) has attained marital apotheosis in fuzz-faced Olly with the flaky skin. Her congress with me, fleeting as it was (if indeed it was), was but an overture to Olly's happy-end opera. If she is anything like the impulsive young women I read about in the *Daily Mail*, she will have had dozens of flings before selecting a life-partner. In the average modern woman's busy sex-life, a tipsy indiscretion with a total stranger would barely register on her score sheet. It is only I, with an archaic set of compromised fidelities, who find the encounter worth mentioning at all. My moral mountain was, for her, a molehill. Speaking of which, a cell of tactile memory calls up a tiny brown mole that greeted my caress to the undercurve of her jaw. Is that a wrinkle on your chin, Sandra, or a cosmetic surgeon's scar? Stop staring, idiot, you're making her uncomfortable.

Checking my pulse, I chit and chat to my fellow judges on common green-room topics. Wasn't that Czech girl smashing in the Proms? Why did what's-his-name resign at Covent Garden? Was it the booze, or the boys? Mrs Olly flickers amiably around the periphery. Is she avoiding me? And what exactly is bothering me – the fear she might identify me and demand another bump on the bouncy frame, or the regret that a woman who once came alive to my practised touch cannot see the extant spark behind my derelict exterior? Either way, the anxiety is affecting both my angina and my stomach, which cramps with tension. Good golly, Mrs Olly, can we clear this up before I suffer a cardiovascular episode? Watch out, she's heading this way.

'A quick word, Mr Chairman, before we go in?' Her breath brings out sweat beads on my cold ear as she outlines my duties in the hours to come. I steal a peek at her features and see nothing beyond dutiful formality. So that's it: a self-deluding fantasy on my part of wishfully misplaced identity. Pathetic, really.

Then, just as we troop into the mock-Tudor Clement Attlee Hall, I feel her guiding hand on my back, just above the coccyx, and the heat of that hotel-room coupling floods my senses with arousal and dismay. Let it rest, I tell myself, there's a night's work ahead.

The hall is packed and the front rows have been well oiled.

Mayor Froggatt burps out a few words of welcome before staggering back to his seat, well satisfied. His guests are port-cheeked and growing merrier by the minute. Three pitchers of water and six glasses await the judges on a trestle table, stage left. At each place-setting there is a mimeographed sheet containing short biographies of the six contestants. We open our ledgers and prepare to judge. This is not the nail-bitten Tchaikovsky Concourse in Moscow, or even the homespun Leeds Piano Competition. There is no pit full of orchestral tedium and suppurating intrigue. There is not even a proper scoring form, just a ream of Tawside Council-headed notepaper on which I draw four columns then circulate it to the other judges, indicating that they do the same. We shall mark separately for technique, interpretation and musicality – or how accurately, innovatively and engagingly they play the seen-better-days Steinway grand piano, or whatever scratchy violins their harassed parents can afford. Add the marks together, divide by three, top average is the winner.

I have done this sort of thing before and never with an easy conscience. Combatants are assessed less on skill and vision than on metronomic exactitude. Personality and artistic penetration would be penalised by the professors as technical faults and by the rest of us as irritating quirks. There is no fair way to rate a winsome ten-year-old against a pimply matriculant, and on different instruments to boot. Injustice is inbuilt, but the public demands a winner and we must deliver one. Everyone knows the system is rotten, but we perpetrate a consensual hoax in the hope of filching a few prime-time seconds to remind viewers that there are greater heights in life than politics, sport and pop stardom.

No one gets hurt by the hoax. The contestants, or so we tell ourselves, have nothing to lose. This, for them, is a one-in-six chance of breaking out of a Tawside council block or semi-detached and reaching for a better life. They look upon music as their ticket to freedom – just as it was for *shtetl*-dwellers in the Russian pale of settlement who, in dire want, turned out a Heifetz and a Horowitz, David Oistrakh and Isaac Stern, Nathan Milstein and Mischa Elman. Tawburn is no Odessa, but its children can dream and we do no harm in encouraging their escapist fantasies.

Our first finalist looks desperate to abscond. Ashutosh al-Haq is thirteen years old, according to his programme biography, his origins in a Bengal village that his parents fled during the 1971 Indo-Pakistan War. Raised, I'd guess, above a textile sweatshop, put to work with needle and thread at six or seven and redeemed, a little, by the old-fashioned English schoolmarm in a faded ballgown who led him to the piano. Ashutosh plays athletically and with reasonable precision, getting through his Bach fugue mechanically and following it with a Busoni reworking of a Bach chorale. What he lacks is incision and colour. He may acquire them in due course, but at this stage the boy is not a contender at the level I have come to expect. I mark him six out of ten for technique, four for interpretation, question-mark for character – be generous and make it five. Sandra Adams squints over my shoulder. A section of the hall, I hear, is roaring, '*Zindabad*,' as if Bangladesh has just won the cricketing world cup. I suppress a woolly-liberal inclination to call the kid back for an encore, undoubtedly in his own best interests.

The next performer, just out of primary school, looks too small for his fiddle. Peter Burbridge, from the village of Oxleyheath, plays more wrong notes than right in the Sarabande of the Bach D minor partita and is almost too upset to proceed with his voluntary piece, Kreisler's 'Liebeslied', with his grey, stray-haired mother as accompanist. I make a mental note to say something nice in my award speech, and mark the miserable urchin three, four and two.

With the third contestant, we have a winner. Maria Olszewska, sixteen years old, is Tawburn born and bred – her father an *émigré* Polish engineer, her mother a North Sea marine biologist. She ripples off a Bach prelude and fugue in C major on the piano as if warming up. Nerveless as one of her mum's nekton, she then plays two Chopin preludes and, when recalled by overwhelming ovations, a dazzling improvisation on the Beatles' hit 'Ticket to Ride'. This girl has got the lot.

Nines for Maria on my sheet and, it appears, more or less all round as we compare notes during the drinks break. Fred Burrows is ecstatic about the girl, and both professors, Brenda Murch and Arthur Brind, are itching to get their pedagogic claws on her. 'We could admit her to the Academy, even though the admission list is closed for next year,' they witter. I make a mental note to tell the girl's parents to take her to Joachim Malkiel in London. All she needs is the final coat of high gloss and a knockout frock, and she'll be ready for Carnegie Hall.

Our glow at her emergence is dulled by Olly Adams, sounding petulant. 'Doesn't anyone reckon on the Asian kid?' he mopes. 'I've got him ahead on points.' I catch a tic of irritation in Sandra's eye and wonder if all is well with the Adams family.

'What about you, Fred?' persists Olly, turning on the director of Music. 'Don't you think the kid's a bit special for his age and, er, background?'

Burrows is in a bind: his budget is controlled by Arts and Leisure Services and he can't afford a falling-out with the director. He likes his job, has no life outside it. I watch his eager brow furrowing in search of a diplomatic formula. 'Oh, ever so good, Olly,' purrs Fred winningly. 'I've got him down as a candidate for one of our junior proms. But there's no question – that Maria is a class apart. She could play for England in the next Queen Elisabeth.'

'Well, can't we give the boy a consolation prize, show his people how much we appreciate his effort?' persists Adams.

'What would be your view, Mr Chairman?' interjects Sandra Adams. I admire her timing, letting Olly have his say but saving him from further foolishness.

'My feeling,' I venture, after a moment's faked reflection, 'is that we must be careful not to blur the Tawside Young Musicians' award with supernumerary presentations. The Mayor is anxious to establish an uncompromisingly high standard. He has charged us with picking a winner, and that's what we must do.

'However, given the encouraging popular response, it might be appropriate to announce that, in view of the exceptional merit of the contestants, the council will tomorrow award scholarships to all the runners-up. That way, you can milk an extra day's publicity and appease the more, er, vociferous sections of the audience.'

'Some of them are a bit fired up,' admits Olly. 'But that's a very helpful suggestion, Mr Chairman, and I'm sure we can find room in the budget. Sandi, will you see to it?' Sandra Adams, as we return to the Clement Attlee Hall, flashes me a wry grin of complicity. I catch her drift. Myrtle, in a marital spat, once accused me unfairly of manipulating my intellectual inferiors. I'd guess that Sandi unthinkingly does much the same, stringing along her tufty spouse like a straw puppet. Poor Olly.

The next two contestants do not detain us long. Both are suburban pre-teens who attack the violin as if it has done them harm. Amanda Garvey and Russell Thornton are products of an Oriental tuition method that takes four-year-old tots and turns them into musical robots. One after the other, this pair hit every note on the nail until the piece is hammered in, five points each. I am bunching my papers and looking forward to an easy night when the last finalist, a fifteen-year-old from Oldbridge, Peter

Stemp, walks on stage, tunes up his violin and begins the opening movement of the Bach G minor sonata, one of the great interior meditations of classical literature.

The boy is too tense to inject much expression, too immature to offer enlightenment. Intonation is good, double-stopping well practised, Grade Eight exam pass.

He finishes the Adagio and pitches without pause into the near-mechanical rhythm of the Fugue, as if fearing we might stop him and send him away. The movement is less than a minute old – I have been reduced to watching the clock – when, on the pure tone of an open G string, my heart stops beating. Turns off. Cuts out.

This is it, I reckon: the moment of reckoning. 'This has come from the Lord,' I hear the sweet Psalmist singing, 'let it be a wonder in our eyes. This is the day the Lord made, rejoice and be happy in it.' Contentment consumes me and I surrender to fate. Davidian hymnody yields to Tudor poetry: 'An end that I have now begun . . . My lute, be still, for I have done.' Picasso's *Guernica*, for some reason, springs to my mind's eye. I am being conducted on a farewell *tour d'horizon* of cultural monuments as life ebbs sweetly away.

Then, with a jolt, the beat returns. Still alive. I exhale, coming to my senses at the close of the second movement, which is all we have time for. The applause is polite, my colleagues inert. 'Nothing special,' I hear one prof carp to the other.

So the heart-stopping moment is mine alone. What was it – an early warning of the inevitable? I run a quick self-check. I took my pills in the proper order and at the appointed hour all day long. Apart from a ridiculous amorous jolt, there has been no serious stress. Diet has been sensible. Pulse ninety-two, breathing normal. It must be the music.

Can't be the piece, the Bach G minor, which has no sentimental history for me, so far as I am aware – a good piece, but not a gut-wrencher. Something to do with the way it was played? Peter Stemp has hit some spot in me, a bullseye unmarked in years. There must be something about the pesky boy. Damnit, he nearly killed me.

The gawky kid is wrestling now with one of those blobs of Saint-Saëns that sound like sticks of candyfloss with added sugar. His mousy-looking mum is at the piano and his tone is unsteady. Marks of six, seven, five, thank you and good night. Yet, back a track, at a certain point in the Bach, the boy did something that almost did for me. If he does not repeat it in the French *petit-fours*, I'll make him play as long as it takes to find out what it is.

As the French froth dies away, I make a sedentary gesture to the other judges and, exercising the chairman's prerogative, call for an extra piece. 'You sure we need this?' scowls Olly. Fred Burrows looks bewildered. Peter Stemp, bemused, whispers, 'Johann Sebastian Bach: Sarabande from partita number two in D minor' and within a minute I know all I have ever needed to know about Bach, the boy and the meaning of music.

Playing Bach on the violin is not child's play. Although the music is generally easy on the ear, the partitas and sonatas are pitted with twists and finger-stretches whose difficulty is masked by the simplicity of the sounds produced. A player can bring off the most dazzling leap without anyone but a fellow-virtuoso knowing what he has achieved. Should he slip or miss a note, however, the least musical of listeners will sit up and spot the error.

Having got the piece under his fingers, the fiddler has then to release the music from its formal chastity-belt and reveal its hooded secrets. The art of interpreting Bach is a book of seven seals that only immortals have unlocked. Bach is not meant to be played competitively. But the transparency of the solo violin works is a gift to competition judges, for no other music so readily separates the meritorious artist from the meretricious.

To bring this music to life, the soloist must overcome the inertness of notes and infuse a gust of his own breath, like a paramedic performing emergency resuscitation. The crotchets and quavers are printed blobs on stave, to be played exactly as written. There is no licence for improvisation or messing around. The only way for a performer to express himself within the strict traditions of classical music is by shading the relative values of the blobs – shaving a nanosecond off one note and adding it to the next.

This underhand form of theft, known as *rubato*, is one way that soloists individualise a piece of music. It is the bottom rung on the ladder of playing alone, the first liberty taken with a composer's text. Great artists surmount such petty acts of larceny as a master burglar would scorn shoplifting. They have no need for subterfuge or sleight-of-hand. They enter through the front door and rearrange the diamond display in the window without anyone noticing the alteration until they are gone. What virtuosi do is take hold of time and create an illusion that, *imitatio Dei*, they control it. They can stop time in its tracks, restore our dreams of youth and defy the march of death. Theirs are the hands on the clock-face of our lives. That is why, know it or not, we lose heads and hearts to master musicians – because they can spring us from the deadly treadmill of daily concerns and transport us to a realm where time is defeated.

I once knew a violinist who made time stand still in the space between two notes. He was not the only one to do so. Kreisler, my father's idol, could do it at will and Jascha Heifetz, the ice-eyed technician, could do anything he liked with a violin. Kreisler would stop time for love and Heifetz for show, but the musician I knew stopped time as an act of power, to exert his will upon the world. Unrecorded, his mastery is known only to me. Pitching my ear to Peter Stemp, I hear it again. In a sea of routinely articulated sounds, the boy picks out another open G and fixes it in the firmament, just so. This is neither a cheap stunt, nor a clever imitation. Stemp could not have copied Kreisler or Heifetz from a recording, because their time-stopping was hallucinatory, unconveyable on vinyl.

What's more, he has something that only my violinist possessed – he sustains the illusion of motionlessness beyond the resumption of motion, as if keeping a pianist's pedal-foot on a fiddle chord. Does this make sense? My violinist made time stop the way a maharishi seems to transcend the force of gravity; however, instead of bumping to earth after a second's levitation, he would leave the sound hanging in the air, or the imagination, until he, and he alone, was ready and willing to let it down. That was the source of his power: the rest flowed from that device.

How can I be so sure, after all this time? Because musical memory does not fade like other faculties. I may have trouble remembering the names of my daughters-in-law, but I can recall every note of the first 'Eroica' Symphony I heard, aged eleven, conducted by the cranky and incontrovertible Otto Klemperer. I may be cheating a bit since I attended both rehearsals and performance. But the fact that I can vouch for every particle of this experience when I could not, if mugged at a cash-point, remember my PIN number to save my life, confirms the indelibility of musical memory.

There is empirical confirmation of this supposition. The neurologist Oliver Sacks, in a case-history entitled *The Man Who Mistook his Wife for a Hat*, observed an elderly musician who was suffering from an advanced form of Alzheimer's disease and unable to tell his wife from his headgear. The only way he could get dressed was by humming a Schumann song whose melody, perfectly remembered, provided a framework in which he could fulfil such complex tasks as tying his shoes and finding his hat. The case-history, converted by Michael Nyman into an effective chamber opera, is a moving testimony to the residual power of music in age-worn minds. In my own case, unimpaired musical memory allows me to compare with a high degree of certainty the sounds I hear today with those I heard as a boy. When I judge that Peter Stemp is employing a device that was patented by a violinist who walked out of my life forty years ago, I do so with full confidence in my judgement – knowing, also, that I am the only man alive who can testify to the coincidence.

There are, as I have said, no recordings of the vanished violinist, nor any mentions in musical literature. He left the stage before the curtain rose, and he took with him half of my being and all of my hopes. I have missed him, unmentioned, every day of my subsequent half-life. I cannot yet bring myself to utter his name, but as Peter Stemp's echo of his trademark trick pricks my ears and floods my eyes, I need no further proof to know that I have somehow picked up his scent and may be on the way to retrieving a part of the life that was stolen from me by that unforgettable time-bandit.

This is not suspicion or surmise; nothing resembling the did-we, didn't-we waltz with Sandra Adams. This is a dead-cert sighting of a suspect who stole the inner, better half of me and left behind the bitter exterior. Hearing Peter Stemp of Oldbridge play a note that defies the passage of time, I know beyond a possibility of doubt that my devourer liveth – and that, come what may, I shall track him down before I die.

As if by way of confirmation, my heart blips again as Peter

Stemp tries his time-stopping trick once too often for good taste. The applause for Stemp's encore is tepid, and I catch a couple of withering glances from the professors. As they troop off for dinner, I stay behind to gather strength and thoughts.

'You all right, Mr Sim?' asks Sandra Adams, with endearing familiarity.

'Yes, yes, go in, be with you in a minute,' I reply, burying my head beneath the green-baize tabletop as if searching for something I have dropped on the floor. The truth is, I am not all right, not even slightly all right, and there is nothing Sandra or whoever she is can do to put me right. I am either dying or reviving, and I'm not at all sure which is the better option.

A man I have long given up for dead is apparently still alive, and I am consumed by thoughts of finding him – as well as by the awful realisation that he has been deliberately hiding from me all these years. Long-dead parts of my past are stirring from sedation. Common sense urges me to suppress them and catch the next train back to London. Vengeance summons me to set out on a man-hunt and pursue it to the mortal end. A civil war erupts inside my control tower, desk-bound caution fighting off wave upon wave of violent adventure. The outcome could go either way. If caution gets blown to the winds, I might be about to expose myself to risk, to ridicule – worst of all, to the possibility of love. I don't think I can cope with love. 'Help me,' I childishly implore, 'please, Dovidl, tell me what to do.'

The utterance of his name – *Dovidl* – precipitates a violent flush of palpitations. He can still unsettle me like nothing on earth. This cannot continue: get a grip, stay cool. I need to get through tonight's business alive before setting out to track him down.

In pursuit of instant calm, I ransack my pockets for pharmaceutical remedies, discovering – too late – that I have forgotten to transfer the pack of Valium from my day jacket to my dress suit. Panic rising, palms sweating, my fingertips claw the bottom of an outer pocket for bits and bobs that may have survived a recent trip to the dry-cleaner's. Into my parched mouth go: two loose Nurofens, a mild laxative and a confectioner's cough lozenge, still in its waxed-paper wrapper. Dear Dovidl, I pray. Let me live just long enough to look you in the eye and reclaim the part of me that is rightly mine.

# 3

# Out of Time

The last time I saw David Eli Rapoport was the last day of my whole life, my life as a whole man. He was leaving the house with his precious Guadagnini in its battered case and a wedge of toast sticking out of his mouth when, on a premonitory impulse, I called out after him. 'Dovidl,' I cried, using our boyhood diminutive, 'are you going to be OK? Do you want me to come along?'

'No need,' he mumbled, through a splutter of toast. 'It's only an acoustic rehearsal. Won't take more than twenty minutes.' And off he hunched into the taxi-cab he had kept growling for half an hour, his black hair glistening in the May sunlight, his Modigliani face tilted upwards to receive its meagre warmth.

It was the morning of his début, an event so momentous that it was the talk of the cultural hemisphere. Telegraphists batted word of it back and forth across the Atlantic. Radio comedians worked it into their routines ('He plays the violin so ruddy well, he can play it Bach to front'). Touts were offering unobtainable consumer goods

('Six pairs of nylons, guv, a lovely Havana cigar?') in exchange for a sought-after ticket. The *News Chronicle* switchboard was jammed for two days after running a competition with a pair of front-row seats as first prize.

The début of this handsome young violinist [warned a *Daily Herald* editorial] is threatening to overshadow next month's buck-you-up Festival of Britain with its striking new concert hall and fun for all the family. The government may think it knows how to put a smile on our faces after years of rationing and austerity, but it takes more than a Royal Festival Hall and a Sky Pylon to inflame the popular imagination. It takes something no government can ever legislate for – it takes a touch of genius.

Eli Rapoport has already been acclaimed by the musical world as the brightest star to appear since the war. He may just be the first of a new British breed of brilliant virtuosos who will go out and conquer the world with flair rather than force of arms. What a boost it would be for our weary people if he turned out to be the first hero of a new era – an age that will put an end to war.

The making of this modern hero had been devised, with military precision and media marksmanship, by the unflappable Mortimer Simmonds. Machiavellian to his bootstraps, he had to break one of his own strict rules to get the campaign off the ground. 'David,' he mused one evening at dinner, 'we may need to make a cosmetic change to your name. Nothing radical, just a modest adjustment.'

'What do you have in mind, Mr Simmonds?' said Dovidl warily.

'Something a little less Jewish,' said my father. 'David, you see, sounds too Jewish. No musician called David or Moses or Abraham ever met with success. Jewish giants don't, for some reason, go down too well – even in America. To get you started, we may have to drop the David.'

'I suspect you have come up with an alternative,' said Dovidl, who knew that my father never mused on an empty mind.

'Eli,' continued Mortimer Simmonds, 'has a nice nondenominational ring to it. He was, as you know, a Jewish high priest, but the name will appeal to Catholics, reminding them of Christ's last words in the Easter service "*Eli, Eli, lamah sabachtani*." The Methodists will think it's Welsh, the Anglicans will find it quaint. It also has the advantage of being short, which means I can print it in a larger font, leading the eye to the trisyllabic surname below. What do you think, boys?'

I sometimes wondered whether my father did not judge every issue by how it might look on a billboard. Dovidl, however, did not seem to mind dropping a name. The more he thought about it, the more he liked the idea of erecting a barrier between his private self and his future public persona. 'That way,' he said, 'I'll know which people know me for what I am and which for what I do.'

That settled, my father sent him out on a confidence-building recital tour around small-town halls, no advance hoardings, no critics invited. Satisfied with his progress after six months, my father took the amiable Neville Cardus to dinner at the Savoy and, over vintage brandys, mentioned to the sybaritic *Manchester Guardian* music critic that a young prospect of his was playing a Bach recital that weekend at the Colston Hall, Bristol. Cardus, who doubled as the paper's cricket correspondent, remarked with faint surprise that he had to be in Bristol to cover Gloucestershire versus Lancashire – a fixture my father had verified in advance.

'It'll probably rain,' said my father.

'Usually does in Bristol,' agreed Cardus.

'I'll leave a pair of tickets at the box-office,' smiled Mortimer Simmonds, 'just in case you have an empty evening.'

Cardus's review the following Monday was headlined 'New Star in the West'. It was the kind of encomium that explodes once in an epoch and is quoted in anthologies ever after. Cardus, who had spent a long day pining for the dotted intricacy of a musical score while the cricket score advanced at a dour thirty runs an hour, was clearly bowled over by Dovidl. He extolled the artist's liquid tone, dashing runs, languid stance and gaunt good looks –

> a combination, if I may mix a metaphorical cocktail, between the wounded Adonis and the young Donald Bradman on his first Ashes tour. Add to these, the eyes of Franz Mesmer and the expressiveness of Laurence Olivier in one of his classical roles – dry, yet infinitely wise – and what we saw and heard in the unadorned Bach recitation was the birth of a comet: the most fully finished young artist I have ever seen astride an English stage, or any other for that matter. My only worry is whether our tiny galaxy is great enough to accommodate his dawning glory.

That morning, the phones went off like fire bells. Journalists clamoured for interviews, orchestras for dates. Mortimer Simmonds refused them all with even affability. 'The boy's not quite ready,' he maintained, his gentle demurral serving only – as intended – to redouble the demand. The cauldron was starting to simmer.

In January 1951, as the government announced the full plans for its Festival of Britain, a three-page story appeared in *The Bridge*, organ of the violin trade. Titled 'Rapoport – Heir Apparent?', the report introduced a 'Polish-born prodigy who will make his London début on the eve of his twenty-first birthday, a milestone in any young man's life'. It noted that 'some have likened the liquescent amber of his tone to the radiance that was Fritz Kreisler's . . .' (and you can guess who planted that comparison in the anonymous writer's mind).

Kreisler's recent retirement at the age of seventy-four, after fracturing his skull in a road accident [the article continued], has left lovers of the violin without an outlet for their ardour. The incomparable Jascha Heifetz excites admiration and wonderment without engaging our affection. The fastidious Yehudi Menuhin is revered at a sterile distance. The gleaming gifts of Nathan Milstein, Mischa Elman, and others of the Russo-American diaspora have been severely rationed since the war. Miss Ida Haendel, marvellous as she is, is but a slip of a girl.

'What we long for,' one hears lamented in the lobby of the Wigmore Hall, 'is another Kreisler, an artist who can warm the cockles of your heart and give a cheeky wink while playing with effortless individuality. They don't breed 'em like that any more, do they?'

Don't they, indeed? It is a dozen years since England heard the last of Kreisler and what resides in the ear is a mist of nostalgia. It is ever thus with living legends: we forgive their latterday lapses and remember them only as they played in their prime. Kreisler the magnificent is a thing of the distant past. We had been waiting for the next Kreisler long before the last one left the platform.

Here, however, we have the glimmer of an oncoming heir. For those who see omens in such things, his début concert at the Royal Albert Hall on 3 May will fall thirty years less a day to the night that King Kreisler made his triumphant return to London after the Great War, a night when the sweet tone of a stringed instrument dispelled agonies of mortal struggle and human loss. The coming 3 May, one has the suspicion, could be another such night.

From what I have seen of the promising Eli Rapoport, in out-of-the-way recitals that he has been giving under Mr Simmonds' careful management in Basingstoke, Guildford and Poole, I can vouch that playing of such communicative felicity and physical mastery, such seriousness and sense of fun, has not been seen since the great Fritz first slipped into our midst like cream into coffee, changing our textures for ever. Young Mr Rapoport has a sound all his own and a style to match: half cocky, half rapt. He will be going places far beyond Basingstoke, Guildford and Poole before this season is out; the sky, one feels, is his lower limit. His approach to Bach, still yet dangerous, resembles a cobra coiled in sunlight on a rock – a thing of beauty that can strike without warning. The B minor partita in particular . . .

There was no need to read on. Critical assessment melted into pure hyperbole, quotable gems cascading down the page. A copy of the article was mailed, 'Compliments of Mr Mortimer Simmonds', to the William Hickey gossip column of the mass-readership *Daily Express*. Two days later it produced the page-lead: 'London Lad Could Be Next Kreisler, Experts Say'. To millions who had never entered a concert hall, Kreisler was still a familiar radio name, an eternal artist. Introducing the next Kreisler to *Express* readers was like unveiling the heir to Rodin in *Le Monde*.

Once the popular appetite was whetted, the media pressure

turned unrelenting. My father policed it to the best of his ability, but his phlegmatism was sometimes overwhelmed and the demands on Dovidl began to mount.

'You must ease up on the boy, Mortimer,' my mother scolded, one morning over breakfast. 'All these inquisitive interviews, endless concerts in God-forsaken dormitory towns and his daily practising – it's taking a toll on his health. Look at him: pale cheeks, rings under his eyes, no appetite. I wouldn't be surprised if he is losing sleep. How long did you sleep last night, David?'

'At least four hours, Mrs Simmonds,' slurped Dovidl, winking at me over the wicked rim of his Wedgwood-blue teacup.

'You see, Mortimer?' exclaimed my mother, expertly wound up. 'You're driving the boy to a breakdown.'

'My dear Violet,' said my father, spreading marmalade equably on brown-bread toast, 'you may rest assured that I have David's best interests at heart. Like you, I stand towards him *in loco parentis* and I shall take every care to shield him from overwork.

'However, you must remember, Violet, that the boy is an artist and I am his manager. I have put all my resources and experience at his disposal, and I am happy to say that he is following my advice attentively – and still finding enough time, I hear, for a certain amount of recreation. Miss Winter told me she saw him queuing at the Everyman Cinema earlier this week with what she described as "a rather forward young lady".'

Dovidl gave a self-satisfied grin, murmuring for my mother's benefit, 'A college friend, impeccably respectable family.'

'So you see, Violet,' Father continued, 'this is no longer first and foremost our domestic concern. It's business. The boy is in good hands, about to become a man. And a man's got to do what his manager tells him to. David, may I remind you of the photo-session tomorrow morning? Be ready at nine thirty. Dark suit and white shirt, please. Violet, will you make sure they have been freshly pressed?'

The fruits of that photo-shoot appeared across pages four and five of the *News Chronicle*, captioned 'Playing on Heart Strings'. Daringly open-necked in a gleaming white shirt, Eli Rapoport sat on the arm of a park bench, gazing over the barren slopes of Hampstead Heath, growing daily into his new public identity and away from the Dovidl I knew.

In March, my father told *The Times* that Eli Rapoport would play, in addition to Bach, the world première of a new 'Peace Concerto' by the modern, though melodic, composer, Vladimir Kuznetsov. New music was usually a box-office frost, but Kuznetsov had just been chosen by Laurence Olivier, ahead of the declining William Walton, to work on the soundtrack of a projected *Paradise Lost*; and interest in Rapoport was now so high that his début had been extended to a week-long series at the Royal Albert Hall. On 31 March, I was sent to paste 'Returns Only' sashes across gigantic placards, taking care to avoid the level stare of Dovidl's deep-set eyes, which hypnotised Kensington passers-by.

The following week, the Royal Handel Society (patron, HM the King) produced what its chairman, Professor Sir Harold Brooke, said was a long-lost Concerto Grosso, dated 1724, that – according to a letter from Handel to the composer Georg Philipp Telemann in Hamburg – contained the germ of what might now be recognised as the first genuine violin concerto, some years ahead of Bach's. The solo violin part in the concerto was not fully realised but, with the kind sponsorship of Simmonds Ltd, Sir Harold was preparing a performing version that would be premièred shortly on a six-nation European tour by that exciting young prodigy, Mr Eli Rapoport.

To launch a new artist with two new works, one purporting to be a major historical discovery, was wholly without precedent and verged on bad taste. But so confident was my father of Dovidl's genius, so emotionally committed to his success, that discretion went out of the window and excess took its place. The press played its part to perfection. Eli Rapoport's first feature interview, in the *Daily Telegraph*, described him as the lone survivor of a family of Polish Jews murdered under the Nazi occupation; he had been raised from boyhood in the family of Mr Simmonds, the musical impresario and publisher.

'I owe my life to the Simmonds family and the British people,' Dovidl was quoted as saying. 'I can never repay that debt. But if I have been blessed with any talent, I will devote it to furthering the values that this country has taught me – freedom, tolerance, and the dignity of the individual.' On a lighter note, the young violinist was reported to enjoy 'the company of pretty girls, the twang of bluegrass jazz and the taste of strong coffee at three a.m. in the Covent Garden fruit and vegetable market'. Journalists in those prudish times refrained from probing any deeper into their subjects' nocturnal proclivities.

The publicity onslaught called for extra hands at Simmonds HQ. In my Easter vac from Cambridge, while revising for my finals, I was conscripted to man a reception desk and cope with callers of many kinds. There were time-wasters, termagants and ticket touts; Swiss news-agency correspondents, paperclip salesmen and Zionist fund-raisers; unpaid orchestral musicians, threadbare composers and an Edinburgh scholar offering to supply syndicated programme notes for every work of music ever written – 'Stimulating essays sell concert seats,' he assured me hopefully.

The musical importuners I dealt with courteously but firmly. None got past my desk, or took more than three minutes of my attention away from Isaac Deutscher's biography of Stalin, which was required reading for anyone working towards a degree in modern history in the early Cold War spring of 1951.

More tenacious were the public officials – Arts Council assessors, local-authority inspectors and cultural attachés from foreign embassies – all seeking more or less the same thing: a brace of seats to the début of the decade. The only caller I failed to fob off was a willowy Eton-and-Oxford type in morning coat and striped trousers who turned up one afternoon at four as the tea-trolley trundled down the corridor, demanding to see the senior partner. 'My name is Alexander Horneyman-ffitch, Foreign Office,' he drawled imperiously.

'I'm afraid Mr Simmonds is in a meeting all afternoon and cannot be disturbed,' I replied.

'Then I shall wait until he is free,' said the official, shooting a crisp pair of cuffs and fractionally adjusting his pearl tie-pin as he took a vacant seat at the desk beside me. I had never seen a Foreign Office man in the flesh before. Neither, it seemed, had Rosalyn, the temporary secretary whose seat he had taken, a flute-cool economics graduate who melted beneath his supercilious stare into a fluttering skivvy, all work discarded as she scuttled down the corridor in search of a 'suitable' cup and saucer for our impeccable guest. Horneyman-ffitch sipped his tea through pursed lips, according her efforts the faintest of nods and addressing his next remarks to the nearest person in authority: myself.

'Perhaps you would be good enough to advise the director of your, er, enterprise,' he said, 'that the Permanent Secretary is anxious to obtain a response to several letters that he has written to this address, having been unable to effect telephonic communication.'

I mumbled something about checking the files and slipped into my father's office where he was, typically, talking away on two phones. It would have been pointless to search his desk for missing crested letters, so the moment he set down one receiver I warned him that a Foreign Office wallah was squatting on his threshold.

'I can guess what he wants,' smiled Father. 'Wheel him in.'

'So good of you to receive me, Mr Sy-monds,' drawled the intruder, stressing the first syllable to underline its Israelite origin and the unbridgeable genetic gulf between us. 'My master, the Permanent Secretary,' he continued, 'has written to you on behalf of his master, the Secretary of State, requesting tickets for a musical evening that you are organising at, if I am not mistaken, the Royal Albert Hall next Thursday. It was intimated that these tickets are required not for personal amusement – although the Secretary of State is an enthusiastic musical *amateur* – but for the purpose of entertaining the foreign ministers of three friendly nations who have expressed an urgent desire to attend the occasion.

'I am empowered to inform you, in confidence, that His Majesty's Government is engaged in rather delicate negotiations with these states with a view to securing our co-operation with an economic union that is being formed among several European states. In order to foster a harmonious atmosphere at these talks, my master wishes to obtain twelve best seats for the concert next Thursday.'

Mortimer Simmonds pressed his fingers together beneath his chin, an ominous gesture to those who knew him well. 'You are aware, Mr, er, ffitch' – he could snub as good as he got – 'that these concerts are commercial promotions, put on at my own risk without a penny of public funding?'

The envoy nodded.

'Then you might also appreciate that, on the night in question, His Majesty the King will attend the opening concert of the Royal Festival Hall, erected at vast public expense and sustained by permanent subsidies. May I suggest that your guests are escorted to the extravagance organised and paid for by His Majesty's Government rather than to our modest private enterprise?'

The diplomat withdrew a silver cigarette-case from his inner jacket pocket, offered us each an exclusive Turkish brand and, when we declined, asked if we minded if he did. Through a puff of faintly perfumed smoke he proceeded to the next level of negotiation.

'Perhaps I should have made myself clearer, Mr Simmonds,' he said, pronouncing the surname correctly this time. 'Our guest from Brussels, Monsieur van Vleeckt, who is himself a capable violinist, has been asked by Her Majesty Queen Elisabeth of the Belgians to report to her in person on this evidently exceptional young artist, Mr Eli Rapoport, whose concert is under your management. Queen Elisabeth is, as you probably know, a pupil of the legendary virtuoso Eugene Ysaÿe, in whose memory she has founded an important violin competition.

'HM Government are most anxious to accommodate our Belgian allies, who are being exceptionally helpful to us in the councils of Europe. The Foreign Office will, of course, purchase the seats at the full ticket price – with,' he dropped his voice, '*any additional premium that may be required for the inconvenience.*'

'I should, perhaps, have specified,' said my father, his tone a degree drier, 'that all three concerts are completely sold out.' This was not strictly true. No concert is ever completely sold out: there are always what are known as 'management tickets' to cater for last-minute emergencies – but that is a trade secret, which the general public and government officials are not supposed to know.

'I have also been asked,' continued Horneyman-ffitch, unruffled, 'to advise you that the contribution made by Simmonds Limited to British cultural life has not passed unnoticed. Indeed, its senior partner may be due – some feel, overdue – appropriate recognition in the King's Birthday Honours List.'

This inducement, finally, hit the spot. My father, like most self-made men, craved public elevation; my mother longed for an invitation to the Palace. A knighthood, even an Order of the British Empire, amounted to temptation on a Faustian scale – strong enough, I feared, to pierce his moral armour.

A timely sunbeam split the dusty air as he shifted a mound of papers from the left side of his desk to the right. 'Mr Horneyman-ffitch,' said Mortimer Simmonds sweetly, 'may I ask an undiplomatic question?'

'By all means, Mr Simmonds.'

'Before you joined the Permanent Secretary's office, to which department of the Foreign Office were you attached?'

'Near East and North Africa, sir,' said the unsuspecting official, exhaling a smug cloud of Turkey's finest.

'And am I right that the Near East and North Africa department of the Foreign Office is responsible for the Palestine Question?'

'Indeed it is, sir.'

'It has been suggested that your department was firmly opposed to the formation of a Jewish state, and continues to support trade embargoes against the State of Israel.'

'These are matters of public record, sir,' said Horneyman-ffitch.

'On another matter altogether,' sighed Mortimer Simmonds, 'am I correctly informed that, in the Near East and North Africa, it is not unknown for officials in your department to give *baksheesh*, or monetary gifts, to local dignitaries and functionaries to help oil the wheels of international understanding?'

Stripey-trousers could see where this was leading, but he had no means of escape. 'I cannot comment on isolated incidents,' he hedged, 'but anything of that sort would be contrary to policy and subject to disciplinary action – although other European nations, less scrupulous than ours, do resort routinely to such practices.'

Mortimer Simmonds rose to his full five foot six. 'Kindly tell the Permanent Secretary,' he declared, 'that his department has just compounded mendacity with hypocrisy. You, sir, have just offered me, in broad daylight, two authorised bribes, pecuniary and titular. Let me suggest that you now revert to regular departmental practice and go buy your tickets through a Lebanese arms dealer with contacts on the Piccadilly black market. Now, sir, I must ask you to leave. I have the French Minister of Culture on the line.'

Every word of that exchange is imprinted on my memory, for it was my father's finest hour (to use the popular Churchillian phrase), and one of his last. Seeing the defeated toff off the premises, Mortimer Simmonds puffed his chest and felt he had scored a small victory for Mosaic rectitude over English compromise, desert rigour over drawing-room courtesies. Next morning, he dispatched a brace of complimentary tickets by special courier to the Belgian, Dutch and Luxembourg embassies, and another pair to the Foreign Secretary, for his personal use. The French were offered two tickets at full price. My father's view of cross-Channel relations had been forged in the First World War.

In the final week, the pressures ran riot. Lofty Rosalyn fainted at her desk and I volunteered to drive her home to Wimbledon, where clean air and a cup of tea effected a rapid recovery. I had grown quite fond over the past fortnight of the leggy, plain-Jane temp, whose blank exterior concealed formidable analytical powers and prejudices. I returned from lunch one day to find her speed-reading my Isaac Deutscher tract on Stalin. 'Conscienceless apologetics,' she snorted, slamming the book on my half of the deak.

'What do you mean?'

'All the excuses he gives for Stalin's forced collectivisation – greater efficiency, equality, productivity, social harmony – are complete eyewash. There was never any economic justification for it, whatever dewy-eyed liberals might pretend. Abolish the ownership of land and you remove the farmers' incentive to produce food. It's a blueprint for famine, which directly resulted.'

'But what of the ideological motivation?'

'The object of Communism, as I understand it, is to spread wealth, not to starve millions. Stalin is just another Hitler wearing an avuncular mask; and this book is fundamentally an academic exoneration of mass murder. Burn it.'

These were bold sentiments to shout at the top of one's voice in a music company where most people thought with their hearts and voted with the left. Stalin, to many of us, was still good old Uncle Joe, our wartime ally with the friendly walrus moustache. Not to Ros. She proceeded to bullet-point each and every one of his supposed achievements and rip them to shreds with her laser-guided mind. I liked her more each day. Away from the office, reclined on a suburban sofa, sipping Lapsang Souchong tea, I sensed an invitation and snaked a tentative arm around her shoulder. Rosalyn inclined her formidable head, ever so slightly, towards me. I asked if she might, one evening, care to go out with me. She ruffled my hair and, half amusedly, accepted. Then we kissed, and she turned serious, stroking my cheek, gripping my forearm. Her mother came home in mid-fumble, and I left on a cloud. Rosalyn was the first girl I had ever summoned the confidence to ask out.

As things turned out, I never did get to date her. A week after our world came crashing down, Rosalyn accepted a post in the foreign-currency department of the Bank of England, where she rose, unwed, to the rank of deputy director. In those prejudicial times, it was considered incompatible for a senior female official to have a domestic life. I met her again, years later, at a barmitzvah, erect and drably dressed. We exchanged tart, wary platitudes.

Pre-concert tension claimed other casualties. The composer Kuznetsov was rushed to hospital with high blood-pressure, which returned mysteriously to normal the moment my father turned up with a missing page of his new concerto. The conductor, a crabby refugee called Matthias Freudenstein, stabbed his hand with a baton in his rage at the alleged illegibility of the full orchestral score. A trombonist turned up fighting drunk; his replacement demanded a bonus for playing a long solo. The Albert Hall bar staff walked out over some imagined grievance, and walked straight back in again when their exit was blocked by a semi-retired heavyweight boxer, Gordy Mills, whom we had hired to stand guard at the artists' entrance.

Scotland Yard sent round a flat-hatted inspector to discuss crowd control. The St John's Ambulance Brigade doubled its complement of first-aiders. My mother began having hysterics about her post-concert reception, which a distant Norfolk cousin of the Queen had graciously consented to attend. 'When do I curtsy,' she quavered. 'And do I call her Your Royal Highness?'

As the frenzy mounted, the calmest man in sight was (David) Eli Rapoport, the object of all attention. Dovidl was unruffled, so far as I could tell, and I could tell better than anyone. He breezed through rehearsals and interviews with a quip and a smile. He had time for mid-morning coffee, and for nights on the town.

'Getting enough sleep?' I asked, mock-solicitously.

'A man's got to do . . .' He winked.

'. . . what his manager tells him to.' I laughed.

Looking back, I have asked myself a thousand times whether his was a preternatural calm, camouflaging a premeditated defection. Try as I may – and I have tried hypnotists, holistic healers and two Jungian psychoanalysts – there is nothing I can recall in his conduct during those last days that suggested anything sinister or destructive. But, then, Dovidl wore his nonchalance like a shield. He was the antithesis of the highly strung artist who goes amok when an old lady coughs in his concert or an oboe comes in late. Dovidl seemed to take life as it came – took what he wanted, and left me to cope with the residue.

So when the police, among others, came asking questions after he vanished on that milky-May morning off the face of the earth, I as his closest confidant was unable to assist with their enquiries. I was as dumbstruck as anyone by his disappearance, devastated by loss, guilt and the smack of betrayal. Where had I been when he was vanishing into the void? Working flat-out, like everyone else, to put his name up in lights. I saw nothing, heard nothing, sensed nothing untoward – except for one jitter of anxiety as he climbed into the taxi and I called out, 'Dovidl, are you going to be OK?' He assured me that he would be fine on his own, back soon.

Time and again, I replayed that moment until the film wore out its sprockets. What if I had insisted on going along in the cab? Might I have saved him from abduction, madness, murder even? The notion that he might have deliberately absconded was still too vicious to contemplate, and I had never seen a vicious side to him. Minor flaws I saw in abundance; motiveless treachery was surely beyond him.

But, then, my view of him had always been blinkered by adoration. He was the light that made my dullness shine, the beam that revealed my best qualities. I depended on him to validate my usefulness and he on me (he said) to mediate with the rest of the human race. We were indivisible, or so he gave me to believe.

Suddenly, we were divided, without cause or warning. When he failed to show up for his magnificent début, I flung myself into managing chaos and staving off catastrophe. It was weeks before I began to grasp that part of me, the better part, had been amputated and my future stretched ahead into a purposeless void. I have searched ever since for him, for me, for the life that died that night.

# 4

# Time Bandit

First impressions can mislead, but my image of Dovidl never altered in the twelve years that I knew him. The sight that springs to mind is the first I saw of him, marching up to our front door as if he owned the house, if not the whole street. It was a sweltering Sunday in August 1939 and we were stuck at home in St John's Wood. Our annual fortnight in Normandy had been cancelled because war was imminent. Parliament had been recalled. Gas-masks were being distributed, tested, drilled. Holiday suitcases were emptied and repacked for evacuation. Sandbags were stacked on street corners and letter boxes were being painted in camouflage colours of green, brown and yellow, their tops coated in a chemical dye that was supposed to detect gas attacks. Barrage balloons sailed in the sky. Trenches were dug in Hyde Park (little did we know they were intended as mass civilian graves); Primrose Hill park was ploughed up and replanted with vegetables. A corrugated shelter was cobbled together by a handyman at the bottom of our garden and covered with the regulation eighteen inches of earth. Blackout curtains were hung on all windows, their panes sticky-taped against blast. The local shops ran out of glue and brown paper. Our domestics, Florrie and Martha, were adizz with excitement. My parents walked around with heads bowed and furrowed brows. I was bored beyond distraction.

This was my normal boyhood frame of mind, unrelated to geopolitical events, which I followed intently. I had begun reading newspapers during the Munich crisis the year before and got hooked on them when the Germans marched into Prague, a move I had gloomily predicted. From then on, I surveyed the slide to war with superior foreknowledge. Let Hitler do his worst: our Empire is invincible, our island impregnable, our parliamentary system strong enough to withstand ranting tyrants. My childish delusion seemed to be shared by just about every national newspaper, with the lone exception of the weekly *Spectator*, whose proprietor and editor, Sir Evelyn Wrench, had known Germany well for forty years and sorrowfully foretold the worst. My father took the *Spectator* every Friday, balanced with the left-wing *New Statesman* and *Tribune*. He seldom gave any of them more than a riffle before settling down with the hatches-matches-dispatches pages of the *Jewish Chronicle*, organ of Semitic communality. Unnoticed, I gathered up the weeklies, lip-reading through polysyllabic commentaries in search of political enlightenment. It was not unusual for nine-year-olds in pre-media days to read Dickens for fun and the Bible for want of anything better in the house. I was one degree more precocious than my peers, insufferably so. Scorning my mother's sentimental novels and the pristine set of World's Classics in the glass-fronted sitting-room bookcase, I used the political weeklies as my guide to the unseen forces that ruled the adult universe, my code for cracking the complexities of evil.

So far as Hitler was concerned, my position was one of studied neutrality. There is a childhood unhappiness that transcends great events, a misery deeper than all the world's tragedies. Mine was a wretchedness of this order. If I read that two million were dying of famine in China, I considered them fortunate beside my well-fed suffering in St John's Wood. Orphans, refugees and the unemployed had, at least, their status to share. I was locked in loneliness, unable to achieve meaningful human contact. Hitler and all his hordes could not, I felt, hurt me any more than I already hurt. Whatever his views on Jews, I was taking no sides in the coming war except to cheer on whichever combatant wiped out my chief enemies – starting with Johnny-Isaacs-next-door, an egregious paragon of a boy who recited Shakespeare at parental *soirées* and played centre-forward in the Maccabi junior league.

I, short of sight and stature, ten pounds overweight and spotty to boot, buried myself in books and shrank from friendship – not that many offers came my way. 'Swotty Simmonds', they called me at school. Where other boys swapped cigarette cards, I read political tracts and dreamed of running for Parliament – an ambition rendered all the more absurd by a sputtering stutter that, to my extreme discomfort, prevented me giving a fast enough answer to pedagogic paedophobes with swishing, impatient canes. Reading was my unreachable refuge from the world's rejection.

Neither of my parents took much interest in my frame of mind. Father was preoccupied with business and I cannot to this day fathom what Mother did with her time. She had a live-in maid and a full-time cook to run the house, one self-absorbed son and a husband who seldom came home. How did she amuse herself? With a Wednesday lover in a Berkshire inn? I doubt it. Middle-class Jewish women in those prim, pre-Pill times had too much to lose in status and comfort to risk a scandal. Divorce amounted to disgrace, a state worse than poverty. Mother maintained a diary of coffee mornings, women's lunches, bridge parties and refugee committees in which to sublimate her vital urges. Sad, really. Had she taken a lover, some of the love he aroused in her might have come my way, if only by osmosis. I longed for a show of maternal warmth. Mother longed for a son she could show off to Lady Rothschild, the Poet Laureate and the Chief Rabbi's wife. Our longings were mutually unrequited.

Strong-boned and with a cut-glass voice, Mother held herself with an hauteur that suggested she had come down in the world through no fault of her own. She wore gloves at all times out of doors, to avoid contamination by *sub speciae humanitas* (her Latin was pure, her Spanish immaculate). In concerts she would not deign to remove a glove to turn a programme page or offer applause. Her hauteur eased only in high society, when it turned obsequious: would the titled ones recognise her for what she really thought she was? She lived in fear of 'the Wood', where we were parvenus – my parents having moved up from suburban Finchley in 1932 shortly after the famous record studios opened on Abbey Road. Mother held open house to artists, whom Father escorted to their dates with destiny, but there was a taint of 'trade' about her and she craved the approval of the district's grand ladies whose husbands did not have to work for a living.

Her parental approach mixed distaste with disappointment. 'Martin, why *can't* you knot a tie in such a way that it sits closer to your throat than your thorax? Come *here*, boy. Let me adjust it once and for all. Spend an extra minute at the mirror before you leave the house in the morning and you might one day turn into an acceptable member of society. Lord knows, I have done my best to make you presentable. Stand still, and stop making those gagging noises.'

It was not just her impatient hand on my trachea that made me choke but something in her very being, an icy mist of frustration that came off her like morning haze off an Arctic lake. I physically feared her embrace, not that she often offered it.

On the Sunday of Dovidl's arrival I was second in her hierarchy of irritants. Father had arrived, as usual, late for lunch, which passed in a wordless clinking of cutlery on crockery, broken only by orders to the staff.

'Florrie, would you pass Mr Simmonds the gravy?'

'The carrots are very nicely done today, Martha, not at all dry.'

'Thank you, Mr Simmonds.'

'Florrie, you may clear the table now.'

'Yes, ma'am.'

'Be especially diligent about cleaning around the boy's seat.'

After iced dessert, my parents rose to take a nap in their newly decorated separate bedrooms.

'I'm bored,' I announced to their receding backs.

'Why don't you go and play with a friend?' sighed Father.

'He hasn't got any,' snapped Mother. 'He buries his head in *Picture Post* and won't make the effort. I don't begin to understand the boy. Why won't he take that football I bought him over to Johnny-Isaacs-next-door and ask him if he wants to play?'

'Hate football,' I mumbled.

'Bone idle, that's his trouble,' grumbled Mother.

'I'll give you a game of chess when I wake up,' promised Father. I knew he meant well, but I expected him to forget, as usual.

'Whatever he does,' said Mother, 'I don't want to hear a peep from him in the next two hours. I think I have a migraine coming on.'

Father and I exchanged a male look and slunk off in our separate ways. A compensatory urge tugged me towards my underbed stash of KitKats, a compulsive treat in irresistibly rebranded red wrappers. Previously sold as 'Rowntree's Chocolate Crisp', KitKat was supposed to invoke the languid grandeur of an eighteenth-century literary club. To my well-read eyes, it suggested something even more exotic than Fry's squishy Turkish Delight – a hint of *khat*, or *qat*, the hallucinogenic drug of the North-west Frontier. I had grown addicted to these milky chocolate fingers, but for once, this vacant Sunday, I resisted their beck.

Instead, I slouched out to the back garden and set up a chair for headier recreation: peeping over the fence at plump Mrs Hardy, who sometimes opened a button too many of her blouse as she dozed in a deck-chair. My peeping procedure had strict rules to minimise the risk of detection. The chair had to stand no less than three feet six inches away from the fence and it was forbidden to stare for longer than ten seconds every four minutes. Mrs Hardy, whose first name I never knew, must have been in her mid-thirties, fair-skinned and barren; Mr Hardy, who wore a three-piece suit even at home on Sunday afternoon, was 'something in the City' and sat with his pipe and papers well out of the sun, twenty feet away. Neither of the Hardys was aware of my mortal existence, let alone my lascivious interest. The satisfactions I obtained were negligible, but the game killed an empty hour and freshened my eyes for the next dose of reading.

In between peeping, I composed and delivered a political oration to an imaginary mass rally. Standing on my chair, aged nine and a half, old before my time, I iterated orotund phrases from parliamentary reports in a utopian vision of social bliss. Mutely, of course, since to have uttered a sound would have betrayed my stuttering, red-faced presence to the neighbours.

'Liberty, equality and fraternity,' I proclaimed soundlessly, 'are inalienable human rights to which we all pay lip-service. But these rights, like tea-leaves, need to be watered with *aqua vitae*. It is not enough for a government to provide health care, full employment and decent pension rights. It must give them the chance to get the most out of life. My administration will help people to fulfil their right to happiness. Millions of people of all ages who have more leisure time than ever before, but squander these precious hours in drink and drudgery, unaware of the opportunities that could enrich their lives – the chance to expand their minds, explore new interests and meet others of like mind.'

I was just getting to my favourite bit – the bit where my party pledges to set up a national leisure network to enable every citizen to find the activity and companions of his or her choice, where no one need ever feel alone again – when I spied through the gap between our house and the Isaacs' a man and a boy marching down the deserted, sun-baked street. Pausing for a final peep at the upbuttoned Mrs Hardy, I hopped off the chair and, hugging the cold brick wall, scampered down the side of the house in pursuit of fresh fantasy. 'Refugees,' I muttered, in the know-all tone of a film detective. The man wore a battered trilby and winter overcoat, the boy a woolly jacket and short trousers that flapped comically below his knees. They could have stepped straight out of a Gaumont newsreel. The boy, beneath his arm, carried a violin case. 'Hit the deck,' I hissed, 'the guy's got a piece.'

The boy looked about my age and half my size, with sleek black hair and stick-thin legs. The father, though sweating heavily, seemed to know his business. He scanned the sultry frontages of Blenheim Terrace and headed, good heavens, determinedly up our path. *Ding-dong,* went the doorbell. Florrie scuffled up from the kitchen. I heard the man ask for Mr Simmonds. Florrie, impressed by the strength of purpose in his voice, showed him to the front room and asked him to wait. This had better be good, I thought. Father won't be pleased to be woken up for nothing.

Peering through the curtains, I noted essential particulars of the strangers' appearance in case I had to identify them in a police line-up or espionage trial. The man, heavy-jowled, wiped a receding hairline with a large purple handkerchief. He talked to the boy in a strange tongue, like German but not quite. The boy listened attentively, but not submissively. When my father entered the room the boy rose and left, as if unwilling to be party to an adult transaction. Father, bleary-eyed, sent Florrie to fetch cold drinks. I crouched beneath the window-sill, ears open for intrigue.

'I thought I told you not to go around snooping, Master Martin,' scolded Florrie, in her Hampshire burr, her sudsy hand tweaking my quivering ear. 'Now, do something useful for once and look after this lad while yer father is dealing with the foreign gentleman.' She pushed the kid at me. 'Take him upstairs, find a game to play and I'll bring you some leftover ice-cream from lunch.' She winked. I liked Florrie; sometimes she mussed my hair when she tucked me into bed at night. No one else ever did.

'What's your name,' I asked the boy, as we climbed the stairs to my room.

'Dovid-Eli Rapoport,' he replied.

'D-dovidl?' I misrepeated. 'W-what kind of name is that?'

'Is Dovid — David you say in English — and Eli,' he responded with a grin. 'But my family says Dovidl for short. You call me Dovidl.'

Discommoded by his unEnglish familiarity, I replied stiffly: 'My name is Martin L. Simmonds. L for Lewis.'

'Mottinl?' he laughed. 'I call you Mottl.'

Introductions over, he demanded to know my age. Well-read as I was, he seemed somehow older and wiser; in fact, he was three months my junior, nine and a quarter to be precise.

'Are you musician?' was his next question.

'I play the piano a bit,' I conceded.

'Me, I am violinist – prodigy. I come to study with Professor Flesch. You know Flesch?' I had heard of him; I realised what was going on. The lad was a boy-wonder, victim of a trade I had heard my father condemn as child slavery. Simmonds, he pledged, would never present a soloist who was too young to buy a drink. Remember that, Martin, when you take over the firm. Yes, Father, I said, wondering how old you had to be to buy a drink.

'Professor Flesch says I am genius,' the boy continued. Well, fancy that. Father was going to be thrilled to be disturbed by a would-be child slave and his pushy parent. He could be frosty when roused: the pair might find themselves escorted smartly to the front door before Florrie could bring us that ice-cream, drat it.

'Do you play chess?' the boy asked, running his long fingers over my ivory set. 'Come, I beat you.'

And so he did, two games in less than twenty moves each, the thrashings sweetened by Florrie's strawberry ice and by the boy's, to me, mystifying refusal to gloat over crushing victories. 'You are solid player,' he said clinically, 'you need good tactic. Me, I am genius, I play brilliant. You, not so genius, must be patient, wait for weakness, go in where other person is blind.'

I was staggered by his analysis. This boy-wonder had, in two brutal games, assessed my qualities, outlined my options and advised me how to maximise my potential. 'I'll beat you at draughts,' I offered.

'Of course, no problem,' said Dovidl. 'Draughts is small game, small possibilities. You play white with correct formula, you win. But chess is big, not possible to make formula. You win, you are 'like God; you make order out of chaos.' He pronounced the word *khu-yess*. 'Is like music. You play good, the notes form structure, make sense. Is good ice-cream.'

Between spoonfuls, his eyes darted round my room like search-lights. He had yet to utter a superfluous word, let alone a definite or indefinite article. He must have had a vocabulary of a hundred useful nouns and verbs, but he used each word like a naked sword, unsheathed of social nicety.

Running his fingers along my shelves, he took down a recent Left Book Club pamphlet on the Danzig Corridor. 'What news?' he asked.

'There will be war,' I predicted. 'The Government is preparing an Emergency Powers Act and we will go to war if Herr Hitler invades Poland. Mr Chamberlain and the Foreign Secretary, Lord Halifax, are hanging back but the rest of the cabinet will force them to honour our international obligations.'

'You have good information,' he said.

'I read voluminously,' I replied, with odious superiority.

'We make good team,' he decided. 'I have genius for interpret-ation but no information. You have good information, but no analysis.'

At this moment, Mortimer Simmonds coughed at my door and asked for the favour of a quiet word. Dovidl deftly slipped outside. Exhilarated by our conversation, the longest and least stuttered I had ever enjoyed, I resented the interruption – even by so rare a privilege as exclusive parental attention.

'I trust I'm not disturbing,' said Father. I shook my head.

'Martin,' he ventured, 'I need to discuss with you in confi-dence a matter I have not yet raised with your mother, who is still asleep. It requires your consent, as much as mine and hers.'

I nodded gravely, encouraging him to continue. Like me, he was not the most liquid of conversationalists.

'The two visitors downstairs,' he continued, 'one of whom you have met, are Mr Rapoport and his son, David, from Warsaw. Mr Rapoport is a trader in costume jewellery. His son, David, is a gifted young violinist who is about to study with the celebrated Professor Flesch, whom you may have heard me mention.

'Professor Flesch, himself a celebrated soloist, has a remarkable record as a private teacher. Almost everyone he accepts as a pupil emerges as a fully fledged soloist. To be accepted by Professor Flesch is a virtual guarantee of musical success. He lives not far from here, in Canfield Gardens, but is presently away at a summer resort on the Belgian coast. The boy you have just been playing with is his latest discovery.

'However, a serious complication has arisen and the boy's father has been directed to me by Professor Flesch for assistance. While organising lodgings in London for the boy and himself, Mr Rapoport has received word from Warsaw that his wife is unwell. He needs to return to look after her and, I believe, other children. He has booked a passage tomorrow and plans to take David with him because the boy is too young to be left here on his own.

'Professor Flesch, with whom I have spoken on the telephone, fears that any interruption of tuition at this stage could be detrimental to his artistic development. He has asked me whether we might look after the boy – whom he strongly recommends as a future prospect – for a few months, perhaps, until Mr Rapoport can gather up his family and possessions and, having secured the necessary permits, return to London once his wife is well enough to travel.

'Clearly, a child of nine years old cannot be left in a hotel or boarding-house, and he has nowhere else to turn in this great city. I have heard what Professor Flesch has to say, and am more than a little impressed. I am willing to accommodate him here and I suspect that your mother, with her notable endeavours in the refugee cause, will not object.

'But the burden of entertaining the boy will fall principally on you, Martin, since your mother and I are so heavily committed. I cannot, therefore, offer to put him up without your consent. I should point out that it would be an act of great kindness and mercy to take him in. Also, that we might be performing an act of some artistic value, since the boy's potential is evidently quite exceptional. But I mention these considerations without in any way wishing to influence your decision, since you are the one who will have to put up with the greatest disruption.'

This was turning into some afternoon. First, my longest chat with a boy of my age; then, the most serious attention I had received from a parent since the day I was rushed to hospital with suspected appendicitis, which turned out to be aggravated indigestion caused by a surfit of KitKats. I threw up in the ambulance, all over my mother's new Liberty two-piece – which failed to increase her sympathy for me. She took a taxi home while the nurses cleaned me up, sending Florrie later to collect me, like laundry, when ready. Where was my father during this juvenile drama? Using the matron's phone for a few minutes, then off to the office.

His interest in this new boy was evidently commercial. If Flesch was able to groom him, Simmonds would have a star on its hands, our first violinist of world pedigree. The opportunity had its humanitarian side as well, making it morally rewarding. I was being called to do my part as heir to the business, and for the benefit of my spiritual education.

What the boy wanted from me was just as transparent. With his talk of making 'good team', he urgently needed me on his side to secure this refuge. I was a guard he had to lull to gain entry to the palace. I might not be a genius, but I saw his scheme a mile off. Nevertheless, recognising all the motives at play, I was suddenly in a position to influence events – and it was a power I relished.

I counted silently to ten before answering my father. 'If this boy stays with us, where will he sleep? Will he go to school with me? Won't he need private tutors in English and history? Where will he practise?'

'Those questions hadn't really crossed my mind.'

'I suppose I'll have to give up my playroom – unless you and Mother were to move back into the same room.'

This was unforgivable, an outrageous invasion of marital privacy. My parents had stopped sharing a bedroom a year before, preserving the formalities of marriage without the intimacy. Whatever spark had first flared between them had been allowed to die, and I was the sullen mourner in a house turned sterile and cold. Sniffing a chance to bring them back together, I plunged presumptuously into prohibited areas and was thrust back with a forbidding look.

'Quite right,' said Father. 'You will have to give up your study for him to sleep in, and David can use the parlour for practising. As for school, let's see what comes to pass in the next few weeks . . .'

'How soon do you need my answer?' I asked.

'Ten, fifteen minutes,' said Father. 'Shall I come back?'

'Not necessary,' I said. 'He can stay. I'll clear out my playroom after tea.'

Another parent might have given me a hug, or a pat on the head. Not Mortimer Simmonds. He stood up, shook my hand gravely and thanked me before descending to give the good news to Mr Rapoport, who left immediately. And that was it. Mother, coming down for tea, found a refugee boy playing Paganini 'Caprices' on the violin in her best room and her son turning the pages, unnaturally contented.

There was to be no more boredom for me that blazing, pre-bellum month. The next day I rode top-deck with Dovidl on the number thirteen bus around central London, introducing him to a city that would soon be blitzed into darkness and dread. We hopped off to pop into half-empty museums and halfpenny-a-head newsreel cinemas. Together, we watched the digging up of rose gardens in royal parks, the pitching of army tents on Hampstead Heath, the hanging out of washing on imaginary Siegfried Lines in the slumyards of King's Cross and Camden Town. We saw tin-hatted bobbies on bicycles wearing placards around their necks and civil-defence wardens blowing whistles in a pathetic charade of air-raid preparedness.

'Git orf the streets, yer little perishers. Can't you hear there's an alarm on?'

'Wot, that whistle an alarm? I thought it was a football referee's.'

On Thursday we rode down to the Houses of Parliament to hear the Commons briskly debate and pass the Emergency Powers (Defence) Act, bestowing a blessing of legality on the violence ahead. The Prime Minister, Mr Chamberlain, rose from his green bench like a sombre walrus and spoke without spirit, a defeated man. 'Who is man in big wig?' whispered Dovidl.

'That's the Speaker.'

'Why he doesn't speak? Maybe he is better than Prime Minister.'

The next morning we jumped off the thirteen bus at Trafalgar Square and found the National Gallery shut, its treasures being carried out by men in brown coats for safe-keeping in country caves. The Changing of the Guard took place unchanged, but up and down Whitehall they were fitting anti-gas doors and shutters on ministry buildings. We ate sandwiches by the Thames, dangling our feet from an embankment wall and waving at passing tug-boats. We returned so close to dusk that the lamplighters were out on our street, kindling the triangular streetlamps.

Father took us to Beethoven Night at the Proms, conducted by Sir Henry Wood at the Queen's Hall, a pleasant stroll from our home across Regent's Park. After a tranquil 'Pastoral' Symphony, Sir Henry turned his great beard to the audience to announce that the BBC was evacuating his orchestra, 'and I am therefore very sorry to say that from tonight the Proms will close down until further notice.' Downcast, we dispersed into the summer's night, the streetlights dimmed. Hitler had invaded Poland that morning and Warsaw was being bombed. 'It will not last long,' said Dovidl expressionlessly.

On Sunday morning at eleven fifteen we huddled around the wireless set to hear Neville Chamberlain's high-pitched whine 'speaking to you from the Cabinet Room at Ten Downing Street.' This morning, said the Prime Minister gloomily, 'the British Ambassador in Berlin handed the German Government a final note, stating that unless we heard from them by eleven o'clock that they were prepared at once to withdraw their troops from Poland, a state of war would exist between us. I have to tell you now,' he paused, sighing, 'that no such undertaking has been received and that consequently this country is at war with Germany.'

At eleven twenty-seven, the sirens sounded: a false alarm, but frightening enough. Dovidl and I cycled over to Euston, gas-masks round our necks, to watch the dispersal to the countryside of thousands of city children; we would remain at home, come what may, my father said. The sirens sounded again after dark;

another false alarm, but we trooped in pyjamas and overcoats into the dank garden shelter. Streetlights would not be lit again for six years. Cars drove without headlamps. All places of entertainment were shut and the wireless was down to a single channel. London was subdued, waiting for untold terrors.

At table, my parents resumed the courtesies of conversation. They talked of a Phoney War, 'just like the last one, when it started'. They spoke brightly, perhaps for our sakes, and mostly of their busy-ness. Mother had set up an informal labour exchange, sending Prague-born dentists and Viennese architects to fill the jobs of called-up bus-conductors and shoemakers. Father, thwarted by the theatrical blackout, sent musicians to play in regional halls and remote army bases. He set up a branch in Bristol, where the BBC had moved its orchestra, and an itinerant chamber opera in Blackburn, Lancashire. His network was national, his ingenuity formidable.

Around the end of September he came home in captain's uniform. 'I have been charged with putting on morale-boosting concerts for His Majesty's idle forces,' he declared, rather proudly. 'I shall give them deadly serious stuff – a chance to improve their minds.' A lunchtime series of Beethoven quartets that he had gingerly broached at the naval base in Plymouth proved so popular that he was obliged to set up loudspeakers to convey the music to civilian crowds outside. Tense and frightened, the public demanded highbrow art – Bach, Beethoven, Brahms, Bruch, never mind their being German. When London resumed its nightlife in mid-October, Simmonds had enough artists and ensembles on call to give concerts across all corners of the metropolitan area, always to packed houses.

The reflective mood was infectious. In the ghostly National Gallery, emptied of its glories, the autumnal Jewish pianist Myra

Hess gave lunchtime Beethoven recitals to a standing attendance, with queues stretching all round Trafalgar Square. Sir Henry Wood turned his wrath on the BBC and belaboured them to restore his Proms, which he would turn into a festival of defiance. 'When this war is over,' Father reflected one night, 'the Government will have to acknowledge the role art has played in winning it. Mark my words: they will have to put public money into the performing arts the way every civilised European country does, not just leave them to be supported by the financial aristocracy.' Mother gave a sceptical sniff as she ticked off invitations to titled ladies for her next charity event. She believed, to her dying breath, that nobility would always oblige.

No one paid much heed to us boys. We were left to roam the school-shut city by bike, bus and lumbering trolley-bus, a brontosauran conveyance that gave Dovidl endless amusement with its stately progress and overhead sparks. 'What is top speed?' he asked the conductor.

'Oh, she can do twenty miles an hour on an open track.'

'Almost as quick as bicycle,' quipped Dovidl, narrowly escaping a clip round the ear.

We jumped off at Lyons' Corner Houses for tea and penny buns, served by Nippies in white hats and aprons. Marble Arch was our favourite, with a waitress from Cracow who slipped us extra jam and as much milk as we liked. We caught the last pleasure-boat down the Thames and sniffed hothouse plants at an empty Kew. We even watched an end-of-season cricket fixture at Lord's, where Dovidl grasped the rules so quickly that over lunch he devised tactics to thwart a rampant batsman by bowling medium-pace seamers, just outside the off-stump, to a packed off-side field.

'If he gets bored and hits out, he will be caught,' theorised Dovidl. 'If he takes time, his side will lose attacking advantage. And meantime, the – how you say? – bowler' – he pronounced it like howler – 'is tearing up earth outside stump for the ball to spin.'

'But that's unfair,' I cried, 'it's not cricket.'

He looked at me pityingly. 'I can see why game takes three days,' he said. 'Nobody is bothered to win.'

His English was improving by the hour, acquiring indefinite articles and starting to shed its boxy accent. By November he was ready for *Julius Caesar*, with Eric Portman as Mark Antony, at the Embassy Theatre in Swiss Cottage ('Smoking Permitted – Abdullas for Choice'). We took shilling seats to the Wednesday matinée and were advised by an elderly usherette that the nearest shelter was five minutes' walk away, opposite the Central Motor Institute on Finchley Road. 'Immediately an Air Raid Warning is sounded,' the programme warned, 'patrons will be asked to rise in their seats but not move until the lights are switched on.' In our ceaseless chatter, Dovidl's and mine, mortal fears were immaterial. We roved from Highgate to Herne Hill, Baker Street to Bow, feeling the pulse of the imperial capital as deadly nemesis approached.

For Dovidl, London was a boundless revelation, its haphazard grid of fine and ugly streets promising fresh vistas at the turn of each corner. Two blocks down from our comfortable terrace with its mock-châteaux, garden gnomes and brass fittings lived the people that Hitler dispossessed, cooking schnitzels on electric rings in one-room Carlton Hill bedsits. One street to the west lay Hamilton Terrace, owned by the Harrow Estate and occupied, in season, by the landed gentry and their marriageable daughters. Two minutes downwind lived the Irish labourers and general layabouts of Kilburn and Maida Vale. All bought food at the same shops, walked the same pavements, rode the same fifty-nine bus-route. The lines of social demarcation were visible only to estate agents.

To Dovidl the intermingling was revelatory. In Warsaw, he said, rich and poor were divided by district. The town was flat as a herring, until it dipped to the Vistula river. Impoverished Jews made their ghetto around the Iron Gate, the Polish middle classes occupied transpontine suburbs and the nobility had the inner city to themselves. The streets Dovidl knew were the squiggly alleys of poverty, bounded by broad avenues designed for fire access and riot control. The apartment blocks had been built, Russian style, around closely watched courtyards, their porticoes shadowed by a caretaker who doubled as a police spy. Inside, one entered a human cauldron where flimsy walls failed to muffle connubial scufflings, and the stench of bodily functions blended with the aroma of simmering soups. Three generations could inhabit a single room, so acute was the deprivation; lavatories were communal and external, a torment in winter. Walls peeled and balconies sagged, but life was colourful and loud. Long-bearded Hassidim jostled bare-headed *maskilim*. Piously bewigged wives bantered with bawdy fish-women. Droshky drivers shared a bath-house seat with decadent poets.

Within most blocks, a vestibule served as an all-hours synagogue, a sanctuary for weddings, circumcisions and memorial services. At no time, day or night, was this room ever empty. An eternal light flickered above the ark and someone – rabbi, Hassid or mendicant – could always be found swaying on a bench, studying the Talmud, praying for the sick or mourning the destruction of Jerusalem. For faithful and faithless alike, the house of study was the hidden heart of the teeming habitation.

To stray beyond your own yard was to risk assault and humiliation – Polish louts loved nothing better than pulling down Jewish trousers and mocking a prepuceless penis – but once inside the gates you were safeguarded and never alone. Somewhere in this haven the infant Dovidl found a disused fiddle and sawed at it so relentlessly that a woman upstairs, unable to bear the racket, took him to a teacher. Aged five he gave a recital in Philharmonic Hall and was showered with bouquets and scholarships.

Back home, he kicked a ball with kids in his yard. His sister, Pessia, two years older and a wizard with crayons, resented his pre-eminence and hissed catty quips away from parental ears. Their younger sister, Malkeh, basked in his gift, begging him to play her a Brahms or Schubert lullaby at bedtime. Between envy and adoration, he struck a middle-child equilibrium. And, all the while, his musical sensibility was being refined by courtyard cries of grief and love, pain and hunger, prayer and mourning. He learned more about life in a Warsaw day than I could show him in a month of London. It was a world where a child grew up half seen and half heard, much loved and yet free.

'You appreciate, David,' ventured my father one Sunday lunch in October, 'that your family may not be able to join you quite as soon as expected.'

Dovidl bit his lip, buying time to formulate a precise response. 'They come when they can,' he replied eventually. 'Until then, I wait here.' It was a statement, not a request. Father nodded benignly and looked down at his plate.

I gathered, though this was never made explicit, that Mrs Rapoport was enduring a difficult, bedridden pregnancy. There was no word yet of whether she had given birth, and my parents' concern was transparent. There could hardly have been a worse time or place to bring a child into the world than Warsaw towards the end of 1939.

'I do hope, David, that you are writing home twice a week, as you promised,' said Mother, with stony lack of tact.

'I always keep my promise,' swore Dovidl untruthfully.

I knew he had given up, and I knew exactly when. At first he would rush to the front door four times a day at the postman's drop. For a week, letters arrived daily from Warsaw with censor-franked Baltic stamps. The German invasion brought a fortnight's fretful silence. Then came a huge delusory bundle, each letter sliced open at departure point and resealed. After that, nothing. When Poland's capitulation was announced on the wireless, Dovidl's sallow cheeks turned grey and he stopped staying up to listen to the nine o'clock news.

His bed, I heard Florrie tell my mother, was wet most mornings at the pillow and in the middle. He wore the same pair of hand-knitted socks he had arrived in until the wool all but unravelled. Each Friday night he knotted the same home-made tie. I never asked who made it for him. His anxiety was angry and private, walled off from well-meant concern. I never asked what he felt or feared, but from gritted comments here and there, I sensed a desperate yearning for his cocooning mother, his occupied city and the illusionary safety of his home courtyard.

My father assured him more than once that Warsaw would be protected by international convention, that the Germans would behave as they had done in the First War, harshly but correctly. Much as we loathed the Nazis, we took German decency for granted. Had anyone imagined the horrors that were taking place from invasion day onwards – round-ups and mass murder in baroque town squares, packed synagogues put to the torch on Yom Kippur, 24 September 1939 – my days with Dovidl would have been shrouded in mourning and I could never have shared with him the rambling discoveries of that dilatory London autumn.

I designated myself to be his refuge from anxiety, frantically planning excursions to distract idle thoughts. Panting on our bicycles, we rode up Highgate Hill, only to be denied entry to the great Victorian cemetery with its grave of Karl Marx, on the absurd grounds that we were too young.

'You have read Marx?' said Dovidl.

'A short extract, he's very dry.'

'Like a rabbi's kiss,' he flashed, and I gasped at his irreverence.

We leaped on our bikes and freewheeled down the hill, narrowly missing a milk float, from which Dovidl coolly lifted two pints while the stripe-aproned milkman went round to calm his horses.

'You know, it's going to be all right,' I told him, arm around the back of a bench on which we sprawled to glug our booty.

'In England, perhaps,' said Dovidl. 'Provided you win the war. In Poland, not all right. Maybe people come through, maybe no.'

'You are in England,' I said sternly. 'Your father sent you here. You have a job to do. The thought of you studying in safety will get them through the war. You will not help them by worrying.'

The steady clip-clop of the approaching milk float made a quick retreat advisable. Skimming along Archway, weaving in and out of sluggish traffic, we headed home in thickening mist that threatened to turn to choking smog. 'We make good team,' said Dovidl, as we turned into Blenheim Terrace. 'I do job and you, Mottl, you take my mind away from worries. Together, we make it work.'

'Does that make us best friends?' I wondered, searching for some orderly categorisation.

'Not friends,' said Dovidl. 'Something more.'

His studies with Carl Flesch ended abruptly, almost before they began. The old professor had returned from his Belgian spa to resume giving lessons at his West Hampstead studio. I accompanied Dovidl the first time, reading old issues of *The Bridge* in the waiting room while Flesch put him through his paces. As I browsed, a cadaverous young man strode in, the next pupil.

'Josef Hassid,' he said, extending a bony hand.

'Mottl Simmonds,' I replied, adopting a friendlier forename.

'Did you see who that was?' whispered Dovidl, as we left. 'That's Josef Hassid from Warsaw, a fabulous talent. He lives here with his father. Did you see? He said hello to me.'

'We had quite a chat in the waiting room,' I pretended.

'Had he heard of me?' said Dovidl. He was turning into quite the little artist.

'I don't remember mentioning your name,' I said, woundingly.

The next week we turned up to find Flesch gone – to Holland for a concert tour, we were told. It was, as we got used to saying, the last we ever saw of him. Holland was a neutral country, and Flesch somehow convinced himself that it was safer than England, that the Germans would bypass it as they had done in the First War. He sent a letter to his pupils, regretting his indefinite absence and urging them to work hard. He promised to write.

When the Germans invaded the Netherlands in May 1940, Flesch was trapped. Arrested twice and fearing deportation to the death camps, he managed to get a visa to his native Hungary, from where, helped by the conductor Ernest Ansermet, he reached Switzerland, where he died in 1944. He left behind a diverse and far-flung set of pupils – Ginette Neveu in France, Alma Moodie in Australia, Henryk Szeryng in Mexico. Three were left teacherless in London – Ida Haendel, Josef Hassid and, the youngest by three years, Dovidl.

Unlike Haendel and Hassid, who had made impressive débuts and were well on the way to becoming practised performers, Dovidl was several years short of concert readiness. He lacked polish, poise and *savoir-faire*, the basic safety standards for setting foot on stage. His artistic personality was embryonic, requiring years of attentive mothering from a master star-maker like Flesch.

'We'll have to find you another teacher,' sighed Father.

'Absolutely not,' Dovidl replied.

'I beg your pardon?' said Mother in her glassiest tone.

'I am pupil of Professor Flesch,' said Dovidl. 'I do not wish to confuse teaching methods. There is risk in changing teachers, even if they are English excellencies. I wait for Professor Flesch to come back. Meantime I work on the material he left me and make good progress.'

'I think we had better be the judges of that,' said Mother frostily.

'I appreciate your concern, David,' said Father. 'I have seen too many good violinists ruined by an excess of teachers. However, we do need to seek guidance in this matter, you and I. May I suggest that we consult Mr Albert Sammons, who is demonstrably the best violinist this country has ever produced, and see what he has to say.'

'Do I come with?' said Dovidl.

'Of course.'

'May I come, too, Father?' I piped up.

'That might be helpful,' he agreed.

Some days later, we caught the fifty-nine to Oxford Street and a seventy-three to the Royal Albert Hall. Skirting the sombre memorial to Queen Victoria's German consort, we descended a steep flight of steps and entered the Royal College of Music, equally marmoreal in appearance and atmosphere.

'Is this conservatoire or cathedral?' whispered Dovidl.

I shushed him earnestly. England's finest was bearing down upon us.

Albert Sammons turned out to be a kindly, lantern-jawed man, sensitive to boys' needs – he gave us sixpence each to buy sweets around the corner while he discussed music business with my father. When we returned with fistfuls of wine gums and Black Jacks, he led us to his private washroom to scrub our hands before asking Dovidl to play something for him. A vignette of

Wieniawski's produced an audible hum of pleasure from the senior virtuoso. A snatch of Ysaÿe brought him leaping to his feet. 'Come, boy,' exclaimed Sammons, 'let's have a go at the Kreutzer Sonata, I'll take the piano part, years since I played it.' The assault on Beethoven collapsed in gales of laughter, Dovidl eleven bars ahead of his hesitant, squinting accompanist, and sprinting for the finish.

'By heavens,' panted Sammons, 'the boy reminds me of meself at his age. Never had a lesson in m'life, y'know. My father was a shoemaker. He put me to work in a hotel band when I was eleven, and I'd been at it for ten years when Sir Thomas Beecham dropped into the Waldorf one night for dinner and heard a few bars of me playing the finale of the Mendelssohn concerto. That was it: I was made. Always play your best, boy, you never know who might be listening – that's the only useful advice I can give you.'

Dovidl nodded respectfully. He knew Sammons was the real thing, Brylcreemed hair and plebeian accent notwithstanding. Father had played us his gramophone recording of Sir Edward Elgar's concerto, a work written for Kreisler but which Sammons had invested with russet English colourings and broad rolling tones in its very first recording.

'Flesch is a damned good teacher,' reflected Sammons, 'and I wouldn't advise you to let anyone tamper with one of his prodigies. The boy's a natural, as I was. What he needs is what the Germans – damn their eyes – call *Bildung*, a whacking great load of musical and cultural knowledge from which he can begin to develop an interpretative style. I dunno who can do that for him. He needs some kind of mentor, a moral tutor more than a technical supervisor, someone who can bring out the inner voice. Look at the boy, he knows what I mean, don't yer? We're brothers under the skin, aren't we, boy?

'Bring him back in a year, Simmonds. No, bring him sooner and I'll take him through the Elgar concerto that I nicked off Kreisler while he had his eye on the ladies. I want to hear the boy play something big like that.' And, with a pat on the head and another sixpence each, he shepherded us generously through the echoing marbled corridors and out into the wintry street.

We sat upstairs on the homeward-bound seventy-three bus, Dovidl admiring the view over Hyde Park, my father deep in thought. This was a critical juncture for Dovidl, and I had to lead the way.

'May I make a suggestion?' I ventured.

'Is it about David?' said Father.

'Do you remember the old man who came to dinner at New Year,' I began, 'the one who was concertmaster of the Leipzig orchestra for forty years until the Nazis roughed him up and threw him out?'

'Dr Steiner, you mean?'

'That's the one. Well, he has a fantastic amount of musical experience, hasn't he, and he seemed to be extremely well read. He talked to me about Goethe, Heine, Karl Marx, Thomas Mann – and who's the chap who wrote *Bambi*? Felix Salten. Might he be the sort of moral tutor you are looking for?'

'Not a bad idea,' said Father. 'Dr Steiner knows orchestral and chamber music inside out – he used to have a famous string quartet – and he is a cultured man. He played Mozart with Albert Einstein, who is an enthusiastic amateur violinist, and he has a doctorate in something esoteric. Icelandic sagas, I seem to remember.

'It would be a noble thing for us to put some work his way, and I am sure he can expand David's mind, if he pays attention. But Dr Steiner is getting on. He can't be expected to exert discipline.

He can do the *Bildung*, not the hard grind of building a career.

'Who is going to keep an eye on his technical progress? Who will make sure he practises every day and doesn't skip the tricky bits? Who will encourage him to persist with Prokofiev, when his fingers are aching and the notes are swimming on the page? Who will inform me of any difficulties that may arise?'

'How about me?' I intruded.

'You?' said Father, politely stifling disbelief.

'I am his friend,' I said boldly. 'He trusts me. I am also your son, heir to the business as you keep saying. Let me help him, supervise him and report to you, should he need anything. I don't think he needs much encouragement.'

'That's a very mature undertaking, Martin.'

'I am,' I puffed, almost ruining the effect I had contrived, 'very advanced for my age.'

'Of course you are,' laughed Father, half proud, half patronising. He patted his pockets for something to smoke, buying himself time to consider my offer. 'This could involve you in a conflict of loyalties,' he warned. 'What if there is something that I need to know but which your friend does not wish me to know?'

'I know where my loyalties lie, Father,' I lied.

And that settled it. Arriving home, Dovidl and I repaired to the piano room and planned a curriculum. Flesch had left him a guide to the repertoire, so we knew what had to be covered, Bach to Alban Berg. The structure was left to us, with weekly nudges from Dr Hermann Steiner, who received us on Wednesday evenings with bitter coffee and dentally ruinous cakes. 'So good of you to visit an old man,' he would say, as his aged wife, slightly demented from exile and loss, scuttled among the cups and saucers. Huddled in front of a single-bar gas heater in a Carlton Hill attic room Steiner, in a frayed grey cardigan, dazzled us with tales of

Nordic heroes, anecdotes of Einstein and his violin, an analysis of quantum theory, an appreciation of the Elgin Marbles, which he admired above all modern sculpture, an account of Max Reinhardt's Salzburg festival, and a wealth of musical encounters. How he had met Brahms on a bicycle; how his father had known a doctor whose father had treated Beethoven for gout; how Gustav Mahler had appreciated his leadership of the Leipzig orchestra. Dr Steiner was, to educated British eyes, an alien from outer space: an intellectually rounded man whose mind-world knew no borders or limitations.

I did not warm to his sagas (or believe for one moment the story of Beethoven's pet cat and the Kreutzer Sonata), but listening to the old man talk affected the way Dovidl played. How, exactly, I as a non-musician cannot explain, but Dovidl's tone deepened and he gave an impression of having more to convey than well-practised repetition. Just as the best conductors imprint their personality upon an orchestra, so Dr Steiner transferred something of his cultural identity to Dovidl. It bypassed me for, while I absorbed knowledge from the old man, my character was unaltered. But Dovidl grew artistically from the exposure, as well as technically from the specific digital guidance that Dr Steiner was able to give for the fingering of intractable passages. Theirs was an artistic transaction, a spiritual transmission, artist to artist. I felt, for the first time, entirely excluded from Dovidl's world. '*Mein Kind*,' said Dr Steiner, seeing my face drop, 'do not be sad. Every artist needs a personal auditor, a pair of ears he can always trust. You will be his listener, the post on which he measures his progress.'

Together, back home in our piano room, we worked through the Bach sonatas and partitas, the concertos and sonatas of Mozart, Beethoven, Mendelssohn, Bruch and Brahms, the chamber music of the early moderns. While he practised scales and arpeggiated runs, I mugged up the teaching manuals of Leopold Auer, Josef Joachim and Flesch himself. It may sound perverse, but in pre-television times clever boys often amused themselves by devouring dense books. My political reading served me well as I devoured the great violin 'methods' and summarised their contents. At nine and ten years old, we brought to our mission the obsessiveness that children apply to building sandcastles and model-train sets. Doing it together redoubled our competitive dedication. Some mornings we set our alarm clocks for six to get in two hours of music before breakfast.

Dovidl's determination was fierce and his self-tuition was assisted by my readiness to plink out rough accompaniments on the piano any time he asked. Before my amazed ears, he invented and perfected his time-stopping *rubato* – which, if memory does not mislead, he adapted from a practical tip by Auer, Heifetz's teacher. With me as personal listener, he picked up speed and mastery without shedding grace and wit. There was no doubt in my mind that he was destined for greatness.

By the end of that first severe winter, Dr Steiner declared him ready for a public début. 'I have such joy from the *Kinder*,' he told my father, who confided afterwards that Steiner's daughter and grandchildren had been unable to leave Germany in time. 'Not only from the artist *Kind*, but from *der andere* as well.' He beamed, indicating me. Dr Steiner had been refusing to accept the envelopes that I thrust on him with payment, which is why I had called Father in.

'Dr Steiner, I cannot let you teach them for nothing,' he objected.

'Is *nichts* for nothing,' said Steiner. 'They are my future.'

A solution had to be improvised. Mrs Steiner was deteriorating fast and Mother arranged for the couple to be housed, at our expense, in a refugees' nursing home in Belsize Park, a Spartan, bare-floorboarded establishment, but one that offered more care, comfort and human company than the leaky Carlton Hill garret. Each Wednesday, after our session with Dr Steiner, Dovidl gave an impromptu ten-minute recital in the residents' lounge to cries of '*Herrlich!*' and '*Wunderschön!*'

A return visit to Albert Sammons reinforced Steiner's endorsement.

'He's ready, y'know,' said Sammons. 'I'd give him the Elgar, Simmonds, and put him in front of an orchestra tomorrow.'

But Mortimer Simmonds performed at his own tempo. 'Not yet,' he told the mentors, 'there's plenty of time. He must grow some more, physically and emotionally. In his father's absence, I have a paternal responsibility towards him.'

The most my father would permit was a private recital with a professional accompanist (At the Piano: Ivor Newton) in our Blenheim Terrace piano room. Father invited Sammons with his star pupil Thomas Matthews, recently appointed leader of the London Philharmonic Orchestra; the famed viola player William Primrose; the Steiners, together with several *émigré* composers; a music-loving Harley Street physician, Dr Edward May; and the conductor Sir Henry Wood.

Mother worked on her invitation list for a month. Her prize catches were two Rothschilds and the Chief Rabbi's wife; the rest of her allocation consisted of Sephardic relatives and wealthy ladies of the Wood. She had an outfit made for the occasion. Caterers were called in. A spare piano was hired, in case our Steinway developed last-minute woodworm. Nothing was left to chance.

Dovidl played the Kreutzer Sonata in the first half, followed by a nonchalant selection of Vieuxtemps, Vivaldi and Brahms. There was a Dvořák 'Humoresque' and something by Tchaikovsky for encores. No one left the room unmoved, or unfed. Sir Henry growled something about a future Prom, and Dr Steiner wept gleaming tears of joy. Johnny Isaacs's mother sulked in a corner. My mother was in raptures. 'She *shlepped* more *naches* tonight from this refugee boy than the poor woman will ever get from her own *shlemiel* of a son,' I heard Mrs Isaacs complain to the Chief Rabbi's wife.

Dovidl, overhearing the comment, asked my father if he could say a few words. A teaspoon was tapped on a cup and he remounted the make-do stage to declare his gratitude to my parents and to his rehearsal pianist – me. He knew, without my saying, the pain of my rejection. He also knew, or sensed, how massively his presence had increased my self-worth. I felt redeemed by his friendship from a cocoon of caterpillar misery.

The only dissentient cough came from my aunt Mabel, a dumpy EastEnder with a gorblimey accent who was married to Mother's dentist brother, Kenneth. She and I were natural allies against Medola hauteur, outcasts who were usually seated together below the salt.

'I don't think much of your fiddle-chum, Martin,' said Mabel.

'What do you mean, Auntie? He's brilliant.'

'A phoney, if you ask me. I tried talking to him in Yiddish, the mother tongue, and he insisted on speaking English. Never trust a man who's ashamed of his origins, my boy. Here, let's split another choccy mouse between us before your mum catches us.'

Mother, as if by osmosis, caught us brown-handed. 'Mabel, I do wish you would stop forcing sweets on the boy,' she snapped. 'A dentist's wife ought to know better. Martin, please remember the desserts have to go round all of our guests. Is that a stain on your tie?'

'She wasn't always such a sourpuss,' explained my aunt, as Mother scudded away on clouds of disapproval. 'Before the last war,' she confided, 'Violet was quite the life and soul of the *soirée*, singing silly ballads and larking the night away. She knew all the latest dances and taught them to the young men. But then Edwin got killed and she thought she'd never get off the shelf, until they found your poor ruddy father.'

'Who was Edwin?'

'Her first fiancé, a Montagu. He went exploring the Hindu Kush and returned to write a rather daring book on puberty and polygamy before getting himself killed in the first wave on the Somme. Violet wore black for two years, never left the house, must have had one of those whadyamacallits, nervous breakdowns. By the time the boys came home, those that did, she was pushing thirty and no poster-girl. I always thought yer dad was a bit of a hero, taking her on, but he never complains, does he? A good bloke, Morty Simmonds, I always say. I knew his family down Mile End. Didn't have two spare beans for a Sabbath *cholent*.'

'Martin, do mingle a bit,' rasped my mother, returning to Wallflower Corner. 'Introduce David properly to the rest of our family.'

Dovidl caught my eye and gave a mock-sigh. He was trapped in a circle with Dr Steiner and other *émigrés* whose efforts to address one another in patriotic English verged on the impenetrable. 'Excuse me, Dr Steiner,' I intruded politely, 'may I take David away for a few moments?'

'Phew,' said Dovidl, as we breathed a gust of fresh garden air. 'As long as you are there to rescue me, I could do this for a living.'

Then, and always, Dovidl insisted that he depended more on me than I on him. He had been, in his way, as lonely as I was, cut off by his talent from other people. With me, he could be a normal boy – or as normal as his genius and my ordinariness would permit. It took a few months to balance those inequalities.

In a relationship founded on mutual dependence, there can be no secrets. Dovidl knew that I knew that he wetted his bed, picked his nose and dipped a licked finger into the bag of icing sugar on the second shelf of Martha's pantry. I knew that he knew where I hid my KitKat stash, that I could not fall asleep without a scrap of baby-blanket wound around my toes and that, once the frost set in and Mrs Hardy had been driven indoors, I had taken shamefully to peeping through the keyhole of the maids' room in an intensified pursuit of naked flesh.

'It's not safe,' he said, catching me one evening as Florrie was getting ready for her weekly night out.

'What would you do?' I demanded.

'You have a mirror, a small one?' he asked. I fetched a compact from my mother's handbag. 'Come to my room,' he ordered.

We tiptoed needlessly down the upstairs corridor, our footsteps covered by a clanking of pipes and a rush of bathwater as Florrie ran her weekly bath before going out with her steady boyfriend.

'Close the door,' said Dovidl, opening his bedroom window. 'This should not be difficult.' He took a wooden coat-hanger from his wardrobe, and taped the vanity mirror on to its edge with blackout sticking-paper. 'Now hold this mirror out of the window at forty-five degrees,' said Dovidl. 'The bathroom window is half open. When the angle is right you will be able to see a reflection of the bathroom mirror.'

He was right, as usual. After a bit of twisting and turning, I saw the bathroom cabinet in my little mirror and, through shifting clouds of steam, the upper half of Florrie as she briskly removed apron, white blouse, her slip and a wired undergarment whose French name I had heard whispered in the playground corner where Johnny Isaacs clustered with his churlish chums. Momentarily, Florrie stood before me in the mirror, her full

Hampshire breasts heaving in the smoggy air before she bent, bouncily, to fiddle with garments below my eye-line and lower herself into the tub.

A breath stuck in my throat, like a fishbone. Thrilling as the sight must have been, I was acutely aware of crossing a barrier from innocence to pubescence, a transition complicated by knowing that the object of my immature desire was a mother-surrogate who tucked me into bed at night. Breaking this incest taboo was bad enough, but transgressing it with the help of Dovidl, my heaven-sent house-brother, was confusing beyond the limits of my modest intelligence. I began to tremble with anxiety and the stutter returned as I handed the hanger-cum-mirror to my accomplice, just as Florrie rose from the bath and wrapped herself in a towel.

'Next show, next Thursday,' grinned Dovidl, breaking the tension. 'Or Tuesday, if you want to see fat old Martha.'

I gagged and giggled at the thought of our bad-tempered cook in the flabby altogether. 'You see?' said Dovidl. 'This is what a little strategy can achieve, without risk or pain.'

'Such a know-all,' I sneered, throwing a cushion at his head. He retaliated with a bed-quilt and we fell about wrestling on the floor until our thumps and yells drew a sharp protest from Mother, who was holding a committee meeting downstairs. We were ordered to straighten our ties, brush our hair and, if David wouldn't mind, come and play something nice for the ladies. Our complicity was complete in its exclusion of the adult world.

The peeping-Tom escapade needed no repetition. It somehow sealed our capsule against intrusion. It also illustrated the practical, even heroic, usefulness of what Dovidl referred to as his 'strategy'. A more telling instance occurred when school reopened in November and we went off together in mauve-trimmed grey uniforms to

The House, a place of detention that groomed the sons of the upper-middle classes for the better class of public school. To me, The House represented seven daily hours of fear, never knowing when I was next to be assaulted by sadistic teachers and playground bullies. I warned Dovidl, skinny and alien as he was, that he must expect to be victimised. He grinned, and told me not to worry.

In the second lesson of the day, a bullet-headed maths master called Horrocks, delighted by my failure to define 'hypotenuse', lifted me balefully out of my seat by the lobe of a twisted ear and began dragging me to the blackboard – only to release his grip with a startled expletive.

'Ruddy hell!' he yelped, glaring around the class. 'Who did that?'

'Did what, sir?'

Rubbing his thigh, he reached again for my throbbing ear – reached, and yelped once more. Swivelling round, Horrocks was just quick enough to catch Dovidl retracting his bowing arm, at the end of which protruded the pointed end of a geometry compass.

'Stand up,' screamed Horrocks. 'Your name?'

'Rapoport, sir,' said Dovidl, unrippled in a sea of terror.

'A foreign boy, new to our ways, I suppose,' snarled Horrocks. 'Well, I suppose it is going to be my English duty to teach you some manners. Tell me, Rabbit-fart, do you know what we do in this great country to boys who assault their masters?'

'No, sir,' said Dovidl. 'But in my poor country we have a name for men who torment children instead of going to war and fighting the enemy.'

Horrocks was dumbstruck. A corpulent specimen in his early thirties, he had evidently failed to volunteer for active service out of cowardice or invalidity. 'I shall ruddy well fight when His Majesty calls me to do so,' he blustered. 'In the meantime, someone has to stay behind and drum some maths into your thick skulls before the Army will even look at you miserable lot as cannon-fodder. Now come over here, Rabbi's-brat, and take your punishment.'

'You will not touch me,' said Dovidl. 'I wish to see the Head.'

Never in the glorious history and voluminous literature of English prep-schooling, from Tom Brown to Anthony Buckeridge's Jennings, has such blank recalcitrance been encountered in a first-morning classroom. If Horrocks was stunned, the rest of us were transfixed by a drama whose outcome could only be epic and bloodstained.

'And why do you think the Head would wish to see you?' growled Horrocks, with the bulbous look of a man who pins living butterflies to an album page.

'Because he has a letter from a higher authority, telling him how I must be treated,' said Dovidl, resuming his seat.

Horrocks flushed, slammed out of the room and did not return before the bell released us for break. At the resumption, Dovidl was summoned to the Head's office. 'What happened?' I whispered when he returned, expecting to see him doubled up in agony after the thrashing of a lifetime.

'Nothing much,' shrugged Dovidl. 'There was a piano in the room, so I went over and played some Schumann, apologising that this was not really my instrument. The Head had a violin from his cupboard, so I played a Bach partita. He tried to look fierce but I saw a tear in his eye and I squeezed the notes until it dropped. He said I deserved the cane for talking back to Mr Horrocks, and what was this instruction from a superior authority?

'I said it was a note I had brought from Captain Mortimer Simmonds, who is on special assignment to His Majesty's forces, perhaps he had not received it? He blew his nose and I played some more. Then he gave me a cup of hot chocolate and asked did I know Mr Albert Sammons, and could I get him to address the school on prize-day?

'You see, Mottl. There is a class system in England, but it is not life class. The real world is divided into two classes of humans: those who make things happen and those who let them happen.

'I,' he concluded, 'belong to first class.'

His avowal of superiority came as no surprise. Dovidl had a way of making people do what he wanted. There had been no letter from a 'higher authority', no request for special treatment. In those authoritarian times, parents or those *in loco parentis* would never have dared to tell a headmaster how to treat his pupils. Dovidl had invented the letter in response to the threat, turning thought into swift action by means of a flowing musical improvisation. Where the rest of us would tackle a problem by resorting to precedent, Dovidl transcended the events at hand and injected the unforeseen. In any crisis, he was wholly unpredictable and hence unconquerable.

Having seen off the maths brute, who departed before Christmas for a post in the pay corps, Dovidl was acclaimed as a class hero and I shared the glory as Antony to his Caesar, Eden to his Churchill. Even Johnny-Isaacs-next-door came seeking my company. Like the explorer H. M. Stanley, I was acknowledged less for my own merits than for having brought forth a popular luminary, a Dr Livingstone, from the heart of darkness. But I did not mind taking second place. It was a role I had been groomed for – being agent to artists, footstool to genius, fixer behind the scenes. For the first time in my conscious life, I felt entirely happy and fulfilled.

Sliding down the banisters one morning, I crashed into a polishing Florrie at the foot of the stairs and crumpled into giggles. 'You're very full of yourself these days, Master Martin,' she chided, sending me into breakfast with a slap to the rear.

'What's that noise?' snapped Mother, looking up from her *News Chronicle*.

'What noise, Mother?'

'That squeaky drone, like a bee in a jam-jar.'

'I can't hear anything.'

'Well, stop it immediately, Martin, whatever it is. I've got a headache and the day has hardly begun.'

It was only then I realised that I had been singing, or perhaps humming, some tuneless expression of inner serenity. This was Dovidl's doing: he had given me a voice, a fuzzy, grating sound of indeterminate tonality, but none the less a means of self-assertion. I was, thanks to him, no longer trapped in mute misery but able to convey my feelings to the world about me, whether it cared to listen or not. I had become a vocal Mottl to his effulgent Dovidl, a vital part of a greater organism. And he lived within me like a futuristic artificial lung, filling me with confidence and contentment when natural organs failed. That's how I thought of him: as part of me. And that's how I loved him – not as a brother in all but blood, but heedlessly and functionally as you love your little finger, or the curve of a cheekbone upon your palm as you drift happily off to sleep.

# 5

# The Time of our Lives

It was the excitements we were about to share – adolescence and the Blitz – that sealed our symbiotic unity. Relative merit was never an issue between us; Dovidl was the instigator of most activity, but he made me feel that I was indispensable to him. It sounds corny, but then so are many of our most cherished musical impressions. Any number of women have told me that their lives were altered by a performance of Beethoven's fifth symphony, because a maestro had gazed into their eyes moments beforehand in a locked green room and told them that he was going to conduct it 'just for you'. Music can be made intensely personal. Dovidl went one step deeper: he gave me to understand that nothing he did could be achieved without me.

How to define our relation except as halves of an indivisible whole? We spent more time together than brothers, yet ours was not a fraternal tie. It lacked the frictional bickering of siblinghood, the inherent rivalry for parental affection. Nor was it, as one might reasonably suspect, a homoerotic involvement. No matter that we flicked wet towels at each other in the bathroom and ran naked down the corridor, willing the deliciously shockable Florrie to run shrieking across our dripping path. We blew raspberry-farts and taunted each other's pimply cheeks and skinny shanks. As manhood descended, Dovidl's limbs thickened and sprouted jet-black hair while mine remained for two long years laggardly boyish and bare. I knew his body as well as my own, yet I cannot recall a covetous thought or penetrative urge. A state of unity, quite distinct from love or desire, was the current and currency of our connection.

An over-serious psychoanalyst (I have paid a few in my time) might interpret this as a sublimation of deeply repressed lust in a neurotically submissive personality. Nothing in my conscious recollection offers any confirmation of this diagnosis. True, we hugged and wrestled as all boys do, but we were far too respectful of each other's dignity to press for submission or consummation. The longer Dovidl stayed, the more assertive I grew, confident in my usefulness to him and, tacitly, to my father. Dovidl, aware of my dual loyalty, never alluded to it by so much as the arching of an eyebrow. He was a hart-like creature of natural delicacy. What passed between us was, it seemed to me, stronger and more elegant than ties of blood or sex. And, as we became exposed to blood and sex in the havoc of Blitz and adolescence, our bond grew tighter and ever more vital.

When the suspenseful calm was broken in June 1940, with northern Europe in Hitler's hands and Luftwaffe fighters swaggering in broad daylight above our heads, we ten-year-olds were nicely placed to observe the excitements. To earn extra pocket money and sustain an essential service, I had proposed that we should take up the paper rounds that were being forlornly advertised by the Blenheim Terrace newsagent, Mr Wilcox.

'Out of the question,' said Mother. 'I will not have you rattling at people's doors like hawkers and common tradesmen. What would your father think of us, David?'

'It is what he does for a living,' said Dovidl quietly. 'He sells costume jewellery, door to door.'

She had the grace to blush.

'Johnny Isaacs does a paper round,' I piped up.

'That boy is turning into a great disappointment, after such a promising start,' sighed Mother.

'It would be a kind of war work,' volunteered Dovidl, 'giving people responsible information and saving them from rumours.'

'I think the boys make a good point,' said Father. 'Let them take a paper round for a probationary three months, so long as it does not conflict with their schoolwork or their music practice.'

'It won't, Father,' I promised, and there passed between us one of those imperishable glances of male solidarity.

Down at the newsagent's, Dovidl and I bisected the district on Mr Wilcox's street map like a halved apple: he took the streets to the left of the core, I the ones to the right. He got the rich blocks of mansion flats and garden houses around Grove End Road; I got the bedsits of Carlton Hill, the terraces of Springfield Road and the council estates of Boundary Road.

'Your friend'll make more in Christmas tips,' warned Wilcox.

'Let's see who's still alive by Christmas,' said Dovidl darkly.

Each morning at seven we loaded bundles of papers into our baskets beneath Wilcox's striped awning, cycling around until the last thin sheet had been shoved through the appropriate brass flap. It took less than an hour, leaving us plenty of time to wolf down Martha's breakfast and wheel off to school before the whistle blew for morning assembly.

If we happened to blow in late, there was no risk of punishment.

Discipline, and much else, was breaking down at The House. With many masters called to the colours, women graduates and retired university dons plugged the gaps and altered the ethos. Caning and sadism ceased; the playground bullies, deprived of adult role-models, turned civilised and considerate. We had Miss Prendergast for history, horn-rimmed but nice legs, and Dr Sedgefield for English, seventy years old and an international authority (it was rumoured) on the semi-colon. These, and others whose names escape me, were founts of knowledge, willing to be dredged, unwilling to be bound by curricular strictures. 'Talk among yourselves,' said Sedgefield, treating six of the brighter boys, bunched around his desk, to his theory of Iago's homosexuality, and Romeo's, for that matter. When the headmaster walked in, alerted by raised voices, Sedgefield looked up mildly and murmured something about college-style tutorials. 'Place is going to the dogs,' I heard the Head mumble, in retreat.

Jewish boys, who made up half the school, were allowed a separate assembly as we could not be expected to feign sincerity in 'Onward Christian Soldiers'. Unwilling to admit actual Jewish ritual, the Head placed us in the hands of Father Edward Jeffries, a brown-cassocked, nicotine-stained Anglican monk who made us recite Psalms in English, Hebrew and Latin. Which is to say that we would read a few verses in King David's Hebrew or St Jerome's Vulgate, and he would then freely translate them into an English more colloquial and compelling than the King James Version. For gravel-voiced Father Jeffries, it must have been a vacuous exercise; he never once met the eye of any of his unbaptisable Jewish brats, or showed satisfaction in our reading. He was a dry old stick with a nasty habit of waggling a finger in his ear and closely examining the waxy yield. But for me, and for Dovidl to a lesser degree, his virtuosity was revelatory in bringing two dead languages to life and both of us closer to the desert source, making us feel its hot-headed Jewishness. Renditions by Father Jeffries lodged in my memory for life.

'Do not fear the night's terror,' he orated in mid-Blitz, 'nor the missile that flies by day. The plague that goes in darkness, the destroyer that ravages at noon. A thousand may fall beside you, ten thousand more at your right – but it will not come near you. Only your eyes shall see it, Simmonds, and witness the reward of the wicked. Carry on, in Latin, if you please.'

'*Quoniam tu Domine spes mea, altissimum posuisti refugium tuum.*'

'Not bad. Next verse, Rapoport, in English.'

'No harm will befall you, no trouble upon your tent . . .'

Back on our bikes after school, we delivered evening papers to about half as many customers. It left us with time to buy a penny ice, pick blackberries from a bramble bush, or simply scoot around the summer streets, still with heat and fear, before resuming work in the music room. On 25 June (I had begun keeping a diary), we came home to the first sign of panic. Dr Steiner was stamping up the front path, waving a sheet of paper and flailing his fine old fiddle-player's hands. 'What is this?' he wailed. 'Why must they deport me? What will be with my wife?'

The poor old professor had been served with an internment order at his front door by two uniformed police officers. As a class C alien under the age of seventy, though barely, they ordered him to report to West Hampstead Police Station next morning, with one small suitcase of personal essentials, for secure detention at an unnamed place of confinement. 'What shall I do?' he appealed to us, his pupils.

I sat him shaking on the living-room sofa, asked Florrie to brew a strong pot of coffee and phoned Father at the office.

'Leave it to me,' he said tersely. 'Keep him occupied until I call back.'

Dovidl took care of that, playing the first Brahms sonata, the G major, with Steiner at the piano and me turning pages, with such an intensity of tenderness that the ringing of the hall telephone came as a resented interruption. 'Tell Dr Steiner the order has been revoked,' said Father, 'and then let me speak to him.'

'How did you fix it?' I asked him at dinner that night.

'A chap I know at the Home Office,' said Father. 'I convinced him that Dr Steiner was essential to the war effort.'

Mother barked a sardonic laugh.

'I didn't have to fabricate much,' explained Father. 'I said he is a cipher expert – which is true, he reads Icelandic runes – and that he is a former colleague of Professor Albert Einstein, which is true in the strictly musical sense. At any rate, the Home Secretary, in person, cleared him within the hour and I have taken the necessary steps to attach him to my unit.'


The skies were beginning to thicken with the growling of aircraft. We saw nothing of the battle of Britain, which was fought above Sussex and Kent in early August, spilling occasionally into south London but never north of the river, no matter how much we craved the excitement. The nearest we got to it were the newspaper front pages that we scanned as we cycled, edited to all appearances by idle hands on the sports desk: 'Biggest Raid Ever – Score 78 to 26 – England Still Batting'.

'Slowly as ever,' remarked Dovidl, who had written off cricket as a futile pastime.

'It could always get stopped by rain,' I chirped.

'Why is it you English treat everything as a game?' he snapped, exposing his cultural confusion at our unchanged habits, our refusal to indulge in the rhetoric of destiny.

'It's not who wins,' I shot back with heavily inculcated cultural superiority, 'it's how you play the game that makes the winning worthwhile.'

We had no concrete sign of the balance of war when, on 20 August, the ebullient Prime Minister, Mr Churchill, famously extolled the decisive achievement of the Royal Air Force – 'never in the field of human conflict was so much owed by so many to so few.' St John's Wood remained, at this point, as untouched as Lake Zurich.

The first action we saw was four nights later when Luftwaffe bombers, perhaps mistakenly, dropped a few loads on the City, reddening our eastern skyline. The RAF retaliated the following night with a raid on Berlin. Sporadic bombings ensued, enough to send us scuttling to the shelter, but not to keep us down for very long. Dovidl and I whined to be let out, ostensibly with bursting bladders, actually to witness the aerial ballet of tracers and planes. 'Just don't go getting yourselves killed,' Florrie would cry, as we ran up before the all-clear sirens sounded.

The war finally came home on 7 September, a summery Saturday, when the Luftwaffe gave up trying to outfight the RAF for aerial supremacy and sent hundreds of bombers to flatten the docks and industries of the East End. Night after night they returned, straying and spraying death indiscriminately all over London, sometimes perishing in a hail of flak. On 9 September, I saw two bombers falling from the sky, pierced and blazing; Dovidl claimed to have counted four. 'Get the Fokkers,' exhorted Florrie, in her Hampshire burr; at least, I think that's what she said. We were quickly learning to tell a Messerschmitt from a Spitfire. The battle of Britain had become the battle for

London and we were thrillingly on the front line, or so we told ourselves.

In reality, we were about five miles from the incendiary epicentre but enough bombs came our way, either in error or jettisoned as the German killer packs wheeled off homewards, to crater the district with crashed houses and casualties. One street after another suffered hits, known as 'incidents'. The stench of burning timbers, brick rubble, broken sewers and putrefaction was inescapable. Death could strike any of us, with the courtesy of three minutes' warning.

'Aren't you scared?' I asked Dovidl one day at sunset, as we gazed down from Primrose Hill on the smouldering city.

'It's so beautiful,' he gasped. 'Look at the tracers, the reds and yellows shooting up through grey smoke, the green fire of those incendiary bombs. It's magnificent, like a ballet, a *Firebird*.'

'This is not art,' I said tartly. 'It's life and death.'

'So is art,' he said, 'when it's good.'

The absence of fear was striking, not just in Dovidl but in our schoolmates and most of the adults we knew. Mortality became matter of fact. Perhaps lack of sleep disabled the panic button, or maybe it was fatalism. A neighbourhood pub, the Queen's Arms, proclaimed itself 'More Open Than Usual' after losing half its roof and the saloon bar. 'We can take it,' was the common slogan, uttered not so much in defiance as in dull determination. Coping with nightly air-raids became a routine like any other.

At home after the afternoon paper round, Dovidl and I would gulp down a high tea, dispatch homework and music and, if the Germans were running late, manage a bath and supper before the sirens sounded. More often, we would head for the shelters unfed, with packs of sandwiches and a Thermos flask that Martha quickly provided. 'All I have to do is put the roast in the oven and those dratted Germans come buzzing over, making a pesky nuisance of theirselves,' moaned our choleric cook. Fiftyish and emphysematic, one autumn morning Martha betook herself home to Devon leaving Florrie in sole charge, promoted from housemaid to house-mother. Father got Florrie exempted from war work by listing her as his army valet.

My parents were seldom around for the early stages of the Blitz, unavoidably detained at essential war work. 'I hope you boys are behaving yourselves and being obedient to Florrie,' Mother crackled down the telephone. 'I shall try to come home tonight, at least to get a change of clothes, but the people here in the East End need our help and solidarity, as I am sure you can understand.'

'I am sorry to be detained for so many nights at a stretch,' said Father from Bristol, or perhaps Liverpool. 'But I gather from the maid that you are coping admirably and not missing us at all.'

We were doing better than coping. We were having, Florrie included, the time of our lives. The Anderson shelter in our garden, popularly named after the Home Secretary who had saved Dr Steiner from internment, was neither safe nor seemly. Several such refuges collapsed on their occupants from the mere blast of a bomb in the general vicinity, and when the first mouse – or was it rat? – scurried over Florrie's face as she drifted off to sleep, we transferred, at the next siren call, to the northbound platform of the nearest underground station, lying down with half the neighbourhood.

You slept with a better sort of person in St John's Wood tube, giggled Florrie. A prissy decorum prevailed, as befitted 'the Wood'. There were none of the heavings and groanings reported from Swiss Cottage, one station up the line, where as many as fifteen hundred souls of disparate origin huddled in garrulous and (it was whispered) carnal propinquity. Ida Haendel, I knew, was shepherded by her father nightly to Swiss Cottage. Josef Hassid refused to descend with his father into that darkness. He stayed at home, listening over and over again, obsessively, to the set of encores he had recorded with the accompanist Gerald Moore, just before the war. HMV had offered him a contract, but his strange behaviour was giving rise to concern. It was the talk of the fiddle fraternity.

On St John's Wood station, one did not speak to a platform neighbour unless formally introduced. The Underground, never officially designated a place of refuge, lacked the most elementary conveniences. Urgent calls of nature were attended to at the edge of the platform, spatteringly over the line. The St John's Wood Society delicately erected a large pair of portable screens, Victorian and lacquered, at either end of the platform (men to the north, women to the south), and a uniformed Bakerloo Line official would appear each morning to hose down the lines before the first trains passed through. But the stench, by midnight, was suffocating and the haughtier type of resident, huddled over coffee cups, sought scapegoats for their discomfort. Foreigners and Jews were the obvious target. I was so relieved that Dovidl had shed his accent.

Florrie, ten years our senior, attended energetically to a burgeoning social life. 'I'm a girl that respects herself,' I heard her tell a soldier in the Underground stairwell. 'He was coming on a bit fast,' she explained next morning. 'Nice fellow, though. I expect I'll be seeing him again tonight.'

Florrie had a responsive eye. She was soon running three other-rank boyfriends, with a fourth in Egypt. Primping and perming her dancing blonde curls as she prepared for the night's skirmish, she regaled us, half comprehending, with the uncomplicated foibles of fighting men on furlough. 'I told Derek we couldn't go any further without us getting engaged,' she prattled. 'Of course, he doesn't know what I get up to with Stanley.' Florrie handled her young men as capably as she coped with us boys, reducing virile masculinity to pliant, amusing companionship.

My parents, after the first intensive onslaught, came home more nights than not. They were needed in their own neck of the Wood as bombs fell and the privileged were imperilled. Father joined a Home Guard unit under Sergeant Eric Blair, whose political essays, signed 'George Orwell', I devoured in the weeklies. The St John's Wood Company met in a drill hall in Allitsen Road and spent its time struggling to master an archaic artillery piece. Most nights Father fire-watched on the roof of Langford Court, a modern block off Abbey Road where Orwell lived in a fifth-floor apartment. His future publisher, Fred Warburg, volunteered to join the unit and the rooftop tone was intellectually elevated. I begged Father to introduce me: Orwell was more of a hero to me than Dan Dare or Winston Churchill – he was the epitome of distilled wisdom.

Dovidl and I were taken round for tea. Mrs Blair, with mournful eyes (Father explained that she had lost a brother at Dunkirk), fussed motheringly about us, but the great writer gave no more than a thin wince from behind his pencil moustache. He fidgeted with a heavy cigarette-lighter while Dovidl played a Vieuxtemps *amuse-gueule*, drawing an involuntary tear from Mrs Blair. Unmoved by the music, his responses to Father's conversational attempts were curt as we gobbled the little treats, ham excepted, that had been laid out for our tea. 'What do you want to be when you grow up, boy?' demanded the polemicist in a high-pitched, schoolmasterly voice.

'A writer, like you, sir,' I crawled.

'They'll need miners and farmers when this lot's over, not pretty phrase-makers,' sniffed Orwell. He seemed as ill at ease in the bourgeois décor of Langford Court as he did in his rangy, six-foot frame, all elbows and edges. His breath was sour and his handshake dank as he bade us farewell before the tea was finished, pleading a looming deadline. Mrs Blair apologised for his discourtesy, explaining that he was under great pressure. I was not offended by his disdain for music, small boys and over-eager Home Guard acquaintances. I knew his to be an inner strength, a moral resolve that made him stay in London while other writers fled to country homes, demanding peace and quiet for their muse. Like many writers I would later meet, he violently resented music as a rival for the public's attention.

Orwell did not remain long at Langford Court, with its dainty fittings and uniformed porters. He moved to Mortimer Crescent, at the Kilburn fringe of my paper round, renting the damp basement and ground floor of a Victorian terraced house where I glimpsed him often at his desk, scribbling in meagre light. He waved at me once, in a vague sort of way, perhaps while in the throes of *Animal Farm*. His move was otherwise unlucky. The house was bombed in 1943 and the Blairs joined the roofless multitude that converged upon my mother's gelid mercies.

This was the role that Mother was born for. Bossing people about came naturally to Violet Simmonds and she had sat through enough charity lunches to know how to handle most human needs. Armed with East End experience and a look that brooked no contradiction, she marched into the district council offices on Marylebone Road and demanded to see the Mayor. Within minutes, she had requisitioned a church hall and taken charge of rehousing and relief in an area that she mapped out, between the Finchley and Edgware Roads. With volunteers from her embroidery class, she descended fearsomely on survivors of bombing raids, located their loved ones (if any were left alive), allocated temporary accommodation and provided food and bedding for their first disoriented days and nights. She treated each needy case with curt efficiency, but felt truly fulfilled when the chance arose to extend a helping hand, from a great height, to one of her social superiors.

One winter's dawn we came home to find Mrs Isaacs (*née* Sassoon), Johnny's mother, wailing orientally, ululating almost, upon the broken slabbery of her mock-Palladian front steps, thick smoke billowing from the wreckage beyond as the firemen wound up their hoses. Her husband, a stockbroker by trade, wrung his hands some feet away while Johnny sucked regressively on his thumb.

'Now, come along, Genevieve,' said Mother briskly. 'No time to mope. Henry' – this to the ineffectual Mr Isaacs – 'you had better go to work if you don't want to miss the markets opening. We'll get this mess dealt with by tonight. Johnny, off to school – Martin, take him to breakfast at our house. Now, dear Genny, I believe I have got just the temporary place for you – a bijou flat in Langford Court, eighth floor, a penthouse the Americans would call it, but quite small. Still, it is admirably situated until you get your bits and pieces in order. Come with me to St Michael's Hall for a nice hot cup of coffee, and we'll get you sorted out.'

The sight of shattered homes never lost its grip on me, and this one was plumb next door. There but for the grace of, so to speak. But there was always more to a bombed house than the destruction of property and human lives, more even than the disruption, often irreparable, of people's illusions of personal security. The bombing of suburban semis, working-men's terraces and well-appointed mansions attacked one of the nation's most treasured myths, a value so innately assumed that it was never enshrined in law. What the Germans violated was the English code of privacy that allotted each householder a castle with his mortgage, sovereign behind the imaginary drawbridge of its front path. Suddenly, privacy was annihilated. A house would be sheared in half by a bomb, exposing half a kitchen, a bedroom, a bathroom to the world. A mirror winked on the wall, miraculously uncracked. Dirty cups were stacked on a draining-board. The pink of a lady's boudoir blushed helplessly at the prurient street.

Dovidl and I were transfixed by such sights. Each morning, on our rounds, we totted up competitive tallies of 'incidents'. The newspapers in our bicycle baskets gave us a kind of journalistic licence to sneak past dazed victims and firemen. Often we arrived in time to join the rescuers, shifting masonry and digging dazed inhabitants out of the graves of their homes. The distinction between men and boys vanished under pressure. 'Over here, boy, lend a hand getting this geezer out.'

'Oy, you there on the bike, take this over to the fire station, double-quick.'

Amid the terror and ugliness of human misery, I was struck by aesthetic novelty. The beckoning glow of a three-storey house in Springfield Road, pulped to rubble and pungently ablaze at dawn, was chilling and thrilling to behold.

'Three new ones this morning,' I would report on the way to school.

'I saw four,' said Dovidl, always one up on me.

'Don't believe you. Where?'

'One on Abbey, one Loudoun Road, two on Grove End Road.'

'Liar.'

'See for yourself.'

'The one on Loudoun's an old one, got hit last week.'

'Look,' said Dovidl reasonably, 'if you won't be sensible about this, we'll have to show proof – one item from each new site.'

'Done,' I exclaimed, punching his arm. 'Bet you I win.'

'Hang on a minute,' said Dovidl. 'Do we count UXBs?'

UneXploded Bombs were a dangerous nuisance, ringed off from gawkers until the sappers came round. Gas explosions were another risk. The first whiff of escaping gas might well be your last. Report it immediately was the rule. A certain heroism pervaded our tally game: we were the first line of detection and defence against gas and UXBs, alerting the nearest warden to anything we smelt or saw. By way of reward, I would pick up a stray penny, a handkerchief, a shard of crockery. Dovidl was more ambitious. He came back with half-crowns, books, a china teacup. I saw something glint in the pale morning sunlight.

'But that's silver,' I protested, 'it could be valuable.'

'Just as well I saved it from looters,' said my friend.

'It's a nice bracelet,' I observed. 'What will you do with it?'

'Nothing,' he lied.

Month by month, our rounds grew longer as houses were pulped and the demand for news increased. Wilcox, the newsagent, doubled our wages to compensate for extra distance and the red chafing of our tender inner thighs against unyielding serge short trousers. British boys were not supposed to wear long pants before secondary school. It was something to do with being hardy in all weathers.

Wilcox bought out his nearest competitor and sent us roaming across the Edgware Road to Maida Vale, where elegant terraces were subsiding into rack and ruin, abandoned by absentee owners. Gapped by craters and squatted by drunks and deserters, these once-handsome avenues were becoming a no man's land that Dovidl and I were warned severely to avoid.

'Be very quick about your business on that side of the road,' said Mother sternly. 'It's full of Fenians and Bohemians over there.'

'The kingdom of Bohemia,' said Dovidl pedantically, 'used to be the southern neighbour of Poland.'

'Not those Bohemians,' sighed Father. 'The Czechs were always very civilised and charming. These are British Bohemians. They are more like gypsies, feckless and immoral. As for the Fenians, I am sure you will come across them when you study the troubled history of Ireland at your next school.'

These admonitions, needless to say, made Maida Vale our pubertal fantasyland, vested with a danger that felt more personal than the metals that rained from above. Alone or together, we cruised this unpoliced domain and got to know its flotsam of unprotected tenants and dropouts. I heard about the successful rent strike that the Communists ('What are Communists?') had organised just before the war, and the dreams of men who drank away their art-school prizes and survived upon the dregs. There were fugitives among them, beyond the law's reach.

Kevin could have been an army deserter or IRA member, we never had the temerity to ask. Fuzz-cheeked with a pepper-and-salt permanent two-day growth, he smelt like a hastily evacuated pub and wore charity handouts that never quite covered the ends of his stick-like limbs. His trousers were pinched at the waist and the tongue of his belt flapped loosely over his fly. But Kevin could be quick on his feet when the rent-collector turned the corner, too quick for a drunk (and for the rent collector), and his reminiscences of the Easter Uprising, glimpsed from his bedroom window, were rivetingly imaginative. The Fenians, from Kevin's point of view, had the most fun. 'All in the past, lads.' He sighed. 'It's a sad world, now, where a bloke can kill yer by dropping blobs from a bus in the sky. You wouldn't have the loan of a florin to tide me over till Monday? The baccy-man is getting a bit stroppy over giving me credit.'

How he got by, I never knew. He never invited us into his basement doss-house, sitting in all weathers on a pavement bench, waiting for anyone with the time of day. He was, like us, neither man nor boy but a creature suspended in-between by the traumas of personal history. I would hear him playing 'Danny Boy' on his battered mouth-organ and beckon Dovidl over to hear. Dovidl was intolerant of bad music. He took the tinny instrument from Kevin and, without bothering to wipe off germs, put it to his own lips and played the Hibernian lament, deepening its yearning with a swaying vibrato and dramatic rephrasing. 'By Jaysus, the boy's a wonder,' exclaimed Kevin. Dovidl, without drawing breath, switched to Beethoven's Spring Sonata, then to 'Smoke Gets In Your Eyes'. 'You want to get him a proper man-sized accordion,' advised Kevin.

One foggy evening beneath a flaking sycamore tree, Kevin lit my first cigarette and watched impartially as I threw up violently on the third inhalation.

'Funny that,' said Kevin, holding my head between my knees. 'Yer mate David took to the Woodbines last week like a Dubliner to Guinness.'

'What's Guinness?' I croaked.

'The very goodness of Ireland,' he replied. 'Here, have a swig. It'll wash away the taste of the fag.'

At the earthy texture of the malted beer, I gagged again. Kevin wiped my mouth with his jacket sleeve, which reeked worse than beer but felt comforting in a comradely sort of way. Kevin and I were at about the same stage of emotional development, less avid for the onset of adulthood than the jet-propelled Dovidl.

At the end of our rounds, beside a plane tree on Elgin Avenue, we would touch handlebars. 'This is ours,' said Dovidl, indicating an oval hollow at the foot of the tree. 'If I need to leave you a message, it will be here. If you want to send me something, here's where you leave it. No one knows about this tree but you and me.' There was never a glow in my life like the glow of his confidence.

Having finished early one spring morning not long before our barmitzvah (my diary-keeping had become sporadic), I waited for Dovidl by our tree and saw him, from afar, on the rim of a smoking bombsite. It had been a vicious night. Fire crews were chasing off to new blazes before they had fully extinguished the last. Mobile canteens patrolled the avenues, ladling out strong tea to victims and rescuers. A sickly Bing Crosby song leaked from a nearby wireless.

I was shaken, in need of companionship. Irish Kevin's dingy squat had been hit by an incendiary bomb. There was no way of telling if he had slept at home that night, but if he had been there he would not have awoken. None of his neighbours had escaped the conflagration. I saw the firemen shaking their heads, nothing to be done.

I never knew Kevin's surname, so I could not post him missing. I was going to miss him, my next-best friend, with his wry anecdotes of rebellion and false dawn. Dovidl, I felt sure, would be upset.

I leaned on my bike, waiting for him to see me. He was in no hurry, scanning the rubble for a trophy. Poised on a jutting beam, he sprang delicately to a safer perch, dipping as he landed to pluck something at his feet. 'As the hart yearns for springs of water,' I heard Father Jeffries recite from Psalms, 'so my soul does yearn for you, O God.' He was sleek as a forest faun, was Dovidl, elegant in his dreadful element. Straining my eyes, I saw him tugging at an object, perhaps a china doll. It was getting late. I mounted the bike and rode towards him. Close up, the thing he was pulling looked almost human – a broken, nightgowned corpse. As I approached, he swooped like a carrion bird and came up with a wallet. His eyes gripped mine in a motionless stare, daring me to break silence as he extracted three large white banknotes and tossed the wallet back into the debris. 'Here,' he gestured, 'one's for you.'

I could not speak. The voice he had given me choked in my throat, asphyxiated by revulsion.

'Go on,' he cajoled, waving the note at me. I could make out large curlicued letters, the figure five, the signature of the Governor of the Bank of England beckoning with spend-me temptation.

'Well, at least give me a ruddy hand off this beam,' said Dovidl. 'The wretched thing's going to cave in at any minute.'

It began to drizzle. I felt sick and hungry all at once, recoiling at the heat of his hand as I helped him off the funereal mound. We wheeled up the hill. Not another word was exchanged until we jostled at the bathroom basin, brushing teeth after breakfast.

'Bad night?' he asked, through a mouthful of Colgate's.

'I saw five,' I replied dully.

'Only four for me.' He shrugged. 'We'd better get to school.'

'Kevin's dead,' I said.

He rinsed his mouth and spat into the sink. 'Get a move on,' he said. 'We're going to be late for Psalms.'

That evening he played the Brahms concerto, start to finish, pushing me off the piano stool for accompanying too carefully and plinking out the connecting bits himself. We had heard Yehudi Menuhin perform the work on the wireless a week before – it must have been April 1943 – and Dovidl felt personally challenged by his star-like descent from sun-kissed California. 'Yehudi Menuhin has come to this country to give his services to war charities,' announced the BBC announcer.

'Some of us have been here all along,' carped Mother.

'I can do better,' said Dovidl, when it was over. All week, on his own, he fretted over tricky arabesques and the faintly gypsy rhythms of the *rondo finale*. That night, he played the chestnut-coloured warhorse for the first time, with me as partner and audience. It was intended as an affirmation of something: a eulogy, perhaps, maybe an apology. 'I shall not die,' echoed the Psalmist in my head, 'for I shall live and recount the acts of God. He may torment me greatly – absolute infinitive, Simmonds – but He has not handed me over to death. So open up those gates of goodness, and I will enter them to thank God. This gate belongs to God, only the good shall enter into it.'

Dovidl leaned on the piano, awaiting my verdict. 'Good, huh?'

'Not bad for a beginner,' I grudged.

'What do you mean, not bad?' he exclaimed. 'I was bloody good, Mottl. Ran rings round that Yehudi.'

Depends what you mean by good, I thought. There is in every artist, my father used to say, a hard core of brute egotism. The talent that wrests music from a contraption of wood and gut is like a natural gas. Funnelled and refined, it gives heat and light. Uncontrolled, it maims and destroys. 'I know musicians of the most saintly countenance who commit unpardonable acts of betrayal in pursuit of some trivial gain,' he mused. 'Confronted with the pain they have inflicted, they shrug and blame it on their art – as if making music relieves them of moral responsibility.

'Faced with a choice between saving the human race and having fluffy towels in their dressing room, they will always go for the towels. Art is their excuse for everything, to us and to whatever they use for a conscience. Remember that, Martin. Never let yourself be overwhelmed by beauty, or some artist will use it to destroy you.'

He gave me this nugget of wisdom in the week before his death, too late to save either of us. I never told him what I had seen on Elgin Avenue, nor did I mention it again to Dovidl, but it served a purpose, drawing me back half a pace from what might otherwise have become a total dependence.

I arrived at a shrewder appreciation of my friend in the aftermath of that incident. He was not the little angel who played partitas to the Chief Rabbi's wife, that I knew already. What I needed to fathom was the depth and drive of his baseness. Dovidl, I guessed, would not knowingly harm his nearest and dearest, but he was single-minded in self-interest and callous about losers like Kevin. He would have no compunction about defiling a corpse and rifling it for a few crinkled notes that would buy him a better grade of catgut. He would never permit morality to impede an artistic imperative. His priorities were: self, art, the rest.

Had he tampered with the body in any fouler way? The odious thought fleetingly crossed my mind. The victim was of presentable middle age, her clothing dishevelled. But I saw no exposed flesh; if he touched her, it was only to thieve, at most to peek. Nastiness could be ruled out. More horrendous to my mind was how Dovidl, desperately fearful for his own family, could manhandle the still-warm corpse of someone else's mother. Did a dead stranger deserve no respect? Was Kevin carrion? Was Dovidl's mind so enclosed in courtyard walls that the rest of humanity counted for nothing?

Disgust wrangling with dismay, I held him at arm's length for some days, fearful of his satanic side. When disgust wore off, I decided he was safe to handle. That Friday, when I checked our tree, I found a red KitKat bar in the secret hollow. And every other Friday afterwards there was another bar, bought with his wages from Mr Wilcox, a treat for the weekend. He continued to say how much he needed me. Having been caught in an abominable act, he was more than ever indebted to my discretion and dependent on my loyalty. I had information about him, a commodity he respected and feared. He was in my power, as I was in his.

Amazingly, our schooling scarcely suffered from lack of sleep and general disruption. At The House, I streaked ahead in history with Miss Prendergast's enthusiastic tuition, and Dovidl scored top marks in maths, thanks in part to the extra guidance he received after dark on Wednesday nights, when we slept over in the bunkered basement of Dr Steiner's retirement home. Two physics professors from Frankfurt would supervise Dovidl's homework, almost coming to blows in their eagerness to introduce him to the higher mysteries of numbers. He would repay them with a short piece on the violin. I, meanwhile, read frail Mrs Steiner off to sleep from historical texts selected by her husband for my edification, mostly translated from the German. I was gripped by Stefan Zweig's account of Mary Queen of Scots, then by Schiller's play of her life. I discovered Thomas Mann by way of *Lotte in Weimar* and Franz Werfel through *The Forty Days of Musa Dagh*, the first novel ever to depict genocide. What struck me about these German authors was their authenticity, their grasp of period detail.

'I love these writers,' I told Dr Steiner. 'They are well rounded.'

'Not too heavy for you?' he quavered.

'I admire their dryness, never a word too many.'

He beamed with the joy of a baptising missionary. I read on: Schnitzler and Hoffmanstahl, Kafka, Hermann Hesse. 'You see the tall lady in the corner?' said Steiner. 'She is a niece of Arthur Schnitzler's. The man over there is a cousin of Max Brod, Kafka's friend. We have a Rilke and a Zuckmayer in this basement, two Zweigs and a relation by marriage of Else Lasker-Schüler, our greatest woman poet. In one London shelter, the whole of modern German literature.' I curled up to sleep against the bare-brick wall, warmed by a culture in exile.

Then there were our Hebrew studies. Dovidl and I were obliged to attend Sunday-morning *Cheder* classes at the sepulchral synagogue on Abbey Road, to be prepared for barmitzvah by a young assistant minister, Mr Goldfarb. A question of precedence quickly intervened. I, by chronological right, ought to celebrate my tribal coming-of-age three months ahead of Dovidl.

'But if everyone turns out for Martin's barmitzvah in February,' I had overheard my father ponder one Sunday afternoon in the sitting room, 'will they come again a few weeks later for the other boy, who has no family of his own?'

'And can we afford to put on two big functions in three months?' said Mother practically.

'I'll talk to the boy,' said Father, meaning me.

Our conversation was a sentimental replica of his first tentative, respectful solicitation. 'This is going to be your day, of course, Martin, and Mother and I would entirely understand if you want to have it to yourself,' said Father. 'However, we are a little concerned that having David's ceremony so soon afterwards will remind him of the absence of loved ones, from which we try to shield him.'

'What do you propose, Father?'

'That you should have a joint barmitzvah on the Sabbath of David's thirteenth birthday.'

'Excellent,' I said. 'He can read the first half of the portion. I shall read the second half, and the section from Prophets.' We shook hands on the deal.

There was only one impediment, raised by the unordained Goldfarb. Was it permissible in Jewish law, he wondered, to delay my confirmation in order to spare another boy's feelings?

Father brooked no cavils from so lowly a functionary. He took me round to the Chief Rabbi's house on Hamilton Terrace, where the learned Dr J. H. Hertz, a world-renowned scholar of notoriously short temper, caressed his well-trimmed beard and pronounced a *psak*, or precedential ruling, allowing the postponement of a barmitzvah for the sake of emotional stability in times of war.

Learning to read tropes and sing the cantillation came easily to us both; recognising curlicued Hebrew letters in a Torah scroll held no terrors for acolytes of Father Jeffries. We were seasoned performers at scripture; we would take barmitzvah in our stride, reading our portions flawlessly and without flair.

The great day, 15 May 1943, passed unmemorably, apart from one dreadful gaffe by the minister who referred to Dovidl, presciently enough, as 'an unfortunate *orphan* of this awful conflict'. Dovidl paled. I clutched his hand. The moment passed. Special prayers were offered for 'our brothers, the house of Israel, who are in grief and captivity'. The synagogue was packed with cousins so distant I barely knew their names, as well as colleagues and contacts of both parents. 'Who's that?' demanded Dovidl, nodding at a woman with a swan-shaped creation on her head.

'How should I know?' I shrugged.

My mother was top-decked in a drama of millinery, a symphony of fake fruits, flowers and creatures of the air. She wore silk gloves up to her elbows and looked, for once, almost content. '*Mazel tov*, Violet,' crowed Aunt Mabel, dislodging Mother's hat with a misfired kiss. To me, she said, 'I still don't trust that pal of yours, Marty. Too smooth by half for my liking.'

'Oh, Auntie,' I protested.

'Don't worry. I've got you both a nice present.'

In normal circumstances, people of our circle would have proceeded to a dinner-dance at the Dorchester, to the music of Joe

Loss and his band. In wartime, we made do with a kosher-catered Saturday lunch in the synagogue hall and whatever gifts our guests had, contrary to the strict observance of Jewish law, brought along. Dovidl and I shared between us five watches, eleven fountain-pens, forty-two books on varied subjects (two presented by the authors), six tie-pin and cufflink sets, a calligraphy kit, a cricket bat, a year's subscription to *Tribune* (courtesy of Mrs Blair), a baroque music stand from a tearful Dr Steiner and one hundred and twenty-six pounds in cheques and cash. Aunt Mabel and Uncle Kenneth got Dovidl an initialled leather music-case and me a printed set of *ex-libris* stickers and a first-edition Thackeray. It took us almost a month to write all the thank-you cards.

Continuing the rites of passage, we left The House a few weeks later to take up places in long trousers at Corpus Christi School, an exclusive Hampstead academy – green blazer, black stripes – that served as gateway to the great Oxbridge colleges. Miss Prendergast kissed me sweetly goodbye. Father Jeffries pronounced Psalmic blessings. To Dovidl he said, 'Upon the ten-stringed instrument and the fading lyre, in meditation on the harp, you have given me joy in your work, O God; I shall rejoice in the works of your hands.' My benediction, from the same Psalm, was: 'A crude man will not understand this, nor a prejudiced fool.' He gave me a copy of the Book of Isaiah, in Greek.

At Corpus we were enjoined to 'work hard, play hard'. Since neither of us enjoyed getting muddy knees, we skipped sports and maintained our extra-mural routines much as before, newspapers twice a day, *Bildung* every Wednesday night. Dr Steiner was sadly ailing. At his wife's funeral, a bleak affair at the Hoop Lane crematorium, we discovered that she was not Jewish; she had gone into exile for love of her Hermann. In the car home, the mourner begged my father to let Dovidl make a public début.

'*Er ist ganz bereits*, Herr Simmonds,' said the old man, lapsing into mother tongue. 'He is quite ready, and I wish to hear him make a success before I die. My Martha was so fond of the boy, almost like a grandchild.'

Dovidl, soon after, followed up with a request of his own. A boy at school had been bragging how much his parents were spending on private education. Dovidl, aghast, asked my father if he could contribute to his own fees by giving a public recital. Father gave the proposal a full day's consideration before delivering a measured refusal. 'For three reasons, my dear David,' he explained, in my presence and for my benefit. 'First, we are not poor. Second, this is not a good moment to put a Jewish débutant on the London stage – I think you know what I mean. Third, I expect to be in a position to give you a more auspicious début once this wretched war is over. So, let's hear no more of it, there's a good chap.'

The second point was more serious than historians of the period are inclined to admit. Culture was flourishing in wartime Britain. Men and women in every shade of khaki craved the comfort of canonic masterpieces and the prospect of self-discovery in the mirror of contemporary art. New composers, writers and performers shot to prominence, despite a shortage of newsprint to report the arts and of shellac and celluloid to record them. A creative dawn was breaking: English art was being reborn.

The anticipation for Ralph Vaughan Williams' fifth symphony in June 1943 was almost tangible, the ovations overwhelming. Michael Tippett's oratorio, *A Child of our Time*, was tumultuously acclaimed despite (perhaps because of) its pacifist agenda. Benjamin Britten's *Serenade* for tenor, horn and strings at the Wigmore Hall quivered with potential; his opera *Peter Grimes*, as the war ended, was universally recognised as the first English masterpiece of lyric drama for two hundred and fifty years.

Marvellous as the revival was, the public response in a robustly John Bullish nation was no less remarkable. Long queues formed to see Laurence Olivier's Shakespeare films, the abstract paintings of Ben Nicolson, the great reclining figures of Henry Moore. Novels by J. B. Priestley and Graham Greene sold out overnight. England, in those Spartan war years, felt like ancient Athens or Venice in the age of the Doges.

The receptivity was, however, restricted to English art, true and blue. Aliens need not apply. The minds that opened to new English writing slammed shut on foreign accents. Writers whose plays had been hits in Berlin and Bucharest sat in cafés along the Finchley Road, lamenting their paradise lost. Fine artists, unable to land a teaching post, became antiques dealers; conductors scraped a living, if they were lucky, as copyists. Soloists talked of catching the first peacetime ship to America. England had given them shelter and oblivion, laced with xenophobia and abuse.

'What is bad about Jews is that they are not only conspicuous, but go out of their way to make themselves so,' wrote George Orwell, my father's night-watch commander. 'Sometimes the Jews make it very difficult to be as much pro-Semite as I am,' yawned the critic James Agate, a theatrical sybarite who used to drop in on my mother for tea, *en route* from his Swiss Cottage apartment to a night in the West End. Orwell blithely acknowledged in one of his essays that anti-Semitism had increased during the war, blaming it on the tendency of Jews to congregate in cities. *The Times* warned that the Jews would forfeit all sympathy unless they dissociated themselves from Zionism. The *Catholic Herald*, which took its line from a collaborationist Pope in Rome, called for a 'solution' to the Jewish 'problem' in the form of mass baptism. As Hitler faced defeat, his cultural victims contemplated a gloomy future.

Stefan Zweig fled from Britain to Brazil, where he took his

own life – 'all too impatient', as he put it, 'to await the dawn'. Oscar Kokoschka, interned as an enemy alien, painted a series of political allegories, 'inspired less by anger than by despair'. Elias Canetti, the future Nobel Laureate, burned a hole in a table at Cosmo's Continental Restaurant, composing the epic *Auto-da-fé* in his head without yet setting a word on paper.

Creative artists could, at worst, inhabit a world of imagination. Performers had nowhere to hide. Ida Haendel had won, before the war, the loyalty of Sir Henry Wood and his Proms audience. She played on at the Albert Hall, through bombs and doodlebugs, growing all the while in confidence and expressiveness. Josef Hassid was less fortunate. The boy who had been billed as 'the most fantastic talent to hit London' grew alarmingly introspective until, one day, he went blazing mad, beat up his father and was picked up by police, stark naked, beside a pond on Hampstead Heath. Dozens of lesser talents dropped silently out of art, never to be heard again. My father was right: this was not the time to present a foreign Jewish débutant on the London concert stage.

There were also personal considerations. With the war nearing its end, the fate of Dovidl's family filled our minds. There had been reports of mass killings in eastern Europe. A million Jews, said the *Manchester Guardian* in April 1942, had been wiped out. The *Daily Telegraph*, in June that year, carried a report about mobile gas chambers that cleansed whole villages of Jews. In November, an American Jewish leader, Rabbi Stephen Wise, brought forth a State Department document indicating that two million Jews had been murdered in an 'extermination campaign'. A place called Auschwitz was mentioned.

Dovidl read these reports for himself in the newspapers he delivered for ten shillings a week, plus tips. The last word he had received from home was a letter routed via Switzerland, many times slit open and resealed by censors. It assured him, in his mother's small hand, that the family were in good health, all things considered. He'd had a baby sister, Basya-Beyla, a beautiful, black-haired little girl who, sadly, had caught diphtheria when she was eight months old and died very suddenly, one night to the next. Pessia had sketched a marvellous charcoal portrait of the baby, but it was forbidden to send drawings abroad so he would have to wait until the war was over to see what she had looked like. Malkeh was growing into a fine young girl, always a great help to her mother.

They were to be resettled soon in the East where they had been assured that living conditions would be less cramped. Missing him terribly, they thanked the merciful Creator that their beloved son was safe, warm and cared-for, making good progress with his musical studies. Dovidl kept the letter in his breast-pocket, ever warm, buttoned up with his pain.

Out of respect for his feelings, we avoided discussing the fate of the Jews in his presence. 'Don't believe everything you read in the papers,' my father warned me, on a summer night's stroll. 'Treat atrocity reports with care, taking into account the possibility of propaganda and the Jewish tendency to hysteria.'

'But it does sound pretty horrible, Father.'

'We shall have to wait and see,' said Mortimer Simmonds. 'The Allies have landed in France, Europe will soon be free, and then we must make every effort to help as best we can.'

I was tormented by several scenarios. If his parents had survived, Dovidl would surely wish to rejoin them. If they had been killed, he might go back to Poland anyway, or go off somewhere else to start a new life. He might go mad like Josef Hassid, who (I heard) had been diagnosed schizophrenic and locked up in a Polish hospital near Epsom. Any which way, I might lose him, and I could not bear the thought.

So I refrained from raising the subject, and Dovidl burrowed ever more into himself. Many mornings, seeing him at breakfast red-eyed and ashen-faced, I jollied him into a sunnier mood. Did I do wrong? Should I have joined him in tortured speculation? Should I have thrown an arm around his thin frame and tried to suction out the pain? Might that, perhaps, have averted the eventual catastrophe?

Retrospection is pointless. Like any adolescent, I was motivated primarily by self-concern. My main fear was losing Dovidl. With him in my life, I was confident, capable, presentable, almost eloquent. Without him, I would revert to being a fat slob with a speech defect. He was the Rabbi to my Golem, the Clara to my Schumann, the valve to my radio. If I failed to invade his privacy, when invasion might have been welcomed, it was because I dared not jeopardise our symbiotic unity. My need, I ignobly reckoned, was more immediate than his. If he could just get me through to full maturity, I would then be equipped to offer help in whatever way he required.

When the ghastly truth came to light, it did so disjointedly. A week after the war ended, Dovidl and I sat in a news cinema near Oxford Circus watching cadaverous scenes of Belsen's liberation. No words could describe what we saw. Nouns like atrocity, barbarity, cruelty, enormity, inhumanity had been rendered meaningless by wartime propaganda. We stumbled out into a mockingly promising spring dusk, the lights twinkling after years of blackout.

'They said they found many prisoners still alive,' I assured him.

'We'd better go home,' said Dovidl.

There was nothing more to say: incoherence bred incomprehension, then shock fatigue set in. What the mind could not grasp, it did not want to know. The statistic of six million was embalmed as a cliché, collectively eulogised, individually unidentified. At Dr Steiner's lonely funeral, in a Jewish cemetery in Edmonton with a bare quorum of ten mourners, I choked back my tears on seeing Dovidl dry-eyed. He had been excised of the ability to grieve.

Months passed before we were able to establish what had happened to his family. My parents embarked on a whirl of activity. Father posted the Rapoports' names at displaced-persons camps and took out boxed advertisements in the *Jewish Chronicle* and *Palestine Post*, in pages that heaved with lost souls forlornly seeking loved ones. Mother activated her refugee networks, distributing search tasks to those she had assisted. Father went to see the Chief Rabbi, specifically to meet his red-bearded son-in-law, Rabbi Dr Solomon Schonfeld, who was running in and out of Poland in search of Jewish orphans. Dr Schonfeld took the particulars, made no promises. We met him weeks later at Victoria station, heading a convoy of bewildered child survivors. When immigration officials blocked entry, he blazed through the barriers with eyes of blue fire. Catching my father's eye, he shook his head slowly with a look of sorrowing exhaustion.

Mortimer Simmonds was not a man to give up. Donning his wartime uniform for the very last time, he descended on the Foreign Office and demanded permission to reopen cultural exchanges with Poland. To his surprise, both governments welcomed the idea. The British hoped a musical overture might offset Soviet dominance in Warsaw, while the Poles were subtly seeking gaps in a descending Iron Curtain. In May 1946, on Dovidl's sixteenth birthday, Father set out for Warsaw, Cracow and Lodz with the Parry Quartet, the soprano Elaine Fielding, reams of scores to be given away to music colleges and an eccentric, diplomatic programme of Britten, Schoenberg, Purcell and Szymanowski. He returned two weeks later, unable to speak through a streptococcal throat and a shattered spirit. 'All I can tell you, David,' he croaked, 'is that not one brick stands of your parental home, or of your family's last address before their deportation. There was no neighbour, no caretaker, no shopkeeper, no eye-witness of any kind who could tell me what had happened. Both streets have vanished from the map.'

'Do you know when they left Warsaw?' asked Dovidl.

'I was able to ascertain that,' coughed Father. 'The date of deportation was 18 August 1942, and the destination, Treblinka. That is not promising. Treblinka was an annihilation centre, not a labour camp. More than a million people were killed there, directly upon arrival. I was not allowed to visit the site – for security reasons, they said. However, I made the acquaintance of a senior official at the Ministry of Culture, Mr Kaczynski, and he has offered to make continuing enquiries at the highest level. He, too, lost relatives at Treblinka.

'I am sorry this does not give us much to go on with, my dear David, but rest assured that I shall not give up the search. And you, David, must promise me that you will not give up hope.'

Dovidl, in a high-backed dining-room chair, waited for my father to expel another souvenir gob of Varsovian phlegm. When he finally spoke, his knuckles were white as quicklime. 'I have no hope, Mr Simmonds,' he said, with mathematical precision. 'Hope is self-deception. One can have faith – in God, in art and in the evidence of eyes and ears. Faith can be validated, or refuted. But hope is futile – an illusion for the hopeless.'

He paused as Father heaved and coughed again. I stared at the tablecloth, feeling useless. 'I had better accept the reality,' Dovidl continued. 'I shall never see the drawing my sister Pessia made of the baby I never saw. My parents are dead' – he rose in a hurry – 'my sisters . . . are no longer alive.'

I knocked at his door late that night. He was lying fully clothed on his bed, staring upwards. I told him that all was not lost, that missing children were still turning up and that any number remained hidden in haystacks and convents. Dr Schonfeld was going back time after time. It was not beyond reason to hope, I argued. The great philosophers did not discount hope: Voltaire, Descartes, even Schopenhauer. Dr Steiner had mentioned a school of thought led by one of his friends, Ernst Bloch. He called it *Das Prinzip Hoffnung*, the hope principle. Hope was part of our human constitution, I protested. It could not be eliminated as irrational.

'Drop it, Martin,' said Dovidl, freezing me with the unfamiliar formality of my name. 'I'm trying to face objective facts. I'm not in the mood for philosophy.'

Wrenched by his misery and terrified that grief would tear him away from me, I gripped his shoulder by way of solidarity and left the room. In the corridor I bumped into Florrie, whose bedroom was opposite mine. She raised her eyebrows in sympathy and shook her irrepressibly curly head. There was nothing to be said.

Assistant Minister Goldfarb of the Abbey Road synagogue came round in black canonicals and dog-collar on a pastoral visit. He urged Dovidl to observe the *shiva* rite of mourning, followed by eleven months of attendance at twice-daily prayers. 'You will find comfort each day in the heart of the community,' he advised.

'I cannot sit *shiva* until I have proof they are dead,' said Dovidl didactically. He turned away when the minister began muttering the traditional verse, asking God to comfort him among the mourners of Zion and Jerusalem. The formulas of faith yielded no consolation.

It fell to my father to mourn by proxy. At seven fifteen next morning, and every morning for the next year, I heard the front door click as Mortimer Simmonds, a man unmarked by religious fervour, went to synagogue to recite *kaddish* for a man he had met only once, for his unknown wife, for their infant daughters and for heaven alone knew how many unnamed others. I joined him on Sundays, saying a silent *kaddish* of my own for Dr Steiner and Irish Kevin, who had no one left to mourn them. Dovidl refused to set foot in synagogue, even on high holy days, for to pray would be to admit the possibility of hope, and he had shut the door firmly on the principle of hope.

Doors closing, doors opening punctuated my nights and ruined my sleep. Father's exit for morning prayers was the last of a nocturnal run of clickings and lockings and swishings and flushings. It began soon after midnight with Florrie, locking the front door after a dalliance with one of her demobbed suitors. Her scuttering of high heels, followed by the squish of stockinged soles on linoleum, ended with a reassuring click of her door-jamb and the creaking of bed-springs. It took Florrie twelve minutes by my luminous watch to shed her glitter and hum herself happily to bed. Minutes later, there would be a faint groan of floorboards and a fresh squeaking of her unresistant handle. Someone in slippered feet was paying Florrie a visit.

At first, I half hoped it was Father, pursuing the carnal comforts long denied him in marriage. But Mortimer Simmonds was too correct a man to sneak sexual relief from an employee, and the footstep was too light to be his. It had to be Dovidl who was creeping presumptuously into Florrie's accommodating arms.

I was hugely relieved at first, delighted that someone was

reaching into his well of grief, easing the alarming grid of fret-lines across his pallid forehead. As I lay in bed alert to any noise, I tried to conjure in my mind an image of their coition, but I had nothing except literary metanyms to go by. It would be years before I achieved sexual initiation and my expectations were harmlessly imprecise. Nevertheless, I felt no envy for Dovidl or animal rivalry, nothing other than an immense surge of sympathy.

This sensation quickly gave way to something more feral, to the grim fear that he was crossing yet another barrier in his flight from me, sheltering in a place where I could never reach him. The erosion of our bond, the crumbling of unity, destroyed my sleep.

His visits to Florrie were irregular: sometimes nightly, then silence for a week. I would wake up thinking I heard a door click, only to find the rain spitting on my window-panes and the house quiet as a coma. Dovidl said nothing. Excluded from his sex-life, fearing that anything I said might alienate him still further, I grew anxious and irritable. I tried bingeing on KitKats, reverting to infantile comforts, but milk shortages had forced Rowntrees to substitute lactate reassurance with plain chocolate in faded blue wrappers. Disgusted, I never broke another bar.

Cocoa, camomile tea and tablets lifted from my mother's bedside table failed to send me to sleep. I lay on my back praying for oblivion, while part of me listened for the C-sharp squeal of an unoiled hinge, the breathy, toneless whisper of welcome.

One summer's morning at four, I heard the front door closing and a footstep on the staircase. This conformed to none of the familiar sounds. Grabbing my cricket-bat, I rushed out to confront burglars. What I met was Dovidl, in his disused synagogue suit, heading up to his room.

'Where have you been?' I hissed.

'Out,' he said, 'to get some fresh air.'

'Where?'

'Up West. Want to come with?'

'When?'

'Tomorrow night, if you like.'

I could not bring myself to accept. Once I would have rushed along with any madcap suggestion of his, but now I was sheltering behind a fortress of suspicion. What did he want of me? What were his motives? Did he need me to cover up for him? Was he inviting me out of pity? He was so much older than me now, in experience and in looks. He probably went to places that would refuse me entry.

Some days later, on our way to school, he made a second approach. 'I'd really like you to come along, Mottl,' he said. 'I need your eyes about me, your ears, your analytical faculties.'

'Where is it that you go?'

'Come and see.'

That night, as soon as my parents turned out their bedroom lights, Dovidl opened my door. 'Suit and hat, let's go,' he commanded.

Moments later we were out of the terrace and chasing the last bus into town, a number thirteen that took us down Baker Street, through Oxford Circus, around Piccadilly and to the seamy edge of Soho, where we jumped off and headed south. Dovidl lit a cigarette on dismounting, the first I had seen him smoke. I inhaled his exhalation and tried to look nonchalant. Covent Garden at midnight was sweeping out the last theatregoers and setting up the odoriferous all-night market. Canvas-covered lorries thundered in mountains of fruit and veg. Street cries that harked back to Chaucer's day split the heady air as porters heaved sacks of apples and hundredweights of spuds for trilbied grocers and ascetic-looking restaurateurs to inspect. Good food was prized above rubies in those rationed times and it was anyone's guess how much of the stuff got knocked off by black-marketeers before it reached the distribution chain. 'See that bloke in the café?' said Dovidl, indicating a Homburg hat above brown coat and wire specs, reading an early edition of tomorrow's *Times*. 'He's a Treasury snoop, drinks coffee all night, never says a word. Here to catch smugglers, mostly booze and fags.'

Tea-stalls and greasy cafés formed pinpricks of light on a periphery of shadow. Short men with sharp features flickered in and out of sight. Restaurants heaved the drunk and merry into the maws of growling cabs. The completely incapable were turfed into the gutter, squatting on the kerbstone where they took up the tuneless ditty they had been trying to sing when the pubs shut. Small pools of vomit decorated the pavement, among cabbage leaves and spent bus-tickets. Powdered old women – prostitutes off the Piccadilly meat-rack, Dovidl whispered – hung around for one last trick of trade, or a free gift of bruised fruit. A cycling policeman purred through pedestrian alleys, to cries of 'Wotcher, Bill, fancy a bit?' The market heaved with wooden crates and ageless ribaldry. I was smitten by the sights and smells, but Dovidl had more pressing matters in mind.

He led me past Bow Street police station along an alley and down a flight of steps to a heavy basement door that yielded at his triple knock. I could barely see inside, so thick was the smoke. When my eyes stopped watering, I found myself in something I had read about in the novels of Patrick Hamilton and Graham Greene but never expected to visit: an illegal gaming club, a den of vice and squalor.

Dovidl seemed to feel at home. He pecked the hat-check girl – on the lips, I noticed – ordered a glass of champagne 'and a lemonade for my teetotal friend' and exchanged a wad of five-pound notes for chips of many colours. Where had he come by so much money?

He strode to a green-baize table and sat down, signalling to the unoccupied croupier to deal him two cards.

'Will your young friend be playing, Mr David?' said the dealer.

'Not so young, Tony,' said Dovidl. 'He's here to learn.'

They played a game I knew from the sixth-form common room as pontoon. Here it was called 'blackjack'. The object was to score twenty-one, ideally in two cards – royal or ten, plus ace – or, if your cards were poor, to bluff your opponent into thinking that you had a better hand, forcing him to 'twist' (take another card) and 'bust' (surpass twenty-one). I considered it a mug's game. If dealer and player had the same total – say, nineteen – the dealer was deemed to have won. The game was stacked in favour of the man with the deck. Why bother to play?

Dovidl, however, seemed to be winning. His pile of chips mounted so fast that I neatly stacked a second pile, then a third.

'Loaded, your chum is,' said a posh-accented man on my right, squiffy with drink.

'Talented, too,' I replied.

'Come on,' said Dovidl, flipping a large green chip to the dealer. 'I'm bored with this. Let's move on to big game.'

We strolled across an expanse of stained red carpet to the roulette wheel, jostling a space for ourselves among a crush of dinner jackets and taffeta dresses. Dovidl scattered coloured discs across the numbered board, apparently at random. He paid scant attention to the scudding ball, the spinning wheel, the call of *'faites vos jeux, messieurs'*. I wondered how French, the language of love, had become the vernacular of chance. When the ball came to rest in a groove, the croupier clawed in the losing chips with a silver rake and paid the winners. Dovidl seemed scarcely to notice. He was chatting to a neighbour and his expensive girl and would miss a round now and then in airy bonhomie. I, too, had leisure to observe the 'membership' of this disreputable place. They were an odd mix of old-school tie and East End toughs, one lot killing time, the other out for a killing. I had never seen men so sharply dressed, girls so strenuously gorgeous.

The repetitiveness of the procedure, the vacancy of conversation, gave me a pain in the small of the back. There was none of the high tension I had read about in Greene and Hamilton, only a want of something better to do. It puzzled me that someone as nervy and hyperbright as Dovidl could squander his nights at such routines. Boredom gave way to anxiety. 'What if there's a police raid?' I whispered, a tremor in my tone.

'There won't be,' laughed Dovidl. 'The boys in blue have been taken care of.' How did he, a schoolboy, know such things?

After an hour or so, he rose, yawned, stretched and strolled off to cash in his chips at the grille beside the door, his pile having redoubled at the roulette wheel. He gave a large chip to the cashier and another to the hat-girl, along with a lingering kiss of the kind I imagined to be French.

'Fancy another club?' he said, as our heads surfaced above ground, inhaling the damp night air.

I looked at my watch. It was three o'clock and I was wilting. 'Never mind,' said Dovidl, 'some other time.'

We stopped for coffee and buttered buns at the Old Teapot and got bantering with two footsore whores, in from the rain for a cuppa.

'Got the time, son?' sniffed one, Mavis by name.

'All the time in the world for you, love,' grinned Dovidl.

'I'll give you a good time,' cackled her friend.

'Time and a half, I bet,' flashed my friend. Where had he learned to banter?

He hailed a cab on Piccadilly and ordered it to St John's Wood. It was the blackest hour of the most vivid night of my sheltered life. Dovidl and I were at one again, but I could not relish the reunion without an attempt at reason.

'How did you begin gambling, Dovidl?' I asked quietly.

'A chap at school took me along,' he replied evasively.

'Where did you get the money to play?'

'Some men I met.'

'Why would they give you money?'

'They saw me winning, and staked me to play for them. I have a system, Mottl, based on simple probability theory. I'll explain it to you some time. Anyway, it seems to work. I keep half my winnings and give the rest to the syndicate.'

'No system is infallible.'

'Try mine,' said Dovidl, rigid with conviction.

His method, so far as I could grasp it, was based on exploiting the freedom of the individual against institutional rules. At blackjack the croupier always wins a tied hand. But the player, said Dovidl, has a much greater advantage. He knows exactly what the dealer is going to do, because the dealer is bound by house rules. 'I know his constraints,' said Dovidl, 'but he has no idea how I am going to play. It's the same as a cadenza in a concerto. The conductor and orchestra follow the composer's score right the way through but I, the soloist, can do as I please when we reach the cadenza of each movement. They cannot anticipate, all they can do is wait for me to let them back into the game.'

'How does that work at cards?'

'If the dealer draws anything from thirteen to fifteen, he has to take another card. This, in all probability, will bust him, since there are twenty cards worth nine or more in a pack of fifty-two. It's madness to twist on thirteen, but under the rules he must do it. I, on thirteen, have a choice to stick or twist. Mostly I will stick and bluff. Sometimes, to confuse the dealer, I will take another card. Three games out of five, on average, I win.'

'And roulette?'

'There is no point in betting on reds and blacks. Fifty-fifty is a fool's bet. I play a spread of five numbers, with in-built aleatory variants.'

'Meaning?'

'Three of the numbers are fixed for the night, the others can vary within a limited range. The combination of fixity and flexibility obscures the mathematical method, making the croupier think I am just another chancer.'

'And it works?'

'More nights than not.'

'And if it fails?' I persisted.

'It can't fail,' said Dovidl coldly.

A shutter slammed down, walling me off from his confidence. Sensing my awareness of the barrier, he rushed to reassure me. 'Don't be such a worry-guts,' grinned Dovidl, pinching my close-shaven cheek. 'I'm not playing for big money. I'm not a compulsive gambler and I am not getting into anything that I can't control.'

'So why bother?'

He stopped the driver on Abbey Road, telling him to keep the change from a ten-shilling note. We walked the last hundred yards home, talking ruminatively in low voices.

'I like the money,' rumbled Dovidl, as we turned into somnolent Blenheim Terrace. 'The money and the kicks. You must have felt it – the high you get when the wheel spins and a hundred quid hangs on the fall of a ball.'

'It didn't do much for me.'

'When you get into it, when you have a secret method that cannot fail, each turn of a card or a wheel dictates your fate: right or wrong, live or die. The blood pumps faster through your veins, your aorta is bursting its walls, and your face is totally calm and smiling. It's a grand illusion. Win or lose, you must give nothing away. It's a triumph of the will, in the Schopenhauer sense of the term: man over situation, individual over massed humanity—'

'That's pretentious nonsense,' I interjected.

'Well, I enjoy taking their money as well.' He grinned.

Amid the overblown philosophising, I sensed, there was a grain of desperate truth. To escape nightmares of loss and guilt, he needed to chase nightly extremes of danger and deception, with a smear of degradation: high risk and old whores. The sensation he sought was the antipode of where he, by rights, ought to be. 'I shall not die, for I shall live,' said the Psalmist. The only way Dovidl could detach his living self from the reproachful dead was by constant reminders that he was verifiably on the right side of the grave. If he felt a pounding in his chest when a card flipped, it was a sign that he was still alive, still defying his intended fate.

'And then there's the money,' he repeated. 'I need money to make a fresh start when I pack in the fiddle. I am planning a new future for us. You and me, the perfect team.'

One taboo after another, I thought. He had removed himself so far from the loving dead that he was now ready to reject their dreams for his destiny. I was not altogether surprised. When my father returned from Poland, something had drained out of Dovidl's playing. It sounded desultory to my ears, rhythmically predictable. The vital edge of innovation had been rubbed to routine. He played well but without panache, as if he no longer believed himself predestined for world glory. Practice times grew shorter, repertorial expansions narrower. I betrayed a pledge to my father, failing to apprise him of the cooling of his hot prospect.

Mortimer Simmonds would be mortified when he found out. I could anticipate the clichés of cultural lamentation bubbling to his lips. A great loss for music, he would groan. The brightest since Heifetz. A blow to tradition, a link lost in the chain of interpretation. Such a waste of golden talent and opportunity.

I, however, was content. The silencing of a soloist seemed a small price to pay for the resumption of my union with Dovidl, my restitution to his right hand. The night's excursion had restored my faith in him; that was all that mattered. Dovidl belonged to me again, soul-damaged and risk-addicted, but needing me to achieve the next stage in his development, as I needed him in mine.

'What's the plan?' I demanded.

'We'll discuss it another time,' he said airily, mussing my hair as we mounted the stairs to bed. I lay awake, unwashed, savouring a redemptive odour of unearthed potatoes and imported cigars. He had assured me that, come what may, I would share his adventures.

A revelatory moment was narrowly averted at his next birthday, which my mother had taken to celebrating with ceremony, as if to represent absent family. We sat around the dining-room table for a festive tea, an Anglo-Jewish hybrid of smoked fish, hot crumpets, matzah crackers, apple strudel and marzipan-cased birthday cake. It was May 1947 and Dovidl was seventeen.

Mother was chatting away about her new mission, raising funds for the beleaguered Jewish *yishuv* in Palestine, which aspired to become a state. 'We're giving a dinner at the Savoy next month,' she said brightly, 'and Dr Weizmann is coming to address us. There will be a kibbutz dance troupe and Danny Kaye to compère. But I want to propose something a little more serious to reflect the solemnity of the struggle. I wonder, Mortimer, if I might ask David to perform the *nigun* by Ernest Bloch, which he renders so meltingly.'

'What do you think, my boy?' said Father warmly. 'It's a private occasion, around four hundred guests, and it would serve to whet the appetites of some fairly substantial supporters for your eventual début, which we must soon start to discuss.'

Dovidl chewed a smoked-salmon cracker, wiped his mouth and took a sip of tea before pronouncing his response. 'I'm not quite in the right frame of mind at the moment,' he said.

Mother frowned: she did not take kindly to being thwarted. Father looked quizzically at me; I glued my eyes guiltily on the marzipan cake. Mortimer Simmonds changed the subject. 'I have been thinking, David,' he volunteered, 'that it's about time we got you a decent instrument. Care for a trip to Baileys?'

Dovidl looked pleased. Baileys, in Soho, were the supreme arbiters of excellence, dealers in fine violins since the early nineteenth century and consultants to the leading performers and collectors of the almost-intractable plaything. With skills passed from father to son, they could tell a fake at a glance, an Antonio Stradivarius from a pupil's model and a genuine virtuoso from the common run of aspirants. Choosing an instrument at Baileys was the preliminary step to launching a solo career, great or small.

We taxied to Frith Street, the three of us, by appointment. 'I'd like you to meet Eli Rapoport,' said my father to the senior Bailey, 'I think you'll be hearing quite a lot of him in future.'

Arbuthnot Bailey, who must have been all of seventy, greeted us in puffed shirtsleeves and a velvet waistcoat, looking for all the world like a Dickensian clock-maker, by appointment to Queen Victoria. He appraised the young pretender with weary eyes that had seen them all, back to the mighty Josef Joachim, for whom

Brahms had written his autumnal concerto. He took Dovidl's right hand as if to shake it, but nursed it instead in his palm like a precious ornament, testing its weight and filigree work. He then took the left hand, holding it by the tips of its long and supple fingers. 'A Guadagnini, I should say,' he finally growled, 'more receptive to your touch than a Strad. At least for the present.'

A player would no more question Baileys verdict than he would a tailor's inside-leg measurement. 'Come this way,' beckoned the old man, leading us into a low-lit backroom, held at constant temperature and humidity by whirring fans and the aura of majesty. 'This,' he said, extracting a violin from a baize-lined case, 'is the work of Giovanni Battista Guadagnini, 1742, the best I have seen. It used to belong to Hubay, the great Hungarian, then to an amateur collector, who let it run riot. It needs to be taken in hand by a young master, trained again and tamed. Here, try.'

Dovidl received the instrument in his right hand, turned it around to see all sides, tucked it under his chin, and picked up a bow. Before playing, he ran his fingers up and down the elongated neck, as if searching for a nodal point that he could choke or snap. Holding old Bailey's eye, he began tuning up. The air in the room stopped circulating. Two employees in the back sat stock still. Dovidl's eyes closed. His fingers barely touched the strings when from the belly of the instrument came a sigh of acquiescence, the sound that every lover strives for in the act of love, the prelude to preordained union. He began the Bach partita in G minor.

Arbuthnot Bailey stepped forward and took the violin from Dovidl in mid-phrase. 'Not too much,' he said. 'There are cracks in the varnish, she needs reconditioning. But I think you will like each other. If you have trouble, we are here to help. I will have the instrument ready for you in a week.'

At no time was money discussed. My father left an open cheque for Bailey to fill in once the repairs were complete. The violin trade functioned on trust and intuition. A Guadagnini of this pedigree would cost, at a guess, three thousand pounds – enough to buy a house in Hampstead. But the act of sale was merely the start of a relationship between vendor and purchaser. Bailey meant what he had said. If the violin did not settle with its new owner, he would take it back, no questions asked. If the player grew tired of its tone or of himself, Bailey would take in the discarded instrument like an orphan and find another to suit the artist. More than the profit from a sale, Baileys valued their standing with violinists, offering a career-long counselling and consumer service, a discreet Soho address for all their woes and insecurities. 'When you come back next week,' he told Dovidl, 'we might take a look at two or three French bows that I have been keeping for the right person.'

'You don't mind not having a Stradivarius?' asked my father as we walked up Wardour Street, which fizzed with the sexually repressed energies of an awakening British film industry.

'Not in the slightest,' said Dovidl happily. 'Strads can sound a bit flash, especially late ones, after 1720. A Guad has depth. It was the favourite instrument of Ysaÿe, did you know?'

'And many other masters,' said Father. 'Arnold Rosé, who led the violins in the Vienna Philharmonic for fifty-six years until the Nazis threw him out, used to play a Guadagnini with his string quartet and bought a second one for his daughter, who led a string orchestra. Jenö Hubay, who owned your instrument, played for Liszt and studied with Vieuxtemps. He was reputed to be the greatest Bach interpreter of his day.'

'It's a magical instrument,' said Dovidl gratefully. 'It will do anything I ask.'

For the next few weeks, he practised like a boy with a new toy, testing its speeds and turns, calling me at all hours to play a piano accompaniment. He loved that violin, wrapping it in a silk shroud like a stillborn baby, closing the coffin-like case with reverence and regret. His engagement with the instrument was exclusive. It slept beside his bed. No one was allowed to touch it, even to open the fastenings on the case. When Mother asked to show it to her committee ladies, he vehemently refused. 'It's a musical instrument,' snapped Dovidl, 'not a museum exhibit.'

Over months, though, the infatuation waned. The Guadagnini slept beside him, but he made love to it less frequently. Apart from the sensual pleasure of playing a beautiful instrument, its presence failed to renew his musical absorption, his once-consuming ambition. The music he practised meant little to him. 'What's the point of all this pretty little patterning?' he grumbled, after sawing with me dutifully through a Haydn sonata. 'It was background music two hundred years ago, and that's all it's good for today. I'm not going to fiddle away at stuff like this just to amuse an audience of idiots. I have better things to do with my life.'

To calm him down, I produced the latest Kreisler recording that my father had just bought. Without reading the red label, I set it on the turntable and shook my head in bewilderment when it started to play. The peer of performers had surrendered to popular demand. He was playing his own arrangement of 'Danny Boy', Irish Kevin's only tune, as well as something called 'The Rosary', with an orchestra made up of off-duty players from the Metropolitan Opera and the New York Philharmonic. 'Pathetic pap for mindless masses,' was Dovidl's comment (though I quite liked it). 'You won't catch me doing that.'

He picked a coming-of-age moment to declare his defection. It was the ceremonial tea of his eighteenth birthday in May 1948 and we were cutting the cake, which Florrie had baked with more eggs than were legally obtainable, when Dovidl dropped his bombshell and all of our lives were blown off track.

'I think I'll go and fight,' said Dovidl.

'No, Edwin,' gasped Mother clutching a napkin to her mouth. I wondered if Father had heard her correctly.

A Jewish state had been declared in Israel that week and seven Arab nations had massed armies to destroy it. Marks & Spencer had turned their head office on Baker Street into a weapons procurement centre and British Jews in their hundreds were answering the call to arms. For many it was a fulfilment of messianic longings, an end to twenty centuries of exile. Others sought to exorcise the agony of genocide with the foundation of a Jewish fortress. Never again, was their watchword.

'I'll go, too,' I chipped in.

'Not yet,' said Father abruptly, 'not if the pair of you want to be of any use. At the moment, you would just be cannon-fodder. Go to university, get some qualifications and then, if you want to build a new Jerusalem, you should be able to do so with skills which will be sorely needed when the independence war is over.'

'But they need men now,' said Dovidl. 'All the papers say the Jews are going to be overrun.'

'Not the *Daily Telegraph* or the *News Chronicle*,' corrected Father, 'and they have the best correspondents on the spot. Listen to me, David,' he urged. 'You were not born with talent in your head and your hands to spill your blood on desert sands. It's not what your father wanted, and I am bound by my promise to him.'

'No one asked if my sisters had talent before the Nazis killed them,' said Dovidl.

That ended the party. Dovidl rose from the table, I knocked over a teacup and saw Florrie weeping as she mopped up beneath

Mother's grim gaze. I never knew whether Dovidl was serious about going off to fight. The plan was not mentioned again. The Middle East war joined the Holocaust, his musical future and all the nocturnal creakings upstairs in a locked family cabinet of unmentionables – until the family fell apart under the strain of suppression.

Florrie was first to go. Her country bloom was fading, along with her zest. A figure that had been sweetly rounded began to sag and thicken as thirty loomed and the search for love yielded diminishing returns. One Sunday at tea-time, Florrie brought into the drawing room a chirpy little fellow whom I recognised as one of her former RAF gear-boxers. She and Derek were getting married, she declared. They were going to sail to Australia on the assisted migration scheme, ten pounds a head. Mother, gazing meaningfully at Florrie's midriff, offered congratulations, waived the month's notice and sent the couple off with a handsome cheque. Florrie packed and left the next day. She hugged me tight by the front door, gave Dovidl a kiss on the lips and shed great rolling tears as Derek's clanking van pulled chokingly out of our driveway. It was, by the still-valid cliché, the last we would ever see of her.

The house felt hollow without Florrie, who promised to write but never did. Perhaps she had found happiness with her devoted mechanic in half-empty Australia, with its beach-eaten turkeys on a baking Christmas and a cup of tea to cure all woes. Perhaps life behind a mock-Hampshire hedge in year-round sunshine was all she had ever wanted, untouched by the agonies of art. Florrie's going felt like a generic rejection. It made me wonder whether the things we valued were not confined to the educated classes, worthless to the uninitiated, a slap in the face of my father's faith in the universally elevating power of art. If Florrie could leave it all without a backward glance, might it count for nothing? Were we admiring an emperor in new clothes? As heir to the Simmonds empire, the thought was disturbing, but the disregard worked both ways. Florrie had declared her role in our lives incidental and she was now declared to be dispensable. An Irish 'daily' took her place the following week, succeeded before very long by a trail of Jamaicans. None imprinted so much as a name on my memory.

It was time for us to leave. Dovidl and I matriculated that summer with what we were told were among the highest marks in the country. Exempted from National Service – I as an asthmatic, he as a Polish national – we went up to Cambridge, he to physics at Trinity and I to history at St John's. Most of our fellow students were ex-servicemen, four or five years older and battle-hardened. There were few girls about, and most were set fixedly on career or early marriage. Our minds were equally end-oriented. The aim was to earn double-quick doctorates. With maths and physics, Dovidl would join Israel's hush-hush nuclear plant in Rehovot. With history and languages, I would join the intelligence and diplomatic services, plying carrots to his explosive stick, partners all the way.

A sun-bronzed, open-shirted attaché from the new Israeli embassy came to lecture at the Jewish Society, presenting himself as the prototype New Jew, arms-bearing, blond and unafraid. He read out a selection of mawkish New Hebrew poetry, not a patch on the Psalms, and recruited shamelessly for volunteer summer workers on his Galilean kibbutz. Dovidl and I exchanged superior grins. 'Spare us the peasant poets,' he whispered.

'Sing unto God a new song,' I chanted ironically, 'his praise is among a commune of devotees.'

We kept pace with one another at college, without much contact. So far as I knew, he was immersed in his studies. I might not see or hear from him for a fortnight, but my faith in him was firm. One Friday evening I went down to the synagogue on Thompson's Lane for social chit-chat and a hot meal, trying to remember when I had last seen Dovidl. He was not at dinner, but as I strolled home with a crowd after supper, he appeared as if by magic from a side alley and asked me back to his rooms for coffee. The Great Court at Trinity was lit by a full moon and ornamented by the orange lights of scholars in their chambers, at study or at leisure. Instead of going up for coffee, we walked arm in arm round and round the adjacent cloister, Nevile's Court, gazing up at glinting galaxies and arguing over ursine particulars: which was the Great Bear and which the Small.

'I love it here,' sighed Dovidl luxuriously.

'But you wouldn't want to spend your life in a place where no one ever grows up,' I countered.

'Why not?' he mused. 'It's safe and sometimes warm. It's a haven.'

'From what?'

'Oh,' said Dovidl vaguely, 'you know . . .'

I did not know, but could not admit it. I suppose he meant the gambling and the whores, the guilt of being alive, the terror of dreams. I was preoccupied with the topic of my dissertation and displayed little curiosity in his escapist fantasy. I felt like asserting my independence of mind. He had no right to disturb my thoughts without warning. I was his friend, not his agent – not yet, at any rate. He did not have automatic first call on my mind.

Should I have given him the full beam of my attention? Pressed him to elaborate? Nursed him through a patch of insecurity? The omission would return to nag me through many sleepless years.

We each won a research grant at the end of the first year, and the Master of John's hinted over a glass of dry sherry that a fellowship was mine for the taking. I flushed with satisfaction. While most of my former classmates were square-bashing in the British Army and saving ration coupons to buy a bottle of cheap booze, I was being ushered into a life of learning and the vintage comforts of high table. It was a passport to privilege. I could make my name as a scholar, stamping my authority on a period in history while teaching grateful generations of acolytes. Yet I would not be tempted by the orange winks of college life unless Dovidl, who had been made a comparable offer, signalled acceptance.

'What do you reckon?' I asked.

'No hurry,' he said lazily. 'We have another couple of years before we need to do anything so strenuous as making a decision.'

'Is Toytown growing on you?'

'It has its moments,' winked Dovidl, suggesting he had got lucky with some Girton bluestocking. One way or another, he had got over that starlit wobble without my intervention.

Nothing else had changed: my tail was hitched to his comet, to follow where he blazed. Together, we would take on the world – that is what he had pledged. So when, the week before Christmas 1949, I came home to Blenheim Terrace and heard him playing Bach with a fervour that had been missing since the war ended, my heart skipped a beat and I was overcome by anxiety.

'What's going on?' I demanded, barging into his room.

'I'm back on the fiddle.' He grinned.

'I can hear that. Why?'

'I need some spare cash.' He laid the Guadagnini crookedly in its case and lit a cocky cigarette from an exotic pack.

'Are you in trouble?' I quavered.

'Nothing I can't handle.'

'Meaning?'

'A couple of bad nights at the wheel. Either I miscalculated the method, or someone rigged the mechanism. Can't quite work it out. I had a suspicion once that my drink had been spiked; I couldn't concentrate. Maybe someone thought I had been winning too much.'

'How much?'

'Oh, I've got four thousand tucked away. But I owe six to the Maltese boys and the interest is wicked, fifty per cent a month. They are being reasonable for the time being, but I wouldn't want to try their patience. I'll pay the Maltesers a thou here and there, as if I'm winning again, until I can earn a few quid on the fiddle, or my method comes good again at the table.'

The colloquialisms that tumbled from his lips were as alarming as the situation he described. Who were these Maltesers, and how could he talk casually about a 'thou', enough to buy a racing car? I felt excluded and clueless. The underside of him had gained an ominous ascendance.

'You could get out of it,' I suggested.

'How?' he scoffed.

'Go to Israel: the Maltesers will never pursue you there.'

'Forget it,' said Dovidl. 'That's off. The last thing they need in a Jewish state is an extra fiddle-player to feed. I'd also be no bloody use to them as the next Einstein if I can't make simple probability theory work on a bent roulette wheel. No, I'm back in training and I need your help mugging up my scores. Ever tried the Sibelius?'

He had not yet looked me in the eye and his pallor was suspiciously grey.

'That's not all, is it?' I persisted.

He coughed twice and lit another Turkish cigarette.

'Go on,' I urged.

'Last week,' said Dovidl, 'I had to go to a research laboratory in Epsom to observe a fission experiment. As I left, I remembered that Josef Hassid was in a Polish hospital somewhere nearby. I had not seen him since we were introduced at Flesch's and I thought he might like to see a friendly face, a *Landsman*. His father, I heard, had sadly died of cancer. So I found the hospital and asked to see him. The blonde at Reception gave me a weird look, but a few words of street Polish got me into the ward.

'I don't know what I had expected. I had this vivid recollection of a solemn prodigy who had the lot: warmth and clarity, light- ness and gravity, technical mastery and natural poise, the whole shooting match on the bloody fiddle. He could outplay Kreisler, Heifetz, Ida, any of us. And then he went off his head, beat up his dad and wound up all alone in a hellhole where they give him electric shocks and insulin comas before breakfast.

'He was sitting, Mottl, in a whitewashed room with an iron bed and bars on the window. Oh, yes, and a crucifix on the wall, no other visual relief. He was rocking to and fro, gabbling syllables, his wonder-working fingers struggling uselessly with a button on his pyjama jacket.

'I greeted him in English, then Polish, and got no response. I had been warned not to mention his father – or the rest of his family, who perished in Poland. The blonde from Reception stood at the door, ready to shout for help if he attacked me. I didn't know what to do, I just wanted to register on his consciousness, or whatever was left of it after the shock treatment.

'On his bedside table lay a cheap mouth-organ, like the one that vagrant – Kevin, was it? – used to play. I reached towards it. He snatched it away, put it to his mouth, breathing in and out – an incoherent music. I remembered his recording of a Dvořák melody and wept within for what was lost.

'I had to get through to him, somehow. I could not leave him alone. I tried Yiddish, the *Mameloshen*, our mother tongue. "Yossl,"

I said, "*vie geyts?*" He looked up at me like a rabbit with its leg in a trap. "*Aroys fin daw,*" he mouthed, "*sakonos nefoshos*" – get out of here, your life's in danger.

'"*Fan vus?*" I asked – what from? – but he said nothing more, just looked down and resumed his swaying and droning, his wailing on the harmonica. He is not much older than us, Mottl, twenty-six at most, but he was hunched up like a pensioner in a bath-chair, waiting for the end.

'What could I do? I kissed him on the forehead, promised to come again and ran – ran like a lunatic down the stairs, through the grounds and out of the gates before I realised I had left my folder with all the experiment notes in his room. When I returned, the briefcase was waiting for me at Reception but Josef was silent – gone to therapy, the blonde said. "Is there hope of recovery?" I asked. "If you believe in miracles." She smiled. "Schizophrenia this severe seldom responds to treatment."

'I was livid, could have hit her. To her, he was just another war victim, but to me he was a paragon, the best there has ever been. And I wondered if he wasn't an oracle, sent to save me from a terrible mistake. He had told me to get out. I was in danger. Israel, gambling, Cambridge was not where I was meant to be. I had to get up on stage and play the violin. That's the place for Josef and me. He might not make it again, so I had to do it for him, to fulfil our purpose. I stood there in the lobby almost in a trance, until the blonde asked if I wanted to see a doctor – and then, believe me, I got out bloody fast.

'I got back to Cambridge, went to the common room, sank into an armchair and tried to gather my thoughts. There was a *Musical Times* lying on the table. In it, I read that Ginette Neveu was dead, had you heard? The plane taking her from Paris to a concert tour in America crashed in the Azores, killing all on board. Her brother,

Jean, was among the dead, and her Stradivarius was incinerated. Ginette was thirty, a virgin by the look of her, and playing like an angel.

'First Josef, now Ginette. It felt as if we Flesch pupils were under a curse – a punishment, perhaps. I may have given up religion but superstition is a different matter altogether. There is hardly an artist on earth who does not carry a lucky charm, get ready in a fixed routine and go "tfui, tfui, break a leg" before going on stage. We live in terror of black cats, and here I had one staring me in the eye.

'I took myself off for a late-night walk around Great Court, and a couple of solitary drinks in my room. It occurred to me that, with Hassid sick and Neveu dead, the odds had shortened. It would be a good deal easier for a layabout like me to make a success. And I wouldn't be doing it just for myself, but for Josef and Ginette and all the other unlucky ones who would never be heard again. So I sat down at my desk, wrote a note to my tutor claiming nervous exhaustion and caught the first train home next morning to start putting in the statutory six hours a day on the treadmill.'

He picked up the violin, retuned it automatically and knocked off a page of what I think was a solo sonata by Ysaÿe. 'What do you think?' he demanded, putting me back in my place.

What did I think? In order of anxieties: where does that leave me? where do I fit in his recast future? what next? For once, though, not even ignominious egotism could sour the joy I felt on hearing the music that flowed from his bow – flowing as if from a natural spring. Ysaÿe gave way to Brahms, and Brahms to astringent Bartók. Each piece was played as if he owned it, as if no other musician had a right to perform it. His authority had grown incontestable.

'Have you spoken to my father?' I asked.

'We're talking,' said Dovidl.

That night Mortimer Simmonds outlined his brilliant plan to create a second Kreisler. The potential was proven, the strategy flawless. All family resources were to be harnessed to the project. Mother duly took Dovidl to be kitted out on Savile Row and had one of her refugee stylists redesign his hair in a Kreisler coiffure. A Medola cousin at St Mary's Hospital took charge of his diet. Uncle Kenneth fixed his teeth, polishing them till they gleamed. The Chief Rabbi's private secretary tutored him in press and public relations. James Agate dropped his name at a meeting of the Critics' Circle; Cecil Beaton took his picture. Nothing was left to chance, no detail of presentation escaped our eager attention.

Albert Sammons, whose career had been curtailed by muscular disease, offered to let Dovidl practise with the Royal College student orchestra any time he liked. 'We've lost so many good players these past few years,' he lamented. 'Old Flesch and young Neveu; Hubermann and Feuermann; Busch and Kulenkampff; old man Rosé and his daughter, Alma; me and slippery Kreisler, who has gone to the dogs with his latest record. This boy will give the blessed art a salutary kick up the backside, set a new benchmark.'

One morning in November 1950 I read of Josef Hassid's death. The newspaper said he had passed away while undergoing brain surgery in Epsom. What, I wondered, had given doctors the right to invade that divinely endowed, desperately damaged organ? It so happened that Dovidl was due in Cambridge that week to explain to his tutors that he was reverting from science to art. Trinity being proud of its renaissance traditions, they seemed charmed by the transition and promised to hold him a place in either faculty. I told him of Josef's death as we walked that night around Great Court. His jaw tightened, but his voice was level as he murmured terse regrets of love and loss. Nothing could now deflect his concentration.

'The thing you have to remember about artists,' said Father, one night at the office, just after Christmas, 'is never to trust their immediate response. Whatever the news, their reaction will be self-protective. The mask goes on, and you see only what they let you see. These creatures carry their emotions around in a violin-case, reserving their only honest expression for the public stage. In private, they turn emotion on and off at will. Never believe an artist when he weeps or declares love. It's all a grand performance.

'Treat their upsets as you would a child's tantrums. Console, then instruct. Show compassion when it is called for, firmness when it runs out. Give them an illusion of your love for them – but never love itself, or they will devour you.'

He was in a rare confessional mood. We were the last in the office, with nothing much to do, and I poured us both a brandy with a view to lubricating his managerial tongue. Father drew deep on a thick Cuban cigar, an infrequent indulgence.

'Sometimes,' mused Mortimer Simmonds, 'we make artists do things they don't really want to do. We tell them it is for their own good, but it's for ours. They resent us and say we exploit them. But even if the things we make them do are purely for our commercial benefit, which is not often the case, the ultimate profit would still be theirs. For if we made no money out of them, they would find themselves pretty smartly back on the street while we turned our energies to estate agency or running a restaurant chain. They need our greed to fuel their ambition.

'Never delude yourself that you do this job for love of music. Every now and then you must take from it some crude satisfaction, purely for yourself, otherwise you will lose interest and incentive and the business will go down the drain.'

He blew a blue curlicue of Caribbean smoke, releasing a fine whiff of masculine gratifications. I did not press the point.

'They don't like to see us making money or having fun.' My father sighed. 'To our faces, they call us brothers. Behind our backs, we are parasites. Artists give managers a bad name, Martin, but where would they be without us? I'll tell you where. In a provincial town hall on a wet November Wednesday, wondering if they can skip an encore to catch the last direct train to London.

'And remember this, Martin: the grubbier we look, the brighter they shine. That is our role, and it is not a dishonourable one. We are the soil-carriers of their souls. They devolve the dirty work on to us, and we accept it with decency and a sense of duty because we hope that they, relieved of common need, will have the power to improve lives. That's all there is to it.

'So keep your distance, my boy, that's my advice to you. Never trust a musician when he speaks about love, never trust a manager when he talks about money.'

I heard out his homily with mild alarm, knowing that in Dovidl's case we had broken all the rules. We had given the artist unconditional love, admitting him to the family. Now, we were about to risk our reputation on his success. If Dovidl let us down, the Simmonds name would be seriously damaged.

Try as I might, however, I could not raise this cavil with my father. We were both too far gone, taken in like bumpkins by the three-card trick of talent, personality and historic justice. I was in love with the artist, Father believed in him, all reservations suspended. So confident was he of the artistic inevitability and moral imperative of our project that, for once in his life, he neglected to insure the concerts against artist cancellation – a routine precaution that would have averted financial ruination when Dovidl disappeared. It is a measure of my father's nobility that he never once uttered a word of self-reproach for that costly, imprudent and entirely uncharacteristic omission.

When, on the afternoon of the concert, Dovidl failed to return for lunch, I called the conductor Freudenstein, the composer Kuznetsov, the leader of the orchestra, the president of the Royal Handel Society – anyone who might have detained or distracted him after rehearsal. An orchestral assistant who dropped in at the office to negotiate expenses said he had seen the evening's soloist leaving the Royal Albert Hall just after noon, violin case in hand, crossing the road towards Hyde Park. He had no umbrella, and it was starting to rain. The stupid clerk had not thought of offering Dovidl a lift.

At five, I went home and called the police. It was too soon, they said, to report a missing person. I checked five hospitals; none had admitted a person of his description. I looked up the gaming club in the telephone directory, but it was unlisted. I heard Mother sobbing in her room. Across the hallway, Father dressed in silence, as if for the gallows. For any other cancellation, he would have been juggling telephones to find a replacement. At this concert, no surrogate would do. The expectations he had aroused were insatiable. People had come from all over the world to hear the next Kreisler: they would not settle for a Menuhin or a Stern.

The roads to the hall heaved with traffic. When we finally got through, I told the hall manager to post signs that the concert had been cancelled 'due to the soloist's indisposition'. Father went out to face the shimmering audience. He offered cash refunds at the box-office and a profound apology; backstage, he paid off the orchestra, the conductor and the hall's eleven per cent commission. We lost ten thousand pounds that night, more than an entire year's profit, but money was the least of our losses. Mortimer Simmonds had lost his good name. He had put his shirt on a spectacular non-runner; his judgement could not be trusted again. Friends avoided his eye; only the press pursued him, like sparrows at a corn-chandler's wake.

Next morning, the fiasco filled the front pages. Inside, columnists crossed swords of speculation. Some suggested the débutant had been smitten by stage-fright or amnesia, others echoed police suspicions of abduction or assault. The headlines darkened next morning with news of 'Nationwide Search for Musical Prodigy' and 'Mystery of Vanished Violinist'. Photographs of Eli Rapoport had been posted at rail termini, airports and harbours. Interpol had been alerted and a reward was being offered for information leading to the artist's safe return. Antiques dealers were being asked to watch out for a 1742 Guadagnini violin, 'worth in excess of three thousand pounds'.

The fiddle belonged, in title, to Mortimer Simmonds, but this was beneath his concern. More than financial loss, more even than professional failure, Father was tormented by fears for Dovidl's safety. 'It's my fault,' he moaned, 'for not exercising closer supervision. I promised the father to look after the boy and I did my best, but I didn't want to smother him. You can't keep an artist under lock and key.' Father never asked for my thoughts, sensitive to my pain and assuming that I would apprise him of any material information. I could not bring myself to discuss Dovidl with him: it crossed too many transgressions, his and mine. The breakfast room at Blenheim Terrace grew chill and lugubrious.

I went off to help the police with their enquiries, of which there were two lines. Either the missing person had, as Inspector Roderic Morgan put it, 'done a runner' – in which case there was no cause for police involvement, unless we wanted to press charges for theft of a violin. Otherwise, someone must have snatched the young chap off the street, bundled him into a car and 'done him a mischief', or was holding him to ransom. Did I, his friend, know of anyone who bore malice towards Mr Rapoport, or perhaps towards my family?

The inspector was an avuncular, overweight fellow whose methodical questions hinted at a propensity, perhaps an appetite, for physical violence. Beneath his bureaucratic Welsh burr I sensed an eagerness to leave his mark on flesh. We sat alone across a metal table in a basement room at Bow Street police station, around the corner from the club I had visited with Dovidl. Was he, I wondered, one of those coppers who were paid to turn a blind eye to such places? He stared at me through a prism of class and saw (I sensed) a child of privilege, a know-all Cambridge student, needs to be brought down a peg or two. I looked him back in the eye and said, truthfully enough, that I could not think of anyone who disliked my friend, let alone wished to harm him. As for kidnapping, he was a penniless refugee. His guardian, my father, was comfortable but not wealthy. No one would expect him to lay hands on a large ransom.

The inspector offered me a cheap Woodbine, lit one himself and asked me to recount, for the third time, Dovidl's arrival at our house, his development and education, habits and relationships. 'What does he do in his spare time? Any unsavoury friends I should know about? Any girl trouble?'

'He likes a night on the town,' I volunteered, 'you know – a drink and a laugh. I don't think he has ever had a steady girlfriend. He was always working so hard on his studies and his violin.'

I lied with an easy conscience. The last thing I needed was the police rummaging around his uncomfortably local night-life.

If Morgan found out about his gambling habits and low-life company, he might leak word of them to the gutter press, destroying whatever chance Dovidl might have of returning safe and with dignity intact. Alive or dead, I had to protect him. If he was in trouble, I felt sure he would find some way to contact me. Here, we were merely going through the motions.

'Are you quite sure, sir, that there is nothing more you know?'

Morgan tapped louringly on a bulletproof cigarette case. He was unconvinced. 'Please understand, Inspector,' I said, turning on the middle-class sincerity, 'that my parents and I are at our wits' end. We cannot think who might want to harm him, unless it is some madman or a Communist agent from his own country – but that's absurd, isn't it? If he was not attacked, he may have suffered some kind of mental breakdown – which has to be taken into account given the dreadful things that happened to his family in the war.

'We are very fond of Mr Rapoport. My parents and I just want him back, safe and sound. Should we increase the reward, do you think? Please help us, Inspector. He could be wandering around, not knowing who he is, or how to get home.'

My tears were sincere enough to terminate the interview. 'We'll talk again at the end of the week, if nothing turns up,' grunted the inspector, seeing me off the premises. 'You know where to find me if anything comes to light.'

I took a taxi back to the office, where Father was distractedly sifting papers and two young constables were interviewing our staff one by one, in the corridor. The phones had stopped ringing. Someone had opened a window. Aunt Mabel was standing at my desk.

'A word with you, young Martin,' she said.

'Of course, Auntie.'

'In private.'

The only secluded place in the doorless office was the ladies' lavatory, with its clanking, dripping cisterns and porcelain wash-basins. Aunt Mabel strode inside, checked the individual closets, beckoned me in and planted her five-foot frame solidly against the emulsified oak door. 'Now are you going to tell me what's going on?' she demanded.

'What do you mean, Auntie?'

'Your father's out there mourning the destruction of Jerusalem, your mother's at home going off her head – "Edwin's gone," she said, when I dropped round. Why did she call him Edwin? Did he have some hold over her? I told you I never trusted that Polish boy. You are the only one in the pack, Martin, who has his head screwed on, so tell me, before I blow my top, what the bloody hell's going on.'

'There's no more to tell than you already know, Auntie. Dovidl didn't turn up for his concert. We don't know why, and neither do the police. They have launched a nationwide search.'

'I can read the newspapers for myself, Martin,' she said icily. 'Now, I'm going to ask you once more, nice and polite, and if you give me any flannel, I'll ram your swollen head down the bog until you cough up some sense. This is my family that's being messed about. Violet and Mortimer have no idea what's hit them and you're just a whipper-snapper with a fancy college scarf. So give me the low-down and let Auntie Mabel see what she can do. Any dodgy business I need to know about? Any nasty friends?'

There was no point in prevaricating. I told her about the gambling, the syndicate, the Maltese debts. 'Thought as much.' She sniffed. 'My Kenneth is a bit of a night-owl. He told me he saw your friend at the Tinkerbell Club, but was too pissed to be sure. Now we know.'

'What will you do, Auntie?'

'First of all, I'm going to send Violet off on a rest cure. Then I'll have a word with some pals from the old days, some faces from the Ball's Pond Road who know what's what. If your boy's in shtook with the Maltesers, the KitKats or the Turkish bloody Delight for all I know, they'll get him back for me if he's still in one piece. If he's running a racket of his own, they might teach him a little lesson before sending him home. Just sit tight and do nothing until you hear from me, got that?'

Someone turned the handle and tried to push the door. 'Sod off,' barked Mabel. 'We're here on business.' She looked almost leonine in a brown two-piece Peter Robinson suit and mangy hat. Mabel reached up and put a gloved hand gently on my Adam's apple. 'Shtum's the word, right?'

'Yes, Auntie.'

Rosalyn had left a message at my desk, asking me to call her at home.

'I am so sorry, Martin,' she whispered. 'Is there anything I can do to help? Man the phones? Make the tea?'

'Nothing at present, I'm afraid,' I replied dully. 'Hardly anyone phones us any more, and the tea sits there getting cold.'

'Well, call me if there is anything I can do,' she said.

That night, with my mother in care and my father under sedation, I caught a bus to Covent Garden to sound out Dovidl's netherlife. The Treasury man was sipping from the same cup, and the same tarts were touting for trade. No one, to my relief, had recognised Dovidl as the face on the newsstands. People came and went in the market, using whatever cover they required, no questions asked. Down here he was Mr David, not Eli Rapoport.

'He's a lovely boy,' said the wrinkled tart, Ava, pocketing my pound note. 'Not in any trouble, is he?'

'Not that I know of,' I said. 'You wouldn't know if he's had any hassle from the Maltese boys?'

'Them half-pint ponces?' shrieked her friend, Jean, joining us at the tea-stall. 'They're all mouth and no muscle, if you know what I mean. Anyway, they wouldn't try it on round here. Mr David's well liked in the market, a proper young gentleman he is.'

'Not too young to make a girl happy,' cackled Ava, and I wondered what happiness he had sought from these tired old comfort stations on their nightly beat. My mind flashed back to the broken cadaver on a bombsite and I wondered how much I knew of Dovidl's darker urges.

Hurriedly, I left the whores and descended to the Tinkerbell where two croupiers and the hat-check girl, four punters and a wholesale costermonger had heard nothing untoward. The girl at the door, who had kissed him deeply, said to give him her best. I looked around, on leaving, to make sure I was not being followed.

The blanks I drew boosted my confidence when, days later, two short men in Borsalino hats turned up at Blenheim Terrace looking for Mr David. I assured them that Mr David had gone away – grateful that, wherever he was, he had eluded his shady creditors.

'Blank,' declared Mabel, back in the washroom. 'Not a dicky-bird. My pals had a bit of a ruck with your Maltesers, leaving one of them in need of a National Health nose-job, but none of my nasties have come up with a sniff of his droppings, worse luck.'

'So what do we do now, Auntie?'

'We try and put your poor parents back together again, that's what. Forget about the boy, he's not worth a tinker's. I can't think why Violet's so upset when she's got such a fine son of her own.

You're doing a good job, Mart. We'll get through this together as a family, got that?'

Inspector Morgan summoned me to another interview, my third. 'An assessment of where we have got to so far,' he said, pointing to the bare metal table. 'It's been three weeks, hasn't it?' His interrogative tone made me uneasy. Two constables entered the room, standing either side of the door, hands behind their backs. The walls had been freshly painted in washable olive-green. The smell was faintly acidic.

'Mr Simmonds,' said the inspector, in sardonically gentle tones, 'when a young fellow goes missing, we keep an open mind if there is no ransom note or body. For the first week, we assume the man maybe lost his way home or met a nice young lady and nipped down to Brighton. The second week, we check out the better-organised parts of criminal society. If nothing seems suspicious, in the third week we start worrying that maybe someone is making a monkey of us, not telling us the whole story, get my drift? Now, Mr Simmonds, are you sure you have told me absolutely everything I need to know?'

The two big coppers at the door, I noticed, had unclasped their hands. Inspector Morgan put his face close to mine, exhaling foul smoke and cheap food. I felt my back sweating like a cellar wall.

'So, Mr Sy-monds, what do you know about a break-in last year at the Jewish synagogue on Abbey Road?'

'What?' I exclaimed, my chest pounding.

'Somebody,' said the inspector, raising his voice, 'nipped in one dark night and made away with antique pieces of silver, insured for ten thousand pounds. Whoever it was knew the building pretty well, set off no alarms. Couldn't be your friend, could it, Mr Sy-monds? He must have known that synagogue, being a Jewish gentleman like yourself. Was he laying up a little nest-egg for when he ran away from home? Did he let you in on the job, eh?'

'That's preposterous,' I interjected.

'Does he have a little hidey-hole somewhere you can take us where we're going to find the missing silver, and maybe the lad himself?'

'Don't be ridiculous,' I retorted, roused by righteous anger. 'The last time Mr Rapoport set foot in synagogue was on his barmitzvah, eight years ago this month. The alarm, I happen to know, was installed only the year before last. Anyway, he would never defile sacred objects. He is too . . . superstitious . . . for that. Is that the best you can come up with, Inspector, a Jewish inside job?'

'Just a theory,' said the inspector softly, rising to let me go.

Angry as I was, I was also unsettled. A seed of doubt had been planted in a field of misery. I raced home to search the drawer where Dovidl kept his bombsite loot, in search of silver Torah bells and pointers. Nothing there, just the trinkets he had kept from the Blitz. They seemed worthless now, without him. After dark, I cycled down to Elgin Avenue to examine our secret tree-hole. Nothing there, either. Suspicion, though, is a persistent rash. I could not purge my friend's memory of its itch.

I extended my enquiries worldwide. I wrote to my supervisor from Cambridge who had gone to teach at the University of Western Australia, asking him to check the Perth telephone directory for a Derek and Florence Mitchell and, failing that, to search the register of births for a baby Mitchell born in the last quarter of 1948 when Florrie would have been due. What if Dovidl had noticed Florrie's pregnancy and, having no living relatives, felt an urge to be united with his child, if it was his, in Australia? Far-fetched, I realised, but worth eliminating.

The word from Perth was grimmer than I had feared. There were no Mitchell births in the period stipulated, my friend replied, but the register of deaths contained a Florence Mitchell who had died in October 1948 of septicaemia, after suffering a miscarriage. Her husband, Derek, had remarried and was running a petrol station in Adelaide, did I require his address?

I enlisted the help of the Israeli poetaster attaché, who responded warmly and energetically. But neither the Tel Aviv immigration service nor the police had seen anyone answering Dovidl's description, dashing my hopes that he had sought a Jewish homeland.

I wrote to my father's ministerial contact in Warsaw and got no answer. I wrote again, with the same result. Much later I learned that the poor man had been whisked off and killed in a Stalinist purge against 'rootless cosmopolitans', meaning Jews.

I applied for a visa to visit Poland, but was turned down. I did my best to keep the story alive in the press, praying for a sighting, but newspapers are not renowned for their constancy. A new story had excited their attention: the sinister disappearance to Moscow of a pair of high-placed British diplomats, Guy Burgess and Donald Maclean. 'Does your story have a political dimension?' I was asked by a news editor.

After three months, the inspector called to say he was closing the file. Mother was spending more time in a nursing-home than out, and Father was staring blankly at his towering pile of correspondence. I was finally free to mourn, in the few months until Father died.

I made one last concerted effort to pick up Dovidl's trace shortly after Father's death, when I became head of the family. Through one of those seedy fellow travellers who thronged the fringes of concert life and contributed occasional reviews to the *Morning Star*, I made contact with a person in authority at the Polish embassy – not the ambassador, but an intelligence officer listed as the junior commercial attaché. The Poles were starved of hard currency. I needed cheap scores. I ordered from them two hundred thousand paperbacks at sixpence apiece, a total of five thousand pounds, which I paid from a pre-war Swiss account that my father had discreetly set up.

This was the riskiest thing I have ever done. British citizens were forbidden at the time to spend more than fifty pounds abroad without Treasury consent; their foreign accounts were supposed to be held under Treasury supervision. If discovered, I would have faced prosecution and a prison sentence of up to three years. Like every illegal act, it exposed me to the possibility of blackmail. My Polish contact knew that I was evading currency controls: he could betray me to the British authorities or pressure me to perform other services for the Poles. I knew the depth of my exposure and took steps to contain it. I slipped the Polish attaché a thousand-pound sweetener, which did the trick.

The scores, obtained at a fraction of union-inflated UK printing costs, paid off instantly and for decades to come. They gave me a competitive advantage in music sales that lasted as long as the demand for my product. Forty years later, I was down to my last ten dozen Polish-pressed scores, falsely stamped 'Printed in the British Empire' and selling at six pounds each, two hundred and forty times their manufacturing cost, bribes included.

The Communists in Warsaw were delighted at the deal, so much so that they promoted my embassy contact to Berlin, world capital of Cold War dirty deals. But leather-jacketed Jaček did not leave without fulfilling his part of our bargain, which was to procure me a trip to Warsaw – ostensibly to sign the contract and raise toasts for world peace, actually to see for myself what remained of Dovidl's world, and if he was to be found anywhere within it.

To ease my conscience and cover my back, I told the Foreign

Office that I was crossing the Iron Curtain in search of musical talent and offered my services as a contact and courier. Independent travellers were rare in those days between London and Warsaw. Under the Official Secrets Act, I am unable to discuss the operational aspects of my trip.

I arrived in Warsaw in the deadliest of March frosts, but with a thaw shimmering on the eastern horizon. Stalin had died the week before and, while Poles queued in their thousands to pay respects under duress, a whiff of relief was in the air. I was allowed to choose the places I wanted to visit, rather than follow a rigid itinerary. Only one request – Treblinka – was declined, on the grounds that 'there is nothing to see there'.

Not that there was much more in Warsaw, where my guide diligently droned out the official history. The Germans had forced the city's three hundred and fifty thousand Jews into a ghetto. Then, they crammed in evacuees from other towns, reducing numbers by means of starvation, slave labour and random shootings. Deportations to Treblinka and Majdanek began in 1941. In the summer of 1942, three hundred and ten thousand men, women and children were herded to a central *Umschlagplatz* and on to cattle trucks. A last-ditch Jewish uprising in April 1943 was ruthlessly crushed and the ghetto was razed to the ground. Other parts of the city were flattened by German artillery when the Poles attempted an uprising in late 1944. What the guide did not add was that the Russians stood by on the outskirts of the town while the Nazis crushed the Poles, just as the Poles had stood by while they put down the Jewish rebellion.

Rampant in rubble, the Soviets redesigned central Warsaw as a proletarian housing barracks, mile upon mile of identical tower-blocks, divided by wide avenues for easy tank access. I could hear the wind howl between these concrete edifices, an inhuman noise.

The Warsaw I saw in March 1953 was a city without character, its flatness aped by the slab-eyed, snub-nosed features of a homogeneously fair-haired citizenry. Where, I wondered, were the black curls, flared nostrils, kiss-me mouths and deep-set eyes of Dovidl's people? Gone to the smokestacks, from which none returned.

Breaking off the tour for lemon tea and sugar-dusted apple strudel in the gilded Hotel Bristol, I was apprised by the guide that it was in a room just above my head that the opera-loving Nazi governor, Hans Frank, sealed the fate of Warsaw's Jews with a whispering pen on a sheet of hotel paper. I have never been able to eat apple strudel since that sick-sweet day.

I returned to find London, still bomb-gapped, in the grip of Coronation fever. A new Queen had come to the throne, fostering roseate dreams of a second Elizabethan Age. Aunt Mabel bought a television set to watch the ceremony, and it was on her sofa during the singing of *Zadok the Priest* that I was introduced to Myrtle, whom she and Mother had selected for me as a suitable life-partner.

'She's got good Medola breeding and a good head on her shoulders,' said Mother, her eyes briefly reanimated.

'Lovely teeth,' confirmed Uncle Kenneth.

'Nice hips,' nudged Aunt Mabel.

Despite these encomia, I liked Myrtle, whom I had not seen since my barmitzvah. She looked me square in the eye and did not simper or flirt, like the Beckys and Hannahs thrust on me at dinner-dances. Her name was unusual, taken from a Biblical plant which is waved on the festival of Tabernacles.

'Mother kept trying to plant some in our garden,' she smiled, 'but it never took.'

'Fragrant and resilient,' I rhapsodised.

'I should be so lucky.' She laughed.

'Better than Hyssop,' I retorted.

'You're the first Jewish man I have met,' she said, on our second date, 'who is tall enough to look me in the eye and make intelligent conversation. The rest are either short and brainy or big and *grob*, like butchers' boys. The aunts are terrified that I will marry a *goy*.'

'Let me offer you a rational alternative,' I proposed.

'I have received more romantic proposals,' she laughed.

'I could drop on one knee,' I said, 'but then I wouldn't be looking you in the eye any more.'

'Keep that girl's mind occupied,' advised Mabel. 'She's the right one for you and she'll be loyal to the death, but she won't settle for charity work and shopping mornings like your poor mother. She needs a challenge. She speaks three languages fluently. She could do literary translations in her spare time.'

'No wife of mine will ever work for a living,' I huffed, in the manner of the time.

'Don't come all pompous with me, Martin,' warned Mabel, 'and don't make me give you another piece of what-for. I'm too fond of you to keep telling you off. Just remember, the girl's not a dolt. You must find something to keep her occupied.'

What Myrtle and I had in common was the hole in the centre of our lives. She, an only child, had recently lost her mother to cancer; I had lost a father and a best friend. She knew of my tragedies from the newspapers and I of hers from Aunt Mabel. There was not much more to tell, though we spent a long evening alone at Blenheim Terrace recounting grief histories. At the end I felt, as Othello did of Desdemona, that 'She loved me for the dangers I had pass'd, And I loved her that she did pity them.'

We decided to rebuild love from our ruins. A Freudian analyst would subsequently enlighten me that I had chosen Myrtle principally for the initial consonant of her name: the Ms of Mother, Mabel, Myrtle, Martin (self-love) evoked my infant ego nuzzling at the maternal nipple. I walked out of that session, roaring with mirth. I have read better theories in *Woman's Realm*. Anyway, Myrtle was unmaternally small-breasted, even after childbirth.

We married at Bevis Marks, Britain's oldest and loveliest synagogue, in a Sephardic ceremony conducted by the *Haham*, or Learned One, with candles borne by six choirboys walking backwards before the bride. '"And he is like a bridegroom coming out of his wedding canopy,"' I heard old Jeffries intone, '"rejoicing like a hero to run his course."'

Dinner was befittingly at the Dorchester, with Joe Loss's band and all the trimmings. Half-way through the soup, I noticed an empty seat at the top table.

'Who's that for?' I demanded. Mother counted heads and declared the place setting superfluous. 'I'll tell the caterer to remove it,' she said.

'No, leave it,' I cried. 'It might be there for a purpose.' In my imagination, I saw Dovidl striding through the door in black tie and tails, elegant as ever, taking his rightful seat at my side. The vision was so unsettling that I could neither sleep that night, nor consummate the marriage.

Myrtle was gently understanding, and we came together contentedly in more relaxed circumstances on the French Riviera later that week. She returned from honeymoon pregnant with our first-born. We named him Mortimer after my father. A second son followed eighteen months later, but Myrtle haemorrhaged in childbirth and was advised to avoid having more babies. Mother asked us to call the boy Edwin, 'a name I have always been fond of'. We compromised on Edgar, less archaic and containing, covertly for me, the *eh* of Eli, the *d* of David and the *ar* of Rapoport, a memorial to the missing. As for the hard *g* in the middle, that was me – a stony consonant encased in phantasms of soft sounds.

The handsome young couple moved into the family home on Blenheim Terrace, converted the large kitchen and scullery basement into a swimming-pool and recreation area, leading out on to a re-landscaped garden that blurred memories of lonely boyhood. We settled into the nuclear routines of a bourgeois Jewish family, all terrors pushed to the past. I had my sanitised work, Myrtle her brilliance at bridge. Our spiritual dimension conformed to Anglo-Jewish norms. We attended synagogue eight or ten times a year, for high holy days, personal milestones and memorial prayers.

Cushioned by domesticity, my existence was ringed by a flat despair that stretched into a horizonless future. My life without the Friend was like the Tsarina's after Rasputin's murder, an empty wait for the inevitable. I slept fitfully, wakened by visions of Dovidl, dead in a ditch, captive in a cell, or wandering mad like Josef Hassid or King Lear around some Epsom heath. Myrtle would rise from our bed and lead me, shaking, into the boys' room, waking little Edgar for a family cuddle that would calm me down, his fear-free respiration restoring the rhythm to my breathing. A string of shrinks, consulted over many years, failed to mend my sleep.

In the mornings I went into Simmonds' depleted offices, dictated letters to the indispensable Miss Winter, departed for lunch, dealt with clients, dressed for the evening's concert or opera, where Myrtle would usually join me. I was engaged in continuous self-sedation, averting my conscious thoughts from the caesura episode of Dovidl's departure and the ensuing disaster. To think about it was to court the unthinkable.

The one option that did not bear contemplation was that

Dovidl had, that sunny May morning, walked out on me as transfiguringly as he had arrived. I could not, then or ever, admit the possibility of willing defection, though the suggestion nagged at my subconscious and eroded my few and insubstantial human relationships. Neither work nor marriage could cover the hole at the centre of my being and I felt impelled to seek casual comforts, albeit infrequently and always out of town. My life was a pathetic sonata built upon an unresolved chord, infinitely tense and unrewarding. Like an amputee, I never lost sensation in the missing limb, or the ache of deprivation. Not a day passed without a remembrance of wholeness.

So when time stopped still on a boy's fiddle in the banqueting hall of a nameless town hall on the night another war ended and the glasses clinked and sloshed, I was terrified by the awakening, by the need to take the inevitable next step. I knew I must follow the evidence of my ears, but I could not bear to discover where, after all these years, it might dangerously lead.

# 6

# Time After Time

Dinner is, as anticipated, execrable. To escape overdone English beef in brown gravy on an untouchably hot plate, I have requested a vegetarian alternative – a selection shared, I see, by the admirable Sandra Adams. The ersatz repast set before me is a bower of lettuce, wilting with stress fatigue and pinned down by four hunks of undistinguished Cheddar. Cream crackers and salad cream complete the feast. This is not untypical for an English province, where non-carnivores are regarded as masochistic misfits. Our slap of leaves is slightingly served on the finest Wedgwood china.

The wine, drunk from Donegal crystal, is a 1986 château-bottled burgundy, a little young and tart to the tongue. 'Bottoms up,' exhorts Olly Adams. 'It's not often I get the key to the Mayor's cellar and we've got lots to celebrate tonight. They announced on the news that the war will be over by morning. Cheers, everyone.'

Sitting at the head of a table that becomes more boisterous by the burgundian glass, I contrive to keep a clear head and work out my next move. Fred Burrows, to my right, respects my introspection and delves into a Simmonds pocket score, humming as he reads. Olly, to my left, lectures me on the iniquities of Thatcherite education policy. I shall need to get away somewhere to assess the state of play on my internal chessboard and come up with a credible end-game. Shuffling the pile of score-sheets beside my plate, I start fumbling for an excuse to leave the table when my haphazard pocket pharmacopoeia rises unbidden to my rescue.

I don't know whether the makers of proprietary medicines ever put them through a dry-cleaning machine but the effects on the human digestive system forty minutes after ingestion are, I can vouch, spectacular. Rushing for the door and reaching a lavatory in the nick of time, I disgorge into the gracious majesty of a blue-veined porcelain Victorian crapper sundry chunks of cheese and biscuit, followed by what appears to be a number of vital organs. Kneeling over the pedigree pan, my sweat-beaded brow grateful for a white-tiled wall to lean on, I wait for the heaving to subside and start to formulate a plan of action. Get the contest out of the way, is the immediate priority, then get to see the boy, Peter Stemp, in private. After that, follow the trail where it may lead. I've got the rest of the week to play with. By Friday, I can expect to have resolved the Mystery of the Vanished Virtuoso. Under pressure, Jews revert to irony. In the washroom mirror, as I rinse my face, the eyes flash back a mocking gleam: Hercule Poirot on the prowl.

Rebuttoning my dinner jacket, I leave the men's room and run smack into Sandra Adams, who is loitering outside. 'I was getting worried about you, Mr S,' she scolds. 'You left the table looking a bit under the weather. Can I get you anything for it?'

'A touch of indigestion, Mrs Adams,' I explain. 'Much better now, thank you. Must have been a funny reaction to the cheese.'

'I know,' she soothes, as we head back. 'I get that way sometimes. Olly likes to have me in charge at his department's public functions, but the stress gets me right here' – she dents a plump midriff with a pink fingernail – 'and I have to make a quick getaway. Embarrassing, really. I never know what to say.'

'But you seem,' I reply, 'so . . . self-assured.'

'I suppose we learn to hide our little vulnerabilities, don't we, Mr S?' she says conspiratorially, her hand nuzzling the small of my back as we re-enter the jury room. 'Are you sure I can't get you an aspirin?' I shake my head, done with all that. A brandy and coffee will do the trick.

There are by now more empty bottles on the sideboard than judges at the table and the atmosphere is rudely elated. I tap my fork on a resonant Donegal glass and set in motion the first part of my washroom strategy.

'Colleagues,' I begin, 'the rules of this contest give me, your chairman, a degree of latitude in conducting our deliberations. We have a good half-hour before we need to declare and I am keen that no one should feel constrained by time or' – glancing at Burrows – 'authority, as we reach our joint and, I hope, unanimous decision.'

'Hear, hear,' cheers Olly.

'The easiest thing for me would be to tally the marks on your sheets and announce a winner. However, I feel the occasion would be better served if each of us briefly explains his or her decision. I, as chairman, will voice an opinion but will not cast a vote. Perhaps, Mrs Adams, you would take a note of the comments? As a matter of record, and to avoid contention.' Sandra nods neatly; Olly looks uncertain, out of his depth.

'Professor Murch, would you mind getting us started?'

Brenda Murch, spinsterly piano tutor and provincial soloist, pushing fifty and past hope, is flushed with wine and bursting to give us the benefits of her limited emotional experience. 'Number three, Maria Olszewska, is the most accomplished young pianist I have heard in more years than I care to acknowledge,' she spouts. 'Setting aside her technique, which is formidable, I was moved and engaged by her intelligent interpretations. Her charm is abundant. She had the audience in the palm of her hand. She is quite a find.'

'Anyone else catch your eye, Brenda?' I ask, eliciting a vigorous shake of that frizzy grey head of unstroked hair.

'Mr Adams?' I proceed, turning to Olly.

'Well you know I think the al-Haq boy is a bit special, but I'm no expert and I was knocked sideways, as we all were, by the lovely Olszewska. She wins by a mile. Just so long as my boy gets some kind of consolation prize.'

'How much can your department afford?' I enquire.

'Will a grand do?' asks Olly.

'Very nicely,' I assure him. 'Your turn, Fred.'

The Tawburn *Kapellmeister* keeps it short and votes for Olszewska. His verdict lacks gravitas and Olly picks his teeth throughout. Without family or political friends, the able and dedicated Fred gets treated – like Johann Sebastian Bach in Leipzig, he once wistfully told me – as a municipal dogsbody, at the beck and call of uncultured superiors and itinerant bishops.

'Arthur?' I continue. Professor Arthur Brind, violin master of the Great Northern, declares vociferously for the pianist Olszewska – 'unquestionably a talent'. 'None of the fiddlers, Arthur?' I tease, knowing that this sour dwarf of a tenured teacher has wrecked many a prospective career by filling young violinists with false dreams and fake methods. 'No flair on the G string tonight?'

'Well, I noticed you took a fancy, Martin, to the last kid – but I heard nothing special,' sniffs Brind, his last contribution before a shot of Courvoisier snuffs him out for the night. The professor will wake up tomorrow in his Manchester rooms, wondering what that fifty-quid Tawside Council cheque is doing in the breast pocket of his dress suit.

'The Stemp boy does have something,' Fred Burrows chips in, trying to be helpful. 'His phrasing was quite unusual. I found it a bit distracting, but it may be worth watching. I'd like to hear him again a year from now.'

'Stemp has something that made me sit up,' agrees Olly, swimming with the tide.

'I liked his playing very much,' adds Sandra Adams quietly.

'I am so glad *most* of you feel that way,' I sum up, tailoring their comments to my requirements. 'I would not wish to dissent from your collective verdict, and I fully endorse Maria Olszewska as the outright winner. Her Chopin was quite exceptional and her aplomb uncanny in one so young. She is almost the complete artist.

'But I am not unattuned to string playing and I did hear a distinct originality in Peter Stemp's articulation, which is what I listen for in young players. Technical proficiency, you see, we take for granted nowadays. Anyone who enters a competition at this level can play, and most can play extremely well. What one hopes for is a spark of personality that will set the players apart from all the competent others on the professional circuit. Stemp did not play blindingly well, but his phrasing was out of the ordinary. I won't bother you with chapter and verse, since I have already caused Professor Brind to nod off. But his *rubato* was sufficiently unusual to prick my ear and I have heard every prince of the instrument from Kreisler on.'

'So, what do you suggest we do?' demands Olly, looking rudely at his watch.

'I suspect,' I continued, 'that the boy is suffering from a lack of intellectual hinterland. He seems to be trying out effects without quite knowing why he does them or what they fit. What he needs is a broader cultural context, the kind of education the Germans call *Bildung*, which I am afraid has vanished from our schools in these materialistic times. With your permission, Director, I should like to make an *extra vires* intervention. In addition to presenting the Tawside prize and the various consolations we have agreed for the losers, I will tonight announce Peter Stemp as the winner of the 1991 Simmonds Foundation Award, with a gift of two thousand pounds as a travel and study grant.'

Olly is chuffed, almost speechless. 'That's incredibly generous of you, Mr Simmonds,' he splutters. 'I can't tell you what it'll mean to people up here to have a Simmonds winner – and what a boost for the event. Everyone will go home with something. There are no losers in Tawside tonight, only winners.'

'All must have prizes,' mutters Brenda Murch, in heavy italics. 'Very politically correct.' Fred Burrows, who is no fool, shoots me a quizzical look. I smile benignly, gather my papers and lead the judges ceremonially back into the Clement Attlee Hall.

The time is ten minutes before ten and the news cameras are winking red as we mount the stage, where a microphone and a mayor are meant to await us. The mike is live, but the Mayor is past it. 'You go ahead without me,' slurs Froggatt, from his seat at our feet. Sandra, flustered, appeals mutely to Olly, whose back is turned, then to me, the chairman.

Terrified as I am of public speaking, I mount the stage, seize the mike and let rip. 'My Lord Mayor, ladies and gentlemen,' the formulae trip off my tongue, 'on behalf of the judges, may I say what a privilege and a pleasure it has been to sample the new vintage of Tawside's renowned crop of musical talent.'

'And the Mayor's best vintages,' burps Froggatt, from somewhere near my toecaps.

'Every age-group in this competition,' I continue, 'especially the youngest, has shown astonishingly high levels of attainment. I shall not detain you very long before declaring the winner –' a hollow cry of '*Zindabad*' rises from the textiles table, '– but when I say we were overwhelmed, I mean precisely that. We were filled with wonderment and admiration at the talent this region produces. Unanimously, to a man and woman, we felt it would be unjust if any of tonight's finalists were to go home unrewarded. So, the Tawside Department of Arts and Leisure Services and my own company, Simmonds Limited, have arranged to present five extra awards – the one-thousand-pound Arts and Leisure Services incentive to Ashutosh al-Haq,' a ragged attempt at '*Zindabad*', 'three council scholarships to the runners-up and the two-thousand-pound Simmonds Foundation prize to Peter Stemp.'

The applause is mildly intoxicating. I haven't orated in public at such length since my barmitzvah, and I am enjoying it so much that Sandra Adams has to nudge me to get a move on before the cameras switch off. 'Ladies and gentlemen,' I resume, 'these are not consolation prizes. They amount to an exceptional recognition of exceptional talent and effort. Now, I have kept you in suspense long enough. It is my pleasure to announce Tawside's first Young Musician of the Year, with a prize of five thousand pounds, a concerto performance with the Tawburn Symphony Orchestra and a solo recital in London. The winner, by a unanimous decision, is . . . Maria Olszewska.'

Popping bulbs, popping corks, sloppy kisses, and a lovely Chopin prelude from the laureate, whose father consults me forthwith about fixing her London début. Peter Stemp and his mother are hanging one step back. I give them each a business card and handshake and slip away, refusing to let ambitious musical parents ruin my benevolent mood. I go looking for Froggatt to thank him for the hospitality, but the Mayor has passed out in his chambers. 'Hasn't been the same since his wife walked out,' advises Sandra Adams. 'Went to Brighton to live with their daughter, couldn't abide public life.'

I arrange to meet Sandra for breakfast at my hotel to organise the supplementary awards ceremony and say goodnight to her with the air of a job well done, not a common reward in my occupation. The night is brisk, the streets busy with youngsters. I walk the short stretch to the Royal, feeling safer than in central London. I need the walk to calm my mind, but my mind will not be calmed. The siren call is too close. I lie in bed, listening to the fading shouts of late drinkers, willing sleep to come. It takes three *Cham. Rads*, a valerian and a Nembutal before merciful blackness descends.

Sandra turns up in the breakfast room on the dot of eight a.m. in soft layers of office wear. Grey angora sweater, pleated skirt, small earrings and a trace of pale lipstick. Freed from her evening costume and inner stiffenings, she smells shower-fresh and erotically alive. We shake hands – air-kissing has not caught on in these parts – and as we sit down I catch myself mentally undressing my pliant partner, raising the sweater over her unbouffed hair, dropping the straps of her shiny slip and stopping my imagination just short of unfastening her (undoubtedly sensible) Marks & Spencer bra. We must get down to business. There will be plenty of time later to play with fantasy.

Sandra sits down at table without waiting for me to draw back her chair. She orders the Healthy Breakfast, sighing, 'It's a losing battle,' and patting her waistline with a hint of flirtation.

'You seem to be putting up a better fight than the Iraqis,' I quip, and she chuckles.

As we wait for food – mine is plain tea and toast – she produces the morning papers. The *Tawburn Gazette* has a triumphant Maria Olszewska beaming across its front page and a full report inside. The awards were too late at night and, I thought, too insignificant to merit national attention, but Sandra shows me an inch on page two of *The Times* and the *Telegraph*, announcing the Simmonds winner. It appears that the moment I took the microphone, she got on the phone to the late editions of the London broadsheets. Her enterprise is admirable; she is wasted, I decide, on Tawside.

Arrangements for the second round of prize-giving are quickly concluded. As an apparent afterthought, I ask Sandra to organise a private lunch in my hotel with the Simmonds winner and his parents. 'I'd be delighted if you could join us,' I tell her, laying a friendly hand on her bare forearm.

'Can't, Mr S.' She smiles. 'I'm supposed to be working for the finance department and they're getting stroppy about my absences. It was all that Olly could do to get me this morning off.'

'How *is* your husband?' I ask, over-courteously.

'Hung-over when I left him, but tickled pink by the awards. He's had Asian businessmen ringing him in ecstasies since the crack of dawn, and he'll be needing their support when he runs for Parliament come next election.'

So that's their game. Olly's the vanity, Sandra the reality. 'What are his chances?' I enquire.

'I can't see him squeezing past the old guard at the constituency party,' she says coolly, 'but don't tell him I said so. When it comes to politics Olly's like a boy with a ball in the backyard, dreaming he's destined to play for England.'

'And you?'

'Me, I'm just a working mum, doing her bit for house and hubby.' She chuckles self-mockingly.

'But you have other ideas?'

'Nothing grandiose,' says Sandra.

'Perhaps we should discuss them, you and I?'

'Another time, perhaps,' says Sandra, brushing crumbs of muesli off her fluffy bosom. 'Gosh, is that the time? I'd better run, or there'll be no prize-giving and no winner's lunch. I'll catch you later, Mr S. By the way, you were brilliant last night.'

'You were pretty sharp yourself,' I purr, calling for the bill. We talk like a pair of first-night lovers, complimenting one another on the foreplay.

Lunch with Peter Stemp and his mother is a stiffer affair. There used to be a Mr Stemp but he, according to Sandra's tingly briefing in my ear, 'ran off with a barmaid from Bolton'. Peter, it hardly needs elucidating, is Mummy's boy. He is dressed in a suit that flaps half an inch over his wrists and ankles, for him to grow into. If his mother has her way, he may never grow up. Mrs Stemp, brown-eyed and tense as a whippet, is recovering from the shock of being invited to lunch with someone as eminent as myself and in the implied majesty of the Royal Tawburn. She has nothing to wear, she protests. 'It's just a working lunch, Mrs Stemp,' says Sandra, steering the awkward pair into the half-empty restaurant before, with a wave, heading back to her mundane employment.

Neither mother nor child has much small-talk, and when one of them musters the energy and effrontery to begin a sentence the other, disconcertingly, leaps in to complete it.

'I'd like the avocado,' says Mrs Stemp.

'Vinaigrette, not prawns,' chimes in Peter. 'My mother can't take seafood, it gives her a turn.'

'What will you have, love?' coos his mother.

'What's Waldorf—'

'Salad,' says his mother. 'Peter loves his salads.'

Her assertion is contradicted by the boy's complexion, which is pasty and pimpled, betraying poor diet and emotional imbalance. Peter is tall for his age, nearly six foot, and has nowhere to put his gangly extremities. He fidgets, picks his scabby chin and kicks me arhythmically under the table as lunch wears on. Service at the Royal, always tardy, has slowed to the point where I summon the sommelier and ask him if the rest of the Mediterranean staff have migrated for the winter. A typical Tuesday in recessional England.

Mrs Stemp – 'Eleanor, please,' – is thirty-five and fading. The veins are visible on both sides of her brow, where the mousy hair has begun to recede. In a couple of years, she will look middle-aged. I wonder if she was ever young. Eleanor Stemp works for an estate agent and lives vicariously through her wonderchild. All her hopes for happiness and security have been invested in his fragile gift for playing the fiddle, a talent he discovered at the age of four, 'just after his father left us'. She wipes her mouth clean of avocado wisp, as if to erase her ex-husband's genetic contribution.

The Simmonds Award is a vindication of all her privations, a first instalment on her earthly reward. She glows with a satisfaction verging on smugness, but the fruits of success are new to her lips and my gentle questioning is greeted with prickly suspicion. Mrs Stemp admits to playing the piano a little, 'but only to help Peter with his practising, and sometimes to accompany him in a recital'.

She is not a real musician, not even an amateur. Peter is the only artist in the family, deserving of all our attention.

Does she ever go to concerts? Eleanor shakes her head. 'I have to be home at night to hear Peter practise and put him to bed,' she says, a flake of cod-flesh falling from her fork. Peter, stabbing an overdone rump steak, keeps interrupting to finish her replies. They are more like a pair of spinster sisters than parent and son, having lived together too long for either of them to own an independent existence. Peter is a dull-witted boy and Mrs Stemp has 'Victim' written in emanescent fret-lines along her ferrety brow.

Over puddings of profiteroles with *crème anglaise*, I raise the subject of Peter's education, gently explaining my views on the need to broaden it. I confide that Peter, remarkable as he is, had not impressed the other judges. Only my intimation of latent talent had qualified him for the Simmonds Award. That gift now needed to be brought out by intensive exposure to art and ideas. I propose that Peter should spend a year at my expense at a music-orientated boarding school – Chetham's near Manchester, for example, or the Purcell in London. It is an offer most musicians would leap at but, from this Siamese pair, it elicits a positively Gilbertian patter-song of protest and refusal.

'Peter won't like that –' says Mrs Stemp.

'– at all.'

'He'd be unhappy –'

'– away from home.'

'His music would suffer –'

'– in a strange place.'

'I couldn't let him –'

'– go away.'

'Not at his age –'

'– not quite up to it.'

'Not yet.'

So much for that. I am tempted to remind them sharply that the Simmonds Award is conditional on a course of travel and study, but I fear that one or both of them might burst into tears. I am not, by nature, a patient man. I long to be shot of this pair, but there is something I need from the boy and I cannot release him without it. Coffee is poured and I am contemplating a less invasive way of lifting the wretched fledgling from the nest when Eleanor Stemp, to my mild surprise, proposes that she and I should discuss Peter's future in private. There is even a hint of collusion in her voice, though Mrs Stemp's bruised eyes, hooded and protective, seem too downcast to portend boldness.

One of the first rules in my line of work is to avoid private meetings with parents of prodigies. Always have a third party present, and keep the door ajar. There is an implicit risk of sexual assault or accusation. Incidents are so common that an etiquette has evolved, allowing music executives to deal with frisky parents without going to jail. Rule number one: never enter a lift alone with a mum. Rule two: watch out if the father wears leather. Rule three: make sure all junior members of staff are chaperoned.

There are, it is true, agents who prey carnally on desperate artists and their parents but, so far as I can tell, the traffic is mostly the other way. Set loose in a glamour industry, clients lose all perspective in their eagerness to assure themselves that they have actually arrived. Time after time, they set upon impassive managers like a pack of defrocked monks and nuns. What is it that provokes previously chaste parents to hurl themselves upon the fixers and finaglers of musical fame? A cocktail of conflicting motives and emotions: gratitude and resentment, ingratiation, blackmail and more. Papa Freud would have identified an urge on the part of the birth-parent to consummate a sexual union with the success-parent.

It's all too squalid to warrant serious attention, but people in my business know the risks and have only themselves to blame if they walk into what I believe is known in Hollywood as a honeytrap.

So when Eleanor Stemp suggests a tête-à-tête, I search her eyes for lustful intent, and find none. Assuring myself that her drabness and my advanced years are ample guarantors of probity, I invite her to dinner the following night. My aim is to interrogate each Stemp separately until I find out what I need to know.

Our lunch has been a complete waste of time. The only intelligence I have gathered is that Peter has two violin teachers: the music master at his high school, a dull fellow called Finch who plays in Fred Burrows' band, and a Saturday-morning mistress called Winifred Southgate, who came twittering at me after the awards ceremony. Winifred also teaches little al-Haq and has failed to endow him with any singularity of expression. That's two down, one to go.

'No other teachers?' I press. Peter shakes his head.

'He does listen to a lot of records,' volunteers Eleanor Stemp. 'Especially the old ones that he borrows from the library. He loves Heifetz, don't you, love?' Of all the useless clichés. Every half-baked would-be soloist reveres Heifetz with his infallible technique, and every aspirant from here to Haiti grows up on his recordings, hoping the magic will somehow rub off on them.

'What Peter has got,' I sigh deeply, 'is not something he has picked up from listening to old masters on library loans. He has in his gift an expressive quirk – like a remote accent, Cornish or Amish – that one does not often hear any more on the standardised, internationalised concert circuit. I am charmed by this accent and would like to help him develop it, both for his own benefit and to conserve a rare flash of colour in the functional concert world.'

'Well, it's all Greek to me,' says Eleanor, putting an end to the lunch by rising, as she puts it, to powder her nose. This is the moment for me to pounce.

Alone with the pock-marked pubescent, I draw my chair adjacent to his. 'Peter, you know that I know a thing or two about violinists.'

'Yes, Mr Simmonds,' he mumbles.

'And you know what it is that I like in your playing.'

'Yes, Mr Simmonds.' He is scratching his chin, hoping for Eleanor to return or the zit to explode all over my inquisitive mug. I run my mind over the geography of the hotel. The ladies' washroom is located at the far end of the basement; it should take Mrs Stemp a good five minutes to walk there and back and do whatever she has to in between. I may just have enough time to extract a confession.

'Peter, you know that *I know* that you did not learn to play that kind of *rubato* in the G minor sonata from a salaried school-teacher or a Saturday-morning handbag who has never left the north of England in her entire life.'

'No, Mr Simmonds.' He is looking pale, precipitately nauseous.

'So who taught you?'

'Does it matter?' He squirms, playing for time, praying that his mother will finish her interminable pee.

'It most certainly does.'

'Why?'

'Because someone has shared with you one of the great secrets of the violin. He has given you a piece of information, a skill, a combustible gift. Use it well, and you can become a great artist. Misuse it, and it will blow up in your face. I happen to be one of the very few people alive who understand this hazardous knack, this clock-stopping form of *rubato*. It's the single reason that I gave you the Simmonds Award, to help you handle this ticking package.'

I pause to let the threat sink in, watching Peter wilt under metaphoric intimidation, seeing the realisation dawn that his prize could be snatched away if he fails to comply with my wishes. He stops picking the scab on his chin, sits still, grows up.

'I'll tell you, Mr Simmonds,' he whispers, eyes scanning the doorway. 'I'll tell you if you promise never to tell my Mam.'

'What's the problem?' I ask.

'She hates them.'

'Hates whom?'

'The blacks.'

At least, that's what I hear, and my brain goes berserkly scanning a catalogue of Afro-Caribbean violinists, of whom there have been no contenders of consequence since George Augustus Polgreen Bridgetower, for whom Beethoven originally wrote the Kreutzer Sonata before withdrawing (as was his wont) the dedication. I draw a blank on blacks and look to the boy for enlightenment.

'Not blacks,' he smirks. 'Black-hats.'

'Come again?'

'Jews,' he whispers. '*Frummers*. Oldbridge Yeshiva – that lot.'

Relief floods my veins: we could be getting somewhere. Oldbridge, a satellite town of Tawburn, has a community of ultra-orthodox Jews who, after the war, set up a rabbinical seminary, called a *yeshiva* or sitting-place, with the aim of restoring the traditions of Talmudical scholarship that had been wiped out in eastern Europe. A bare handful at first, the seminarists proliferated rapidly, with families of ten or twelve children and an open door to scholars from all over the world. Although they number no more than five hundred and live in an enclave of four streets around a Georgian square, their stubborn separateness and their strangeness sets them apart – not just from gentiles but from most Jews, who shudder at the authenticity of their medieval lifestyles and dress-codes. There but for the grace of, we imagine.

The *frummers* of Oldbridge have their own schools, shops and entertainments. Those who work for a living engage in middleman occupations. They are estate agents, travel agents, import-export agents. Agents, I suppose, like myself, but untouched by external ideals. They work in order to finance their community, their *yeshiva*, and they work mostly with one another. Cars and houses they interchange internally. Kitchen units and bedroom furniture they buy from a *frummer* wholesaler in London, ten families at a time. They have their own driving instructors, dentist and midwives, using public utilities only in sickness and emergency. Should one of them die in Tawburn General, they whisk away the body while still warm to avoid the dishonour of an autopsy.

They would like to exist unnoticed, but one bearded man in a black hat and his pregnant, bewigged wife stand out in Tawburn Station like Apaches on Wall Street, quaint and vaguely menacing, as if they hold some prior title to the place. Their archaic trinity of monotheism, monogamy and monochrome attire is reproachful of the modern way of life, an unuttered rebuke to sluttish girls in slit skirts and their can-swigging consorts. There have been ripostes from loutish modernity – bricks through front windows, 'Jews to Auschwitz' scrawled on walls – but, this being England, nothing murderous. The *frummers* – an Anglo-Yiddish form of the German *fromm*, meaning pious – are protected by English privet-hedge privacy, secure in their self-walled ghetto, shuffling about like Martians on our social margins.

Their seclusion is infringed only by Channel Four documentary makers and the occasional pair of Jehovah's Witnesses. They, for their part, regard gentiles with fear and commingling Jews with contempt. Their conservationist rigour, they believe, is all that preserves the Jewish race from extinction, paving the path for Messiah. They may be right. It is always the zealots, not the accommodators, who define a people's character and give it jarring protrusions that protect from erosion. In middle-road Jews like me, the *frummers* arouse complex emotions of fearful prejudice and secret pride.

Could it be that my vanished friend has fallen among these extraterrestrials? Dovidl, erudite and sybaritic, alive among relentless sectarians? Surely not, though I feel unsure. The route to obscurantism has become alarmingly popular in recent years. The son of one of my Medola cousins went *meshugga-frum* under the influence of a proselytising sect that entrapped him, friendless and disoriented, on campus at Berkeley, California. He spent years in some intensive Israeli *yeshiva* and was ultimately hitched to a nineteen-year-old bride he had never met before at a wedding where men and women were segregated by a trellis wall and danced for joy in single-sex circles. Myrtle and I found it all perplexing and distasteful.

'My mother says they are filthy speculators,' confides Peter Stemp. 'They buy up any property that's going in Oldbridge and either keep it for their own lot or, if it's in a nice area near the river, convert it into luxury flats for yuppies and weekenders. They're pushing prices out of the reach of ordinary people, and pushing local estate agents out of business. Drives my mam wild, it does.'

'And how did you get to know them?' I prompt.

'Not them – just one,' he whispers. 'Watch it, here she comes.'

'Sorry to keep you so long,' says Eleanor Stemp, her hair brushed and fluffed, her lipstick repaired. 'The toilets in this hotel are a disgrace. The one downstairs was flooded and I had to go all the way across the road to the railway station, and that's no Savoy, I can tell you.' She surveys us shrewdly, sniffing betrayal. 'What have you two men been talking about?' she wonders, mock-cheerily.

'Nothing much, Mam,' blurts Peter, far too fast.

'We have been getting along famously, Eleanor,' I assure her, using her first name to emphasise our familiarity. 'So much so that Peter here has agreed to stay for tea and tell me more about himself, isn't that right, Peter?'

The boy nods blankly.

'But he's normally so shy,' says his mother, flushed with anxiety. My heart goes out to her, hovering in her gaberdine raincoat and her heel-worn flat shoes, so fearful of life, so restricted in her range of options (good for the boy, or bad). Downtrodden and close to hysteria, she presents a sorry contrast to confident Sandra Adams, her close and class contemporary, who copes so capably with everyday matters and gives herself scope to plan a future. Eleanor is one of life's losers, and I dislike myself for exploiting her fragile faith in me. 'You are most welcome to stay for tea, my dear,' I assure her, with utmost insincerity, 'but, then, you and I are going to have our little chat over dinner tomorrow night, aren't we? Shall we say seven?' And all the while I am steering her to the main exit, where my day-hired chauffeur-driven Jaguar is dutifully waiting. 'Alfred will drop you wherever you need to go, and he'll come back at six to take Peter home, in time for supper.' I kiss her hand with the unctuousness of a Viennese head-waiter. 'Until tomorrow, then.'

Peter, detached from his parent, improves appreciably. He may never win a prize for charm, but he can give a good account of himself. His narrative is pointed with deft turns of phrase. There is character in the boy; my eye has not erred. He is alert, astute and more than adequately ambitious.

Which is not to say I like him any the better. Candid as

Peter contrives to appear, there is a shiftiness about the boy that is probably embedded. He has already broken faith with his suffering mother and he is about to betray a further confidence under my gentle pressure. I ought to be pleased at his compliance, but I deplore his baseness. He is cultivating me because I represent his ticket to the next station up the line. The instant my usefulness expires, he will discard me like a broken string. Peter Stemp, fifteen years old, is grooming himself for the conscienceless career of a classical virtuoso.

'Tell me how you got to meet the *frummers*,' I resume in the lounge as tea is served, a tower-tray of ham and cheese sandwiches, tinned biscuits and gooey cakes.

'Just the one,' he repeats. 'This man, Mr Katzenberg, and a couple of his neighbours.'

'Carry on,' I encourage him, pouring dark tea from a chipped china pot.

'I do a paper round before school every morning.'

'Do you?' I interject. 'Used to do one myself when I was your age, during the war, it was.'

Peter ignores me. Having resolved to sell his story, he will do so without my participation. 'I started it a couple of years ago, to pay for a mountain-bike that I really wanted. My mam said we couldn't afford it, so I saw this ad in the newsagent's window and suddenly I had money to burn.'

Some things in England, I mutely reflect, never change. I bet he buys himself a KitKat at the end of the round. He expertly unwraps a chocolate Swiss roll.

'My round,' he sputters, 'takes in the up-river half of Oldbridge, including Gladstone Square, where most of the black-hats live. Four streets are almost totally *frum*: Canning, Palmerston, Disraeli and Chamberlain. None of those people takes papers; I don't know if they even speak English. All except one. In Canning Street, there is one house, number thirty-two, that takes the *Telegraph* every morning and the *Jewish Chronicle* on Fridays. It's a real drag to go down a whole street just for one customer, but Mr Amin the newsagent says an order is an order and you don't turn good money away. Anyway, with a ten-speed mountain bike I can scoot down the street, drop the papers, and be out on Salisbury Avenue inside a minute. Fifty-three seconds is my personal best.

'Who lives there, I have no idea. I never see anyone, and I'm hardly likely to ring their bell for a Christmas tip because those people don't even celebrate Christmas. Mam says they killed Our Lord, but that seems a bit . . . much.

'Anyhow, one Friday morning, I'm pushing the *Telegraph* and *Jewish Chronicle* through number thirty-two when the door opens with the papers jammed in the flap. I try pushing them in, he's pushing them out, and we both burst out laughing. He's a big man, huge grey beard, silk-black skullcap on his head, deep eyes and – the thing I spot straight away – amazing fingers. Never seen hands like that, long and thin. While he's laughing, I'm thinking, This man must find it so easy to play the fiddle.'

Those fingers, how could I ever forget? Slender, supple, white as snow, trim nails, tapering to the narrowest of tips. Not so much fingers as tendrils, sensitive as nerve-ends, swift as lightning. Invisible at speed, angelic in repose. His fingers.

My pulse is pounding and I can feel the arteries protesting at the added workload. 'Carry on,' I say. Peter scoffs a quarter-sandwich. With his mother gone, he eats like an aboriginal, storing strength.

'I must have looked a bit shocked,' he continues, 'because the man steps back and says, "Forgive me." See what I mean? *Forgive me*, not 'scuse me, or sorry, or watch it. "Forgive me," he says, meaning – if I have upset you in some way, let me put it right. Those words, "forgive me", take my breath away. My mam made me swear not to talk to the *frummers* and never to go into their houses. They kidnap Christian kids, she said, and kill them for Passover blood, can you imagine? She read it in a book somewhere. So I'm being very watchful and not leaving the doorstep. But there's something about this man that makes me feel incredibly safe. I don't know how to describe it, Mr Simmonds. He shows such respect for my feelings – like a saint out of the Gospels.

'"Forgive me," he says again. "Did I give you a shock?"

'"A bit," I say, or something of the sort.

'"I have been trying to catch you all week," he says, "but I wasn't planning on a tug-of-war over the *Daily Telegraph*." He has a lovely rich laugh, you just have to join in. "May I ask you a favour?" he says to me.

'"Go on," I say.

'"Tomorrow morning, when you deliver my paper, would you mind stepping inside for a moment to switch on my gas fire?"

'"Can't you do it yourself?"

'"Not on Saturday," he says. "It's our Sabbath and we are not allowed to kindle light. It says so in the Bible, in Exodus, I can show you. But on winter mornings it gets cold and my kids come down to a freezing living room. You would be doing me a great service by lighting the fire on Saturdays, and I will pay you for it."

'"How much?" I ask.

'"Fifty pence?" he suggests.

'Brilliant, I think, I'll be able to pay off the bike by Easter.'

Peter drains his tea and rearranges his gangly legs, tripping a passing waiter as he does so. He does not apologise. Peter is not the type to say, 'Forgive me'. Self-obsessed, he feels only how things affect him, never the impact on others. He is about to betray his mother again.

'Next morning I ring the doorbell and he comes running all flustered to the front door in his woolly dressing-gown. "Please don't ring," he whispers, "just knock. Ringing disturbs our day of rest. It activates an electric impulse and changes, however minutely, the serene state of God's universe."

'Wow, I think. Everything he says has a reason, some kind of proof that he can find in one of those big books. "There is order in God's world," he told me once, "and it is our task to appreciate it. Just as there is a fixed order to the musical notes we play, so there is a heavenly plan governing all our actions, no matter how small. If I raise my hand to scratch my nose, that is because God arranged for me to do so five thousand seven hundred and forty-nine years ago at the moment of Creation. I am just an instrument that God plays at His will."

'"But we learned in science that the world has been going for millions of years," I say.

'"Not according to our calculations," he insists.

'Anyhow, that first Saturday morning, Mr Katzenberg takes me into this front room that seems absolutely poky because there's a huge bookcase along one wall and a massive dining table in the middle. Bending down to light the fire, I spot a piano in the corner and think, Right first time – the man's a musician. Then, on top of the piano, I see this terrific violin case, knocked about a bit but really classy. "D'you play?" I ask, pointing at the fiddle-case.

'"Sometimes," he says.

'"Professionally?" I ask.

'"Once," he says.

'"Can I hear you?"

'He shakes his head.

'"Why not?"

'"Sabbath," he says.

'So the next day when I call for my money – fifty pence from him and an order to light Sabbath fires for his neighbours on either side – I ask to hear him play.

'"Are you a violinist?" he wants to know.

'"I'm going to be a famous soloist," I tell him.

'"Come in."

'He opens the case and unwraps the violin from its silk scarf. I tell you, Mr Simmonds, I have never seen anything so gorgeous. Wood the colour of a bronzed medal and a sheen that seems to come from right inside. It's a 1742 Guadagnini that the great Joachim used to own, you know, the man who inspired Brahms to write his concerto. It's like something so holy you hardly dare look at it. I want to touch it, but I don't even dare to ask. You can almost hear it breathe.

'Mr Katzenberg draws his bow, and the walls start to bulge with the sound he makes. He does this little étude by Sarasate, and I almost pass out, can't believe what I am hearing. The room has grown as big as Tawburn Cathedral. His eyes are shut – not in concentration, the way you or I play, but sort of looking inwards, inside himself.

'"Teach me," I say.

'"I don't take pupils," he replies – just like Jascha Heifetz.

'"Teach me," I repeat, "or I won't be your *Shabbes-goy*" – that's what they call anyone who lights their Sabbath fire. I'm amazed at my nerve – I've never talked like that to a grown-up before. He could throw me out, or drown me in his Passover soup. I can see that he, too, is a bit startled.

'"You're a good boy," he says – meaning, Don't make me

dislike you. "Come back next Sunday and maybe I will show you something."

'So the following Saturday I light fires at three houses in Canning Street, and on Sunday, I ring the bell at number thirty-two and march into the parlour with my fiddle under my arm. "Teach me," I say.

'"Just listen," he replies.

'And that's all there is to it. Every Sunday for two years I'd go to his house at the end of my round and he would play something – Bach, Mozart, Brahms, Debussy, Vieuxtemps, Ysaÿe, anything he fancies, he knows it all by heart. And the way he plays is out of all time. A minute étude can seem to last an hour, a whole sonata is over in a flash.

'Afterwards, he'll pour me a fizzy drink and talk about the violin – the only instrument, he says, that reveals everything about a player: his good points, the nasty side of him, everything down to the way he wears his pyjamas, if he wears pyjamas, that is. "What you hear on the violin," he explains, "is the naked truth about a person. It cannot be faked and, like a fingerprint, it cannot be mistaken for anyone else." I might try to imitate him, but my own character will always stick to the sound I make.

'After six months he lets me play him some Mozart. He is not impressed. "Take your time," he keeps saying. "Ignore the score. A musician is the master of time – subject to God's will, that is. Imagine you are holding the arms of a clock on which the world turns and that you can make them rush ahead, or stop dead, as you wish. Do it now, in your own time."

'I am so knocked out by this that I start bending the music towards me, sort of, and he smiles. Then I bend it away from me, and he gives a big grin. And once I have started I can't go back to the way I was. It completely changes how I play. And that was fine until that old witch Miss Southgate goes whingeing to my mam that I'm messing about in her lessons, won't play the proper tempo. So I have to develop a split style – one to please my teacher and my examiners, and a private way for me and Mr K. At the competition last night, I got carried away and showed too much of my private way – which is why you've got me telling you now all about thirty-two Canning Street.'

He repeats the address ghoulishly as if it is a scene of crime, a place of notoriety. The boy looks pale, drained by confession and consumption. Sweat is beading between his acne spots. He sneaks a glance at my expression, keen to see if I am satisfied. My colour has risen, my nostrils are aflare. I am closing in for the kill. Ordering a fresh pot of tea, I resume the interrogation.

'Did you, Peter, ever ask Mr, er, Katzenberg how he knows so much, how he arrived at his particular philosophy of playing? After all, it scarcely befits the rather secluded life he leads.'

'Lots of times I asked him, Mr Simmonds,' says Peter. 'At first, he changed the subject. Then, when I nagged, he said, yes, he once studied under a great master, Professor Flesch, but he never had the urge to make a career. "You have to want it more than anything on earth," is how he put it. "More than love, more than money, more than faith, more than life itself. Myself –" he said – "I never wanted it that much."'

I am now so close to home that my metabolism begins to shut down, slowing and cooling my reactions to protect the weakened aorta – or so I imagine. Whatever is going on inside my chest, my brain is receiving and processing information with deadly clarity. A strategy starts to form. I am now convinced that Dovidl is still alive, and not far from here. What I do next will determine the rest of his life, and mine. 'Did you believe that?' I asked Peter.

'Sort of,' says the boy, no fool. 'I looked up Professor Flesch in *Grove's Dictionary* in the reference section at the public library, and there is a list of all his successful pupils, but none by the name of Katzenberg. So I reckon he must have dropped out before he made a début, though I don't get it.

'Sometimes when I turn up on a Sunday morning, he is still sitting at breakfast saying grace with his youngest kids – he has eleven, amazing. Seeing him like that, I suppose he prefers a quiet life to the risk of playing a live concert where anything can go wrong. Maybe he had a breakdown, or lost his nerve. But then he'll pick up the fiddle and play the Beethoven concerto, with Joachim's cadenzas, me picking out accompaniments on the wonky upright. And I think, Wow, what a loss.

'The only thing he ever asks is that I mustn't tell anyone, specially not my mam. I must have mentioned that she hates folk like him, and neither of us wants her turning up on his front doorstep accusing him of stealing my blood for Passover. He tells me, quite sharply, not to make fun of her fears, that she does her best for me and I must respect her. I hope he won't mind my telling you all this, since you're Jewish also, just like him.'

Is it so obvious? Or has his pathetic mother warned him of my malevolent race? I am tempted to choke the boy and drain his blood just to fulfil her loathsome prejudices, but there are higher priorities to hand.

'And what if Mr Katzenberg does mind you telling me?' I needle.

'Can't be helped,' says Peter.

'You have fallen out with him?'

'Other way round,' he says.

'What happened?'

'He told me to go away.'

'When was this?'

'A month ago,' says the boy, looking queasy. I retract my chair in case he vomits and squeeze out one last gobbet of intelligence.

'He caught me outside the Jewish grocery shop on Canning Street talking to his daughter, Basya-Beyla, she's about my age, dark hair, keen on maths. "Not fitting," he says. "Our girls do not mix with boys, even our own. If my child is seen talking to a stranger, no one will want to marry her. Please go now, forgive me."

'I swear to you, Mr Simmonds, there was nothing between us, me and her. We were just chatting about schoolwork, for heaven's sake. But the old man puts me in quarantine, as if I'm a dog with rabies. "Please leave now," he says. "It is best." He's not angry. Just detached, and dead set. He cancels his papers from Mr Amin. Then I find out he's switched to another newsagent. He just wanted to get rid of me, that's all.'

'I'm sure he'll be glad to see you back some day,' I tell the boy misleadingly, leading him from the tea-table to the purring Jaguar outside. 'Come, Peter, it's time to run you home. Your mother will be getting worried.'

'You won't tell her, will you?' he checks.

'Don't worry,' I reply, hearing his gasp of relief, 'but I may drop in on Mr Katzenberg tonight to discuss your progress.'

'I don't know if he's in of an evening,' says Peter, 'and he's kind of leery of strangers.'

Confused and exhausted, Peter bites his nails during the short drive to his home, on a council estate revitalised by the right that Margaret Thatcher gave tenants to buy their own flats. Mrs Stemp is peeking through net curtains. I would be happy never to see her again, her and her disloyal little boy, but I shall play the game to the end to avoid hurting their feelings. No need to pour fuel on their dry-stick racism.

'Oldbridge,' I tell the driver. 'Canning Street.'

'You're sure you mean Canning Street?' says Alfred, an amateur cornettist and semi-retired chauffeur who turns out for regular clients but refuses the new breed of Thatcher entrepreneurs.

'Something wrong with Canning Street?' I ask.

'That's where the funnymen live.' He coughs.

'Funny?'

'Weirdos, wackos, men in dressing-gowns, women in wigs.'

'Know any of them?'

'Not me,' growls Alfred, his neck reddening above the uniform. 'Not my slice of pork-pie, if you know what I mean.'

'Well, I'll let you know how I get on,' I say quietly, as he opens the rear door to let me out. 'Wait for me here, I may be a while.'

A church clock is tolling six as I stand in the yellow glow of a street-lamp outside number thirty-two, taking deep breaths and listening for confirmatory sounds. There is no one on the street, but I feel I am being watched. The house is a two-up, two-down pebbledash terrace, built by a patrician mine-owner for deserving pit-workers. Modest as it is, it has two doorbells, indicating multiple occupancy. A foot-long *mezuzah* decorates the right-hand doorpost, which needs a coat of paint. The *mezuzah*, I know, contains four passages of Scripture, a reminder on entry and exit of the bond between God and man. The devout plant a kiss on it in passing.

I raise my arm towards the lower bell, marked 'Katzenberg'. Then I hear the sound of a violin being expertly tuned, each string touched with the bow and tweaked at the nail. I wait for the music to follow.

It is a *nigun* from another world, a soul-wrenching lament with Hebrew words by the martyred Hannah Szenesz, who parachuted into Nazi-ruled Hungary, was captured, tortured, put to death. *'Eli, Eli, she-lo yigamer le'olam,'* she prays. 'My God, my God, may it never end . . .' And I am thinking, in perfect metre, 'Eli, Eli, who never came home from the hall . . .'

Pressing the bell sharply, I stop the melody in mid-note. Heavy footsteps approach. The door opens. The man's features are obscured by the hall light behind him. He wears a large skullcap and a belted black gaberdine, a *capota*. Daunted, I murmur, 'Good evening.'

'Can I help you?' he asks, in an unmistakable resonance.

'Dovidl?' I venture.

'Mottl,' he replies serenely. 'I have been expecting you.'

# 7

# Still Alive

The house is as Peter Stemp has described it, dark and narrow, extended rearwards to provide extra bedrooms. It feels overcrowded yet uncramped, the corridor and staircase bare of clutter. The smells intermingle; it is impossible to tell at a sniff what is being cooked among the myriad human emanations, but the effect is not malodorous. The house feels at ease with itself.

Its master leads me down three short steps into a congested front room, with an upright piano in one corner and tightly packed glass-fronted bookcases around two walls. His library consists, at a glance, entirely of Talmudic tomes and commentaries. There is not one book with non-Hebrew letters on the spine, let alone a music shelf with lovingly leatherbound albums of favourite pieces. The room is a den of religious studies and I feel as intrusive within it as a carnivore before the Buddha.

Dovidl gives me a high-backed chair beside the gas fire that Peter used to light on Sabbath. He calls, 'Mama!' to summon someone, presumably his wife. He has, typically, stolen the initiative and left me lagging in his slipstream.

'What do you mean you have been expecting me?' I demand wintrily.

He picks up a newspaper from the outsized dining table. 'Look here in the *Telegraph*.' He points. 'The Simmonds Award given to my former *Shabbes-goy*, Peter. I thought you might recognise his *rubato* – and that Peter wouldn't keep his mouth shut. Did you ever know a teenage boy who could keep a secret?'

'I could,' I declare.

'You were different,' affirms Dovidl. 'We were different ... Anyhow, I saw you were in the area and thought you might drop in, so I arranged to be home tonight. Normally I teach late at the *yeshiva*.' He makes it sound so simple, as if no other explanation might conceivably be required.

A woman in her late forties enters the room, a dozen years younger than Dovidl but prematurely stooped, perhaps from many pregnancies. Her cheeks are lined, her lips chapped. I cannot discern more of her disposition since her forehead is covered to the eyebrows by a headcloth and her eyes religiously refuse to engage with mine. Her husband, by open contrast, seems unaffectedly happy.

'Mama,' says Dovidl, 'this is Mr Martin Simmonds, from the family I stayed with in London during the war.'

'Pleased to meet you, Mrs Rapo – Katzenberg,' I greet her, rising and extending a hand. Mama keeps her hands pointing downwards at her sides. I remember that ultra-orthodox women avoid touching men – even, at certain times of the month, their own husbands. She registers my presence with a nod of her makeshift bonnet.

'Mr Simmonds was my boyhood companion,' Dovidl tells her slickly. 'We grew up together but we have lost touch over the years.

We have much to catch up. Perhaps some refreshments? Thank you, Mama.' I wonder why he does not address her by name. Then I remember that the devout reserve the use of personal names for private moments, fiercely shielding their love from prurient ears.

'Where does Katzenberg come into it?' I demand, once his wife has left the room.

'A criminal alias,' grins Dovidl. 'Actually, the married name of a cousin of mine who was murdered in Majdanek. As you know, we remember the dead by giving their names to the newborn. I lost thirty-nine members of my immediate family to Hitler – that's parents, siblings, aunts, uncles and cousins. I have been blessed, thank God, with eleven children. I gave each one three forenames, but was left with six relatives who remained unnamed – my cousin Fayge, her husband Chaim Katzenberg and four children. By chance when I came here and had to forge a new identity, I unthinkingly took Fayge's married surname, as if by divine will. So everything has worked out for the best, no name has been forgotten.'

'Except Rapoport,' I nudge.

He shrugs, expressionlessly. 'A surname is meaningless,' he rationalises, unwittingly contradicting himself. 'We only took the wretched things in the eighteenth century because the *goyim* needed to tell us apart from one another for the purpose of collecting taxes. It's Hebrew names that matter. Each one is home to a soul.'

A lissom girl of sixteen or so – long black hair to her shoulders, long black skirt to the floor – knocks at the door and enters with a tray of coffee, biscuits, liqueurs and dried fruits. 'My daughter Basya-Beyla,' introduces Dovidl. 'Named after my baby sister, the one I never saw.'

The girl, Peter's unattainable beloved, smiles at me shyly and steals a fig from under her father's arm, giggling as she runs from the room. Dovidl pours coffee and Cognac for us both, murmuring a benediction before he sips. I, bareheaded, murmur amen. 'Technically speaking,' he reflects, 'I should have taken something to eat first and said a blessing over it before I had a drink, but I was gasping for a Cognac and I wanted to toast your arrival with a *lechayim*. It has been a long time. Tell me, do you have children? Grandchildren? Have you brought pictures? It is so good to see you, it has been too long.'

He is taking charge again, denying my right to outrage. 'For heaven's sake,' I expostulate, 'there are more important things we need to clarify.'

'Not tonight,' says Dovidl quietly. 'All in God's good time. Tonight we will go back to being brothers, enjoying each other's good fortune. Tomorrow, I will tell you everything.'

'How do I know you will be here tomorrow?' I snap.

'Look at me,' he chuckles, 'I am an overweight sixty-one-year-old grandfather with a dozen dependants and a car that won't run more than fifty miles without packing in. Where do you think I am going to disappear to?'

He has lost none of his charm, or persuasiveness. I can never trust him again, but his arguments are irrefutable and I have no choice but to play at his tempo. So for the next few hours we exchange family trivia, avoiding contention, as children and grandchildren troop in and out, some replenishing our refreshments tray, others depleting it. The young men sport curly sidelocks and wear shiny *capotas*. The women wear housecoats and headscarves. The hubbub is constant – doors slamming, kids yelling, water flushing, someone singing – but there is a calm about the house that is absent from my own, a sense of shared contentment and earthly purpose.

Dovidl explains that he has converted the upper floor into a separate flat for his eldest daughter, Pessia, and her husband, a *yeshiva* student whom he has undertaken to support for five years.

They already have three children – 'The last of my names,' he smiles – with a fourth on the way.

His progeny regard me with mild curiosity. '*Iz der choshuvdikke gast a Yid?*' one of the little kids pipes up, in Yiddish vernacular – is the important guest Jewish? In my own eyes, and Peter Stemp's, unmistakably. But with head uncovered in the house of devout Jews, I could be a passing Mormon for all the tribal affinity they sense. Dovidl assures them that I have a Jewish heart and that my family saved his life during the terrible war. They look at me again, as if at a museum exhibit, and whisper behind cupped hands. One of the older lads engages me in polite chit-chat in basic English – did I have a good journey? where am I staying? is my hotel comfortable? Dovidl beams patriarchally over his brood.

'"A righteous man",' I compliment him, '"will flourish like a palm tree, like a cedar in the Lebanon he will rise."'

'"*Plantati in domo Domini*",' he replies in near-Vulgate, fresh from Father Jeffries' class, '"*in atriis Dei nostri florebunt.* Those who are planted in the House of the Lord will flourish in the courts of our God."'

'"They will still bear fruit in old age",' I reply, nodding at his ample patriarchy, '"fat and vigorous they shall be."'

'"*Lehagid ki yoshor Adonoy*",' pipes up a teenaged son in yeshivist Hebrew. '"*Tsuri veloy avlosoh boy.*"'

'Meaning?' demands Dovidl.

'"To tell",' says the boy, in diffident English, '"that Hashem, our God, is upright. He is my rock, there is no . . . injustice in him."'

'Do they play an instrument?' I ask the patriarch.

He shakes his shaggy beard. 'They study Torah, it takes up all their time.'

'*Tateh zol spielen eppes?*' squeaks a grandchild on his knee.

He beams again, delighted that the Yiddish-raised infant has intuited his way into an English conversation. No, he chides, he will not be playing tonight, for this is a night of reunion.

At ten, I stretch and prepare to leave. 'What time shall I come tomorrow?' I ask.

'I will collect you from your hotel at eleven,' says Dovidl, a half-beat too hastily.

'I have a car and driver, I can come here,' I offer.

'No, better that we should discuss things somewhere private and undisturbed,' he insists. 'This house, you can see, is like Piccadilly Circus.'

'Or Covent Garden market,' I mutter, loud enough for him to hear.

He shoots me a withering look. That pleases me. The past, then, is a faraway country for Mr Katzenberg, but not a neutral state. It has the capacity to strike, through me, at his mask of serenity and monochromatic garb. Missiles and misdeeds from our common locker can still hurt him. He shows me to the front door with almost indecent bustles. I ask him to say goodbye for me to his wife, and walk out without a backward glance.

Alfred grumbles all the way back to the Royal – how could I have kept him waiting so long without so much as a cup of tea, and in a part of town where no one speaks the lingo? I tell him to take the morning off, ignoring his moans now that my quest is accomplished and my riddles are about to be resolved.

The sensation that fills me is not so much elation or relief as raw empowerment. I am no more than moderately pleased to find Dovidl alive, having long given him up for lost. What thrills me beyond the symmetry of reunion is the breathless edge of discovery and the weapon I wield over him. Albert Einstein must have felt like this the night before relativity was revealed.

I am about to grasp the mighty truth and, with it, the capacity to destroy a world.

His destiny is finally in my hands. Should I wish, I can avenge myself by exposing his nefarious past to the pure souls he has raised. He will not want them to know of his market tarts and gambling dens, less still of his broken obligations to the family that gave him a home and treated him like a son. My presence has, after the initial welcome, made him uncomfortable. He will not sleep soundly tonight. That is a first payment. But there is more to my elation than the tick of debt collection. For the first time in our relationship, I find myself in control. For the first time in forty years, I have ceased to be a victim of circumstance and can begin to dictate the course of events. Starting tomorrow.

The telephone in my suite at the Royal signals 'message waiting', but I cannot be bothered to check it. I turn on the teletext for world news, and flick through the diplomatic debris of the now-ended Gulf War. In Israel, people are dancing in the streets at the lifting of the Iraqi Scud-missile threat. I rejoice with them, for a cloud has drifted from my skies and I can sleep without fear of further catastrophe.

On my bedside table I review a plastic parade of homoeopathic and chemical relaxants and sleeping pills, ready for ingestion. I sweep up the lot in the crook of an arm, march into the bathroom and empty each container down the toilet, flushing and reflushing until the last pill has disappeared. No more props for me. I will take life as it comes and take my rest when I am ready.

The telephone jangles next morning at eight. It is Myrtle, in the accusative.

'Where were you last night, dear? Why didn't you ring me back? I was worried.'

'Everything's fine, dear, just went to bed a bit late, interminable meetings and late supper.'

'Well, never mind that. I need you to come back tomorrow instead of Friday. The Brents are coming to dinner and I'd like you to help me with some shopping and choosing the wines.'

The Brents are her trophy guests: Lord and Lady Brent, formerly Simon and Joyce Whitehill (Weisberg), a pair of Finchley creeps who got ennobled for donations to Mrs Thatcher's party and took their lordly name from the local shopping centre. Simon is an empty-headed accountant, Joyce a bridge-player too far. Myrtle flutters about them like an Edwardian scullery-maid, mopping up their spilt drinks and *bons mots*, all but bloody curtsying. I refresh their drinks, mutter, 'That's interesting', slump back in the divan and think wanly of England. The Brents make me want to emigrate.

'Sorry, dear, simply impossible.' I sigh with maximum sincerity. 'Far too much to do up here, all sorts of interesting possibilities emerging. I'll fill you in when I get back.'

'Nonsense, Martin,' she insists. 'You're never going to make any money in that dismal heap of potholes, and you're far too old to be getting into new ventures. You should have retired two years ago, when the doctor told you. You promised me you would take it easy, but on the one occasion I need your help, you pretend that a tiny bit of business is more important. That's so inconsiderate. I sometimes wonder why I still put up with you.'

She has not quite finished, so I place the receiver on the pillow as I get dressed and murmur formulaic emollients each time I pass by. When her irritation is played out, I take the phone and assure Myrtle that she is the most important person in my life. That seems to do the trick.

'You must be back no later than four on Friday.'

'I will be, dear.'

'And for once in your life listen to me and retire.'

'We'll talk about it when I get back.'

'Take care of yourself.'

'And you, dear.'

Retirement is strictly off the agenda: I'm about to start anew. In the toe-tingle moments of descending sleep, a plan of action has begun to form in my mind – a sweet redemption of my empty existence and a satisfactory settling of old scores. I have Dovidl where I want him, and the world will be a different kettle of fish: my oyster, at last.

Wednesday is my favourite day, half-way through the week, a nexus of work and anticipated leisure. Sipping juice and coffee on a tray in my room, I call Sandra Adams, who sounds pleased to hear from me. We fix breakfast for the next morning, and she promises to let me give her career advice. I have an avuncular role to play there, perhaps more.

There is still an hour to kill before Dovidl arrives, and I spend it filling sheets of marbled paper with fervid calculations.

He draws up on the dot of time, in a battered blue Volkswagen camper with a fixed table and benches in the rear. 'Useful for family holidays,' he explains. 'I thought we might take a spin along the coast.'

'Not the ideal time of year.'

'True,' he acknowledges, 'but private.'

He does not want to be seen with me by any of his *frum* friends. I belong to a hidden past. I must be exorcised or placated in a secluded spot before he can resume his orderly, devotional, falsified identity.

Out of Tawburn, up the A529, under the railway bridge and we are soon chuntering along the fringe of a raging North Sea.

The wind is short of gale force, but the waves do not need much whipping to come crashing over the sea defences and on to the esplanade. We are the only idiots driving along this elemental stretch of road.

'It's a test of faith,' I tease.

'I have been out here in worse,' says Dovidl, nerveless as ever. He leans forward on the wheel, peering through rain-slashed patches of windscreen clarity.

I suddenly remember where this road ends. It stops dead at the region's number-one suicide spot, a promontory known as Deadly Head from which a dozen desperate souls, on average, leap each year to certain destruction. The edge is two hundred feet above the sea, which is studded with protruding rocks.

There used to be a fence along the edge, but it was knocked down so often by suicide couples in speeding cars that the council gave up trying to stop them. The only safety measure is an official sign saying, 'Danger – Do Not Approach', and a lifebelt stand that mocks the purpose for which it is intended. Beyond this point, hope can be safely abandoned.

Dovidl pulls up ten feet from the edge of the Head, leaving his engine running. 'To keep us warm,' he explains.

'Turn it off,' I insist, for safety's sake.

Clambering into the back of the van, he produces a Thermos flask of scalding hot tea, two plastic mugs and a packet of home-baked biscuits, which he lays out methodically on a checked tablecloth, which he has spread on the plywood table.

'"God forbid you should die hungry," is my wife's motto.' He grins, seeking male complicity.

'She looks after you well,' I reply.

'I could lose a couple of pounds,' he shrugs, 'but so could you.'

We have nothing, after forty years, to say to one another.

'You owe me an explanation,' I state actuarily.

'I am aware of that,' he says, his bifocal glasses misted by tea, his eyes concealed from inquisition. We are locked in silence in a tin camper, unable to move on until confession has been extracted, and restitution made.

'I owe you more than an explanation,' he says after a while, his Guadagnini-rich voice thickened with winter phlegm. 'The question is, where do I begin?'

# 8

# Time To Tell

The story he has to tell – and he is aching to tell it – rings with the acuity, excitement and self-mockery that I recognise as typically Dovidl. Some of his phraseology belongs to a former age, as if retrieved from a time-capsule, but there is nothing dusty about his tale. He speaks not in the heavy cadences of a rabbinic patriarch but in the breathless snatches of a lad on the make to whom each experience is a half-open door, inviting penetration. Some of his story sounds over-rehearsed, as if he has been held in custody for many years, waiting for his day in court. Other parts sound freshly awoken, as if the revelation that removed him from the real world is daily renewed. 'I cannot tell you,' he says, 'how I have longed to tell someone about it.'

'Your wife?'

'Not a word.'

'Your children?'

'I thought some day, perhaps.'

How much can I believe? Given that one can never trust a traitor, I coat each phrase in suspicion and give him no encouragement to elaborate. Knowing the outcome, I am immune to suspense and scrutinise the details for inconsistency and dissimulation. But his account is so fervid that I find myself accepting, for want of counter-evidence, its impulsive logic. He has, after all, little left to hide and much to fear. For if he deceives me now, he will have denied himself the last chance to face the truth. And if he prevaricates, he knows that I can play havoc with his holy life by exposing him to the faithful as a philanderer and a thief. There is no love left between us. The only enduring bond is truth.

He begins, crumbling a biscuit between his tentacular fingers, twenty-four hours before his disappearance. Leaving the general rehearsal at the underground studio in Kingsway Hall, Holborn, on 2 May – 'a doddle, so easy the music hardly touched the sides' – he was at a loose end for amusement. He rode back to the office with the conductor to cash an expenses chit and, while there, got flirting with Rosalyn, my deeply reserved desk-mate. Rosalyn had been given the afternoon off and, it being sunny, accepted his invitation to a sandwich and a stroll in Regent's Park. They discovered a common aptitude for higher calculus and a shared disdain for western liberalism. Dovidl suggested that since they were having such a good time, why not carry on chatting over tea at our place, which he knew to be empty all afternoon. He was a practised seducer and she, innocently or knowingly, acquiesced.

'Were you aware that I was going out with her?' I interject, with an unbidden growl of sexual jealousy.

'I suppose so,' he grunts. 'I think she may have mentioned something about a date with you.'

'And?'

'And what? You were a student. I was a full-grown artist. I

had certain physical and emotional needs. I am not proud of it, but that's how I was. Can we move on?'

'You deceived me, you took my girl-friend—'

'Whatever I took,' he replies acidly, 'you would have given me, had I bothered to ask for it.'

This assertion is so cuttingly accurate that I decide to ignore it.

'Was she worth it?' I demand.

'Is anything?' he shrugs.

With Rosalyn dressed and gone, he moped around the house in a state of post-coital *ennui*.

'Not your type, then?' I persist.

'It was myself I didn't much care for.'

'You preferred the more motherly sort . . .'

He winces from the depths of his shaggy beard at the reminiscence of his tarts. I proceed to wreak further vengeance, revealing the wretched fate of Florrie, his domestic comforter. He betrays no emotion. 'She was very good to us,' he murmurs collegially, as if to regain common ground. 'Can we move on?'

That evening, he wandered down to his usual haunts but found few distractions. Heeding my father's injunction for once, he was in bed by midnight but tossed and turned until daybreak. When he finally fell asleep, he had a fleeting dream about his mother and awoke to the sound of the doorbell, feeling blessed. Keeping the taxi waiting, he showered and consumed half a grapefruit before grabbing a slice of toast and his fiddle and rushing out. 'I had never felt so calm in my life,' he murmurs. 'It was as if my mother had told me in the dream, "Everything's going to be all right."'

The acoustic rehearsal was over in fifteen minutes. They had done the concerto to perfection the day before in Kingsway

Hall; now all they had to do was check the balances in the cavernous Royal Albert Hall. Dovidl played a short passage with the orchestra while the conductor checked the sound from the auditorium. Then the leader of the orchestra played a theme while Dovidl listened from different parts of the hall. In the turnarounds, they exchanged chippy banter.

'Wearing your lucky socks tonight, Rappo?'

'I'm playing barefoot – remember? I'm a penniless refugee.'

'Well, just make sure the band gets paid.'

'Not unless you chaps pitch in and buy me a nice bunch of flowers.'

'Cheek-y.'

The conductor called for another test, but Dovidl was packing away his instrument and the musicians were huddled around him, alert to his promise. He was superior to any British violinist and they were keen to collar him for future concerts. 'Come across the road for a quick one?' said the leader. Dovidl shook his head, hungry for sunlight. But when he left the artists' entrance at the rear of the hall, the sun had gone and a chill wind was blowing off the Hyde Park tundra.

He shivered in a light jacket, momentarily disconcerted, as red buses rumbled past and a party of black-capped private-schoolgirls clip-clopped their horses towards the park. Fishing in his pocket, he found he had come out without money for a cab. The conductor was in a sour mood after being cut short and there was no one from the office from whom he could cadge a lift. So he crossed the road and stood at the bus-stop, remembering from our boyhood explorations that the seventy-three ran to Oxford Street, from where he could catch a thirteen or fifty-nine to take him home.

A man in a flat cap stood at the stop, a plumber or suchlike by the look of his overalls and tool-kit. He struck a match on a lamp-post and lit a Woodbine. Dovidl patted his pockets and found he had left his cigarette case at home with his wallet. 'Fancy one?' said the plumber.

'Don't mind if I do.'

A cheap fag and a waft of war memories melted most barriers in those frugal times. The plumber had been a bomb-disposal man; Dovidl recalled their skill and courage with UXBs. 'Not English, are you?' said the man, too inquisitively for comfort.

'Good as,' said Dovidl.

'What's that in your toolbag?'

'My whole life,' said my friend, uncomfortable under scrunity.

Three buses growled up together in convoy. The Germans, Dovidl reckoned, would have made the London buses run on time. He let the plumber take the first bus, then mounted the second, climbing up to the smokers' deck and claiming a front seat, the better to enjoy what he told himself, melodramatically, might be his last anonymous journey. By tomorrow, he would not be able to ride public transport unrecognised.

Traffic was heavy and progress slow. A police convoy was escorting some visiting Arab potentate from Buckingham Palace to the serious business of shopping at Harrods, snarling up Knightsbridge in a cloud of exhaust fumes. Dovidl was in no hurry. As the Wellington Arch hazed into view, the sun came out again, tweaking the urban mood from moroseness to light. He felt, like London itself, suspended between glamorous past and uncharted future. No longer an imperial hub, not yet a cosmopolitan lure. Still pitted and pocked from recent trauma, never perhaps to acquire the astutely plotted magnificence of Paris, or Kreisler. He felt at one with London, for the last time in his life.

Looking over his shoulder, he found himself alone on the

deck and sprawled his legs across the front seat. Securing the fiddle-case between his back and the wall of the bus, he closed his eyes contentedly for a moment, expecting to be alerted as the bus gathered speed.

He awoke to find the bus stationary and the engine dead. He was alone on the top deck, looking out over a grubby patch of common ringed by drab Victorian terraces. He shook his watch frantically: one o'clock, nothing to worry about. Where was he? He must have slept through the whole route and wound up at the end of the seventy-three line, which he recalled as being somewhere in nondescript north London, midway between the Arsenal and Spurs football stadia. Not to worry. All he had to do was wait for the next bus into town and he would be home by two, in plenty of time.

He stumbled down the winding staircase, fiddle-case in hand, and checked in with a gloomy bus inspector in a tin cabin, who told him the one-ten 'up West' had been cancelled 'due to staff sickness' but there should be another at one twenty-two. Lacking a book or score to browse he took a stroll in milky sunlight, relishing the mild adventure. He turned into Stoke Newington High Street and was assailed by a familiar smell. Salt pickles, untasted since Warsaw.

An open-fronted shop, the Egg Stores, was selling cucumbers from a barrel on the pavement. He bought one for a penny and ate it on the street, savouring the acrid rush of vinegar, the soft flesh trapped in tight skin. The genuine article, he happily concluded. Next door was Berkovits's, purveying boiled *gefilte* fish, calf's-foot jelly, *gedempte* cabbage, chopped liver.

'Try some?' said Berkovits.

'I've come out without my wallet,' said Dovidl.

'Try today,' said the deli man, 'buy tomorrow fresh for *Shabbes.*'

The taste was intoxicating, transporting him to his grand-mother's Friday-night table with its speckless white cloth, sparkling candlesticks and endless parade of delicacies. The peppery jelly, or *ptchah*, smacked his head like a shot of heroin – yes, he had tried some in the club – and sent him reeling on to the street, giddy with gourmet thrill and painful memory. He took another look at his watch. He could afford to miss the next bus and catch the one after; he no longer needed lunch.

He veered off the busy stretch of shops and took a left, or perhaps a right, then another left, reaching the dead end of a railway embankment with no living soul in sight. The afternoon had turned warm and still. He strode ahead, turned another corner, then another, searching for a way back. There were no cars on the road, no pedestrians on the pavement. If this were not London, it could have been siesta hour in Santa Cruz.

Quickening his pace, he spotted a store shield on the corner ahead: a grocery shop, Frumkin's. He entered to seek directions. Hunks of cheese and butter crowded the marble counter, half covered by fly-paper. The shelves were sparsely filled and there was no civilised hum of refrigeration; a cellar light spurted through gaps in the floorboards. Frumkin, a tubular man in soiled apron and curly sidelocks, was busy with a customer, a black-bearded giant in a frayed greatcoat that kissed his dusty shoes. From what he could gather from their Yiddish burr, Dovidl decided that they were not buying or selling comestibles but discussing a fine point of Torah commentary, the illuminations of some eleventh-century Tosafist on the weekly reading.

'Excuse me,' he coughed.

They ignored him. He peered through the grimy window in

search of passers-by, but the street was tropically deserted. 'I'm sorry to bother you,' he said, slightly louder, 'but could you direct me to the seventy-three bus-stop? I seem to have lost my bearings.'

Neither man looked up. They had to be either deaf, rude or so immersed in their study that the prophet Elijah could ride by on his white donkey without disturbing their concentration. What was he to do? Dovidl was an artist. He knew all a man needed to know about magnetising public attention.

'*Sholom aleikhem!*' he declared. The Hebrew salutation did the trick, coming as it did from a smart young man in a three-piece suit, silk tie, cocky hat – the trappings of gentility, of the hostile, gentile world.

The tall man swerved around and surveyed him with a black-eyed glare. Dovidl returned his stare unblinkingly, pride for pride.

'*Fin voh kimt a yid?*' demanded the shopkeeper, conventionally enough – where does a Jew come from?

'*Fin Varsheh,*' said Dovidl, denoting his birthplace.

'*Und vus mit die mishpocheh?*' came the inevitable corollary: and what's with your family? A family is what people lost, over there.

Dovidl turned his hands outwards, signalling acquiescence to a collective fate. The big man sighed, then asked his name. 'Perhaps I can help you,' he said.

'Some other time,' said Dovidl evasively. 'Right now, I need to find a seventy-three bus. I am expected in town.'

'You don't want to know if, perhaps, any of your people survived?'

The challenge was so direct, it struck him beneath the breast-bone. His heart pounded in response. 'What do you mean?'

'We have people here who were in the Warsaw ghetto, later in the camps. They have excellent memories.'

'You were there?' said Dovidl.

'I was there,' echoed the giant, introducing himself. 'Chaim-Yossef Spielman, once from Medzhin, then Warsaw, Treblinka, Auschwitz, displaced-persons camp, Antwerp, Stamford Hill, *sholom aleikhem.* Peace upon you.'

How sheltered his world had been, thought Dovidl. While this man had gone from freedom to slavery, from hell to redemption, he had gone from St John's Wood to Trinity College, Cambridge. Spielman was his first survivor from Warsaw. He looked nothing like the cadaverous victims shown on the newsreels. Spielman was burly, self-possessed to the point of insolence. He outshone Dovidl in confidence, as Dovidl had outshone me. Against his nature, Dovidl felt himself turning from pack-leader into submissive follower.

'I must be home by four thirty,' he stipulated, calculating his time to the last free moment.

'Don't worry,' said Spielman, in carelessly accented English, 'we will get you home once we have helped a Jew to find his family.'

They walked together into the warren of streets that bordered the railway bank. Step by step, Spielman took his history with terse, impersonal questions. When had he got out? How many left behind? Cousins? Second cousins? All in Warsaw? Anyone in America? The questionnaire sounded practised, unnervingly routine.

They stopped at the open door of a run-down residential house and walked inside. The ground-floor room was unusually large. The partition walls, he realised, had been removed to create a low-ceilinged prayer-hall. The street windows were whitewashed to deter snoopers and the only light was artificial, two strips of neon and a pair of tinny candelabras. Two dozen men and boys sat around the perimeter of the room, swaying and chanting at single lecterns. Spielman strode to the centre, slapped his hand on the Torah stand known as the *bima* and announced: 'I have a Rapoport from Warsaw.'

The chanting dimmed, there was a furrowing of brows. A smooth-cheeked boy slipped out, returning a moment later with a stooped thin man, straggle-bearded in a shining-clean silk *capota*. He was not more than a year or two older than Dovidl. All stood.

'This is Dovid Eli Rapoport from Warsaw, Rebbe,' said Spielman, inclining his head respectfully.

'Sit,' said the man he had addressed as 'Rebbe', indicating chairs. Dovidl inspected him frankly, searching for the authority to which the powerful Spielman had deferred with such humility.

'*Sholom aleikhem*,' said the Rebbe, shaking Dovidl's hand.

'This is the Medzhiner Rebbe,' explained Spielman, unedifyingly.

'They call me the Young Rebbe,' smiled the leader thinly, switching to guttural English. 'My father, peace upon him, was the Alte Rebbe who never lived to grow old. He died in Treblinka, of typhus, God preserve us, just before the liberation. Towards the end, he gave me the task of keeping the book of souls, where we preserve the names of those who died in the sanctification of God's name. That is where we shall search for your loved ones, Mr Rapoport.'

Dovidl looked around. The walls were lined with heavy books, but the Rebbe did not reach out for any of them. His source of reference was, like his authority, invisible. He took Dovidl's hand again, holding it between his own chill palms.

The Alte Rebbe, Spielman explained, had reacted resourcefully to persecution. Powerless to resist by force of arms, he charged his followers to keep a record of every death they saw from the day the Nazis entered their doomed village. The first killings came in his own prayer-house. On the sixth of the ten Days of Penitence, three soldiers shot the Rebbe's *shammes*, his beadle, before selecting twelve men who were taken to the forest, ordered to dig a pit and, when it was deemed deep enough, were beaten to death with their own spades. One, Spielman's elder brother, was kept alive to fill in the grave and spread the terror. He was shot the next day. When the order came for evacuation to Warsaw within the hour, the community was too numbed to flee or resist.

Herded into the ghetto, the Medzhiner Hassidim numbered no more than a hundred families among a hundred thousand, but the Rebbe had given them a mission. Every man, woman and child who died, whether of brutality, starvation or natural causes, every corpse passed on the street, every verified fatality, was to be identified, recorded and written down on lists that were to be sewn into the linings of Medzhiner garments. 'If we cannot perform our duty of purifying and burying each departed soul,' ordained the Alte Rebbe, 'then we must keep its memory alive until a relative can be found to sanctify its memory by saying *kaddish*. That is our special *mitzva*.'

Fearing that their lice-ridden clothes with the sewn-in lists might be stripped from them by so-called hygiene patrols, the Alte Rebbe ordered his Hassidim to memorise the names by reciting them at night after evening prayers. To stimulate the memory he invoked the methods of the *Baal shem tov*, Master of the Good Name, founder of the Hassidic movement. Gathering the simplest of Jews, the shepherd-boys and shleppers who never had a day's education, the *Baal shem* (known by his initials as 'the Besht') proclaimed that literacy was not a prerequisite of piety. Sincerity was more precious in God's eyes than scholarship. 'If you cannot read the words in the prayer-book,' he preached, 'sing unto God a new song.' And the Besht would vocalise a melody of his own, one tune after another, rapt and ecstatic in alternation as he turned dumb hearts to heaven.

The Medzhiner Rebbe, in graver circumstances, resorted to similar means. He composed a *nigun* to the names, solemn but catchy. As the list lengthened, he wove variations on his original theme. Then he added a contrapuntal extension, livelier and foot-tapping. A third melody grew out of that tune, then a fourth. Night after night, it was joined to evensong. On the choking cattle-truck to Treblinka, in the quarries and the barracks, the Alte Rebbe led his Hassidim nightly in *sotto voce* renditions of his deathless Song of Names.

'What were the parents called?' said the Young Rebbe softly.

'My father was Zygmunt,' said Dovidl, 'my mother Esther.'

The Rebbe smiled, and shut his eyes. He began to hum, then to sing, tunefully in a low tenor voice. 'Rapoport, *ay* Rapoport, *ay* Rapoport,' he rhapsodised, patting the arm of his chair. '*Vir hoben* Rapoport, Avrum, Rapoport, Berel *und* Chayeh-Soroh, *mit Kinder* Yossl, Yechiel *und* Leah.' The men and boys in the prayer-room chimed in, a ghostly chorus: 'Rapoport, Chaim-Dovid, Rapoport, Shua-Chaim, Rapoport, Yerachmiel *und* Soro *mit* Yehiel, Shloime, Shneyur-Zalmen *und* Rivke, Rapoport, *ay* Rapoport, *ay* Rapoport, *yehi zikhrom boruch*, may their memories be blessed.'

Dovidl swayed with the melody, wondering if he should take out his fiddle and accompany. The Rebbe's eyelids were unwrinkled, his face tranquil. On and on he sang, *a capella*, running through the Hebrew *aleph-bet* one Rapoport after another. It was not an uncommon name. Rapoport, Dovidl knew, was a conflation of Rav d'Oporto, a rabbi from Portugal, whence thousands of Jews fled the Inquisition in 1497. There were Rapoports all over Poland and the Baltic states, linked only by place of origin and common fate.

The second *nigun* was more intricate than the first. Dovidl found himself harmonising under his breath, assimilating its cadences. Music, these rabbis must have known, clings to the brain like a barnacle. In the aged and confused, it is the faculty that fades last, the final memory. For the faceless victims, it was a lasting memorial that could never be denied or vandalised. The swirl of names continued in song. When the Young Rebbe reached '. . . Rapoport Shimon-Zelig *und* Esther *mit Kinder* Pessia, Malkeh, Basya-Beyla', Dovidl started in recognition. The Rebbe gave a *fermata* gesture, ending the chorus with 'Rapoport, *ay* Rapoport, *ay* Rapoport, *yehi zikhrom boruch.*'

'Zygmunt was Shimon-Zelig in Hebrew?' he asked.

Dovidl nodded, tears spilling from his eyes.

'Blessed be the Judge of truth,' said the Rebbe. 'My father knew him. He was in our transport to Treblinka, August 1942,' he confided, still swaying. 'When we arrived, they put women and children to the left and sent them to the gas. The date of your mother's death and your sisters', the date for you to say *kaddish*, *ay* Rapoport, is the seventeenth of the month of Av, remember that, seventeenth of Av, *ay* Rapoport.

'Some men were spared for maintenance tasks. Your father, Shimon-Zelig or Zygmunt, was in the same barracks as the Alte Rebbe, on the same work-detail, the same forced march when the camp was closed. He gave up his holy soul, on the twelfth of month of Shevat, the month of Shevat, on the twelfth you must say *kaddish*, *ay* Rapoport.

'And one more Rapoport, a cousin Chaye-Rivke, came out alive from the place of destruction. *Ay* what happened to her, Rapoport. She was set free by the Russians and set out to walk south, to the south, until she came to a port and hid in a ship that took her to the Land of our Fathers. And there she met a man called Shteinberg, who changed his exile name to Har-Even in Hebrew and worked on a farm near the Holy Town of Safed, *ay* Rapoport. And she married, *ay* Rapoport, and she has a child, God be thanked, *ay* Rapoport. May God wipe a tear from all faces and remove His people's disgrace from the earth, for that is the word spoken by the mouth of God.'

The Young Rebbe fell silent, opened his eyes. His face, like the prayer-room, looked as if it had never seen daylight. 'Ich bin der Welt abhanden gekommen,' came to Dovidl's mind – the title of a lonely *Lied* by an Austrian Jew, Gustav Mahler: 'I am removed from the world'. This unworldly rabbi, barely older than himself, had experienced all the world's evil and emerged, somehow, secure in his unworldliness, brandishing his father's song like a shield against oblivion. He was, in the prophet's words, 'a brand plucked from the burning'.

This was, Dovidl knew, no time to quote Scripture or *Lieder*. He should have felt a wave of relief at the post-mortem verdict. His parents and sisters were dead, as he had feared; but a cousin, a scrap of flesh and blood, lived on as a pioneer in Galilee. He was not alone, not without kin. In the song of death, there was life. He could seek consolation and, freed of uncertainty, start anew. But relief was refractory, denying him ease. He felt no lifting of burden, rather a great weight settling on his shoulders, rendering his arms leaden and useless. How will I play if I can't lift a bow? he wondered briefly.

A razor blade flashed expressionlessly in the Young Rebbe's right hand. 'What's that?' said Dovidl impassively.

'I am going to make a cut in the jacket, and another in the shirt,' said the Rebbe. 'The mark of bereavement.'

Spielman's arm extended protectively, possessively, around his shoulders as the cloth was cut, then ripped, and a verse uttered: '"May His presence comfort you among the mourners of Zion and

Jerusalem."' The men and boys echoed the benediction, lining up to shake his hand, and look away.

'Where will he sit *shiva*?' said the Rebbe, in Yiddish.

'*Bei mir*,' volunteered Spielman.

'But I must leave,' protested Dovidl.

'First one must mourn,' said the Rebbe, incontrovertibly. It was upon those words that Dovidl's life turned.


The gale that rocked the camper van has given way to spattering hail, blown in gusts against the tin walls. Katzenberg rises, flexes his legs, pours another mug of tea and offers me a polite biscuit, mutely declined. 'I make no excuses,' he insists. 'I do not want you to feel that I was acting under duress of any kind, physical or moral. I was alert to what was going on and could, at any moment, have asserted my will, got up and left. I was not their prisoner. But I was in awe of the Young Rebbe and his terrible song, and I felt sheltered by Chaim-Yossef Spielman, by his great size, his gentleness and self-assurance.

'When I saw this giant of a man doing unquestioningly as the Young Rebbe told him, and the Rebbe himself acceding to the wishes of his dead father, whose authority stemmed from a hundred generations of rabbis and scholars stretching back to the editors of the Talmud, I felt like a foot-soldier on the field of battle, a cog in a towering machine, driven by vastly superior forces.

'All my life, as a musician, I had been trained to see myself as a remarkable individual, a unique voice. Suddenly, I was relieved of that responsibility. I had nothing to prove. I was just a Jew, subject to the same observances and obligations as any other – joined, as a Jew, to all that we had shared and lost since the Exodus from Egypt, from the Holy Land, from Spain and Portugal, and now from Poland and Germany. I had no singular purpose: and I no longer suffered alone. This is what captivated and detained me. That is why I stayed. Does that make any sense, Martin?'

I refrain from giving him encouragement, but of course it does. It sounds like a typical late-twentieth-century epiphany. My susceptible friend was enticed by a fanatical sect, stripped of his individuality and reconditioned as a zombie. No, I correct myself, that's not quite right. He is, even now, too sharp and self-questioning to suspend irony and accept the immutable yoke of faith. His surrender must have come in several layers – impelled by the trauma of his family's fate, the aura of the Young Rebbe and the insidious interference of this Spielman who, he had decided, could walk him through the minefield of life more effectively than I could have done. Envy invades my entrails at this extra betrayal.

'When you stepped out of that prayer-house,' I cross-question him, 'was there not a moment when you looked at your watch and thought, I need to be somewhere else, I have a concert tonight, people are depending on me? Did you not give the real world another thought?'

'Once I left the Rebbe,' he replies evenly, 'I was never for one instant alone, or undistracted.'

He was taken to sit on the floor of the living room of Spielman's cramped flat, the top storey of a cold-water house that the big man shared with four Medzhiner families. Spielman, his heavily pregnant wife and their two infant sons had three rooms and a kitchen; the toilet and bathroom were two floors down. Mrs Spielman – her husband addressed her as Havaleh – wordlessly served refreshments and meals through the week of *shiva*. When Dovidl apologised for the inconvenience, she gave a tired smile. 'It's a *mitzva*,' she said briskly. 'May you know no more sorrow.'

Three times a day, morning, noon and night, a dozen men arrived for prayers, at the end of which he recited a stumbling *kaddish* and they intoned ragged amens. The rest of the time, he sat on the floor and received visitors – strangers who confided their histories and asked after his loss. Between visitors, Spielman would amble in to keep him company. He talked about the travel agency he was setting up, selling passages to Israel and America. He displayed no curiosity about Dovidl's circumstances, nor about the violin that was stowed beside him. His chief concern was that his guest should have the correct conditions to acquit his eternal duties of mourning.

Spielman explained the rules of *shiva*, stringently and sensitively. The mourner is forbidden all pleasures, even the relief of the marriage bed. He may not wear shoes or clean garments, shave or shower, work or cook. His reading is confined to the books of Job and Lamentations. He may leave the house only on the Sabbath, when sorrow and suffering are imagined to cease even in the furnaces of hell. The week of mourning, explained Spielman, is a tunnel of anguish with light at its end. To Dovidl's rational mind, it sounded like a ritualised deterrent to morbidity and suicide.

When Dovidl questioned Spielman about his own history, the big man was unforthcoming. 'I have mourned the past,' he said. 'Now I look ahead to the days of redemption, to the coming of Messiah.'

'Your faith never faltered, even in the camps?'

'Someone in Auschwitz,' said Spielman, 'a Communist, once said to me, "Your God must be evil to inflict such torments on innocent children." I replied, "It is man that is evil and inflicts torments. God we cannot understand. If we could, He would not be God."'

'Does He answer your prayers?' asked Dovidl.

'Always,' winked Spielman. 'Generally in the negative.'

On the seventh day at noon, the Young Rebbe came by. He raised Dovidl by the hand from his stool and led him to the dining table, where cold fish was served, with potato salad. Blessings were recited and the Rebbe quoted passages from the Sages about the end of days and the promise of redemption. The Song of Names was sung, start to finish. Dovidl recited *kaddish* and the men rose to leave.

'What happens now?' he asked Spielman, who looked to the Rebbe.

'That is the guest's decision,' said the Rebbe. 'He has fulfilled the ultimate duty of the commandment to honour his parents. Now he can remain with us, study Torah and become an *ehrliche Yid*, a true Jew – or he can go back where he came from, in peace.'

Twelve pairs of Medzhiner eyes turned upon Dovidl as he weighed the options for the rest of his life, his first cognitive act for a week. He stroked his chin and found it prickle-bearded. He looked for guidance but the Rebbe's eyes were averted. He had noticed that the Rebbe avoided the use of personal pronouns. To address another person directly would be a discourtesy, an intrusion on his four cubits of privacy. To determine another's life was unthinkable. The Rebbe, when pressed, gave principles, not performance instructions. Decisions were a matter of individual conscience. His was the least prescriptive of leaderships.

It was Spielman who forced the issue. 'Forgive me, Rebbe,' said the big man, 'but our guest cannot go back. The police are looking for him.'

At the mention of 'police', the Rebbe flinched. Dovidl was not surprised. He had learned by now that certain nouns, innocuous to him, were loaded for Medzhiners with negative meaning. A necktie, for instance. None of the Hassidim wore a tie, even on the Sabbath. When he wondered why, Spielman explained that in knotting a tie a man inadvertently made the sign of the cross, and that was to be avoided at all costs.

He choked on his toast one morning when, after grace, Dovidl had casually quoted a Psalmic verse in Latin. *'Vus iz dus?'* barked Spielman.

'A classical language,' said Dovidl.

'Classical?' thundered his host. 'It's the tongue of the destroyer who laid waste our Temple. May it rot and be forgotten for ever, amen.'

Dovidl did not quibble with the prejudice, reinforced as he knew it was by memories of incense-choked churches from which priests preached murderous pogroms upon harmless neighbours. Spielman was a village Jew from the old world: he lacked the serenity of a classical education. The gulf between his response and modernity's was unbridgeable. Similarly, the Young Rebbe's suspicion of metropolitan policing was understandable. To him, the word 'police' did not mean bobbies on the beat and flat-hatted inspectors with departmental budgets. It meant oppressor, enforcer, agent of hostile authority. The Rebbe's pallor turned cadaver-grey at the mention of police and his eyes shrank within their sockets.

Spielman had laid out on the table a broadsheet newspaper with Dovidl's portrait on the front page. He recited details of the nationwide search for the missing violinist, a thousand-pound reward offered for information leading to his safe return. The Rebbe listened mutely, fingering the outer margins of the page as if he expected to find peripheral commentaries by the Tosafists.

'You could turn me in and claim the reward,' said Dovidl

jocularly, smiling at the nervous Medzhiners. In his own mind, he was free to turn up at our house as if nothing had happened. He would explain his disappearance as a temporary amnesia, of the type suffered by the crime writer Agatha Christie in 1926 during a crisis in her marriage. Such episodes occasionally befall artists under stress and are readily forgiven. He would simply walk in, claiming to have slept rough for a week. In his ripped and grimy clothes and unshaven face, the story would ring true and the immensity of our relief would absolve him from detailed investigation. The prodigal's return – not, perhaps, the most apt of metaphors to mention in Old Testament company. He must take care to avoid apocryphal allusions in the Medzhiners' presence.

'I can handle this,' he told Spielman. 'The police will be relieved to shut the case and no one will ever know where I have been.'

Spielman looked to the Rebbe, who shook his head. 'It is not safe,' frowned the Rebbe. 'The police might beat him with sticks, or stand him all night in a barrel of freezing water until he confesses.'

'But this is England, Rebbe, not Poland,' objected Dovidl.

'England,' said the Rebbe, witheringly, 'is also a Christian country.'

A huge hand fell upon his shoulder. 'The Rebbe is unhappy,' said Spielman. 'We must do what the Rebbe deems best.'

A week before, Dovidl would have scorned such meekness. Now he found it liberating. He no longer needed to belong to the class that 'makes things happen'. He could sit back and let them happen, confident in the protection of Chaim-Yossef Spielman and the wisdom of the Medzhiner Rebbe. Together, they had relieved him of the unbearable expectations of talent and admitted him to a world where all were equal in the sight of God and subject equally to His eternal laws, as interpreted by rabbis down the generations.

'He may remain, perhaps, until the fuss has died away,' murmured the Rebbe who, Dovidl noted, was culturally incapable of issuing an order. For all the immensity of his authority, the Rebbe ruled by inference. The Yiddish he used knew no words of command.

'Stay with us,' urged Spielman, 'and we shall teach you the whole Torah while you stand on one leg, as the sage Hillel did with a sceptic. You will discover the ways of your fathers—'

'My father was not *frum*,' interjected Dovidl.

'But your grandfather was, forgive me, and his fathers before him. Did they hand down myths and lies, father to son, generation to generation? Your father, peace upon him, may have departed from tradition as many Jews did when they moved to the city and into the twentieth century. But this was an aberration. After Hitler, many who survived are coming back to Torah. This is the only truth we possess. Come, learn it a while, then go. What do you have to lose?'

Nothing, thought Dovidl. Nothing of value, beyond world fame and more money than he could spend in six lifetimes.

'Nothing much,' he told Spielman.

'It may be a good thing that he should stay indoors for another week,' said the Rebbe, 'until the beard is thick and black and no policeman or informer will recognise him on the street.' In another week, thought Dovidl, he would not know himself in the mirror.

The Rebbe's concern, Spielman confirmed privately, was not so much for the fugitive's safety as for the welfare of certain of his Hassidim whose passports and livelihoods were not, as he put it, 'strictly kosher'. Many had arrived in Britain on false papers. They made a living by shifting untaxed diamonds between the great cutting and trading centres of Antwerp, Johannesburg, Tel

Aviv and Manhattan's 47th Street. As survivors, they did what was needed to eat and live. When desperate, they resorted to fraud and theft, justifying the acts as needful and non-violent. No bones were broken; none stole more than he required for subsistence; none worked more than was minimally necessary to provide food, clothing and a roof over his family's heads.

Work was incidental to the Medzhiners' lives. These Old Believers lived from one Sabbath to the next, rushing to market on Friday mornings, then to the ritual bath, the *mikve*, and finally home to change into a golden *capota* and fur *shtreiml* hat. All week long they scrimped and denied themselves luxury. On Friday night the table was decked with delicacies, the silverware shone in candlelight, the Song of Songs was chanted, eyes sparkled and husbands and wives renewed their marriages in an erotic compact with the holy Sabbath. Relieved of mortal stresses, they came together in mutual harmony and cosmic unity.

From Friday sunset to the counting of three stars on Saturday night, mundanity was suspended. No kettle was boiled in a Medzhiner kitchen, no light-switch flicked, letter opened, telephone answered or doorbell rung; no object was carried outside the house, even in a pocket; nothing was allowed to disturb the unearthliness of the Sabbath. And when, on Saturday night, the silver *kiddush* cup overflowed with sweet red wine and a blessing bade farewell to the beloved Sabbath, a spicebox was sniffed to restore men and women to wakefulness, as if from a dead faint.

Such was the trance of transcendence in which Dovidl passed his month with the Medzhiners, absorbing their archaic rhythms. He likened it to discovering a medieval manuscript, its music a daze of hieroglyphics and its instruments rough to the unattuned ear – 'like swapping my Guadagnini for a sackbut'. It required him to suspend his perception of what is beautiful and what is music.

Only when such preconceptions were set aside could he appreciate the marvels of a different value system.

Hassidim who had visited him in mourning now came by daily to teach him Torah with Rashi's exegesis and, in the afternoon, *The Well-laid Table* of the sixteenth-century Safed sage Josef Caro, the catalogue of the laws and customs for observant Jews. It reminded him, in its clarity of purpose and timeless certainty, of Johann Sebastian Bach's *Well-tempered Clavier*, which contains preludes and fugues for each of the major and minor keys – a mode for every circumstance. He did not articulate this allusion since none of the Hassidim would have recognised Bach's name, but the affinities between religious and musical practice seemed to him more than incidental. Both demanded daily hours of application and a comparable single-mindedness. He wondered briefly if he were not exchanging one servitude for another.

By way of relief, the Hassidim told him fabulous legends of former rebbes, recited in a sing-song that evolved, at times, into actual song: their melodic legacy. Had the *Baal shem tov* (1696–1760), it suddenly occurred to him, ever come across J. S. Bach (1685–1750)? They were almost exact contemporaries, ten years either way. Both had travelled widely: imagine an encounter at a wayside inn, Bach and the Besht. And why was the *Well-tempered Clavier* known to pianists as the 'Old Testament of the Keyboard'? Bach was not the tiniest bit Jewish, but had it not taken a Jew, Felix Mendelssohn, to revive the performance of his music after a century of neglect? Dovidl kept these speculations to himself, swallowing his cross-cultural confusion. Over time, the distinctions dissolved in his mind and he came to the conclusion that one form of devotion was not that different from any other, and none had a monopoly on divine revelation.

Dovidl's Hebrew, barely functional at his barmitzvah, picked up fluency and speed under continuous usage. His Yiddish, forgotten since infancy, returned intact. His appetite for knowledge was ravenous, overwhelming several of his teachers. They referred his questions, some heretical, to the Young Rebbe, who knew all but did not always vouchsafe an answer. The Rebbe was their repository of all knowledge but, like Josef in Egypt, he eked it out according to need, saving enough in his granary for future famine. Dovidl felt sure that, if he approached him with a musical problem, the Rebbe, with his fine ear and brilliant mind, would resolve it by force of logic without being able to read a score. And if, to master the issue, he needed to decipher notes on the page, he would learn to read music in an hour from a printed tutor. No musician that Dovidl had ever heard could crack a theological conundrum or speak meaningfully about the origins of the universe. The Rebbe, he reckoned, had a wealth of information and an analytical ability that was superior to anything he had encountered. The very qualities he had once admired in me were, once more, outshone.

One morning, as Spielman was coaching him in the Aramaic vernacular of the mystic *Kabalah*, the Young Rebbe came over to their synagogue lectern. Both rose.

'It may, forgive me,' said the Rebbe, 'be necessary to transfer the guest to a safer place.' He held in his trembling hand a letter from the president of the Board of Deputies of British Jews, alerting the Medzhiner community to their concern for a missing Polish-Jewish violinist and asking for any information to be conveyed, through the Board, to the Metropolitan Police. There was nothing to connect the Medzhiners to the absent musician, but the embossed letterhead made the Rebbe uneasy and the mention of police aggravated his anxiety. 'Away from London,' said the Rebbe. 'In the north of the country, there is a new *yeshiva* with forty students. All of them have dark beards and long *capotas*. A new person will not be noticed there.'

'How long shall I stay?' said Dovidl, marvelling at his own will-lessness.

'A month, a year, as long as you like,' Spielman assured him. 'Then you will come back a *talmid chochem*, a learned man, and we will find you a *shidduch*, a nice girl to marry.'

'When do I leave?' said Dovidl.

'There is a vehicle outside,' said the Young Rebbe, extending a skeletal hand in benediction. No blood seemed to pass through its veins as Dovidl bent to kiss it. It was, he sensed, another of those partings when he would never see the other person again.

It took him a few minutes to collect his violin, his prayer-kit and a change of clothing from Spielman's house. Returning to the prayer-house, he saw a workman on the other side of the street in blue overalls and flat cap, about the same height and build as the plumber at the bus-stop. He ducked into the waiting car, covering his face with a *talit*-bag and telling Spielman, at the wheel, to get a move on. Was he being followed? It hardly mattered now, but he longed to get away and breathe a different oxygen.

They slipped through London's suburban sprawl, past Edmonton where Dr Steiner lay in his lonely grave. Avoiding the A1 highway for fear of police checkpoints, they sidled up through flatland East Anglia to the industrial north-east, stopping three times for petrol, prayers and a chance to admire the yellowing beauty of an early-summer countryside. Two dark men in long black coats swaying over a crop-filled meadow might have aroused local suspicions, but the pair felt safeguarded by the merit of their journey and in the car, for much of the way, they sang a medley of Medzhiner tunes.

It was dark when their Vauxhall pulled up outside Oldbridge Yeshiva, a thriving college concealed behind the residential front-ages of three terraced houses. It consisted of a prayer-hall, tutorial rooms, kitchen and dormitory quarters. Dovidl was assigned a bed in a box-room, shared with three others. It was so narrow that only one man could rise and dress at a time, but the cellmates were courteous to the newcomer and he experienced no friction.

His formal instruction commenced the next morning, after prayers and a generous breakfast, with a Talmud session that left him floundering. It began with two men clutching a prayer shawl, or *talit*, each claiming ownership, so far as he could tell. But the text veered off the disputed point into unconnected byways: the validity of an oath, the meaning of money, the nature of sacrifice, the prophet Elijah – all without pause or punctuation, and with contrasting opinions coming left and right from rabbis in different centuries and countries. At the end of two hours he felt dejected, defeated, ready to leave.

After coffee, the students paired off in the prayer-hall to revise the half-page they had just been taught. Dovidl was put together with Yoel, formerly of Vilna, to whom he expressed bemusement. 'But that's what makes Talmud so engaging,' said Yoel. 'There are usually three separate issues being discussed, linked by one, or more, of the thirteen recognised methods of exegesis. Each issue has at least two sides, and to each side there are conflicting opinions. On each opinion, there are fifteen centuries' worth of commentaries, right up to the present day. The trick is to keep the main issue in mind while whittling down subsidiary arguments, one by one. When you get it right, there is nothing more satisfying.'

Tackled in pairs, with much adversarial cross-questioning, the students teased the text into manageable strands. It was, thought

Dovidl, not unlike studying music with Dr Steiner, hearing him apply experience and intuition to the inner meaning of notes. There were more staves to this score, however, than in any opus he had ever seen, more possibilities of interpretation. So complete was his absorption that he yelped with frustration when they had to break for the afternoon prayer.

'Carry on later?' he asked Yoel.

'Not today,' said the Lithuanian. 'Much tougher tractate after lunch – ritual purity. You'll have another partner for that.'

Tuition ended at seven, but most students returned after supper to the study hall, swaying over outsized tomes until midnight and beyond. Resuming with Yoel next morning, Dovidl resolved to test him with a Cambridge conundrum about the act of creation: 'What happened *before* the beginning, when God created heaven and earth?'

Yoel dismembered the proposition effortlessly. The question was founded, he sighed, on a Greek mistranslation of the Hebrew words *bereshit bara* – a phrase that does not mean 'In the beginning God created', but 'In the beginning of God's creation'. The act of creation is continuous, he explained, a process in which humanity is privileged to participate. Before the beginning, there was God. Should the world ever end, He will still be there.

But what, persisted Dovidl, of the idea advanced by some Christian theologians that all God created was order among elements like fire and water, which pre-existed Creation – that order is, as the poet Alexander Pope put it, 'Heaven's first law'? That's irrational, said Yoel. If elements existed before God, how did He get control of them? The organisational hypothesis of Creation contradicts the fundamental Judeo-Christian belief in a *creatio ab nihilo*, which Jews call *yesh me'ayin* – something out of nothing.

'You don't mind me asking?' said Dovidl.

'Ask what you like,' said Yoel. 'Nothing is ruled out in the search for knowledge. You want to know whether the world is a hundred million years old, or five thousand seven hundred and ten, according to our calculations? For us, it's not a burning issue. The Torah tells us that the world was created in six days, but those days are not literal units of time, twenty-four hours each. The Hebrew word for days – *yamim* – is the same as that for seas: immeasurable lengths and depths. A day can be as long as you like. Time in the Torah is relative, as Einstein well knew.'

'Don't you have to believe in some fixity?'

'Our own rabbis are forever challenging the Creation passage. Some of them mischievously decontextualised the second and third words to read: "In the beginning He created God." That, too, is no problem for us. God is *sui generis*. He was, is, ever will be. Now, can we get back to the question of who, exactly, owns this contested prayer-shawl? Rabbi Yossi says . . .'

Dovidl was dazzled. This Lithuanian *yeshiva* student, untutored in science, mathematics and philosophy, had just ripped apart a riddle that regularly confounded divinity scholars at Trinity. His open-door defence of creationism was rooted in rock-solid faith, but it was supple enough to confront contemporary ideas. Where had his partner acquired such analytical skills? 'In Vilna,' grinned Yoel, 'you learn logic before you can walk. The Vilna Gaon, who detested the ecstatic path of the *Baal shem tov*, taught that faith must be founded on iron reason. He abhorred music, mysticism and other sensual stimulants. The road to truth was paved with knowledge.'

That nearly clinched it for Dovidl. The intellectual satisfactions of Talmud – wrestling with a many-headed dispute until clarity broke through – engaged his mind with a totality that music had failed to ignite. The sensation of cracking a problem was almost hallucinogenic, raising him from mortal stupidity into a seemingly higher realm of understanding. The experience was addictive. The more he studied Talmud, the more his mind craved its fix. On fasts and days of mourning, when learning was prohibited, he felt physically deprived.

He was soon marked out as a fast-track candidate for *semicha*, the laying on of hands that would make him a rabbi and teacher, joining him to a continuity of textual interpretation that stretched back to Moses. His first *vort*, or oral dissertation before the entire *yeshiva*, was received with hums of approval and dart-like shafts of brilliant refutation. Oddly, to Dovidl's Cambridge-trained mind, no one ever tested his faith. Belief in God was taken for granted. What mattered was the observance of His commandments. What did Dovidl believe? Not much, at this stage. In my view, he was a victim of post-traumatic stress disorder, acutely vulnerable to the persuasive consolations of a closed community.

Spielman came to visit him after six months, bringing news of the Medzhiner and their devastating tragedy. The Young Rebbe, newly married, had died of a brain haemorrhage at the age of twenty-four, a delayed victim of genocide. His Hassidim were paralysed by grief and fear. The Rebbe had left no child, no dynastic heir. The sect was too small to survive unled. It would have to merge with one of the greater Hassidic courts, losing its autonomy and identity, in order to preserve its melodies, its song of martyred names. There was no home, Spielman regretted, for Dovidl to return to.

He took the dispossession calmly. The *yeshiva* occupied him body and mind. It accommodated his quirks, defused his nefarious urges. He thrived in its cloistered masculinity, feeling safer between its walls than anywhere since leaving his parental courtyard. He was too sharp to be popular, too mysterious to become a teacher's pet. But when he brought out his violin at wedding feasts and twirled off traditional melodies, with his own variations and intuitions, more celestially than these sheltered souls had a right to imagine, Dovidl was accepted on their terms as a *yenuka*, a young genius, whose gift must be sheltered and nurtured.

Days before his *semicha* was confirmed, the *Rosh yeshiva* called him in and, wasting no words, offered him the hand in marriage of his seventeen-year-old daughter, Broche. Dovidl was astonished. 'But you know nothing about me, my family, where I come from . . .' he stuttered. Scholarly lineage was paramount in arranging rabbinic matches, followed by piety and wealth. As a suitor, Dovidl failed on all counts.

'I know enough,' said the *Rosh*, an austere scholar from a Baltic seaport expunged of its Jews, 'and what I do not know, I have closely observed. You are going to be a great rabbi, a light that will shine from our *yeshiva*.'

'He was wrong,' chuckles Dovidl, as the storm blows out the last of its energy across the North Sea. 'I was never ambitious to excel in sacred studies. I had no urge to publish *responsae* and small-print commentaries; my stimulus was the chance to ignite the joy of learning in new classes of students. What I loved best was to watch a young man awaken to the cerebral and sensual love of Torah.

'After my father-in-law passed away they asked me to become *Rosh*, but I did not want the administrative burden, or the representative duties within the *yeshiva* world. He wanted me to be a beacon for the institution, more outgoing than he had been. He recognised my extrovert qualities, but did not appreciate why I could not let them radiate beyond our four cubits. I must have been a bitter disappointment to him, as I was to all my mentors. On his deathbed, I refused his last request.'

His narrative is coming to an end. Account has been rendered, the books balanced. All that remains is to scan the entries, and then – the reckoning. He recounts through tight lips the power struggle that raged on the death of the *Rosh* when the *mashgiach ruchoni*, the spiritual guide and dean of studies, proposed to turn the *yeshiva* into a more modern, outgoing institution. The *mashgiach* wanted to introduce one-year residencies for Jewish grammar-schoolboys after their matriculation, before they entered university. Dovidl opposed the plan ferociously, forming an alliance with fellow recusants to run his Lithuanian study-partner, Yoel, as their candidate for head of college. It was, he wryly reflects, not unlike the election of a new master at Trinity, a bitter, rule-bound contest of principles, personalities and tough practicalities. Yoel was elected Rosh by a nine-to-six majority on the rabbinical council and Dovidl accepted the vacant post of *mashgiach*, mainly to fortify Yoel's resolve to reserve the *yeshiva* for those who intended to dedicate their entire lives to the study of Torah. In the intro-extrospective schism that afflicts every belief system, Dovidl won the battle of the navel-gazers.

'I could not have stayed here, had it become a place of comings and goings, of parents from London dropping off and collecting their classically educated sons,' he admits. 'I wanted no part of the outside world. I could not bear the need to avert my eyes for fear that some nosy parent might recognise my former self and start asking questions. Even now, I cannot go shopping without looking over my shoulder to make sure I am not being followed. By whom? I haven't a clue. But if I see a workman loitering on a street corner, or a teenager staring at my quaint outfit, I think of the inquisitive plumber at the seventy-three bus-stop and quicken my pace or hail a cab. Behind the happy face, Martin, I am a haunted man, hiding a guilty conscience. It has not been as peaceful for me as it may seem, and sometimes I have prayed for it to end.

'My father-in-law, peace upon him, wanted me to make a name as a scholar, but any name I might have made would not have been my own. I hardly know who I am. Chaim-Yossef Spielman furnished me with false papers, as he often did for his travel clients. I got married as Katzenberg. That is the name my children know, and the one that went on my passport when I eventually made a journey to the Holy Land. I wanted to see my only cousin, Chaye-Rivke Har-Even, but in the end I dared not risk exposing my real identity. So Spielman visited her on my behalf while on a pilgrimage to Safed. He reported that she seemed to be a militantly secular Zionist, who served milk and meat together at her table and scorned our sacred faith. We would have had nothing in common, she and I – not even a name, which both of us had changed to suit our post-traumatic circumstances.

'And that's about all there is to say. I have lived here forty years, raised a family, earned a little respect, maybe some affection. My eldest daughter is married to Spielman's son, who is a rabbi in a seminary in New Jersey. The rest of my children, thank God, follow the same path, down to the youngest who studies here in our *yeshiva*. That's the whole story. I am what I have become, not what anybody else has ever wanted me to be.'

He opens his palms on the table-top, a gesture of transparency, of relief and resignation. How much do I believe? Most of it, I suppose, but the question of belief does not bother me much, any more than it does his fellow-rabbis. What a man feels in his heart of hearts is inscrutable to the human eye, therefore immaterial. What counts is his conduct, what he does with his life. Account has been duly rendered. Now it is time to calculate penalties and the methods of repayment. A plan of action is forming in my mind.

I purse my lips and allow a haze of tension to cloud the cabin. I stare him in the eye, challenging him to flinch. Dovidl refuses the childish dare. A long minute of silence elapses. He releases a sigh in instalments, *ay-ay-ay-ay-ay*. I feel an urge to sneeze, and rustle about in my pocket for a handkerchief.

He rises suddenly, announcing that he must step outside for a call of nature. He slams the door of the camper-van and strides away in his billowing black coat, halting with his feet apart at the edge of the cliff, two hundred feet above the wintry sea. His back towards me, he looks up at the scudding sky and bends slightly at the knee, as men do when they are about to let go.

# 9

# Payback Time

Waiting for Dovidl, I uncap a pen and sketch a rapid plan on the back of a makeshift score-sheet from the Tawside Young Musicians' Competition, which seems so long ago. There will be calls to make, budgets to calculate, staff to engage and train. This will not be a minor operation, but it is within my grasp. The skills to bring it off have been lying dormant. I can hardly wait to start.

Looking up after several minutes, I see a great emptiness of sky and sea at the spot where Dovidl last stood. Alarmed, I step outside and look around. The wind, much becalmed, whips me almost off my feet. I cannot see or hear a living soul, just the shrieking of gulls and the howling of gusts. Something he had said about 'praying for it to end' sends a shiver up my spine. I take an agitated few steps towards the precipice, but stop well short of the edge. Instead, I turn round and walk behind the van where, shielded from the wind, I find him swaying and praying the nineteen blessings of the afternoon service. He points to his lips, and I acknowledge with a nod that I know he cannot be interrupted.

'We must go soon,' he says, on uttering the concluding affirmation of God's oneness and kissing his curling prayer-book as he returns it to an inner jacket pocket. 'It gets dark at six and I have to pick up my youngest from *yeshiva*.'

He is back in the van, packing away the Thermos. 'There's plenty of time,' I say, authoritatively. He opens his hands, in that characteristic gesture of simulated resignation. 'I have some questions,' I begin.

'Ask away.'

'When, exactly, did you accept this identity?' I demand, pointing to his beard, his garments, his ghetto. 'Not the outer trappings, but the actual faith. When did it overcome your healthy scepticism and become the new you?'

'Who knows?' He shrugs. 'At some point, perhaps in London, perhaps up here, I stopped asking such questions. It was easier to buy the whole package on trust and stop searching the ingredients. Once the wrapping was off, there were no further problems. Anything that was unanswerable could be accounted to the Creator. Knowing that it was beyond human comprehension, the pain was taken away.'

'Like having an appendectomy under hypnosis?'

'If you like. Or treating cancer homoeopathically. If you believe in the older, herbal therapy, there is a chance it will work just as well as radical surgery. And if it fails, the end result is the same either way.'

'It relieved you of taking responsibility for your treatment?'

'If you want to extend that metaphor, yes. Into His hand I yielded my soul, as we say in our prayers. And the auxiliary care was an unexpected bonus. The wordless devotion of my colleagues and the *yeshiva* community nursed me back into feeling part of the human race, or at least their microcosmic part of it.'

'You never felt connected to people when making music?'

'Momentarily,' he admits, 'but only with a strapped-on culture, a prosthetic device.'

He is enjoying this hospital game too much for my liking; presumably, he cannot indulge mild pleasures of free association with his severe, book-blinkered colleagues. I bring him smartly back to business with a confrontational proposition. 'Music, I suppose, gave you no spiritual shelter?'

He strokes his beard, like a security blanket, before sighing a reply. 'What does a Dovidl from Warsaw derive from Johann Sebastian Bach and Ludwig van Beethoven?' he ventures, in Talmudic sing-song. 'When a Dovidl needs to mourn, does he sob a *kaddish* or intone a *Dies Irae*? In pain, we become tribal. I love music, of course I do, but Bach and Beethoven do not heal my wounds.

'With Rashi and Maimonides, on the other hand, I share a heritage of suffering and an ironic turn of mind. Their approach to life is much the same as mine, albeit often above my reasoning. I used to think I had a good mind until I attempted rabbinical exegesis, the whole world predicated on a pinhead. How did medieval scholars achieve such insights? Read Freud on grief and guilt; then read Rashi on Jacob's remorse after the death of Rachel. It's the same idea, expressed eight hundred years earlier and in a single, devastating phrase.'

It is my turn to play for time, rustling in my pockets for a roll of sweets as I wonder whether to mount a defence of modernity, or lunge again for the bobbity jugular. Offering him a fruit gum which he declines, not certifiably kosher, I fight both fronts at once.

'I am aware,' I affirm drily, 'of the consolations of scholarship. But your actions were not the outcome of a mystical epiphany, a eureka moment. They were a conscious substitution of one way of life for another, modern for archaic. You stepped back in time, liked it and decided to stay there.'

'Not entirely,' he objects. 'I did not shut out the world I knew before. I recognised certain parallels between Brahms and Rashi, the Vilna Gaon and Strindberg. To me, privately, they were all honest searchers for truth, brother pioneers in the fight to make sense of suffering. I could not share this thought with fellow-rabbis, who would have thought it heretical. But for me this calm acceptance that there are many paths to understanding was the nexus on which my old self acquiesced to the new, the answer to your original question.'

'You make it sound so rational.' I sniff. 'But face it: you were running away in some kind of blind panic, or breakdown, and simply walked through the first open door. Just tell me this, I have a right to know. What were you fleeing most? Your gambling debts, the obligations of talent or the intolerable expectations of those who loved you – my parents, me, your own dead parents?'

He winces, but does not flinch. 'My mentors,' he replies, 'had become my tormentors. They idealised me, demanded more than I could give. But I assure you that I was not running away from any one of them. It never crossed my conscious mind to escape. True, I was a bit worried about the debts I had run up—'

'Some interesting-looking Mediterranean types came by Blenheim Terrace after you left.'

'I hope you sent them packing. Those villains double-crossed me. I found out that they owned two of the clubs where I lost money and were just using me to test their defences against method gamblers. I had no reason to pay them back, since the money they lent me I lost to them. I let them think they scared me, but I had friends who were watching out for me . . . I was in no immediate danger.

'As for other pressures, I was not afraid of my talent; it was something I was born with, like a kidney. I never gave it a second thought. My greatest regret has been the distress I must have caused you and your family, who showed me nothing but kindness and love – what we call *chesed*, one of God's attributes. Looking back, I don't believe I had an alternative. What happened, happened. After that, there was no turning back. Having defaulted on my début, I could hardly turn up months later expecting forgiveness. Having chosen another way of life, there was no point in making contact. Look at us Martin: we are worlds apart with nothing to say to each other. I am sorry, truly sorry, but we are resilient people and I imagine you managed to get over it in the course of time.'

It is time for me to apprise him of the damage he did, then to present the bill. Briskly, I run through my mother's madness, my father's death, the near-bankruptcy of Simmonds Ltd. He listens mutely, fingertips pressed together. 'Forgive me,' he murmurs, when I have finished.

'You owe me,' I retort.

'I know,' he sighs.

'You will have to make good.'

'What do you mean?'

I need to call another pause. I plead a full bladder, step outside and rehearse my next scene. I shall have to play it not with my father's silky persuasion but with Aunt Mabel's enviable bluntness, some gene of which I have hopefully stored within me. I shall slam him, metaphorically, against a door and grip his windpipe in my unyielding hand.

'You have in your possession,' I remind him, shutting the van door carefully, 'a valuable Guadagnini violin, which my father loaned you. It is worth, at today's values, around three million dollars.'

'Really?' he exclaims, seemingly astonished. 'I shall return it tonight. It is your property. Can you recommend an affordable modern instrument that I can continue to play at our communal celebrations?'

'I don't need you to give me back the violin,' I snap.

'What, then?'

'I intend you to play it.'

And he sits aghast – there is no other word for it – as I outline the plan I have sketched on the back of the competition score-sheet. 'You have a debt to pay, a date to keep,' I begin. 'You ducked out once and destroyed my family. It may be a bit late, but you are going to keep that début date, and as many others as it takes, until restitution is made. *Wiedergutmachung*, as the Germans call their payments to Holocaust victims: making good again.'

'How do you expect me to play? Like this?' he demands, pointing to his *yeshiva* greatcoat, his unkempt beard.

'If you insist,' I say icily. 'It would certainly enhance the publicity value.'

'Come on,' he chides, 'who is going to pay to hear a sixty-one-year-old rabbi sawing through a Bach étude he has not practised since he was so high?'

'That's exactly what they will pay to hear,' I reply. 'When I put out an announcement that the legendary Rapoport has returned from the dead, every violin fancier in the world will demand tickets and every sensation-seeker in the press will be on your case. We will keep that side of things under control, protecting your privacy. The rest is up to you.

'Music lovers will flock to hear you because you play like no one alive. And having heard you once, they will flock to hear you again because they will not believe that such playing is still possible. What you represent is a freedom of expression that has been forsaken in modern times.'

And I proceed to enlighten him in the ways of jet-age violinists, who play a hundred and twenty concerts a year and, looking out at a packed house, have no idea if they are in Boston or Brussels. Most of them are multi-millionaires with bulging investment portfolios. They play like zombies, deaf to music, dead from the waist up. Even the young bloods burn out before they reach thirty.

'When I announce Rapoport is back,' I continue, 'people will think: Kreisler, another world, a better world. My father gave you a brand name and a brand association. It won't matter how rusty you are, people will queue for hours to be connected to the innocent past, to their youth, to a vanished, halcyon era of art. You will be a sensation – short- or long-lived, it's your choice. What you do will be different from any living performer. It will be like going to the theatre to see Kenneth Branagh as Hamlet and finding Laurence Olivier in his place.' I have to explain to him who Kenneth Branagh is; Olivier he remembers from the wartime *Henry V*.

He will make his return, I inform him, in three months' time at the Royal Albert Hall – on 3 May, forty years to the day since his disappearance. The hall happens to be vacant that night; I made the call and reserved it this morning. He can play whatever he likes, solo recital or concerto with orchestra. 'They will queue to hear you play "Baa, Baa, Black Sheep",' I hyperbolise. I will pay him ten thousand pounds per concert. He will also sign a two-year contract for up to forty performances in Europe, the United States and Japan. I will keep fifteen per cent of his overseas fees, record royalties and broadcast payments, the standard industry terms. By 1993, I predict, when he passes his first million, I will write off the rest of his debt – to me, to my family and to his own destiny. 'Who knows?' I say. 'By then you might be enjoying it so much that you will want to carry on. I had better make the contract renewable.'

His response delights me. This most self-assured of men is fidgeting like a boy who has forgotten his homework. His fingers flutter around the roll of unkosher gums I left lying on the table. He is not so much distressed as disabled, his laser-beam intellect stalled by an insurmountable force. He wriggles this way and that, searching for an emergency exit. I lean back against the locked door.

'You don't seriously expect me to play before an audience,' he implores.

'Not one audience. Many. Internationally.'

'But can't you see that's completely impossible . . . for a person in my way of life?'

'I foresee no problem. You will not have to travel or work on the Sabbath, festivals and fast days. Kosher food will be provided at all venues. No scantily dressed girls will appear on stage. All religious requests will be treated sympathetically. I will disclose no more than the bare fact of your forty-year retreat to an unnamed contemplative community. You have no need to say anything more, and I will ensure that your family is kept out of it. No one will have any reason to connect Rabbi David Katzenberg to Eli Rapoport.'

'What will I tell my wife, my children, my colleagues?'

'Try the truth for a change. They won't love you any the less for bringing home a million dollars.'

'And if I refuse?'

'I don't think you have that luxury. You have legal obligations to my firm, quite apart from a moral debt to my family. Should you be foolish enough to try to evade them a second time, I will take steps to ensure that your wife and children are introduced to your interesting past: the clubs, the whores, the betrayal, the theft of a violin. A mysteriously well-researched article will appear in the *Jewish Chronicle* on the fortieth anniversary of your disappearance. A *Daily Mail* reporter will turn up on your doorstep. Must I elaborate? It would be a terrible *chilul Hashem*, a desecration of God's name. The *yeshiva* will never live it down.

'On the other hand, when you make your appearance as the vanished virtuoso rabbi on the stages of Carnegie Hall, the Concertgebouw in Amsterdam and the Musikvereinsaal in Vienna, fearlessly scaling the summits of European culture without concession to its corruptions, you will be fulfilling a *kiddush Hashem*, sanctifying the Holy Name with a fusion of piety and art. You will be a credit to your faith, vindicating by way of bonus the final wish of your last mentor, the *Rosh yeshiva*. Those are the binary alternatives – it's not much of a choice, is it?'

He squeezes past me and, without another word, clambers into the driver's seat and revs us back on the road to town, his jaw clenched. As he drops me off around the corner from my hotel he asks, 'How long have I got?'

'Until Friday morning,' I reply, 'I shall need an answer before I go back to London. I'm catching the nine-seventeen.'

'I'll come by tomorrow before lunch,' he suggests.

'Thank you, Dovidl,' I say sweetly. 'I am sure we can work something out.'

Bristling with vigour, I march into the lobby, pick up my room key, no messages, and take the stairs two at a time, whistling the main theme from the Bruch concerto. So much to do, so little time. I phone the Albert Hall just before close of business to confirm the booking. I call a colleague to check current rates for orchestral sessions. I alert a printer that I am about to place a large order for handbills and programmes, and then obtain competitive quotes from two others. A quick doodle on the bedside telephone pad tells me I can clear a hundred grand on the first concert alone, assuming a seating capacity of five thousand. Then there will be radio and recording rights, possibly television, Sky the limit. These tasks accomplished, I pour myself a double malt from the mini-bar and run a deep bath, the better to contemplate my magnificent future.

Hardly have I sunk my chilled limbs into the water than the phone rings. I am inclined to ignore it, but there is an extension on the wall above the bath and it is no great effort to stretch out a frothy arm.

'Excuse me, sir,' crackles Alfred, my chauffeur, 'I have brought the lady you invited to dinner.'

Damn and drat. It's the scrawny Stemp woman. She will want to talk about her precious Peter all night, when I have bigger things on my mind. Still, she is unlikely to stay late with the lad all on his own at home, and I suppose I owe the pair of them a small favour for leading me to the end of my trail.

'Show her to the bar, Alfred, and order her a glass of best champagne. Tell her I'll be down in fifteen minutes.'

Dinner with Mrs Stemp – 'you must call me Eleanor' – is not half as dreary as I feared. Detached from her pimply offspring and dressed in a stiff dark suit with a white silk blouse, Eleanor Stemp can hold her own in an intelligent conversation and tell a good yarn against herself. Over singed salmon Hollandaise and a slightly-too-tart Pouilly-Fuissé, she tells how she rushed into marriage with an irreproachably 'suitable' man to get away from a drug-riddled rock guitarist whom she loved to distraction. Her suitable husband left her cold in every way and she was by no means upset, one evening when she came home, to find him gone, leaving a letter beside the hall telephone telling her that he wanted to marry Helen, a schoolgirl waitress at Happy Burgers. Peter was, by this time, displaying exceptional musical aptitude and practising his child's fiddle more than an hour each day. She decided to help the lad make the best of his gift. She lacks social life and job satisfaction, but she enjoys watching Peter's progress and she finds flight for her fantasies in a surprisingly elevated taste for contemporary European literature.

Over crème caramels that might well have been made from leftover Hollandaise, we discuss Jorge Semprun, Patrick Süsskind, Thomas Bernhard, and Ivan Klima. She has just discovered Czeslaw Milosz. I mention my distant visit to Poland and she demands to know more, more, her eyes sparking with static energy. I praise the Warsaw Yiddish novels of Isaac Bashevis Singer, scanning her face for prejudice. But much as she might loathe the *frummers* of Oldbridge, Mrs Stemp's racial hatred stops at the books on her bedside table. As coffee is sullenly poured, she looks at her watch and exclaims, 'Is it ten o'clock? I must be going. Peter will be beside himself.'

'We haven't begun to discuss his future,' I gently remind her.

'Oh dear,' she groans, turning fretful and mousy.

'There is not much to get concerned about for the moment,' I assure her. 'I will arrange for him locally to see a first-class teacher, who will prepare him for a public début and enable us over the next couple of years to make a realistic assessment of his prospects.'

'Is he going to be a great soloist?' she wants to know (as they all do.)

'It's too soon to tell. It depends, as much as anything, on what erupts from the crumbling Soviet Union. Classical music is a shrinking, fiercely competitive market, with only so many concertos and recitals to go round. If half a dozen Heifetzes were to emerge over the next decade, Peter would be wiped out, but so would the rest of the West. Give it time. In a year or so, we should know better. We'll do our best.'

'I'd like to see him launched so I can reclaim my life,' she confides, much to my surprise. 'I don't intend to be one of those smothering mothers who follow their prodigies all around the globe. I have read about them in biographies and reject the role. I have given Peter some of my best years. The rest I want for myself.'

Well, well, there's uncrushed spirit in Eleanor Stemp. She makes to rise. Moving smartly round the table, I pull out her chair.

'Thank you for a lovely evening, Mr Simmonds—'

'Martin, please. Allow me to call you a cab.'

'I had better phone Peter to tell him to go to bed, and then I must find my way to the ladies' room to powder my nose.'

'Why don't you make the call from my room?' I suggest. 'That way, you can avoid the hotel's remote and antediluvian public washrooms, which you may recall from our lunch yesterday.'

I collect her coat from a somnolent cloakroom attendant and lead her to the first-floor suite where, long ago, I bedded a giggly girl who called me 'Daddy Bear' and who might, or might not, have a part to play in my far-reaching plans. I hang Eleanor's coat on the wardrobe rail while she telephones Peter, then turn on the television news to drown out any tinkling noises from my capacious Victorian bathroom. The room is large enough to convert into three in an efficient modern hotel.

Eleanor emerges, freshly lipsticked and slightly flushed, her smart jacket half-way unbuttoned to reveal the billowing white blouse. She is fuller than I might have imagined, and comfortable with it. I reach for the phone to summon a cab. 'Thank you, Martin, for everything,' she repeats, laying a hand on my outstretched arm. I turn and kiss her, full on the mouth. She responds slowly, eyes shut, compliant. Without further ceremony, I lay her across the king-sized bed, hoist her skirt to her hips and take her full-length on the unturned counterpane, rhythmically, proficiently, rewardingly.

An hour later I escort her downstairs to a cab with a buss on the rosy cheek and a farewell wave. I leap the stairs upwards three at a time and climb, unwashed, into bed with a smirk on my lips. All parts appear to be in good working order, would you believe? I have taken, as my father prescribed, 'some crude satisfaction, purely for oneself'. Was this what he meant? I wonder, as satiated sleep descends. No matter. It's a token of things to come. Simmonds are back in the music business, back with a taste for the takings.

# 10

# Time for Action

The bedside telephone rips me from the smugness of sleep.

'Martin, major disaster, you must come home right now.'

'What time is it, Myrtle?'

'Half past seven. I had to get you before you left the room. The thing is, Lord Brent has cried off for tomorrow night. Tonsillitis, Joyce says. She's coming, which is really nice of her, but that leaves two spare women at table. What are we to do? Martin, are you awake?'

'Just thinking, Myrtle.'

'No time for that. I need action.'

'All right. Phone Dr Rodriguez. He's usually free for a meal at weekends and can be good company if you keep him off golf. Doesn't eat much, either. Then there's that South African lawyer we met at the Solti concert. His card is on a pile at the right hand of my desk. He's definitely single, probably gay. Pity. I'd like to see someone make a pass at prissy Joyce in the absence of his pompous lordshit.'

'Martin, that's unforgivable. No wonder nobody of any consequence will accept my invitations.'

'Try Doc Birdie and the Queen Boer, Myrtle, but at a more
civilised hour than this if you want them to accept.'

'Is something the matter with you?' my wife twigs, her suspicion
snaking through the telephone line. 'You're sounding very frisky
for the fourth day of a sales trip. I'll book you in for a check-up
with Rodriguez first thing Monday morning.'

'That'll be nice, dear. See you tomorrow.'

After replacing the receiver, my fingers trail a cheering odour
of stale sex, stranger's sex, past twitching nostrils. I savour the
conquest and prepare for the next. Quickly out of bed, I shower,
shave, select a vivid green tie and flip through the under-door
*Telegraph* until it is time to go down. Sandra Adams is due for
breakfast at eight thirty, and my mouth is watering.

'Mr S, I'm not late, am I?' she greets me effusively, in a snazzy
pink two-piece, an inch too tight for her amplitude.

'Mrs Adams,' I protest. 'I thought we were on first-name
terms.'

'Oh, you can call me Sandi, but I'm sticking to "Mr S". Martin's
so dusty, not at all your kind of name.'

The Royal can just about manage a competent English breakfast.
I remember Sandra's frugality on Tuesday, but today she has blown
diet to the winds and loads up on fried proteins and bread. I make
do with orange juice and muesli, returning a second time to the
buffet for a prohibited Danish, all sugar and starch. I need to
replenish lost energy if I am going to continue at this pace.

'We are meeting to discuss your future,' I remind her. 'Let's
dispense with preliminaries. I'm offering you a job.'

'What makes you think I'm available?' she retaliates.

'You tell me.'

'Well, I'm in a dead-end position that was created for me by the General Purposes Committee so that I can take time off to be Olly's dogsbody at his evening dos and not feel too hard done by. My youngest has just started secondary school and my husband wants to run for Parliament but won't get selected. Yes, I might just be prepared to consider a lucrative alternative. What's on offer?'

'How much are you earning at the Council?'

'Fourteen four,' she replies, meaning fourteen thousand four hundred pounds a year, before income tax, national insurance and compulsory pension contributions – say, a hundred and forty take-home a week. A pittance, in plain English.

'You have been knowingly undersold,' I tell her.

'What am I worth?' She smiles coquettishly.

'Twenty basic, plus a share of profits.'

Her colour rises and drops like the thread of a thermometer. Is she too transparent for my kind of work? My doubts are balanced by the booster-rocket of her pent-up ambition.

'What's involved?' she demands. 'Nothing illegal, I hope.'

'More immoral than illegal,' I chortle. 'We're talking music business.'

I give her the broad outline of my grand plan. I am setting up a new subsidiary, Simmonds Artists, and I shall need her to run an office in Tawburn, looking after our first signings, Olszewska and Stemp – along with another performer whose identity I will disclose in due course. She will also look after northern sales of Simmonds scores and instruments to provide cashflow. She will also maintain contacts with conservatories to monitor new talent and she will visit London weekly to report and co-ordinate with me.

She will receive, on top of salary, twenty per cent of net profits from any artists she signs. If the business prospers, she will be made a partner in two years, with the right to buy out my share when I retire.

'When do I start?' she beams.

'How much notice do you need to give in your present job?'

'A statutory month, but I am owed six weeks' holiday. If I call in sick today, I can drop a letter of resignation at the town hall and start working for Simmonds in about two hours flat.'

'What about your husband?'

'Olly knows I can't bear the bloody Council any more.'

'He won't mind you staying overnight in London, as needs arise?'

'He'll get used to it,' she smiles. 'Or not, as the case may be.'

I congratulate her on her decisiveness. Sandra will be an asset, quick as a whippet and keen to prove herself. I can't wait till she meets Myrtle, who will bridle at someone so flashily underclass, bluntly provincial and upwardly mobile – all her social nightmares encased in a throbbing pink outfit.

'More coffee?' moans the waiter.

'Not for me,' says Sandra. 'I've got a heavy day ahead. Let me have sample contracts for the young artists, Mr S, and I'll get them typed up and signed by the parents before you leave. I'll also type up a letter of engagement on the terms we have agreed for you to counter-sign. Mr S, I'm so excited, I could burst my bra straps.'

'Not in a public restaurant,' I implore.

'Oh, you know what I mean. We're very down-to-earth around here. You know, as a kid in this godforsaken town I used to dream of being in a backing group or becoming a disc-jockey. I was smitten by showbiz, but this is worlds better: it's got class. Do I get to meet the Queen?'

'Prince Charles, perhaps.'

'He'll do. One last thing, Mr S, before I dash. This is a bit weird. I know we only met three days ago, but I feel we've known each other for ever. I have a terrible memory for faces. Can you remember, Mr S, have we ever met before?'

'Maybe,' I reply truthfully, 'in a previous life.'

There was once a Liverpool youth called William Roberts who, rejected by the Indian civil service, went to work in a bank but longed to become a music critic. When he got a job on the *Manchester Guardian* in 1904, he took the name 'Ernest Newman', signalling that he had become, in all earnest, a completely new man. I met Newman in his dotage, when he was the doyen of British critics, a world authority on Wagner and castigator of all things modern, a man locked in what he had made of himself. I am beginning to grasp the limits of metamorphosis. Dovidl has changed his name, location and way of life, yet he cannot cast off his past. I have altered no part of my identity, merely embalmed it for forty years. Now, by restoring Dovidl to his true self, I can reclaim mine. I feel like a new man – no, not new: whole again. Like Sandra, I can't wait to get cracking.

I return to my room and busy myself with paperwork, faxes and phone calls until Sandra comes by to collect contract forms. Together, we ring the thrilled Olszewskas, offer them world representation for little Maria and arrange for Sandra to call. I undertake to phone Eleanor Stemp and tell her that Sandra has taken over her son's personal management; she will not be pleased, which is just as well. It will put the previous night's digression into proper perspective.

'Is that the radiator?' asks Sandra, resplendent in her straining pink sweater. 'That droning noise.'

'No, it's me,' I confess. 'I often hum when I work.'

'Nice to see a man who loves his work.' She beams.

Nice to have my lightness back, I think. Thank you, Dovidl.

We order a business line over the phone to be installed in Sandra's spare bedroom, nip round to the nearest bank to open a joint account and collect enough cash to buy her a personal computer at the shop next door. Simmonds must be seen to be doing its bit for local businesses: we shall need them to sponsor some of our local artists. The latest line in Japanese radio gadgets catches my eye: I buy one for Myrtle, for the kitchen, a guilt-offering.

No sooner do I get back from shopping than a call from Reception advises me that Mr Katzenberg is waiting for me in the car park.

'Well?' I demand, climbing into the camper-van.

'What choice have I got?' he sighs.

'Excellent, that's settled. Now tell me, how long is it since you were last at a symphony concert?'

'I think you can guess.'

'Good, because we are going to a midweek matinée in Manchester. On the motorway, at this time of day, we should make it in an hour.'

He has brought along sandwiches and tea, expecting an outing, and we consume them none too daintily along the route. Our conversation is neutral and wide-ranging, touching on the weather, the recent war, the fate of Israel, the economic downturn, the trouble with the younger generation, the scarcity of talent, the kind of drivers they let on motorways these days, just look at that Vauxhall – anything except the past, which is enemy territory, never to be re-entered.

Beneath the beard, I see a sore patch on the underside of his chin. Excellent, I tell myself. He must have been practising for hours.

We pull up a block away from the Free Trade Hall, a mock-Victorian mausoleum that no one could mistake for a house of pleasure. I purchase a pair of ten-pound stalls seats for the Manchester Chamber Society's all-Mozart matinée. The bulk of the audience is already seated – several busloads of pensioners trawled in from care homes and day centres in a well-intentioned initiative to preserve them from turning into sodden lumps. Some of the women are dressed in worn finery; the men have barely bothered to climb out of carpet slippers. 'What time does it start?' quavers one chap, a former military man in blue blazer, stained grey trousers. 'Will we be home in time for *Coronation Street*? Is it *Corrie* night tonight?'

A flock of students has been let in for free, but their gaiety is subdued by geriatric blankness and the hall's inbuilt gloom. The orchestral musicians, drifting on to the stage in their English couldn't-give-a-toss way, take one look at the audience and slump into their seats. The concert is conductorless, cheaper that way, and mortally clichéd. 'Eine Kleine Nachtmusik' is followed by the clarinet concerto; tea interval, then the G minor symphony. I am grimly regretting having brought Dovidl to such a despondent event, but the instant the hackneyed music strikes up he leans forward to the limits of his seat, chasing the sounds with the ends of his nerves, inserting himself at the centre of the performance. In the clarinet concerto, I fear for one nasty moment that he is about to jump up and start conducting, so ragged is the ensemble. When it ends, amid shuffling applause, his face is suffused with pleasure, as if he has just consumed a gourmet meal, or made love. 'We can go now,' he grins, 'it is not going to get any better.'

I apologise for the miserable experience. 'On the contrary,' he exclaims, 'it has been wonderfully instructive. First, I have been relieved of the temptation ever to attempt Mozart again – it's too subtle to be played with anything less than total conviction. Second, I have no urge to play with an orchestra.'

'There are better bands,' I protest, 'and fine conductors for hire.'

'Save your money.' He laughs. 'I intend to play solo Bach in the first half, like it or leave it. After the interval, I might try out some of my own compositions, variations on various themes by Hassidic masters. Something different, what do you think?'

'Sounds good, cross-cultural sells well. Do we need a support act, a singer, a pianist?'

'No, if they want Rapoport, they can have him neat, no ice.'

'You're sounding a little more enthused,' I venture.

'Why not?' he responds, in the Jewish interrogative. 'How many men of my age get to top the bill at the Royal Albert Hall?'

I mention Frank Sinatra, Dizzy Gillespie, Pablo Casals – pointlessly. He gives a blank look, as if he remembers none of them.

'Will we have royalty in the Royal Box?' he wants to know. 'Your father often did.'

'It may be short notice, but we'll try for a duke.'

'Will I have to curtsy?'

'Cut it out . . .'

We are almost back to boyhood banter, swept along on the crest of his excitement. I gently suggest that he may need to prepare more than one programme, and that an evening of unadulterated violin playing might prove too tiring for most ears. He should consider doing one of the two Mendelssohn trios, which, Dr Steiner used to say, he understood better than any fiddler ever born. A chamber-music first half would spare him the unrelieved glare of critical attention and whet the public's palate for a violin-piano and violin-solo second half. I can recommend two or three outstanding pianists in the region for him to try out; good cellists are ten a penny.

'It will take the pressure off you,' I advise.

'I'll give it some thought,' he concedes.

'It's for the best,' I nudge. He has been through a similar negotiating process before, with my father.

'Best for me, or best for you?' he demands.

'There's no difference,' I reply. 'In the act of presentation, you and I are on the same side. That's why we have to discuss and agree the programme – your instinct, my experience.'

'"A man's got to do what his manager tells him to,"' he quotes, with whimsical irony.

'Mendelssohn first half, Bach and Besht post-interval?' I press.

'Could be.'

Then, just as we reach the van, he sees across the street three bearded Jews dressed in black coats and hats, scurrying to some sacred purpose or other. Manchester has several Jewish districts, north and south, some of them aggressively ultra-orthodox. 'Do you need to attend evening service?' I enquire considerately.

He shakes his head, but the *élan* ebbs from his voice and the return drive to Tawburn is colourless and quiet. He is going to be under great strain, I warn myself. It will be difficult to strike a balance between his introverted life and the exposure to public acclaim and self-realisation. I am the one who has put him under pressure, and I shall have to watch him unobtrusively every pace of the way. He is going to be a high-maintenance artist, but the results, both artistic and financial, will be worth every effort and expense. The world will rediscover a lost wonder, the violin will be restored to its glory days, and Simmonds will be renowned once more as the premier name for musical talent.

'Do you have copies of your own compositions?' I ask, as we cross the road bridge into Tawburn. He shakes his head again, and points to it. 'They are all up here,' he says, alarmingly, 'but

I shall play them to you before we go public. You remember how Kreisler used to write pieces in the style of baroque composers? It's a bit of a fraud, but I do something of the sort with the Hassidic masters.'

'How do you mean?'

'They are my own tunes, but I ascribe them to great rabbis of the past, which accords them instant reverence and popularity in the *yeshiva* world.'

'Are they preformed, or improvised?'

'A bit of both. Sometimes I can do twenty minutes of variations on a wedding tune.'

Jumping Joachims, I tell myself. He has developed a skill that has been gone from concert halls for a century, the art of a Paganini or a New Orleans jazzman, who makes up his music as he goes along. If I can only bring him once before a discerning audience, I will have done more to regenerate the art of music than any puppet-master since Diaghilev.

'I long to hear you perform it,' I assure him. 'I have to leave for London first thing in the morning, but I'll be back soon and I'll make immediate arrangements for you to audition suitable pianists and cellists. I shall also hire rehearsal premises near your home.

'I have just taken on someone to assist me up here. If you need anything urgently – new strings, scores, paper – call Sandra Adams on this number and she will get them to you without delay.'

His face falls, and I grasp the immensity of my error. 'I'm so sorry,' I splutter. 'You cannot possibly have dealings with a gentile woman, what will people think? Stupid of me. Forget I spoke. If there is anything you need, call me in London and I will get Mr Woodward, the manager of the Royal Tawburn, to hold them for you at the reception desk. He does little favours for me, lets me use his vault between visits, to save me shlepping my stuff up and down the railway line. I'll tell him to expect requests from a Mr Rapoport of your description. Whatever you do, don't worry. We will work this through without offence to your faith or family. We have not come this far, you and me, in order to fail.'

He seems swayed, but shaken. Did he think I was setting a honeytrap for him? Does he associate sex automatically with strange women? Has he no sense of proportion? 'Look,' I tell him, 'no one has ever done what we are about to do. No artist has ever risen from forty years of rest, no orthodox Jew has excelled in a famous concert hall, no impresario has staked his shirt on a patriarchal débutant. We both have a lot to learn. Let's take it step by step. Trust me, I can make it work. I can grant you forgiveness.'

'You won't let me back out?'

'Back out? A few minutes ago you were sounding pretty keen. You want to play. You also want to make good, to stop looking over your shoulder, to do what you were born for. What's the point of being alive if not to fulfil your purpose? God gave you a gift. Use it.'

We are antagonists again, but the air has cleared. His poker face, softened with scholarship, relaxes at the corners of his jaw. 'I'll say good night, then,' he murmurs, pulling up a few yards from the hotel, 'and thank you for the concert.'

'There will be bigger and better ones ahead.'

'God willing.'

'You said it.'

A malt from the mini-bar, the last miniature bottle, settles my nerves as I run through the faxes and voice messages. Myrtle has secured her spare males and is happily stewing over the discovered nuisance that the Cape Town bore is a strict vegetarian. Sandra has signed up Olszewska and Stemp, and is wondering if she should hire Fred Burrows as a talent scout. Good idea: the cathedral organist knows his onions. She reminds me that we need to start planning Manchester, Leeds and Newcastle recitals for Maria Olszewska, building up her confidence before she makes an international début in London. We will make a good team, Sandi and I.

Weary, I decide to avoid further company and follow my past routine of a drink in the bar with a light snack for supper. The *Telegraph* crossword should untangle my mind and leave me ready for bed. It is past eight when I descend and the snug is near-empty. 'Not a good night, Thursday,' says the barman, 'everyone saves up their money for the weekend.'

Suits me, I think, nibbling peanuts while waiting for a cheese salad to settle my diet of fine whiskies. I hardly notice the woman until she slips in beside me and nuzzles my cheek.

'I was just passing,' lies Eleanor.

'What a lovely surprise,' I lie back. 'Can I get you something?'

'Just an orange juice,' she says primly.

'Peter all right?'

'That's what I wanted to talk to you about,' she says, instantly naked in her anxiety. 'Why did you send that Adams woman round?'

'Because it is not appropriate for me to deal with personal management. Sandra is a very caring, efficient agent. She will look after everything we discussed for Peter.'

'But I thought we had an understanding, you and I . . .'

'Of course we do, my dear, and a very warm understanding it is, if I may say so. But as head of the firm, I must be careful to stand above the interests of individual artists in order to resolve any conflict, should one arise. Do you understand? If ever there is something on your mind that Sandra cannot satisfy, you must get in touch with me and I will sort it out. But I cannot take day-to-day responsibility for managing what

I hope will be a most propitious career. You do appreciate my position, don't you?'

She appreciates all right, bedraggled and mouselike, with no cards left to play. I am tempted, in masculine ways, to console her, but that would not be good business. So I sip my drink and she gulps hers, slipping out into the night with a mumbled farewell and just enough dignity to refrain from offering me a kiss. I feel appropriately sorry for Eleanor, but that's the music business. You give the rough and dispense the smooth, as the situation requires. Only fools and artists are ever on the receiving end.

# 11

# Time's Up

Ever anxious about missing connections, I have spent many a wakeful night waiting for the alarm to go off, unable to take a sedative for fear of oversleeping. Renewed as I am, I am not sufficiently rearmed to face the threat of Myrtle's wrath should I fail to catch the first train. So I set the bedside alarm for six forty-five and the TV set to come on at seven with the wakey-wakey news on BBC 1. That should give me plenty of time to shower, pack, have breakfast and catch the nine-seventeen to King's Cross from the station across the square.

The night is restful and the news undisturbing. In the Gulf, they are counting the cost of war and uncovering atrocities. The defeated Iraqi leader vows defiance. The Americans swear they will strip him of weapons of mass destruction. A human-rights activist warns that punishing the Iraqi regime will inflict unjust suffering on millions of innocent citizens.

As I return from the bathroom wrapped in a towel and rubbing my torso, the transmission switches to a Tawburn studio for three minutes of local news delivered by a mop-topped girl with a severe case of adenoids, or what might be a pungent sub-regional accent. 'Police in Oldbridge,' she begins, chilling my steaming skin, 'are investigating an incident early this morning when a camper-van plunged off the A821 at the entrance to the town. Police divers have been called in to search for the driver, a middle-aged man who appears to have been alone in the vehicle. Roger Middleton is on the scene. Roger?'

The picture switches to dawn on the Taw, shimmering with frosted dew. A cub reporter in a bear-sized duffel-coat has gleaned a few details. 'Well, Tamsin, police are mystified by the cause of this incident on what is a very well-lit and heavily used stretch of highway. The van apparently left the road fifty yards before reaching the bridge, at a point where there is no fencing. It slithered down the bank and into the river, sinking before any other motorist could pull up and give assistance.

'No one was seen getting out of the vehicle and, in sub-zero temperatures, police say there is very little hope of finding a survivor. Police believe they know the driver's identity, but they cannot release it until the family has been informed.'

'So is this just a tragic accident, Roger, or are police looking at any other cause?'

'The question troubling investigators is whether the driver lost control, maybe fell asleep at the wheel, or whether he was forced off the road by an oncoming vehicle. Hopefully, we'll have more in an hour. In the meantime, it's more misery for motorists. One-lane traffic on the A821 all day, I'm afraid. Be prepared for long delays into and out of Tawburn. Back to you, Tamsin.'

I have heard enough. Packing my bag, I am out of the room within two minutes, heading downstairs to check out. Woodward, the manager, presides at the reception desk. I ask him to deliver my suitcase to my reserved seat on the nine-seventeen and slip him a twenty-pound note in a parting handshake for this and other services rendered. 'Always good to see you, Mr Simmonds,' he murmurs, 'I do hope you had a good time with us.'

Missing the hotel breakfast is a bonus. At the revolving doors, a flunkey hails me a cab. Oldbridge is only ten minutes away, even in rush hour, not long enough for my mind to circumferate the possibilities. 'Wait there,' I tell the driver, striding to the riverbank. The area is cordoned off with striped plastic tape, but I step over it authoritatively, flashing a Metropolitan Police press pass that I was once given by a music-loving commissioner.

'What's the latest?' I ask the BBC's Roger Middleton, pretending to be a passing colleague.

'Nothing much. The divers are about to go in to locate and retrieve the van. May take all day. No hope for the driver.'

'Do we know anything about him?'

Middleton nods to a knot of men standing on the bridge, swaying and keening raggedly in black hats and coats. 'One of them, it seems.' He shrugs. 'Can't talk to those guys – too busy shaking. Anyway, don't suppose any of them speaks English.'

Skidmarks define the van's descent. It's a sixty-foot drop and no more than a one-in-eight gradient, gentle enough for a driver to slam on the brakes and, had they failed, to jump clear before he hit the water. But there are no brakemarks on the mossy bank. The furrow is smooth all the way down. If the driver had his foot on either of the pedals, it was the accelerator, not the brake. Not an accident, then. Something more contrived.

'Any address for the victim?' I ask the sergeant in charge.

'Not yet, sir. Must wait till next-of-kin are notified.'

'Terrible thing to happen . . .'

'Never had one go off this part of the road before.'

My suspicions are hardening, but there is not much more to corroborate here. As my eyes imprint the scene, my ears and every gene in my ancestry tug me towards the Jews on the bridge, nudging me to cover my head and recite psalms for the salvation, or soul, of the missing man.

'"I lift my eyes to the mountains, from where my help shall come,"' I hear the leader cry, each Davidian word stressed to the point of fracture.

'"My help comes from God, who made heaven and earth,"' the others respond, dragging out the final syllable, refusing to accept no answer to their prayer.

The next psalm is the Song of Steps for all forms of distress. '"From the depths I have called you, O God. God: listen to my voice; let your ears be attentive to the voice of my supplications."'

And from the depths of memory I hear a mocking echo, a Latinate recitation: *De profundis clamavi ad te Domine. Domine exaudi vocem meam, fiant aures tuae intendentes in vocem deprecationis meae . . .*

'"And He will redeem Israel,"' chants the leader of the Hebrew huddle, '"from all of its sins."'

I yearn to join them, to lose myself in familiar verses, to commune with brethren in pain. But I cannot join. I am responsible for their distress. It was I who propelled that van into the river by pushing the driver into a position from which he had no reverse gear. Always leave an artist room to back out, my father would say. That way he can later come crawling back. I had overruled Father's voice in my head, forcing the issue to achieve instant results. I was pressed for time; I had failed to achieve the illusion that I was master of time.

No point in prayer or tears. I can feel the beginnings of regret, but no ache of remorse. Everything must come to an end. This, at least, has ended without further damage to my family interests. It's over, I tell myself, over at last.

'Canning Street,' I direct the shivering cabbie, 'centre of Oldbridge.' The pavement outside number thirty-two is thronged with women in black, but there is no hearse to be seen. That is all the confirmation I need. 'Station, please,' I command.

I have half an hour to buy coffee, a croissant, the *Spectator* and think about flowers for Myrtle. No, that would be overdoing it, in addition to the radio gadget; anyway, she has already smelt a rat. The train is stationary at platform four. My suitcase has been stowed in the rack above my seat. Good old Woodward, never lets me down.

The first sip of coffee is so hot it brings tears to my eyes. I remove my specs and dab away with a white handkerchief, checking an imaginary emotional pulse to see if I feel grief. Nothing yet, too much else on my mind.

Several options need to be sifted. Accident, or suicide? Certainly no accident. The apparent speed of descent suggests a predetermined act. Also, the van slewed off at the only unfenced stretch on the whole riverbank. Presumably the driver was aiming for it.

Suicide, then. Couldn't face public exposure, one way or other. Saw no way out. Maybe left a note? We'll know soon enough.

But suicide is a capital crime in the Torah, equivalent to murder. Dovidl would have had to renounce his faith before charging into the depths. Did belief mean so little to him? And why now? He had weeks to spare, time to put his affairs in order before I came to drag him into the limelight. Dovidl is not an impulsive man; he is never pressed for time. Keep this option open, I warn myself. There is more here than meets the average intelligence.

Murder? Faint possibility that some racist lunatic rode him off the road, shouting, 'Ingerland, Ingerland,' as the bearded Jew went into the river, flailing behind his rolled-up window. Can't be ruled out, but there are not many drunken bigots about at six o'clock on a February morning. And what was Dovidl doing out so early, when he did not need to be at morning prayers until seven thirty?

How did the rabbis and their disciples come to be swaying on the bridge so soon after the 'accident'? They were chanting in the background on the BBC news report, at seven twenty-six when they would otherwise have been on their way to morning prayers. They should have been unaware of Dovidl's absence until he failed to show up for devotions, certainly not before eight. There may be a red herring here, and it's starting to stink.

What about his wife? Had she rolled over in bed after six, found her husband missing and called out a search party? Surely not. Married couples in the ultra-orthodox community do not share beds. They sleep in twin singles, separated by a bedside table, to keep them apart during times of impurity. So the chance that Mrs Katzenberg missed him and raised the alarm is remote.

What, then? An ugly precedent springs to mind. Yossele! I exclaim. Yossele Schumacher was an Israeli child who was kidnapped in 1960 from his Sabbath-breaking parents by a heart-broken grandfather and a rabbi's wife, Ruth Blau, intent on raising him in their stringently religious way. He was hidden for two years in ghetto homes in Bnei Berak, Brooklyn and goodness knows where else until common sense and threats of prosecution persuaded the zealot kidnappers to release him, on assurances that he would continue to receive a religious education.

For months on end, while Interpol searched in vain and the state of Israel squirmed with embarrassment, *yeshiva* students in Jerusalem danced on the streets, taunting police with cries of 'Where is Yossele?' sung to a Purim festival tune. Set against the might of a modern state and international law, the medieval walls of rabbinic orthodoxy had managed to hide a wanted child for as long as they liked – until they were good and ready to give him up on favourable terms.

It does not take a great leap of memory to recall that Dovidl, too, had been successfully concealed and transported by Hassidim during a British police search. Have they done it again? Is it conceivable that he got the *yeshiva* community to conspire in a second disappearance, persuading them that he was being harassed by a pursuer from his former life – me? Or has he simply done a runner all on his own, telling no one, not even his wife?

Easily done: drive the van to the top of the bank, with no risk of being seen so early. Change clothes, shave beard. Step outside. Wedge accelerator down with a piece of wood. Take off brakes. Stand well back. Then walk a short mile to the station and catch a bus or train to anywhere. A Labour Cabinet minister, John Stonehouse, dumped his clothes on a deserted beach, disappeared, and turned up years later in Miami. Lord Lucan, a gambling aristocrat, murdered a nanny and fled his Belgravia home, never to be seen again. Every week, some innocuous farm-worker or bank clerk walks out on wife and family without further trace. It does not require exceptional brilliance or vast wealth to vanish and stay hidden. A genius like Dovidl could do it twice, unaided.

So, what next? Wait for clues. The nine-seventeen sighs deeply and starts pulling out of Tawburn station. It crosses the river within seconds, overlooking the accident scene. A dripping blue camper-van is being hauled by crane from the water. It's Dovidl's, all right. No mistake.

As I crick my neck at the window, a pinstriped young man enters the first-class compartment, asking if this is Carriage D. He is carrying a violin case. All senses flare alert. What has Dovidl done with the three-million-dollar Guadagnini? If he has absconded, as

I am starting to suspect, he will not have left it behind. It would show up in the estate, be sold at auction to pay living costs or death duties, and be claimed by me with a police warrant, exposing the missing man as a thief and liar, to his children's disgrace. He would not want that.

The violin is on an Interpol watch-list. It cannot be legally sold. If he has taken it with him, it will have no value. If not, it must soon come to light.

'Is that an old instrument?' I ask the loose-limbed young fellow, pointing to the violin case that he has laid carefully on the seat.

'Oh, I should say so,' he drawls, in fluent Eton-and-Oxford. 'Italian eighteenth century. I'm taking it to Sotheby's for a bit of spit and polish before we sell it.'

'Mind if I take a look? I'm a bit of a connoisseur. Got a Testini at home. Used to be my grandfather's,' I blabber.

'I can't let you touch it,' says the agreeable chap. 'They'd murder me at Bond Street. But I'll open the case and give you a peek, if you like.'

My heart starts pounding, the way it mortally used to until this week's renewal. Have I uncovered a flaw in his posthumous plan? I pat my pills pocket, find it empty and manage to survive unaided.

'There,' says the auctioneer's runner. 'What do you think of that?'

Not a lot, is the truthful answer. To my jaded eye it looks like a nineteenth-century French copy of a Cremona original, common as muck and worth no more than a hundred grand. Phew.

'It's gorgeous,' I tell the clerk. 'Have you tried playing it?'

'Oh, no, I can't play the things, just sell them.'

'Where does it come from?'

'Usual story. Country estate, been there for yonks. Old man used to play a bit, dead now. Kids just want the money.'

'No respect for tradition . . .'

'Shame, really, but I suppose they need the cash.'

Inside, I am effervescent with delight. It would have been far too sloppy, too unlike the Dovidl I knew, to try to slip a key piece of traceable evidence out of town while the heat is on. He will have made more sophisticated arrangements for the tainted instrument. Patience, I tell myself contentedly. Be patient and all will become clear, all in your own good time.

# 12

# In My Own Good Time

Losing him a second time is the best thing that has ever happened. It has taken me four years to say that, but there it is. My life has been redeemed more by his second disappearance than it was shattered by his first. Past the statutory retirement age, just about, I am brimming with ambition. My business booms, my private life glows, and a confident whisper has reached me that I am to be offered the Order of the British Empire in the Queen's Birthday Honours, for 'contributions to British culture' – contributions that have been made, overwhelmingly, in the four years since my friend's second vanishing act.

This is not what I tell my wife, who plays a more prominent role in my considerations than heretofore. Since my return from Tawburn, Myrtle has changed in response to my changes, as a good spouse must. Say what you like about Myrtle, she has the antennae of a spy satellite and the discretion of a chessmaster. Not once has she asked me what happened during that week up north, or why

I have swept out a cupboardful of quack medications, refuse to visit the osteopath and seem reinvigorated none the less. I, for my part, have revealed nothing of the causes of my restoration. She observes the sparkle in my eye, and starts to twinkle in response.

The arrival of Sandra Adams presents a challenge to her resilience. Sandi is swift and hungry. She claims a desk in the corner of my office and is soon spending as many as four nights a week in London, in a flat that I have rented for her. Without consulting me, she enters Maria Olszewska for European Young Musician of the Year and, when the girl blazes to victory on continental television, is swamped with offers of dates and recordings. Everyone is gasping to hear Maria, who will not finish school for another year. A Dutch agent, Hans Derks, comes up with an interesting proposition. He will give us world rights in an energetic Russian pianist in exchange for the right to present Maria in the Low Countries. It looks good on paper and soon turns into the best swap since Jacob's lentil-soup-for-birthright deal.

Maria was never likely to make a mint for us in Maastricht, but the Russian, Anatoly Gudzinsky, is a veritable dynamo. He plays like a wild legend of yore, a long-haired Paderewski or a lip-contorting Pachmann, with heedlessly sloppy technique and on-stage idiosyncrasies that make him a box-office sensation. He walks on to the concert platform chewing gum, which he sticks ostentatiously to the underside of his polished stool. Between movements, he hawks and spits like a footballer. His pink flared silk tie with an outrageous pudendum motif collars column inches in the popular press, then column miles. He recognises neither tact nor restraint. He responds to ovations with an impromptu speech, often defamatory and profane, and gets involved in a Wimbledon love affair with all-England's latest rose-cheeked loser – an on-off, off-on, love-fifteen rally – that keeps the slavering tabloids in perpetual titivation. 'He was Sophie's only true love,' screams the *Sun*, 'but Rat Gudzi was scoring her doubles partner.' The *Mirror* dubs him 'Gudzilla' and exposes his 'steamy night' in the locker room with two first-round contestants from Sweden. How much of this is true is none of my business. Gudzinsky, that egregious philanderer, makes the most of it and sells his ghosted off-court memoirs for a dollar fortune, pumping ten per cent of the advance and royalties into Simmonds' vertical growth.

The Dutchman Derks, whose Russian connections are distinctly shady, feeds us a ceaseless stream of post-Soviet hopefuls, all of them tuned way above western concert pitch. Sandi and I select six fine specimens – three pianists, two violinists and a seductive Kazakh cellist, who proves irresistible to conductors of a certain age. Top orchestras beat a path to our door. Sandi promotes eastern promise via Hook of Holland with such enthusiasm that I am obliged to enquire whether her relationship with Mr Derks is strictly professional. 'It is now,' she grins disarmingly, 'but we had some high old red-light nights in Amsterdam early on. Have you ever done it on hash, Mr S?'

I mutter something about generation gaps and carefully avoid asking after Olly. Sandi cheerfully volunteers that he is happier without her around. After giving the kids supper, he goes out most nights to press male flesh in Tawburn's Royal Victoria Park, relieved to be rid of the lash of spousal disapproval. Olly has abandoned his political ideal in favour of self-gratification. Sandi is content and when Derks mysteriously disappears, to be dredged up in several butchered pieces from a Leyden canal, she gives up studying Russian and seeks no further close alliances, carnal or commercial. Success, I conclude, means more to her than libidinal satisfaction – exaggerating the hairline fracture in her unequal marriage.

As soon as Maria matriculates, Sandi moves the Olszewska family to Switzerland 'for tax purposes' and her own sons to Corpus Christi School in London, sloughing off Olly and her regional roots as a rattlesnake sheds its skin. When I mildly question her rejection of past, Sandi smiles tolerantly and murmurs something from Pushkin about 'the snows of yesteryear'. She is quick to pick up cosmopolitan chic. She flies twice a year to Milan to buy her outfits from Versace, from Gianni himself. Sandra Adams is going places.

Myrtle, alert to her ravenous ascent, announces that she is giving up bridge and is joining me in the office as financial controller. 'Someone has to keep an eye on the comings and goings, especially the outgoings,' she states briskly. Her remark calls to mind the milling corridors of my father's open-door office and I, in a depressed property market, swoop on the ailing next-door neighbours and buy back the rest of the suite.

Myrtle applies the rigour of common sense to our fetterless advance. Her budgetary veto is unbudgeable, and Sandi is obliged to back off a number of stylish acquisitions. But Myrtle is no killjoy or scaredy-cat. She, too, is fired by expansionist desire. Her fluent ancestral Spanish cracks open lucrative overseas markets. She escorts Gudzilla on a riotous Latin-American tour and returns with five tango composers under contract. My warm congratulations are reciprocated by her with rekindled amorous ardour in, ahem, a carnival outfit. Business draws us closer than marriage has ever done, much to the bemusement – not to say embarrassment – of our adult sons.

Mortimer, the elder, undergoes a mid-life upheaval, walks out on his wife and children and buys into a gynaecological practice in Beverly Hills, where (I gather) he receives patients in a flowery shirt. Edgar, the barrister, suffers a precipitate decline in libel work after the suicide at sea of the litigious rogue publisher Robert Maxwell. He comes to me for advice, for the first time since boyhood, and I recall the nights when Myrtle took me into his room to salve my loss in his gentle breathing. I recommend that he should think of turning his formidably trained forensic mind to entertainment law, with particular reference to the contract and copyright implications of new media and the dawning Internet.

He takes to virtual music like a shark to shipwrecks, slicing through standard publishing agreements that have stood unaltered for a century. A submarine treasure-chest of unclaimed electronic rights is uncovered by his beaming eye. There is a fortune to be made from unexploited musical applications. I frugally repossess the visible future of the composers I once sold off as dross. Edgar draws up a precedential contract that licenses *Dawn on the Dnieper* to a cyberspace bookseller as website aural wallpaper. We find ourselves navigating an uncharted sea with no longitudinal measurement. The horizons are limitless and unforeseeable.

Simmonds is the first music company to enter e-commerce, light-years ahead of the rest of field. My competitors accuse me of sharp practice and all manner of chicaneries. I am flattered by their fear. No longer the respected doyen of my trade, I have become the ferocious pace-setter, the market leader. The attendance at my funeral, not a subject I have much leisure to contemplate any longer, will be depleted and the eulogies less fulsome. So much the better. Edgar relocates his chambers from Gray's Inn to the floor below me, acquired on the cheap. He joins the Simmonds masthead as legal director, a hedge against Sandi's uncorked rapacity.

Mrs Adams's attention now turns west, to the greatest market of all. She plans Maria Olszewska's Carnegie Hall début with meticulous foresight and the best PR that money can buy. Maria goes on NBC's *Today* show in a white confirmation dress and plays 'Ave Maria' over the closing titles. On ABC's *Good Morning America* she reveals that, aged eight, she saw a vision of the Virgin Mary rising from the North Sea, telling her to put her talent in the service of Jesus. Every note she plays is an ode to divine goodness in an ugly, graceless world.

At Carnegie, the regular recital audience is crowded out by Catholic grandees, led by the Cardinal Archbishop of New York in a pre-Easter parade. Maria plays an all-Chopin programme 'with immaculate chastity', as the *New York Times* reviewer puts it, Jewish tongue in cheek. No matter: she is made for life on the incense circuit; she has played powerfully enough to satisfy the half-dozen hard-bitten bookers who dominate the concert circuit. Her native charm is the more compelling for having shed its disabling encumbrance of Englishness. Sandi has wisely engaged an expensive elocutionist to mould her tangy Taw accent into expressionless middle-American.

A week or so after Maria's début, Anatoly Gudzinsky, while playing the Schumann concerto with the New York Philharmonic Orchestra at Avery Fisher Hall, rises from his stool to inform the audience that the conductor is an excremental homosexual half-wit who cannot be bothered to rehearse and that they, the public, know 'fuck-all' about music. As security men rush on to subdue him, he rips off his pink vaginal tie, throws it to a front-row dowager and strides off through rows of open-mouthed subscribers. The press besiege his hotel, but Gudzinsky refuses to emerge until second-serve Sophie, ranked eighty-ninth in the world, flies out and agrees to marry him. The ceremony takes place on the cover of *People* magazine. Gudzinsky need not fear for future American celebrity.

Sandi, her hands full with enquiries, suggests that the time might be ripe to take on a couple of assistants and establish Simmonds

Inc. in a vacant shopfront on 57th Street, opposite Carnegie Hall. I accept her proposal with alacrity and relief, glad to remove an outsider from the heart of our firm while retaining her eagerness, expertise and uncorseted goodwill. Sandi becomes chief executive of Simmonds Inc. (USA), renouncing (in an Edgar-drafted letter) all shares and entitlements in Simmonds (Symphonic Scores and Concerts) Ltd. She is gone from our story, her catalytic function fulfilled.

Myrtle's relief is conveyed by a cocked eyebrow and the immediate reallocation of Sandi's London space to a new publicity director. She points out that I now employ more people than my father did at his peak – eight more – and with greater focus and efficiency. Our growth is controlled, in every sense of the word. Work is kept in check, never being allowed to overwhelm us as it did my parents. Myrtle and I have time to travel to exotic destinations, to read, to share. We will never spend another summer in a deadly Swiss resort.

All of this fills me with an immense satisfaction, a satisfaction so great that it almost vindicates my wasted years and obliges me to reassess, *da capo*, the assumptions on which my previous life was lived. Losing Dovidl a second time has granted me a second life. Could it be that he destroyed the first? Is it conceivable that he was, from the day he arrived, a malignancy that blighted my youth and condemned me to subservience? The thought is heretical enough to keep me awake through two miserable nights.

Consider, I urge myself over a milky dawn cocoa, how your life might have proceeded had he not invaded it. In two or three years, I would have overcome puppy-fat, beaten up Johnny-Isaacs-next-door and emerged from social isolation. In another four or five years, I would have brazened my way into bed with the maid and brainstormed to Cambridge. Admired and loved by my parents, I would have nursed my mother back to health from menopausal depression. In time, I would have inherited the firm and taken it to greater heights, or dominated a different field of endeavour, lucrative or contemplative. In short, I would have enjoyed a rewarding existence, coping with ups and downs like every other competent and reasonably fortunate adult.

Dovidl obviated all that. The first words he spoke put me in my place: a slave to his destiny. I was to be Sancho to his Don, the *mashgiach* to his *Rosh*, with no right of reprieve or parole. By flattering my intelligence, he had fooled me into thinking I was indispensable to him, a partner to his genius. I was, but only as Leporello is a partner to Don Giovanni's exploits, vicariously and without corporeal pleasure. In truth, I was his dupe. He needed me so much, he made me his prisoner, his emasculated acolyte.

In every corner of my being, he shackled and disabled me. At school, I basked in his glory. At play, he led the way. At home he, not I, was the apple of my parents' eyes. Nor could I even protest at my neglect. He was a genius, a tragic orphan. Only a heartless ingrate would have objected to helping him.

When his adolescence turned turbulent with grief and rage, his mode of rebellion denied me the right to rebel. Aware of my parents' concern for his wellbeing, I could not burden them with any wildness on my part. I was forced into a pattern of obedience that persisted all my adult life, a coerced kind of fake compliance that sought evasions in marital infidelity in dingy railway hotels, destabilising my domestic contentment.

My dominator could not permit me the relief of sexual intimacy for fear it would allow me to escape his grip. So he screwed my first girlfriend, not because he especially wanted her but in order to keep me in a state of servile eunuchism. He left me no life to call my own. When he left altogether, he took with him the keys to my cell. I was incapable of initiating love or pursuing an ambition. I was reduced to sackcloth and ashes, unable to rise from an endless *shiva*, eviscerated of confidence. And all those years that I mourned the loss of my redeemer, I never once saw him as he really was: my devourer.

What he performed on me was a classic musical operation. It was the disempowerment that Richard Wagner practised on his acolyte Hans von Bülow, fucking his wife, Cosima, and forcing the sickly *Tristan* conductor to deny his own cuckolding before King Ludwig and the whole sniggering state of Bavaria. It was the enslavement that Arnold Schoenberg imposed on his pupils, Alban Berg and Anton von Webern, making them copy out his music instead of composing their own. It was the contempt that Mozart displayed for his fellow man, the scorn that Brahms heaped on his friends, the sinister way that Igor Stravinsky exploited everyone he ever touched.

And think of the suffering families – the wives of Puccini, Janáček and Sibelius, the children of Liszt, Berlioz and Schumann, the damaged relics and offprints of the divinely endowed. They say the devil has the best tunes. Wrong: he has the lot. The greater the musician, the closer he communes with the source of evil. Managers in the music business have a reputation for toughness. Many of us start out as music lovers, but we grow an asbestos coating to protect us from the dragon's flame that lurks within each and every maker of mellifluous noise (with the exception of cellists who are unusually gentle and accommodating). *Ne tirez pas sur le pianiste*, we are exhorted. On the contrary, it's the pianist (violinist, conductor, composer) who deserves to get shot for the lives he wrecks. I ought to make a movie called *Ne tirez pas sur le patron*.

We managers stand unprotected in a rocket-pocked no man's land, between giver and receiver of harmony. I got off lightly, hit by a minor comet, and am finally in the process of recovering. Perhaps I should set up a counselling service for survivors of musical abuse. I'll apply to UNESCO for a grant and to Carnegie Hall for a first-aid room for victims of the sado-masochism that is central to the provision of serious music.

So what now? In place of fraternal love for the musician who stole my life I feel . . . not hate, but a growling resentment and a surge of self-assertion. I can now be me, come what may. Do I wish him dead? Not yet. There is unfinished business to be settled. The question that nags me midway through the second night is, what if? What if he had never turned up on that scorching August day in 1939? What if my life had run on unbroken rails? Would I want to have missed the thrill of bonding, the intimacy with music in the making, the time-stopping, spine-chilling thrill that I shall take with me to the grave? Or am I for ever in his debt for those gifts, paying an extreme price for a rare, illusory bliss?

In the grey self-accounting of a recovering insomniac, I am obliged to admit that I would not have missed a minute of it. What Dovidl brought was the revelation of intensity. He showed me that passion can invade dull lives, that my place on earth need not be suburban – so long as it is lit by a star. Even the mundane can be elevated, overturned, by a spontaneous burst of music. I cannot expunge that idea, nor would I wish to. It is a *raison d'être* that I have clung to through the empty years and one that must be reapplied in my age of triumphancy. I owe him something for that: I owe him the right to be left in peace, once the debt is settled.

It has taken four years for that recognition to sink in. At first, I could not let him go, the more so since my original plan hinged on his public subjugation to my managerial will. His return was to have been the making of me, the reversal of our roles. I craved that arching of triumph, though not as desperately as I first thought.

For the month after he vanished, I had the *Tawburn Gazette* delivered daily to my office.

Police divers have called a second search of last week's A821 crash site after dredging an empty van from the River Taw. The body of the driver, believed to be Rabbi David Katzenberg of the Oldbridge Talmudic College, has not been recovered.

Colleagues of Rabbi Katzenberg say that he rose before dawn on Fridays to purchase fruit and vegetables for the Jewish Sabbath which he distributed among needy members of his community. Rabbi Katzenberg's wife and eleven children were said to be in deep shock and mourning. Friends told the *Gazette* that he was a much-loved teacher who would have laid down his life for others. Born in Poland, he was the only survivor of a Jewish family murdered during the German occupation in the Second World War.

Nothing new there, just the evidence on which the Tawburn coroner, Dr Ali Medahi, must return an open verdict. For deeper insights, I study *Hameir* and the *Jewish Mail*, weekly journals of rival sects of ultra-orthodoxy, published in English and Yiddish with a sprinkling of classical Hebrew and Aramaic to throw sand into prying eyes, like mine. *Hameir* is by far the better informed.

The *yeshiva olam* has been devastated by reports from Oldbridge that its much-loved *mashgiach ruchoni*, Reb Dovid Katzenberg, has been *nifter* in a tragic motor accident. Reb Dovid made it his *mitzva* to visit the fruit and

293

vegetable market early on *erev shabbos* so that he could buy the best produce and give it away to the poor. On his way home, his vehicle went off the road and into the icy river. That such a disaster should occur while a righteous man, a *tzaddik*, is in the midst of performing two *mitzvos* – the duties of prayer and charity – is beyond the understanding of mere humans, *rachmono litzlon* (may His mercy protect us).

Reb Dovid leaves behind his beloved *rebbitzen*, Broche, daughter of the first *Rosh yeshiva* of Oldbridge, Reb Menashe Hershkovits of blessed memory; and their eleven children, all of whom are *oskim* in Torah and *mitzvos*.

Reb Dovid was sent to Oldbridge by the Medzhiner Rebbe, may his memory protect us, after losing his whole family in Poland. His great love of Medzhiner and other Hassidic *nigunim* was witnessed at many Oldbridge weddings where Reb Dovid, the revered teacher, would take off his *capota* and play a cheap violin to bring joy to the hearts of the young couple. He used to quote from *Tehillim*: 'Serve Hashem with joy' and 'Sing to Hashem a new song.' These verses, said Reb Dovid, teach us that the Creator of the World gave us music for a divine purpose – to worship Him and to renew His treasury of songs for every generation.

Mr C. J. Spielman of London N16, the Medzhiner archivist and a close friend of the *nifter*, notes that his *petira* took place on the 12th of Shevat, which was also the *Jahrzeit* for his father as dated in the Song of Names by the saintly Medzhiner Rebbe, who shared with him the sufferings of the Nazi camps. The Oldbridge Yeshiva will hold a day of prayer and learning for the soul of Reb Dovid Katzenberg on a date to be announced *iy'h*.

IYH – *im yirtseh Hashem*, God willing. Nothing can be accomplished on earth without divine volition – including mass murder and sudden disappearance. I examine *Hameir* in the ways its writers study the Talmud, more for what is omitted than for its disclosures. The technical phrase, I recall, is *megaleh tefach umechaseh tefachayim* – reveal one measure and conceal two – and it refers to husbandly practice in the act of love. But the metaphorical implications for observant Jews need no elaboration.

*Hameir* (the *Enlightener*) is not in the business of enlightenment, but of maximum concealment through which chinks of hints and gaps in narrative will allow the faithful to complete its puzzle-pages. It makes, for instance, no mention of the statutory seven and thirty days of mourning for the *nifter* (dead one) – either because, in the absence of a corpse, the next of kin are not yet permitted to mourn, or because he is not really dead but has been whisked away.

There is no mention, either, of rabbinic eulogies, which normally swoop around rabbinic losses like gulls to a fleet at sea. My suspicions are aroused. 'Where is Yossele?' I ponder, humming the black-hats' abduction song.

I now understand why Dovidl rose early that morning – he always did on Fridays – and why he chose that particular day to go. The Hebrew date of his father's death will have acquired extra significance at a stressful moment, precipitating a hastier disappearance than was rationally necessary. That much is clarified to my pernickety satisfaction.

But unconnected wisps trail from his evanescence like chords from an over-pedalled piano. The victim set out to buy fruit and vegetables, but the van was empty when hauled out of the river. What did he do with his shopping? A child of poverty, Dovidl would never have wasted a vanload of food. A double-escapologist, he knew the police would seek to reconstruct his last movements and he had to make them appear routine. So he must have visited the market that morning as usual to leave an illusion of normality and a body of eye-witnesses. A scan of the *Gazette* produces corroborative evidence from the trading fraternity:

> 'Always bright and breezy he was, whatever the weather,' said Fred Trimble, 46, a wholesaler of Eakenfield. 'He were one of my best customers, always paid cash, regular as clockwork,' said his brother Arthur Trimble, 48.

Having completed his purchases, Dovidl must have arranged to dispose of them before pitching his van into the river. In the hour between the market opening and his 'accident', this was more than one man could have managed unaided. He needed an associate, maybe more. I design a flow-chart to plot his final hour. Let's assume D-one goes to market at six, places his orders, loads up the van then slips away, presumably into the car of a co-conspirator. A Jew of similar physical build and beard, D-two, is seen boarding the van and driving away. He offloads the crates of fruit and veg at some quiet roadside into a third vehicle, probably another blue van, whose driver, D-three, distributes the stock around the community. D-two then drives the empty van into the river. By this time, Dovidl is being dropped at Manchester Airport by D-four, just in time for the Tel Aviv, Newark or Miami flights. The three other Ds return safely to base. The *yeshiva* world closes ranks tighter than a Sandhurst parade. No one may ever know the full story, but I have gained enough insight from two days in Dovidl's company to tell when someone is laying down a trail of *schmaltz* herring.

Two questions remain: where is he now? and what has he done with the Guadagnini – the *Enlightener*'s slightly 'cheap' violin? I could proceed in hot pursuit. Three million dollars is no small incentive, or reward. There are detective agencies in Israel that specialise in ultra-orthodox investigation, sifting one bearded fugitive from another. I consider the option, and reject it. I cannot see an Israeli private dick uncovering the wiles of my double-Houdini. Leave it, I tell myself. Give up the search. Let him be. As for the violin, he can never sell it. Let him take it to the grave, good riddance.

But the lack of resolution, like an unfinished symphony, will not give me rest. 'What's bothering you?' asks Myrtle, as I toss sleepless for a third wintry night.

'I'll tell you when I've cracked it,' I promise.

'It can't be that important,' she murmurs. 'Everything is going so well for us.'

'You're right,' I say. 'It's not important, just some untied odds and sods from the business up north.'

'I never quite understood that.'

'Me neither, dear, and there's not much to be done about it.'

'So devolve it,' she proposes sensibly. 'If it's trouble, let Edgar deal with it. And if not, just forget it.'

'Good idea.' I take another camomile, snuggle into her warm back like a cat into a cushion and try to think of something else.

And then, just as I start to despair of ever regaining an unmedicated night's sleep, the next morning brings a letter from the north that puts a wry smile on my face. 'Weeping may endure for the night, joy comes in the morning,' sang the Psalmist, 'and I said in my tranquillity: I shall never give up hope.' The letter is from Eleanor Stemp, requesting an urgent meeting to discuss the future of her son, Peter. 'I am sorry to trouble you when I know you have bigger stars to fly,' she begins, with a faint whinge, 'but since you were good enough to take an interest in Peter's talent I would be grateful for your advice at this difficult stage.'

I call for the file. Peter has made halting progress. Fred Burrows reckons he will never make the grade as a soloist, but he likes playing in the local orchestra and might have the character to become a concertmaster. He is nineteen now and in the middle of his second term at the Royal Cardiff Academy of Music, where the principal, an old contact of mine, has delivered an encouraging report – but, then, music colleges always do. They hate to admit that any member of the human race might not, with proper tuition, qualify as a professional musician. I had better see for myself, and bring the episode to an honourable close.

'Book me on the nine-oh-three to Tawburn next Monday,' I tell my bright young secretary, all IT skills and no graces, 'and let's have a table for two for lunch at one o'clock at the Royal Tawburn Hotel. Better make it three, in case the boy turns up. Ask for Mr Woodward, the manager. He will see to it.'

'Will you be staying the night?'

'No, book me back on the early-evening express, it used to be the sixteen-forty-two. First-class day return, facing the engine.'

And so, four years on, I find myself swimming against the Monday-morning incoming tide on Euston station to begin a journey that, in terms of profit and loss, is not strictly necessary. This time, however, I tell Myrtle an approximation of truth. 'I'm going up north to sort out those loose ends. Back for supper.'

'Wrap up warmly,' she exhorts. And I do. February is funeral time for my generation. I have just paid last respects to two close friends.

Shunning the 'concessions' granted to senior citizens who are prepared to travel in cattle-cars at unsocial hours, I plump down in a first-class carriage and accept a complimentary newspaper from a grumpy attendant, along with unasked-for coffee in a grimy china cup. No point complaining. Country's going to the dogs. Used to be the finest railway in the world, now look at it. Government is selling it off to greedy so-called investors, as if that will do us passengers any ruddy good. I grin self-mockingly at my advancing curmudgeonliness.

No time, either, for reveries. My briefcase is full of plans to open a Simmonds office in united Berlin, marketing our list of thirty-two artists across both halves of Europe. Clicking open my laptop like a twenty-something yuppie, I start working out budgets for the string-quartet cycle that I plan to promote in London's tomb-like Barbican Centre, touring onwards to seven European cities. There's a livelier future in flexible chamber music than in the lumbering orchestral juggernaut my father used to employ. Tawburn arrives all too soon. I look out wistfully: no band on the platform. Mayor Froggatt, ousted in the last election, is wasting away of liver cancer, I hear.

Striding across the square to the Royal, I continue crunching the numbers over a Scotch in the snug bar. When the clock strikes one, I rise to face an uninviting lunch. It is only now that I notice the changes that have befallen my old haunt. The bar has been remodelled in chrome and equipped with a bouncer, a sure sign of rejuvenation. The lobby has been extended with an atrium and the dining room has lost its sickly hue in a pastel-smart colour scheme and concealed lighting. The menu, posted at the entrance, has been tarted up with *nouvelle cuisine* dishes. I imagine the cooking is just as vile, but I won't get much of it to eat.

'Your guests are seated, sir,' says the smart maître d', with a local accent, a reconditioned ex-miner by the look of him.

'How many are we?'

'Three, as you ordered, sir.'

So she must have brought Peter along for a sulky reassessment, I assume wearily. As I approach the table, Eleanor Stemp levers herself up with both hands and obvious difficulty. She is heavily pregnant, eighth or ninth month at a guess. She must be, what?, about forty. 'My dear Eleanor, this is a wonderful surprise,' I greet her. She blushes prettily and accepts my kiss on her cheekbone. Behind her looms Fred Burrows, squinting protectively.

'Frederick and I are getting married next week,' declares Eleanor, 'hopefully before the baby is born.'

'This calls for champagne,' I exclaim. 'Why, Fred, you are a dark horse, I thought you'd never make it up the aisle.'

'I was very choosy,' burrs the Tawburn choirmaster, 'but I knew it was the real thing when I met Eleanor – and we have you to thank for bringing us together by getting me to keep an eye on Peter.'

'And how is Peter taking this?' I venture.

'Sourly,' says his mother, through pursed lips. 'He has been an only child too long for his own good. But he does respect Frederick and I hope we can all get along.'

Truth to tell, I am relieved to have Fred here. I would not have relished another obsessive exchange with Eleanor about a boy who is evidently going nowhere. We order quickly. The aubergine pâté is an acceptable caviar surrogate and the salmon-avocado roulade is bland but firm, a distinct improvement on the old Royal. The wine is an 'eighty-seven Chablis and I am feeling quite mellow when the future of Peter Stemp is finally broached over dessert of poached pear and vanilla ice, a leftover from the previous cookbook.

'He's unsettled,' begins Eleanor.

'The Welsh not treating him well?'

'Unsettled in himself,' she continues. 'He's not pleased about the new baby, he's jealous of Frederick and he wants to give up music and study computers.'

'Would that be such a terrible thing?' I say mildly.

'I cannot authorise it without consulting you, after all that you have done for him.'

'Fred, what's your view?' I enquire.

'The boy's confused,' says Fred. 'Not keen on his mum having a life of her own. Bit frustrated, never had a girl-friend, so far as we know. Might do him good to study something else, meet a different set of people. He can always come back to music. The foundations are solid.'

'Excellent,' I conclude. 'Then we are agreed?'

'Thank you, Mr Simmonds,' says Eleanor Stemp quietly. 'I am grateful for your understanding.'

'Was there anything else?' I demand, signalling for the bill.

'Mrs Stemp and I were wondering if you could shed light on a bit of an enigma in Peter's past,' says Fred, curiously employing his fiancée's formal name.

'Go ahead.'

'When you gave him the prize,' recalls Fred, 'you heard something in his playing that none of the rest of us picked up. Then you had a private word with him, and he directed you to a Jewish bloke in Oldbridge who had given him some informal tuition. What do you know about this man? Mrs Stemp thinks he may have had a bad influence on Peter, and may in some way have affected his estrangement from the study of music.'

Ah, so that's what she's after. Eleanor does not need my say-so to let Peter drop music, but she suspects I know a secret that he never shared with his mother. Tricky, this. I wonder how much she has squeezed out of the pimply brat, or whether she is implying that he was corrupted by contact with those hateful, reclusive, bearded Jews. I vividly recall her anti-blackhat prejudice.

'There is not much to say that I couldn't have told you on

the phone.' I shrug with feigned irritation. 'Peter, when I first heard him, echoed a style that I had not heard since childhood, an expressive freedom that I thought might develop into something significant and worthwhile. I was anxious to trace its source, which seemed authentic and untouched by modern distortions. He led me to a kindly old rabbi in Oldbridge who gave him remedial lessons during breaks in his paper round. I visited the rabbi myself and found nothing untoward. He represented a defunct tradition and we had a nostalgic chat. I gather that he is, sadly, no longer alive.'

'That's right,' snaps Eleanor. 'I caught Peter trying to visit this man not long after he won the prize. He came home all upset, refusing to practise or eat supper. He had rung the bell and found different people living there. Never heard of the rabbi, or of his daughter who, I suspect, Peter fancied. There were blank stares when Peter mentioned their names, no speaka da English.

'I read that this man, Rabbi Katzenberg, drove his van into the Taw while running a fruit and veg round. It was in all the papers. I told Peter the man was dead, and he went berserk. Said he was a holy man, a musical genius. I said, "Don't be silly: these people are primitives, barely out of the Middle Ages. What can they know of Bach and Beethoven, with their long beards and thick wigs?"

'Peter wouldn't listen. He went into a slump, almost failed his exams. Then Frederick moved in with me. Peter's playing changed, it sounded hollow. He did not seem to be trying so hard, he had lost his ambition. I'm no musician, but it seemed to me as if something had gone out of my boy, as if this dead rabbi had taken his soul.'

'That's a bit metaphysical, isn't it?'

'You tell me, Mr Simmonds. I read the Isaac Bashevis Singer

novels you mentioned. They are full of strange occurrences, of men and women being occupied by *dybbuks* – isn't that what they're called? These people are a menace. They dabble in the occult. They possess unnatural powers and prey on innocent folk.'

'These people?'

'You know who I mean.'

A dirty silence settles over the disordered table. I know all too well who she means, and I imagine she includes me in the generality of soul-stealers. Did I not make secret approaches to her precious son? Was I not the devil's spawn? Had I not penetrated her long-neglected private parts? Heavens, she can count herself lucky that I took only her virtue and not her Christian soul when I shagged her diagonally upstairs, on the bed of the Palmerston Suite.

I survey her through hooded eyes, savouring her fears – so archaic beside the multi-layered intellectual lives of the 'primitives' she despises. I owe her nothing, nor shall I see her again. She and her boy have been stepping-stones on my path to truth. I have trodden on them, and moved on. However, we are not savages. I could not have reached my destination without them and, remembering an ethic of my father's never to give gratuitous offence, I resolve to allay her odious prejudices with a sophisticated dose of bromides.

'So far as I am aware, my dear,' I ooze, 'the late Rabbi Katzenberg was, in his youth, a promising pupil of the distinguished Professor Flesch. The murder of his family in Nazi concentration camps propelled him towards a spiritual life, as I am sure Peter has told you. I had hoped to persuade him to become a mentor to Peter. Tragically, the accident intervened, and I was unable to find a substitute. Had Rabbi Katzenberg lived and continued to teach him, Peter might now be on his way to a glittering career.'

'I was quite upset to read about his death,' interjects Fred, 'not that I knew anything of his background.'

'Let's leave it there,' I conclude. 'It has been good to see you both, and I hope all goes well with the birth. Please give Peter my good wishes. Goodness, is that the time?'

I have an hour left before my train. A brisk walk would do me good. There are no waiters around, so I take the bill to the reception desk and ask for Mr Woodward.

'Doesn't work here any more,' says a trim young woman with a name-badge on her navy lapel. 'Woody took early redundancy – sorry, retirement – last year. Can I help? I'm the new manager, Sue Summerfield. As you can see, we're smartening the old place up for the millennium.'

Ms Summerfield graciously accepts my appreciation of her improvements. She recognises my name from the mailing list. I mention that Woodward allocated me a locker in the vaults, to save me shunting stock to and from London. 'We'd better take a look,' she says. 'Good thing you came today. I put up notices two months ago warning customers to remove all their possessions by the end of this week. The builders are about to convert the basement, in phase two of our renovation, into an executive health club and swimming-pool.'

I descend, for the last time, into the Victorian bowels of a once-great institution. Thunderous pipes run above my head. The walls are tiled in morose shades of brown and yellow. I pass storerooms, kitchens, lavatories, sculleries, fenced off for demolition. Near the end of the corridor, the agreeable Sue Summerfield produces a master-key and throws open my locker. 'I'll be in Reception if you need me,' she reports. 'No need to lock up. It's all coming down on Monday.'

A mound of tatty purple paperbacks, 'Printed in the British

Empire', is all that remains of my former wares. Couple of dozen, hardly worth shlepping back home. I cannot see anything else in the gloom and my ears prick to a scurrying nearby. Near an English river, always expect a rat. I grope inside the base of the huge locker, hoping I am not going to get bitten. It has been years since my last tetanus jab. Three feet in, I touch a leather case, rounded at either end, hollowed in the middle. I locate a strap and pull it out, trembling with anticipation. The light is too poor to see much, but the worn leather tells me that this is not one of my mass-produced Chinese fiddles. It feels like the genuine article, the missing object, the final satisfaction.

Back upstairs, I thank Sue Summerfield for her help, assure her of my continued custom, and ask to hire an office for twenty minutes, which is all I have left before the train leaves. She shows me into a brand-new business suite brimming with computers and telecommunications. I put the violin case on the table and wait until she has left before, fingers fumbling, I crack open the clasps.

Without being Arbuthnot Bailey I can tell a Guadagnini by the orangy varnish and fine-cut scroll. It is looking slightly the worse for wear, not having been played (at a guess) for a good four years, but with new strings and a nice brush-up at Baileys it will return magnificently to full resonance.

So excited am I by its aura, its welcoming smile, that I almost miss the sealed letter, tucked into the roof of the violin case, beneath the bow and sticks of resin.

My dear Mottl,

Since I am leaving without saying goodbye and it is unlikely that we shall ever meet again, I have arranged for the safe return of your property and would like to offer you, for want of an apology, an explanation.

You must have known, when demanding my return to centre-stage, that this was an entirely untenable proposition. It would have compromised my position in the only society I care for and exposed me to the pressures and scrutiny from which I had fled once before.

Looking back at those events under your intense though sensitive examination, I am obliged to conclude that my defection was no accident or coincidence. It was an act of sheer cowardice that took advantage of a chance encounter to secure a refuge. In all honesty, I was terrified of all that lay ahead – of the fame, the fortune, the certainty of failure.

I was made out to be the best violinist since Kreisler, but I did not feel that way. I knew that others would discover, sooner or later, what I already knew – that my reputation was many times greater than my ability. I blame no one for that, least of all your father or mine. I was born with the curse of an intelligence larger than my talent. Other artists could fool themselves through a rich and glorious career that they were God's gift to suffering humanity. Not me. I had seen the suffering, and I knew myself. I knew every flaw in my technique, every gloss in my half-wrought interpretations, every flimsy imitation of genius. And if I knew these shortcomings, some discriminating ear would surely flush them out and expose me as second-rate. I could not face that disgrace.

After the hullabaloo of my début, I suppose I might have settled into the routine whirl of a top violinist, one of the best, but not the best. That is not what I was cut out for. If I could not be supreme, why bother? Call it performance anxiety or the worst case of stage fright in history, but I could not live with being less than I was cracked up to be.

So I took the emergency exit. I could have left my Medzhiner friends at any time and returned home to Blenheim Terrace. But, hearing the Song of Names in my head, I knew that I could never face an audience with less than absolute truth. I was a fraud. I was not the equal of a Hassid, a Neveu, a Haendel. I might fool the masses, but inside I would be an impostor – mocking those things that I held most dear. I had to get away.

And now, for much the same reasons, I have decided to take the escape route once again. I hope you won't be too disappointed. I was both dumbstruck and uplifted by your scheme to put me back on stage – until I realised that it was, for the most part, an angry imposition of your will over mine. If that was the game, you won and I quit. Congratulations.

It happened to coincide with an urgent circumstantial need – not that there is such a thing as coincidence in God's pre-ordained plan. My colleagues at the *yeshiva* have been making themselves sick with worry over a financial embarrassment. An Australian alumnus has given us a hundred grand – I am not sure in which denomination – to build a new study wing in the name of his late mother. He is about to turn up for a visit. The wing, however, has not been built and the money has been spent on other exigencies – entirely germane to the *yeshiva*'s operations but not fulfilling the purpose of the donation. When the man arrives from Melbourne and there is no wing with his mother's name on it – always a name at the heart of the matter – there will be an almighty row and, God forbid, a police investigation. My dear friend, Reb Yoel, has suffered a minor heart-attack. As *mashgiach*, I am next in line of authority.

Although I have nothing to do with the *yeshiva*'s finances, I summoned my senior colleagues and offered to take written responsibility for the missing funds, provided they helped fake my abscondment and put me beyond reach of police – and you. My friends joyously agreed, showering me with thanks. Some may have been relieved to see me go. My mind was sometimes too questioning for their orthodox comfort. Be that as it may, they offered every covert assistance, along with an assurance that my wife and youngest children will rejoin me shortly under a foolproof new identity: my third and, hopefully, my last.

I told my wife, by the way, that I was facing outrageous demands from someone in my former life, which is not a world away from the wholesome truth.

Anyway, as young Peter Stemp (give him my best) would say, I'm out of here. I was glad to see you alive and well, Martin, and sad that we could not spend more time together. I loved you dearly at a desperate time in my life, whether you choose to believe that or not. I repent the harm I caused your family and wish you the happiest of lives, or what remains of life for men of our years.

Be well, Mottl, as I am. May God be with you, *Deus noster et non est iniquitas in eo* (which I can hear you quoting back to me in the original Hebrew).

Dovidl.

There is no time to digest the letter. I shut the violin case, race to the station and catch the train as it pulls out. Panting on my flash new mobile phone, I tell Myrtle that I am on my way, and all is well. As we cross the Taw, I see the site of the 'accident' and smile. Where is he now?

What does it matter? It's over, settled, restituted. The last debt has been cleared. The violin that he loved so much it never left his side has been returned to its rightful owner. Off to Baileys tomorrow and then up for sale or put out on loan to a promising newcomer – like that distant Odessa cousin of David Oistrakh's whom we have just signed. Mine alone to decide.

And that's when I spot the trap, the revenge for his displacement. What will happen when I take this fiddle in for repair? Bartholomew Bailey, grandson of the great Arbuthnot, will receive me with unctuous expertise. But the moment I leave the shop, he will search the card files. Haven't we seen this Guadagnini before? Isn't this the Hubay that Mr Simmonds senior bought for that young virtuoso, Rapoport, in, when was it, May 1947? And didn't the violin vanish with Rapoport, four years later, no trace of either of them ever since?

If this is the Guadagnini, where is Rapoport? Was the insurance ever collected? The police will have to be informed. The violin is a piece of evidence in a missing-persons investigation. Now, Mr Simmonds, where did you say you found this violin, and would you mind telling us exactly where you were and who saw you on the morning of 3 May 1951, when Mr Rapoport disappeared? Take all the time you need. We never call time on a possible homicide investigation.

Phew, I congratulate myself, that was close. I could have gone to jail. Dovidl must have been testing to see if my strategic brain is still ticking over. Damn. I cannot take this violin into a restorer or put it up for sale without bringing the plods to my door, followed by the press. Dovidl has released his grip on me but he has made me the prisoner of his instrument, his most cherished possession. I lay the violin case beside me on the seat. When I die, I suppose, I shall have to have it buried with me to end the matter once and for all. I lift up the case and see my coffin.

No, that's ridiculous. I can get out of this.

The next morning I call a man I know, Norman Lebrecht by name, a newspaper columnist notorious for his acerbic exposures of musical skulduggery. We fix lunch, and I proceed to lay some of my cards on a white tablecloth at the Langham Hotel, where Puccini, Janáček and Sibelius used to stay.

'I wonder if you remember,' I begin, 'the strange case of Alma Rosé.'

'Of course I do,' he replies, in the know-all way of journalists. 'Wrote about it not long ago. Her father, Arnold, was concertmaster of the Vienna Philharmonic Orchestra, married Mahler's sister, wound up penniless in London after the *Anschluss*. Alma went back to Holland in pursuit of a no-good Austrian boyfriend. She was trapped by the invasion, tried to escape and was deported to Auschwitz, where she formed a women's orchestra and was murdered.'

'And what happened to her violin?'

'One day in 1946, according to reports, two nuns turned up on her old father's doorstep in Blackheath, presented him wordlessly with Alma's fiddle and vanished into thin air.'

'A Guadagnini, if I am not mistaken?'

'That's right. What's all this about?' he demands.

'Any idea how that instrument got from Auschwitz to south London?' I persist.

'No one knows.'

'Well something of the sort has just happened to me. Does the name Eli Rapoport mean anything to you?'

'The prodigy who vanished on the day of his début?'

'That's the one. Disappeared with his Guadagnini, never seen

310

again. Last week, two rabbis turned up at my office after dark, handed me the Guadagnini and, without a word, scuttled into a waiting taxi. Rapoport was my boyhood friend, almost a brother. I don't know what became of him, but I want you to have the story, see what you can track down. Interested?'

The journalist sips his wine, strokes his chin, directs a volley of quickfire questions. 'It'll take months of investigation,' he eventually warns. 'I'll need unfettered access to company and family documents and any contacts you can provide. I cannot promise where it will lead. I may turn up things you won't want to see in print, but once they are in my hands I can't ignore them. Are you sure this is what you want?'

'Do what you have to do,' I tell him softly. 'It's your story.'